DANGER RIDES
THE RIVER

DANGER RIDES THE RIVER

A Frontier Story

LES SAVAGE, JR.

Five Star • Waterville, Maine

Five Star First Edition Western Series.

Published in 2002 in conjunction with Golden West Literary Agency.

Cover design by Thorndike Press Staff.

Set in 11 pt. Plantin by Minnie B. Raven.

Printed in the United States on permanent paper.

Library of Congress Cataloging-in-Publication Data

Savage, Les.
    Danger rides the river : a frontier story / by Les Savage, Jr.
        p. cm.
      ISBN 0-7862-3543-8 (hc : alk. paper)
     1. Frontier and pioneer life—Fiction.   2. Mississippi River—Fiction.   3. Natchez (Miss.)—Fiction.   4. River boats—Fiction.   5. Steamboats—Fiction.   6. Boatmen—Fiction.
    PS3569.A826 D36 2002
      813'.54—dc21   2002019946

Editor's Note

"Danger Rides the River" by Les Savage, Jr., as it appeared in *Zane Grey's Western Magazine* (3/53), was a short novel set against the brawling and exciting days when steam-powered boats were first being introduced on the Ohio and Mississippi Rivers, only a few years before the War of 1812. However, when the author decided to expand this short novel into a major historical frontier story, he was beset by editorial interference. His editor at Doubleday insisted that the story be treated as an historical romance, even if this meant that he had to betray the integrity of the characters he had created in order to bring about the conclusion desired by the editor. The author was profoundly disappointed with what he was forced to do to his story. Now, at last, *Danger Rides the River* has been restored so it can be published as Les Savage, Jr., originally intended it.

Chapter One

Owen Naylor rose on that May dawn of 1809 to find a silver curtain of fog hanging over the Ohio River. Like a furtive cat it crept among the line of shabby taverns on the Louisville waterfront and turned them to gray and ghostly illusions; it settled in woolly banks over the countless boats, creaking and sawing at their moorings in Bear Grass Creek; it completely hid the Falls and seemed to muffle their roar as they rushed forever over their limestone reefs beyond Goose Island. It gathered in clammy dampness against Owen Naylor's gaunt young cheeks as he came down First Street and turned toward the anchorage, his boots beating up a sodden echo on the wet planks of the deserted levee.

Another figure materialized from the veil of mist ahead of him. He saw that it was Evadne Archer, standing at the head of his keelboat. She was a big woman, almost as tall as Naylor. Even the shapeless covering of a long, wool carrick-like dress couldn't quite hide the bountiful promise of her boldly curved body. Her enamel-black hair was drawn plum-tight against her head, and the mist had dampened her vivid red lips till they shone wetly. As he reached her, she held out a pewter mug. The fragrance of strong coffee steamed out of it, mingled with the faint scent of rum.

"I thought you'd need something to warm you," she said. "I bet you didn't even eat breakfast."

He took the coffee gratefully. "I guess not," he said.

Her lips were full and pouting, touching the mature beauty of her face with a hint of sulkiness. "I hear Danny

Blackwell's taking your keel downriver, Owen. You shouldn't't've hired him."

Naylor sipped at the coffee. "Too late in the year to get my pick of patroons, Evadne."

She was watching him steadily, a smoky look to her black eyes. "I guess I'm like your mother, Owen. I just hate to see the river get you."

It made him look past her toward the invisible town and the graveyard beyond. There was a new cross planted in that graveyard, with a legend he had carved himself.

SARAH NAYLOR
BORN NEW YORK, JANUARY 6, 1755
DIED LOUISVILLE, MAY 2, 1809

The thought of it made his face go dark. Twenty-three years old, a man's size had already come to him. He was six feet tall, and years of arduous labor in the boat yards had turned his broad shoulders thick and bunchy with muscle. His features tended to gauntness, all sharp angles and secret hollows. His jaw and cheek bones ran in definite ridges against the sun-browned flesh, his eyes as jet black as his shaggy hair and set so deeply beneath his brow that they always seemed to look from the shadows. It touched his face with a melancholy streak and a hint of some restlessness running beneath his somber surface.

He finished the coffee, handing the mug back to Evadne. "I'll thank you once more for all you done. I don't know where Ma would've turned without your friendship."

Before she could answer, a feeble light broke into the fog from farther down the levee, and the waterfront was suddenly filled with the hoarse curses and rough calling of the men leaving the pleasant warmth of a tavern. It was

Naylor's crew, coming down the levee like a pack of roving hounds—a dozen Kentucky boatmen, half horse, half alligator, as wild and raw as the frontier could make them. In the lead was Danny Blackwell. He was taller than the average, but the immense breadth of his torso made his height hard to judge. His blue eyes were pale and shining disks set deeply in the primitive bones of his face, and his hair was a shaggy blond mane, bleached out in white streaks by years of sun. On the back of his head sat a round fur cap with the red feather sticking cockily from its band, proclaiming him bully of the river and champion of his crew—a challenge to any man who thought he could spit farther, jump higher, curse louder, or chew more hide off a grizzly than Danny Blackwell.

"All ready to cast off, Owen!" he called. "Here's your supercargo. Kenneth Swain. Knows the river like a keeler, won't give us a lick o' trouble."

He halted before Naylor, jerking a thumb at the man with him. In the dim light, with the rush of boatmen jostling past him, Naylor got a vague impression of sartorial elegance—a coat of Spanish blue with gilt buttons winking slyly in the pearly mist, a scarlet waistcoat of quilted cassimere, nankeen trousers carefully tucked into gleaming Hessian boots.

"We've outfitted your cabin at the stern of the cargo box," Naylor told Swain. "We're shoving off as soon as the Falls pilot gets here."

Swain gave a patronizing nod of his narrow head and proceeded to follow the last of the crew across the gangplank, trailed by a Negro manservant stooped beneath a load of trunks and bags. Blackwell turned to look at Evadne now, and a brazen grin spread his lips wolfishly away from his teeth. The woman's eyes, sullen, heavy-lidded, showed him nothing but a smoldering resentment. Blackwell threw back his head to emit a gust of laughter, then turned to swagger aboard the keel. At the same time, Captain Abner came hurrying down the levee. He was one of the men appointed by the courts to pilot the boats through the Falls, a bowlegged bantam dressed in a shabby white fur hat and stained green frock coat. He stamped officiously past Naylor, wiping a thumb across his runny nose.

"Let's go, let's go, my bones ain't fit to stand these early mornin' chills very long."

Naylor looked at Evadne. She touched his arm; it sent a disturbing current through him. Her lips pressed together, growing full and heavy.

"Come back, Owen."

"Thanks, Evadne. It's good to have somebody waitin'."

He looked into her smoky eyes a moment longer, then turned to clamber aboard. They were the race horses of the river, these boats, sixty feet long and only eight feet wide, laid on a keel of solid oak and pointed like an alligator fore and aft. The cabin and cargo box were forty feet long, with eighteen inches of cleated walkway on either side. The crew had taken their positions in this walkway, six men to a side, their poles tossed high. Naylor joined Captain Abner in the bow and turned to watch. It was the moment he had dreamed of for half a lifetime; he must have watched a thousand keels set off for the downriver voyage, from his vantage point in the boat yard, with the longing to follow them building up through the years till it was an almost unbearable pressure. Now it was his turn.

At the after end of the cargo box, the steering sweep was set in its tholepin, extending ten feet back over the stern and into the water. Blackwell took his position there and cupped his hands to shout the first order. "Set poles!"

A dozen poles, twenty feet long and tipped with iron, dropped into the river, digging into its sandy bottom. A dozen shoulders were pressed against the leather buttons at the upper end.

"Down on 'em!"

As one man, the crew bent against their poles. The boat groaned, shivered, scraped against the bottom. Then it was sliding into the water. The two lines of men walked down the catwalks from the bow to the stern. When the first two had reached the stern, Blackwell bawled: "Lift your poles!"

The pair tossed their poles free and turned to climb up on the cargo box, clambering back to the bow, while their companions passed them by on the walkways below. As each pair reached the stern, they in turn ran back over the cargo box to the bow and started their journey all over again. As the keel slid gracefully into the river, Naylor took a last look at Evadne, a dim wraith in the fog, standing alone by the stone bridge.

Again he knew his wonder of her. He had been a boy most of the time, and she had come to their miserable shack on the outskirts of Louisville as his mother's friend. But a year ago her husband had died, leaving her the Red Feather Inn.

Captain Abner saw where he was looking and made a sucking sound with his toothless gums. "There's one you could've had, Owen."

"Could I?" Naylor asked. He watched the fog close about Evadne's figure. The thought suddenly made him restless, and he turned to clap Captain Abner on the back. "What're we talkin' about women for? Ain't a steamboat purtier?"

Captain Abner's eyes began to shine. From his pocket he fumbled a handful of dirty papers, covered with a maze of figures and crude plans. "I got a new idee fer goin' without

11

that condenser. Evans says you kin git twenty pounds more pressure by exhausting steam direct into the air. . . ."

He stopped short, his filmy eyes swinging past Naylor's shoulder. Kenneth Swain stood at the head of the cargo box, looking down on them. The mist made his pale face look like a waxen mask. A pair of polers reached the head of the catwalks and scrambled onto the cargo box, forcing Swain to back up till he was out of earshot. Captain Abner hurriedly stuffed his plans into his pocket, looking worriedly at Naylor. "Who is he, Owen?"

"Tarascon is shipping twenty hogsheads of flour on consignment. He sent Swain along as his supercargo."

Captain Abner's eyes swung toward the patroon, standing by the sweep. "Tarascon OK Blackwell, too?"

"Why shouldn't he?" Naylor said.

The old man took out an immense handkerchief to blow his nose. Then he shrugged, and turned to call. "Head two, Blackwell! We'll take Indian Chute!"

Blackwell repeated the order in his deafening bawl, and a pair of polers ran past Naylor, scampering over the four rowing seats, taking their stand in the bow to fend off the rocks. The other men on the catwalk tossed their poles high, shouting and hollering as the boat gained speed in the quickening current. They swung around Goose Island and were caught up by the two-mile stretch of rapids. Foam shot over the side, spraying against Naylor's face. He sought a place by the cargo box to brace himself against the pitch and yaw of the boat.

"A point to larb'rd!" Captain Abner shouted. "Head two and brace off!"

A black rock seemed to spring from the fine spray, gnashing at the bow. Blackwell was already swinging his steering oar, and the two boatmen had jumped to the larboard side, jamming their poles at the rock. Iron squealed against stone, and the keel swung sharply in answer to the sweep. They took a sheer around the rock, and then shot into the roaring rapids again. They raced on through a spray that hung over them like a white mist, hiding the river half the time. The crash of the rapids was so loud in some places it drowned the shouts of the boatmen and Captain Abner's shrill orders. The boatmen scrambled crazily back and forth along the catwalks, their iron-shod poles clanging against the limestone reefs. Then, surprisingly, they were through the Falls, and the boat slid into smooth water.

Shippingport appeared on the Kentucky side, a line of brick buildings and log cabins huddled along the waterfront, dominated by Tarascon's towering mill. Blackwell drove the keel into Rock Harbor, landing Captain Abner just above Armstrong's ropewalk. As the old Falls pilot made ready to jump ashore, Naylor put a hand affectionately on his shoulder.

"Keep working on the engine, Captain. When I come back, we'll build that steamboat."

The man grinned at him. It was a joke they shared, a gentle joke between friends. "Keep sayin' it often enough, people will believe you."

"They do now."

"Just once, Owen, I wish't you meant it."

"Maybe we can't build a whole boat, Captain. But I'll have some money when I come back. I promise you enough to keep experimenting with that engine."

The man grasped his hand, eyes shining with gratitude. "Thanks, Owen. Fer that and everything. You'll take 'er all the way. I know you will." He looked aft, and the light left his eyes. "All the same, I wish you'd got somebody beside Blackwell."

★ ★ ★ ★ ★

The river was a tawny banner unfolding before them, mile upon mile, with the tree-lined shores forming a cañon that opened endlessly far ahead and closed endlessly far behind. Now and then a meadow broke through the timbered bluffs and spilled down to a beach in an emerald-green rush. There were banks like yellow gold where the tickseed flowered, and river birch stood in mucky bottoms with a soft wind fluttering its papery bark. Behind it all was the frowning mass of the forest, unfolding its green-black billows of foliage endlessly across the land.

For the most part the Ohio's current was enough to impel the boat, carrying it along sometimes at four or five knots an hour, but the keelers had to stand in their catwalks on constant watch for the snags. Every year the flood tides carried down thousands of uprooted trees that sooner or later caught on the bottom. There were the planters, their roots imbedded so deeply that they stood solid as growing trees. A keel running upon one of these would rip her bottom out in a second. More dangerous yet were the sawyers, whose roots were not caught so solidly and whose free ends bobbed erratically with the current. They often remained hidden below the surface, rearing their heads suddenly to strike like vindictive snakes. These snags stood alone in mid-channel or gathered in veritable forests along the shallows and the sharp turns, forming lethal shoal waters that were feared by every boatman. As soon as they were sighted, the boat would rock and shudder to the passage of running men, and the patroon's bawling voice would issue in the few moments of madness.

"Head six, two on the larb'rd! Throw your poles and brace off! Heap, git to the starb'rd! Pandash, make a reverend set on that snag by the sandspit! Hump, you 'gators!"

They reached Salt River that night, sliding into the rotting jelly that stood before a miserable huddle of log buildings set on a sloping mudbank midway between forests and river. The men leaped ashore and made her fast, and then spread away to help the cook set up camp. Blackwell was the last off the keel. He saw Naylor standing alone by the bow and came to him. The muscles lay with a beefsteak thickness across Blackwell's chest beneath his dirty red shirt, and he stank of sweat and rancid bear grease.

"There's a tavern in this town," he said. "After dinner, I'll let the men go in for a drink."

"No."

Blackwell looked surprised. "What?"

"We made an agreement," Naylor told him. "We don't let them into a town till New Madrid. I'm not a-goin' to lose half my crew in these deadfalls along the way."

Blackwell's lids crept together till his eyes were merely silver slits in the dusk. "You ain't going to give me trouble so soon, are you, kid?"

"If you don't want to keep your word, you might as well go back to Louisville and find another keel."

The man stared intently at him. Naylor's face looked gaunt and dour, and there was no relenting in it. He could almost hear the cogs of Blackwell's elemental mind turning. Finally the man settled back, letting a chuckle flow from him on a rough gust of expelled air. "All right, Owen. New Madrid it is."

He wheeled about and walked toward the fire, ponderous as a swaggering bear. Naylor watched him go, realizing that had been the first test. Blackwell still thought he was a kid and was going to take advantage of him if possible. Naylor knew he'd been lucky there were no men about. Blackwell could not have stood to lose face with the crew by backing down in front of them.

Naylor turned toward the keel. He gazed at it a long time, with Blackwell's antagonism fading from his mind and the pride of ownership making his eyes shine. There was a prime cargo in that long box—Onondaga salt in five bushel barrels; twenty hogsheads of flour from Tarascon's Shippingport mill; ten tons of Juniata iron from the Pittsburgh rolling mills; twenty kreels of hemp spun on the Louisville ropewalks. It could be added up that way, or it could be added up in the years of grueling labor he had given to the boat yards since he was sixteen. His father had died that year, smashed to bits on the rocks at Big Chain. Before that, Naylor had lost three older brothers to the river. It had filled his mother with a bitter hatred of the boatman's life. She had done all within her power to keep him from following in their footsteps. She had been sick those last years, and the necessity of taking care of her and of making their living had kept Naylor tied to the shore. But there had been something else. As young as he was, Naylor had already begun to see the almost universal pattern of the boatman's life. A wild and profligate lot, they looked forward only as far as the next spree ashore, spending their meager earnings in the dives and bordellos of Natchez and New Orleans or losing them to some bandit as they returned home along the Natchez Trace. His father had been at it for twenty years— a dollar a day in the spring and fall, starving to death in a miserable shagbark cabin when winter ice locked the river in—and not a fip in his pocket when he died.

It seemed to Naylor that such a vast river could be more bountiful to a man. It was to some—those who owned their own keels and cargo, sailing them down to New Orleans and selling all at a handsome profit. Naylor had told his idea to Heap, a boatman who had been his father's friend

16

for half a lifetime. He argued the keeler into helping him. They rented ways in the boat yard and worked after hours and on Sundays, building the hull, while Naylor put aside what he could for the cargo. It was a bitterly discouraging process through the years; the hull growing so slowly there on its ways became as big a butt for the townsmen's jokes as Captain Abner's steam engine. More than once Heap had gotten disgusted and shipped out on a downrigger keel. But he always returned, sooner or later, to help Naylor again. Finally, almost the very day they had finished the boat, Sarah Naylor had died.

A step behind broke into Naylor's reverie. He turned to see Heap approaching, holding a pair of tin plates piled high with parched potatoes and meal cakes and roasted salt pork. He was a lean and pigeon-breasted man with knobby arms and sinewy brown hands, dressed in the traditional leather jerkin and tow-cloth trousers of the keeler. His face was as smooth as varnished mahogany till he grinned, then it was etched with a million lines, fine as chicken scratches in the sand. He was grinning now slyly.

"I bet you're thinkin' about that woman."

Naylor frowned. "What?"

"That Evadne. I seen the way she was standing on the bridge, watching you go." Heap handed Naylor a plate, squatting down like an Indian. "You'll forgit her soon's we hit Natchez-Under-The-Hill. I'll be a 'gator's tit if you don't. The women there!" Heap's Adam's apple bobbed in his turkey-thin neck like a cork. He licked his lips, and his eyes shimmered white as marble. "You ever heard of Charlotte Dumaine, hoss?"

Naylor smiled wryly. "Who hasn't?"

Heap talked with his mouth full, pork juice dribbling down his chin. "You'll see her, Owen. But you won't touch

17

her." He put the plate down, making shapes with his hands.
"Jist like that, I swear. And make meat? Worse'n high
yaller. Walk up Silver Street and them keelers and shack
bullies line up behind her, thicker'n black bugs on spiled
bacon ham. Ain't a keeler on the river wouldn't give a heap
o' plunder t' count coup with that chil'e. . . ."

He broke off so abruptly it made Naylor look up. Kenneth Swain stood not six feet from them. Firelight winked
against the gilt basket buttons of his Spanish blue coat.
"You must be speaking of Charlotte Dumaine," he said.

Heap snorted. "Who else?"

Swain's secretive smile deepened the wound-like grooves
bracketing his mouth. There was a sense of spurious aris-
tocracy to his pale and chiseled features. He spoke to
Naylor. "They tell me Captain Abner is a great friend of
yours. Do you really think a steamboat can be built to stem
the river?"

Heap belched disdainfully. "Comin' up these rivers is
like tryin' to climb a greased pole heels upp'rd. Ain't no
steam engine strong enough to haul a boat fernenst a Mississippi current."

"Fulton's done it with the *Clermont*."

"That's on the Hudson," Heap said. "Them Eastern
rivers got a current like a millpond. The only thing that'll
ever haul a boat up this river is muscles and poles, Mister
Swain."

"Then,"—Swain indicated the keelboat with a patrician
hand—"when you sell this cargo in New Orleans . . . ?"

Naylor rose without a sound. The firelight made secret
pockets of shadow in his gaunt young face. "We'll come
back and buy another cargo," he said.

"Ah?" Swain pursed his lips. "Well . . . that's an admirable idea." He smiled at them. He tipped his narrow head.

18

Then he turned and walked idly toward the fire. Blackwell was sitting in on a game of old sledge near the blaze. Swain bent and said something to him. Blackwell shook his head, without looking up, and went on playing. Naylor was still watching Swain.

"Tarascon recommended him, Heap."

"Then he must be all right," Heap said.

"And Blackwell?"

"The best patroon on the river till he gits drunk. Then I'd rather git locked in the cargo box with a grizzly."

"Evadne jumped down my craw about him this morning. So did Captain Abner."

Heap grunted disgustedly. "Abner'd have everybody from Moses to Mike Fink tied up with them boat wreckers at the Ivory Bill. So Blackwell takes a drink down there now and then. I do, too. Does that make me a river pirate?"

Naylor sat down and began eating again. Slowly the night crept in from the forest. It came in satiny shadows that swallowed the sycamores and the oaks and the chestnuts towering like giants with their feet snared in the impenetrable tangle of creepers and vines. It came in the sounds of turkeys gobbling sleepily from some far-off creek bottom and a great owl high in the trees groaning like a man in pain. Once a panther screamed, so far away it sounded thin and shrill. All the other noises stopped for a while. Then, timidly, they started again. Over it all, murmuring, whispering, rippling, was the sound of the river, soft and silken as a mistress sighing in her bed.

Chapter Two

On May 26th, they passed Hurricane Island and Lusk's Ferry and the Three Sisters. On May 27th, it was the mouth of the Cumberland and Smithland and Fort Massac, on the 28th, Little Chain, Wilkinsonville, Big Chain. They were old names to Danny Blackwell, for his world was the river. He didn't know the exact date of his birth there in the shagbark cabin in Redstone. Sometime in the 1770s, son of a waterfront harlot and a river rat, orphaned by malaria so young he couldn't remember either of them, then scavenging and stealing in the streets of Pittsburgh till he was old enough to stow away aboard a downriver keel. From then on he had been molded by the river—its violence, its barbarism, its cruelty. Following the fixed and endless pattern of his life, driven by a primitive cycle of appetites and lusts, knowing neither how to read nor write, but dimly conscious of the outside world, he was closer to the animals in many ways than to men, and the river—more than two thousand miles long and a mile wide—was his cage. He paced it restlessly from end to end, and, when the pressures of its confinement became too much, he sought release in the savage revels ashore. Those pressures had begun to build up as they neared the mouth of the Ohio, turning him restive and morose as a rogue bull. They had been on their way for ten days, broiling under the sun, battling the snags, with the emptiness and loneliness of a vast wilderness pressing closer and closer around them. The whole crew was beginning to show the strain, quarreling among themselves, taking his orders sullenly.

They reached the confluence of the two great rivers on the 30th, fighting their way through the yellow whirlpools and into the chalky rush of the Mississippi. It took them two more days to reach New Madrid, the first town of any decent size since Louisville. It lay like a miserable jade stretched out on the low bank above the river. The town had been founded in 1788 by a Colonel Morgan from Pennsylvania who had planned to make it a famous and glittering metropolis, but malaria and politics had defeated his dreams, and all that remained was a squalid collection of log houses, a crumbling church, a half dozen ugly taverns that catered to boatmen and the river trade.

A dozen boats lay against the muddy levee. Blackwell maneuvered his craft between another keel and an emigrant's broadhorn. This huge craft, with its sweeps sticking out on either side like a pair of great horns, was carrying a whole family downriver. The cabin on its afterdeck was as big as some of the houses ashore, and the pen near the bow held a pair of cows, three horses, and half a dozen goats. A ponderous farmer in tattered linsey-woolsey stood by one of the sweeps, gazing with unveiled hostility upon the boatmen.

As soon as the keel bumped the levee, the crew dropped their poles with a clatter, looking expectantly up at Blackwell. He jumped off the cargo box and strode to Naylor, standing in the bow. Taking orders from such a youth had undermined his childish pride, and he had taken every occasion to assert his authority on the downriver trip. He stopped before Naylor, his massive-boned face set and belligerent. "We're goin' ashore this time, by God, and no argument about it."

Surprisingly Naylor smiled. "That's our agreement.

21

Have your frolic. Heap and me'll stand watch."

It took the wind out of Blackwell's sails. He glared at Naylor a moment, at a loss for words, then he wheeled about, bawling roughly at the men. "Tumble out . . . and save some o' that rotgut f'r me!"

The crew scrambled ashore, stringing out up the main street in a shouting, hooting gang. They were like a bunch of brawling schoolboys who could only stand the restricted confines of the boat so long, then they had to be released or their sheer animal spirits would explode into some dangerous violence. Blackwell followed them, swaggering and shouting and laughing with the anticipation of what lay ahead. He was halfway up the main street when Kenneth Swain joined him.

"So you really think that Naylor means to use the profits from his voyage for a steamboat?" Swain asked.

Blackwell laughed hoarsely. "You been hearin' too much tavern talk at Louisville."

Swain pursed his lips. "More than tavern talk, Danny. Captain Abner's an old friend of the Naylor family. I understand Naylor's father put some money into his experiments with steam."

"What does that prove? A 'coon smart enough to have his own keel at twenty-three ain't goin' to waste his money on such crazy doin's as a steam engine."

"On the contrary. A man that shrewd is liable to be just the one with the vision to foresee what steam can mean to the river."

Blackwell frowned at the man. He didn't like dandies. He didn't like the fancy language, and he didn't like fancy clothes. "Just what could it mean to the river?" he sneered.

Swain studied his gold-headed cane as he twirled it between slim fingers. "If steam comes to the Mississippi,

Danny, you'd be out of a job. Every boatman on the river would be out of a job."

Blackwell made a guttural sound. "I been a boatman all my life. Nobody's takin' that away from me."

"Captain Abner is closer to a steamboat than anybody dreams. All he needs is the money. And Naylor will have that when he comes back from New Orleans."

Blackwell slowed down, with his shrewd and primitive mind picking the implications to pieces. His face darkened till the scars of a hundred river battles stood out white as chalk on his blunt cheek bones. He came to a full stop and swung to face the other man. "Who are you, Swain?"

The man smiled at his cane. "Shall we say a friend of the boatman?"

"The hell you are!" Blackwell leaned toward the man, his voice low and thick with anger. "I think I know what's in your mind, and I won't have none of it. I been a patroon for ten years, and I never lost one keel in that whole time. I don't know what you got against Naylor, but, if you try any of your crummy schemes aboard my boat, I'll bust you open like a sack of meal and pitch you to the 'gators."

He wheeled from the man and stalked down the middle of the street. What the hell kind of shoal had he run into? If Swain had it in for Naylor, why didn't he get the kid himself? Blackwell felt no particular allegiance to Naylor; in fact, he knew an insidious jealousy of the youth's achievement. Somehow it wasn't right a kid should get ahead so fast. Blackwell had been on the river all his life and what did he have to show for it? A few fips in his pocket, a red feather in his cap. But his feelings for Naylor did not conflict with his allegiance to the boat. He'd been signed on to take it to New Orleans and, by God, that's where it would go. No damned dandy was going to spoil his record.

The confused anger Swain had raised in him only quick-ened Blackwell's need for some release. He reached the Shawnee Tavern, its taproom a gloomy, low-ceilinged chamber beamed with unpeeled logs. The light was supplied by a few hog-fat candles that added their stink to the gagging reek of stale whisky and damp wood and unwashed bodies. Most of the crew were already lined up at the plank bar along with the men from the other keels and flats at the levee. Blackwell joined them and was soon roaring drunk. He began beating on the bar with his mug.

"It's time for the wimen. Who's goin' with me to La Fleur's?"

By the time he had gathered half a dozen of them, drunk and shouting, Pandash and another keeler came shambling in the door. Pandash's saturnine face was flushed with liquor and a vindictive anger glittered in his black eyes.

"Ain't no wimen in town," he told them. "The gals at La Fleur's heard we made a landing and ran out on us."

Blackwell stood by the end of the bar, swaying a little, memory of a year ago at La Fleur's coming to him. They had left the place in a shambles, and one of the girls had been hurt pretty bad. But it didn't ease the aching need in him. Weeks without a woman now. Weeks on that damned river. It ate into a man. It filled him with an intense frustration, a sense of awesome pressure, building up inside, that had to be loosed.

Somebody had moved to his elbow. Kenneth Swain. Smiling. Twirling his cane. "No women, Danny?"

"Shut up."

"Maybe Heap warned them."

"What's he got to do with it?"

"He's Naylor's partner, you know. Helped Naylor build the keel. Maybe he plans to help on the steamboat hull, too."

"Will you shut up?" snarled Blackwell. He slammed the bottle on the bar. He had to blink to see straight. "I got to do somethin'." His voice rose to an enraged shout. "I'm so full of pus and bile my seams will burst wide open if I don't do somethin'. . . ."

"Why not Heap?" Swain asked. He smiled, looking down at the gouging nail on Blackwell's thumb. "A blind man couldn't build a steamboat, Danny."

Blackwell stared blankly at him. A rush of new rage swelled the veins in his neck till they stood out big as a man's thumb. He swung a wild blow at Swain, shouting: "You bastard!"

Swain ducked back, and Blackwell spun on around till he was facing the others. He lunged at a keeler, and the man dodged aside. Blackwell crashed into the bar; he swung around, letting his venom out in a wild roar. "I'm the child of a snapping turtle!"

It killed the sound instantly. The shouting, the hoarse curses, the rough scuffle of boots on the dirt floor—all of it ceased. He saw their faces, a score of them, gleaming with sweat and contorted with their surprise, turned toward him.

"Come on, somebody," he bawled. "Come up to taw. This is me and no mistake." Like a tiger in his cage he paced across the room, glaring at them as they spread away from him. "If I can't have a woman, I got to have a fight." He picked up a chair and smashed it against the wall. "Come on, you 'coons. I'm all brimstone. I'm a volcano. If I don't git my bottom scraped, I'm a-goin' to explode."

He was so drunk he almost tripped over a table. He made a pass at Pandash, but the man spun free. He sensed someone moving on his left and spun back with blinding speed, catching him with an outflung arm. The swiping blow knocked the man backward into a table; it spilled be-

25

neath him, and he fell heavily to the floor amid the wreckage. Only then did Blackwell see that it was Heap. In his drunken state Blackwell was no longer capable of resisting Swain's insidious suggestions. It flooded through him on a tide of rage. No son-of-a-bitch was going to build a steamboat on his river. He jumped at Heap with a wild cry, trying to kick him in the head. Heap rolled away and scrambled to his feet. He was drunk, too, and his challenge came from him in a squealing shout of anger. "I was weaned on alligator milk!"

Again, for an instant, the intense silence fell. Every man knew what it meant. Blackwell had found his victim. Then a scuffling sound began. It sounded like rats scampering across the hard dirt floor, as the crew began to circle the two men. Their faces were shining, their lips parted, their eyes wide in an avid expectancy.

A gusty sigh of satisfaction flowed from Blackwell. He spread his boots, crooked his arms out, began to circle the man. Heap leaned toward him, matching his movements. The drunken anger still made a putty-colored stain against Heap's cheeks, but the primitive eagerness was beginning to varnish his eyes, for this was a pattern fulfilling itself, as necessary to their child-like lives as food and drink.

"Maybe you don't know who Killin' Danny is," Blackwell announced. "I'm a poor hoss, that's a fack, and must smell like a drowned polecat from a hunnert miles off. But I can't be whipped. I'm the identical personage what grinned a whole menagerie out of countenance, the same 'gator that made the ring-tailed chimpanzee hang his head in shame. Whoop!" He jumped into the air, cracking his heels. "Maybe you heard about the time I spit too far and put out the sun."

Heap flexed his arms, circling Blackwell. "I'm a pretty

severe colt myself. One squint of mine would singe the pelt off a catamount. Bare my teeth and the shine would blind a man in New York. Cock-a-doodle-doo!" He matched Blackwell's antics, jumping into the air, flapping his arms like the wings of a rooster. "I'm your toughest sort. I was born in hell, raised on brimstone, suckled by a grizzly, got nine rows of back teeth, I'm so all-fired helliferocious I rumble like an earthquake every time I open my mouth!"

A ritual. A tradition. A catechism of boasts and taunts adhering to the exaggerated specifications handed down by the river bullies for decades. A burlesque to the uninitiated, yet deadly in its implications as a pair of rutting bulls trumpeting their blood lust to the moon, for beneath those flamboyant taunts all the savage cruelty of the river was boiling closer and closer to the surface.

"I'm the very 'coon which out-grinned Davy Crockett."

"I'm the identical colt which whipped Mike Fink."

"I'm half hoss, half alligator, clumb a streak of lightnin', and slid down a locust tree a thousand feet tall, ain't even got a splinter in my rump."

"Come up to taw, then, and quit braggin'."

The crowd took up the chant. "Come up to taw, come up to taw, come up to taw!"

Both men were almost within reach of each other, circling for an opening. Blackwell's shirt was drenched with sweat, plastered wetly to the beefsteak thickness of the pectoral muscles across his chest. Heap was grunting and wheezing like a stallion at a fence. "I'm the original 'gator that chawed up the pup."

"I'm the bear that ate the 'gator."

"I'm the catamount that clawed the bear."

"I'm the buff'lar that gored the cat."

"Come up to taw, come up to taw . . . !" It swelled from

the crowd like a pagan chant, and Blackwell could suddenly support it no longer. He rushed against Heap with a hoarse roar. Heap spun away like a top, but Blackwell swung with him. He saw the man's contorted face in front of him and came up from beneath with a blow.

It snapped Heap's head back and knocked him into the press of the crowd. A dozen hands caught him, shoving him back at Blackwell. Heap reeled drunkenly, a glassy shine to his eyes. Blackwell was but a foot away and lunged in to strike again. In the last instant, Heap doubled over. Blackwell knew the daze had been feigned, and tried to stop. But it was too late. He ran right into Heap's butting head. The pain slashed through his middle like knives, and he heard all the air leave him in a hissing gasp as he jackknifed over Heap. Heap straightened up and was on him like a wild thing, clawing, biting, slugging. A lashing boot caught him in the crotch. Blackwell doubled over, incapacitated with the sick pain, and fell on all fours. Heap danced around him, kicking him in the ribs, the head.

He caught Heap's foot and heaved. Heap came down on him. Heap slugged at his face, trying to tear free. Blackwell felt his teeth break under the impact of bony knuckles, but he had Heap grappled to him now. Locked together, they rolled back and forth, each struggling, shifting, fighting to gain the leverage that would give the advantage. The taste of blood was like brine in Blackwell's mouth. Heap tore a hand free, sank a blow deep into his belly.

Gasping sickly, Blackwell countered with his elbow, smashing it into Heap's face. Dazed, Heap could not block the following shift of Blackwell's body. Blackwell caught his shoulder, ripping the shirt as he twisted the man beneath him. He was on top of Heap, a knee in the small of his back, an arm hooked under his throat. It arched Heap like a

28

bow. One good pull would snap him like kindling. The pain and the outrage of punishing blows and the primitive excitement of battle had ripped the veneer of civilization from Blackwell, robbing him of all reason, taking him back to the animals. The muscles rippled and bulged across his back as he gathered himself. With a stertorous grunt, he started the sudden jerk that would break Heap in two.

He didn't complete it. He checked himself, with Heap arched beneath him, eyes straining from his head like a frog's. Something had been pressed against Blackwell's temple, something about the circumference of a coin.

"Blackwell, I've got a pistol against your head. If you don't leave him go and get up, I'm a-goin' to shoot."

It was Naylor's voice. All the youth was gone from it, and he sounded a million years old. Somehow, through the drunken rage firing Blackwell's brain, he realized what he had to do. He released Heap. He got to his hands and knees, then stood up, swaying. The pistol was taken from his head, and he stepped off Heap, wheeling to face Naylor. He had to blink his bloodshot eyes to get the youth in focus. The gun was still pointed at his head. Behind it, Blackwell could see a gaunt face, the cheek bones and the brow making white ridges against the dark flesh. Blackwell swayed forward in a sort of sodden rage, breathing like a man at the end of a long run. "I'll break you up for this, Naylor," he said. "I'll kill you."

Naylor did not answer. Some trick of the treacherous candlelight made his eyes flash green as a cat's. There was something dour and utterly baleful about it. Heap staggered to his feet, and Naylor took his elbow, swinging him around and guiding him to the door. Here he stopped, speaking in a metallic voice. "Be sure you're sober when you come back to the boat, Blackwell. You won't get aboard drunk."

Chapter Three

Naylor and Heap stood watch aboard the keel for the rest of the night. While Naylor sat on top of the cargo box with a pistol loaded and primed in his lap, Heap rubbed lard and gunpowder into his wounds, and hunkered down in the catwalk with his back against the box, grumbling and complaining.

"You shouldn't o' done that, Owen. I would've whipped him. I'm a pretty severe colt myself, you know."

"Helliferocious."

Heap spat. "I guess I do owe you some thanks. It jist gits a man's pride, that's all." He squinted up at Naylor. "How'd you come to be there?"

"Wheeler come running down and told me you was fit to git snapped in two." Naylor grinned through the night at Heap. "I couldn't do much with a partner in that fix."

Heap did not answer. It was all they would express of the bond between them. It needed no words. Naylor felt as close to this man as he had to his own family—an attachment that went back through the years of heartbreaking labor together, of working and planning and hoping and building toward a common dream.

A distant sound of another fight issued from the Shawnee. The broadhorn creaked, next to the keel, as the farmer shambled restlessly from his cabin. Naylor knew what worried him. There were enough keelboat crews ashore to make for a full-scale riot if it got started. The rampages of the boatmen were the scourge of the river towns. Naylor had seen it happen more than once, spreading through a village like wildfire—the raping and the killing and the destroying. They could wreck a town in a short time, and the local police were powerless to stop it.

Shortly after midnight, a figure approached the gangplank. Naylor challenged him, and the man answered that he was Swain. He came aboard, a narrow shape in the darkness, and stopped below Naylor. "You'd better hope Blackwell gets drunk enough to forget what happened tonight," he said.

"We'll take care of that when it comes," Naylor answered.

Swain stood peering up at him a moment longer, then made his way around Heap to his sleeping pallet up in the rowing benches.

Some of the crew straggled back through the early morning hours and fell into a drunken sleep along the catwalks. The last one was Danny Blackwell. He must have slept off his drunk in the wrecked tavern. His broad, slope-shouldered figure materialized out of a pale dawn, stumbling across the levee. Naylor stood to his full length on the cargo box, a hand on the mahogany butt of his big Cherington pistol. "Are you sober, Blackwell?"

The patroon stopped at the gangway, glowering up at Naylor from red-rimmed eyes. He blinked stupidly, running his blunt fingers through three inches of honey-colored beard. "What happened last night?" he asked.

"Don't you remember?"

Their voices had wakened some of the crew. They sat up, blinking their eyes. Heap rose from the catwalk, watching Blackwell closely.

Blackwell shook his head stupidly. "I must have got pretty drunk," he said.

"You was going to break Heap's back. I stopped you with a gun."

Blackwell gazed blankly up at Naylor. The scars made a chalky crisscross pattern on his square cheek bones. Suddenly he laughed. "That's a good brag," he said. He walked across the gangplank and onto the catwalk, throwing his head back to let the laugh roar out of him. "That's the goddamnedest brag I heard since Pepper Annie claimed she took on seventy-three keelers in one night." He shoved past Heap and walked among the men, kicking them awake, still laughing.

Heap gaped after him. Then he looked up at Naylor. "He don't believe you," Heap said wonderingly. "He don't believe a kid like you would have the guts to pull a stunt like that on Danny Blackwell."

Light as a cat, Blackwell vaulted onto the cargo box and strode to the head. His bawling shout shattered the morning. "Whaddaya gapin' at, you 'coons? Jist fer gittin' drunk last night you kin shove off without breakfast. Now stand to your poles. We're goin' to N'yawleens!"

South of New Madrid, it was a river with shores of soapy-looking clay that lay close to the horizon and swarms of mosquitoes that rose from every thicket to plague the boatmen and long green islands inhabited only by birds that filled the day with their clamor. South of New Madrid, it was a new world to Naylor, day upon day of floating down the great sluggish river that curled and dipped and twisted and looped back on itself and flowed endlessly through a country where for weeks on end they didn't see one single human being. Some days they fought like wild men against the snags and the overwhelming current and the dangerous turns. In one stretch a mile long they made ten crossings to stay in a safe channel; in another reach they floated all day without need of a pole, lying stripped to the waist on deck, playing twenty-one, yarning, sweltering under the merciless sun. Pelicans swarmed the islands and cranes rose whooping from the muddy banks and jays and parakeets chattered in the trees. Near Council Island, they saw Indians darting their canoes alongshore in search of the vanishing swans whose fine down was so fashionable in Europe.

It was cane country now, where the canes grew as big around as a man's leg and clattered like an army in battle when the wind blew. Alligators looked like scaly logs, sunning themselves on the sandbars, and the roar of the bulls made the brakes hideous at night. In some places the river flooded the bottom lands for miles back of the shore, and the cypress stood in these swamps like gnarled old men, gray-bearded with Spanish moss, festooned with vines and creepers, filtering the light till it had a pale green glow. Heap had been cutting a nick on his pole for every day on the river, and by his calculations it was June 16th when they reached the Big Black River, with Natchez only two days away. They beached the boat on a dirty sand spit half a mile above the river and pitched camp back in the cypress. The men sat around a snapping fire, consuming vast quantities of roasted salt pork and parched potatoes, the first course drowned in bear grease, the last swimming in molasses.

Naylor saw Kenneth Swain approaching the fire. The man had a certain charm about him and was a seasoned traveler, but had revealed little of himself on the long journey. On the other hand, he had done nothing to perpetuate Naylor's first suspicions. He stopped at the stew pot, making some comment Naylor could not hear. The cook looked up with a frown. He was built squat and thick as a keg of Monongahela in his dirty red shirt and blackened rawhide leggings. He had curly black hair, a saturnine face, and his mouth was mean as a knife slash. He answered Swain in a truculent voice and went back to his cooking.

The other keelers gathered around the fire, helping themselves to more salt pork. They had begun to talk of Natchez-Under-The-Hill, and the women there. It excited the cook, and he wheeled around and jumped into the air, clicking his heels together. "Talk about your other gals all you want. I say it's a shame to have Charlotte Dumaine runnin' around loose in Natchez-Under."

A whoop arose from Wheeler. He was a big, red-headed man from Brownsville who had lost his right hand on a pole and now wore an iron hook in its place. "Quit jumpin' around, Pandash," he jeered. "Somebody give you a dose of Spanish fly?"

The cook threw his head back and crowed like a cock. "Don't need none of that. I'm horny as a goat right now. It's Charlotte Dumaine for Pandash this time."

Nicolas Fry strutted into the circle. Big and potbellied, his swarthy face was pitted by the pox he had contracted in New Orleans. "I'll lay a month's wages you don't even git near her."

Naylor watched their antics with subdued humor. It was an old ritual to him. When he'd been a kid, it had been Pepper Annie and her legendary feats in the bordellos of New Orleans. When he'd first gotten his job in the boat yards, it was the Queen of Tchoupitoulas Street and her lurid perversions. Charlotte Dumaine was only the most recent in a long line of women who had excited the boatmen's childish imaginations. Through the chronic exaggerations of the river men she had become more legend than reality, a strange combination of shining symbol and salacious dream upon which the men could dwell during the long, lonely days along the river.

"Is she really as beautiful as they say, Heap?"

Heap's grin gave him a satyr's face. "You never clapped your peepers on nothin' like it, chil'e. Like that." His hands made bulbous curves in the air. "And that." His eyes shone lecherously. "And that. . . ." He broke off and rose abruptly, pacing a restless circle around Naylor. "Talk like this makes me feel plumb sergiverous." The word, from some strange convolution of language, was derived from the name of a 1st-Century Roman voluptuary.

Naylor grinned at him. "You better break out Zadoc Cramer. This is getting' you exactly nowhere."

Heap licked his lips and hunkered down again, pulling out his tattered copy of Zadoc Cramer's NAVIGATOR. It was the bible of the boatmen, this little navigation manual, with its white line woodcuts charting the river on a scale twelve miles to the inch. Cramer had been publishing it since 1801, selling it for a dollar a copy at his bookstore on Market Street in Pittsburgh. Every change in the river—the new snags and the new cut-offs, the slightest alteration in any channel, the formation of new sandbars or the disappearance of old ones—all these and a thousand other things were reported to Cramer by the boatmen and patroons. Each new issue incorporated the constant flood of information, and in this way Cramer kept the guide up to date. Naylor watched Heap as he studied the page with squinted eyes.

Palmira Island, No. 106. Lies nearest the left side—channel right. It is 4½ miles long. A settlement at the head.

No. 107. 2½ miles below. Channel good either side—

2 miles long. In very low water the left pass of 106 goes nearly dry. Right side is main channel in all stages.

Heap shook his head, marking the page with a stub of a pencil. "Have to tell him that left channel on one-oh-seven won't even be good in high water no more. Never seed such a mess o' snags." He fished a twist of garlic from his filthy shirt pocket, thumbing it into his mouth.

Naylor turned his head away. "Don't you stink enough?"

Heap's chuckle shook his lank frame. "Black Vomit country now, hoss. You better have a chaw, too."

"I'd almost rather have the fever."

Blackwell crossed in front of them, carrying his empty plate toward the fire. The blunt ridges of his cheek bones had been burnt raw red by the sun, and his eyebrows were bleached out till they ran like shaggy white hedges above the silvery disks of his eyes. He glanced at Naylor, scowling thoughtfully, and then passed on.

"He's still tryin' to recollect what happened in New Madrid," Heap muttered. "I wish you'd keep that gun in your belt, Owen."

Naylor smiled humorlessly. "I don't think he'll do anything till he gets the boat safe to New Orleans."

Heap made another mark in the NAVIGATOR, grumbling to himself. Naylor saw that Swain was no longer by the fire. He looked around the camp and could not see the man. He rose restlessly. "If we're sleepin' aboard tonight, I think we better turn in."

Heap rose and followed Naylor back through the thick fringe of canes that cut them off from the boat. They emerged on the long spit of sand, stopping abruptly. Clouds scudding over the moon left but a fitful yellow light shimmering on the river. The keel was already twenty feet from the shore, wheeling around into the current. Heap was the first to run for the water, shouting wildly: "Keel adrift! Keel adrift!"

They ran as far as they could into the muddy brown water and then started swimming for it. Naylor was the stronger swimmer and reached the keel before the current could pull her away from him. He caught the gunwale near the bow, pulling himself up. As he bellied over the side, dripping and gasping, he glimpsed a speck of red caught where the binding strake met the stem. It was a triangular piece of cloth. In that single instant the significance of it reached Naylor. The boat had been beached too solidly to have slid off into the water by itself, and a man pushing her off from the bow could have torn a piece from his shirt on the jagged point of the strake. A savage look filled Naylor's face. As he scrambled to his feet, he pulled the piece of cloth loose and jammed it in his pocket. Then he ran down the cleated walkway till he reached a pole in the scuppers.

Heap was pulling himself over the bow as Naylor straightened with the pole. The keeler rolled inboard, gasping, drained. "Go down on your pole," he panted, " 'fore we lose the bottom."

Naylor drove his pole into the river. He was bent double before it struck bottom.

Heap got another pole, and joined him. "Got to turn her back to shallower bottom." He groaned. "Shoals ahead at the Grand Gulf. They'll eat her keel out in a minute."

They could see the crew, running down to the shore now. Several of them ran into the water and struck out for the boat. Heap and Naylor strained at their poles, but they were fighting a swift current, trying to do the job of a dozen men. Even a full crew would have had trouble turning her

now. She swept on downriver, pulling away from the swimming men. Then the bottom went out, and Naylor and
Heap dropped to their knees, pulling their poles high to
save them.

Heap climbed to his feet, staring ahead. As Naylor rose,
dizzy from the struggle, he could hear the growing rush of
rapids ahead.

"It's too late to leave her," Heap said. "We're right in it."

Under the pale moonlight, Naylor saw the river churning
itself to scummy lace over the snags ahead. The first one was
a planter, a huge oak sunk solidly in the bottom, its skeletal
branches sticking five feet above the surface, waiting like
twisted spears to impale an unlucky keel. Both Heap and
Naylor rushed forward, driving their poles at the water-
logged tree. Steel bit into oak. The leather bottoms at the top
of the poles drove into straining shoulders. The boat yawed
aside from the planter, and the current swept her around.

"Git back on the sweep!" Naylor yelled. "Try to keep
her in the channel!"

Heap scrambled atop the cargo box, and ran to the stern.
The long arm of the steering oar was swinging wildly on its
tholepin. Heap caught it and threw his weight against it,
trying to swing the boat into the main channel. From his
greater height he could see the snags ahead. He shouted at
Naylor: "Sawyer on our larb'rd, Owen! Head up and brace
off!"

Naylor ran through the rowing benches to the other side.
The free end of a river birch bobbed erratically up and
down with the current. He drove his pole at the fork, but it
bobbed high, and he missed. He had to drop his pole and
go to his knees in the scuppers to keep from pitching overboard.

The keel ran her thwart against the tree. There was a

scream like a woman in pain, and the whole boat shuddered and leaped like a wounded buck. Naylor was thrown back against the cargo box. He saw the birch sweep by. Branches cracked off like gunshots. The keel righted itself, racing on down through the froth of white water.

Heap's voice came thin and shrill. "Take another pole! If we can get her through them shoals, there's smooth water around the bluff."

But as Naylor regained his feet, he heard a roar like a waterfall. They were right on the shoals, a veritable forest of snags raising their gaunt arms above the froth. Dripping wet now, battered and gasping from the battle, he scooped another pole from the scuppers. Heap was leaning with all his weight against the sweep, trying to use the eddy to swing them away from the shoals and into the main channel, but the boiling rapids sucked thcm in like a vortex.

A sawyer bobbed high above the bow, not a foot away. Naylor lunged for it, driving his steel tip for the fork. It bit deeply, and the boat took a sheer, almost pitching Naylor off his feet. As the keel swung around the sawyer, a planter loomed ahead.

Naylor shifted his weight and tossed his pole. Before he could drive it home, there was a rending crash. The world rocked on its axis. The moon spun over the horizon, and the wet deck slid from beneath Naylor. Pitched into mid-air, he was deafened with the shriek of snapping strakes and the wild crash of smashing timbers. The gunwale passed beneath him, and he went headfirst into the river. He came up once, convulsed with a paroxysm of coughing. Then branches tore savagely at his body, and he shouted with the pain. His head struck something with a sharp crack. The roar of the rapids seemed to spread through him in a violent black rush. It was the last thing he heard.

Chapter Four

The morning was already hot when Charlotte Dumaine awoke in her room above Pepper Annie's Inn. A heat that drew out all the noisome stench of Natchez-Under, sucking it from the very boards and walls of the building, bringing the old dismal depression to Charlotte as she rose and dressed.

She stood a while at the window, gazing listlessly out on the town that had been her life. There were two towns, really. On the top of the bluff was Natchez—the town of wealth and comfort, pleasure and ease, rich cotton merchants and indolent planters and beautiful women. Beneath the bluffs was Natchez-Under-The-Hill—the town of sin and violence, shack bullies and harlots, drunkenness and despair. Here, three hundred miles up the Mississippi from New Orleans, seven hundred miles downriver from the mouth of the Ohio, an irregular shelf of soft earth had been formed against the base of the cliffs, half a mile long and a few hundred yards wide. There was but one road winding down from Natchez above; as soon as it reached the shelf below, it became Silver Street, the main thoroughfare of Natchez-Under, criss-crossed by alleys that ran through the welter of weather-beaten shacks covering every available foot of ground on the mud flat.

Fronting the river was the half-moon landing, crowded with scores of vessels, sometimes anchored four and five deep against the levee. Flatboats from Pittsburgh and keels from Louisville; barges and arks and broadhorns carrying emigrants downriver; *pirogues* piled with St. Louis furs; and even seagoing brigs, bringing cargo from the Caribbean Islands and Europe, their spars rising in a naked black fretwork against a sun-bleached sky. From the boats, a constant stream of traffic flowed up Silver Street to the town above. Drays and wagons loaded with barrels of corn and salt and flour groaned through the milling crowds. Long lines of slaves clanking in their chains carried cotton and sacked potatoes and kegs of rum and hogsheads of salt and New England furniture. The boatmen were everywhere, singing and cursing, brawling and bragging, staggering in and out of the countless dives and brothels that lined the street.

For the downriver boatmen it was the first real taste of a town since New Madrid, hundreds of miles behind, and for the upriver keelers it was the last chance for a genuine revel ashore in four long grueling months. Natchez-Under was dedicated to giving them what they wanted. Since the beginning of the flatboat era, it had been known as the wildest, most vicious, most lawless town on the continent, a place of thieves and cutthroats, gamblers and prostitutes, con men and murderers, all purveying to the primitive appetites of the boatmen. Yellow-skinned hawkers sifted through the mob, calling out the joys to be had on Silver Street. A half-naked woman bent from the second-story window of a log building, shouting raucously at a red-shirted flatter below. Pepe stood just beneath Charlotte's window, an oily young man resplendent in a frayed blue coat with double gilt buttons. As a keeler wandered by, Pepe darted out and seized his arm.

"I got just the girl for you, keeler. You won' fin' nothin' like her on Silver Street. You know what I mean. Like a cat, keeler, jus' like a cat."

"Furry?"

As their voices were drowned by the shrill cries and the cacophony of tinny pianos issuing from a dozen barrel houses, Charlotte turned away from the window. It was an old picture to her. She had been born to it, born south of New Orleans, out in the miserable shacks on the mud flats where the shrimpers eked out their precarious living; born of an Acadian father who had been driven south with his parents when the British forced the French settlers out of Nova Scotia in *le grand derangement;* born of a red Irish mother who had been orphaned at sixteen by a Spanish musket ball that had killed her father in the first battle of Baton Rouge. The sea took the Acadian, when Charlotte was eight. Her mother, unable to support the two of them, had taken the girl to their only relative in New Orleans, Pepper Annie, who had a houseful of girls on Girod Street. It was where Charlotte's first real education began.

She didn't know exactly when the visitors to Pepper Annie's began pinching her buttocks and offering her a piece of candy or a fip to go further, for she had bloomed young, with breasts round as apples. But the rough boatmen, stinking of river mud and cheap whisky, were repulsive to her, and the affected dandies, scented with women's perfume and cackling like excited hens, made her crawl inside. She never tasted the candy or took the fips, and none of Pepper Annie's inducements could make her accept their sly offers. Then the cholera swept the town, taking her red-headed mother and half the girls in the house, and Pepper Annie had fled New Orleans along with thousands of others. That had begun the succession of dreary river towns, Pointe Coupée, Tunica Village, Clarksville, Baton Rouge, Pinkneyville, all the way up to Natchez. . . . Charlotte tried to drive the repugnant memories from her mind, moving to the cracked mirror and combing out her hair. It was rust-red hair, falling in a luxurious cascade to her shoulders, massing there, curling in shimmering abundance, with enough feeble illumination creeping through the window to start amber fires in its depths. It formed a hoydenish frame for her face with its haunted shadows beneath the oblique cheek bones, its eyes that seemed to tilt up at the outer corners with some elfin mischief. She was nineteen, but her body had matured long ago. The flimsy sarsenet dress did little to hide her insistent curves. Her beasts were bold and out-swelling, and her hips curved like a lyre against the skirt.

"Charlotte!" Pepper Annie's shrill howl came from the depths of the building. "Where the hell are you? You got some shopping to do this mornin'."

Reluctantly Charlotte put the comb down and started down the narrow stairs to the taproom below. Another day. The beginning of another day on Silver Street, like a hundred before it, a thousand, a lifetime. It seemed to drain all the life from her, leaving her sodden and apathetic and hardly able to face it. The taproom was a long, low-ceilinged chamber, typical of these taverns, with a splintery bar made from flatboat gunwales running the length of one side and a cluster of rude tables and benches on the other. At the bottom of the stairs was a landing, four feet higher than the main floor, a sort of dais that commanded the taproom. Upon this sat the chair. It was a Queen Anne chair, with its upholstery of frayed crimson damask, its brass-studded tacks, its tattered lace pelisse trailing down over the arms—and ensconced in this dilapidated throne was Pepper Annie. She was an immense tub of a woman, dressed in a soiled white blouse, a tawdry green velvet skirt, with a fringed shawl of yellow India silk pulled over her head. Her face was a crumbling façade of dissipation and age from which peered a pair of bloodshot eyes imbedded in seamed pouches of flesh. Wattles hung slack and furry on either side of a gray-lipped mouth, and she kept wiping her bulbous, blue-veined nose with a corner of the shawl. She blinked her eyes as Charlotte stopped on the landing.

"Whaddaya doin'?" she asked querulously. "Wastin' your time in front of the mirror again. Primpin' an' fixin' . . . an' waitin' fer a man that'll never come."

Charlotte saw a pair of keelers at the front end of the bar, gaping at her, and spoke in a low voice to keep them from hearing: "He'll come. He promised me."

Her aunt snorted disgustedly. "What does a promise mean to a puke like Louis Reynaud? Why'ntcha give up? Wastin' the best years of y'r youth. Could've set y'self up in the finest parlor house in New Orleans by now. What good has all them gentlemen down from off the bluff done? You know what they're after."

"Annie, I don't want to talk about it. . . ."

"So you and Louis wait around like a couple of ghouls for Grandpa Reynaud to die. . . ."

"What else can we do? He'll never consent to the marriage as long as he's alive."

"You'll never git off Silver Street, Charlotte."

"I will. . . ." Charlotte broke off, biting her lip. It was an old argument between them. She had promised herself a hundred times she would not be drawn into it again.

Then she realized that a man had entered the door. He stood just inside, accustoming his eyes to the gloom. He was a tall man, his buff tailcoat and kerseymere trousers impeccably tailored to a lean frame. He had removed his tall beaver hat, and the light behind him made a tawny nimbus of his carefully groomed hair. His features were marble-pale, chiseled into a mold of chronic cynicism. That mold broke when he saw Charlotte. His thin lips formed a smile of genuine pleasure, and he came toward her with long strides that sent the tattoo of his boots echoing through the whole room.

She went down to the main floor to greet him. "Swain," she said. "Your keel arrived early."

Kenneth Swain halted before her, performing a gallant bow. "As a matter of fact, Charlotte, my keel didn't arrive at all. It went down on the shoals of the Big Black, and I had to borrow a horse from Leland at Bayou Pierre."

"You weren't hurt?" she asked quickly.

"I wasn't aboard. Only two of the crew were lost. A man named Naylor and a boatman." He grimaced. "But enough of this morbid talk. I can't tell you how good it is to see you again. How is Louis?"

She gave him an ironic smile. "He still comes down to see me . . . if that's what you meant."

"It isn't exactly what I meant," he said. "But if he ever stops coming, my dear, I am always available."

The faint crevices at the corners of his tawny eyes gave them a searching quality as he looked at her. As ever, she didn't know if he was joking or not. She had known him for years, as one of Louis Reynaud's closest friends. His position in Natchez had always been obscure. Some said he was a professional gambler; others claimed he lived on a remittance from England. He was equally at home among the brawling bullies of Natchez-Under or the fine dandies on the bluffs above, and was accepted in the innermost circles of both classes. Charlotte had always enjoyed his company; he was an intellect and a wit, and every moment was a new surprise. Yet it had always been this way between them, this veil of mock gallantry and badinage, this constant fencing. Sometimes, she thought, he took secret delight in keeping her guessing; sometimes, she thought, he was afraid to let her see behind the mask. Yet she enjoyed the game.

"You know, sir," she said demurely, "that I will marry only for money."

"We shall buy the most fabulous mansion in Natchez," he said. "We shall put the finest *chacalatas* in town to shame. Our extravagances and our profligacy shall become legend."

"You must have done well in the East."

He sighed. "On the contrary, not a fip. A group of Federalists hired me to assassinate President Jefferson, should he be reëlected."

She was shocked into laughter. "Swain, you're terrible."

He bowed. "A blackguard, *mademoiselle.*"

A pair of men entered the front door. Swain raised his head, sending them a casual glance. Then his eyes widened in surprise, almost in shock.

The two in the doorway had halted, blinking in the gloom. One was about forty, egg-bald, with rawhide clothes that hung filthy and grease-blackened against his loose-jointed frame. The other was younger, black-headed, the muscles of his shoulders bunched thickly beneath a torn linsey-woolsey shirt. His face was bony and gaunt, all sharp angles and secret hollows, with a melancholy darkness to his deep-socketed eyes. His glance circled the room, stopping abruptly at Charlotte. A definite change ran through his face. It was an expression Charlotte had seen a thousand times before, when the boatmen looked at her, the slackening of the lips, the little lights burning in the eyes. Then he seemed to become aware of Swain. His expression changed again. Some trick of the light, as he moved his head, made a luminous green flash against the surface of his eyes. He started toward Swain in a long, hard stride.

46

"Naylor," Swain said. "We thought you were dead. We stayed there a whole day, looking up and down the river. . . ."

He broke off as Naylor reached him. There was a smoldering anger on the young man's face. Without a word he grabbed Swain's waistcoat, unbuttoning it in vicious jerks, tearing it open. Swain recovered from his astonishment and caught Naylor's hands, jerking them away. Then he stepped back, his nostrils pinched and white, his hand gripping the gold-headed cane tightly. Charlotte knew it contained a sword.

"My young cock," Swain said in a brittle voice, "if you put such a small value on your health, step out in the alley with me and I will accommodate you with dispatch."

The youth's grim anger seemed to make him oblivious to Charlotte. He pulled a triangular piece of red cloth from his pocket. "I'm lookin' for a man with a hole in his shirt," he said. "When I find him, I'm a-goin' to kill him."

Baffled, Swain turned to the older man. He had regained his control now; some of the droll cynicism was back in his voice. "Heap, will you tell me what this young maniac is talking about?"

The keeler licked his lips, squinting at Swain. "We figger somebody pushed the keel off the beach, Swain. He got his red shirt tore on the bow. If we ever see it, we'll know him."

Swain buttoned his scarlet waistcoat, speaking to Naylor. "If you keep looking for him this way, you won't last long enough to find out who he was. Have you thought of Danny Blackwell, seeking revenge for New Madrid?"

"I'll look at his shirt, too," Naylor said.

"How did you manage to get out of those shoals?" Swain asked.

Naylor settled back a little, still staring intently at

47

Swain's face, searching for something. "I got pitched overboard and knocked out. Heap come in after me. Dragged me ashore. We got lost in them swamps east of Grand Gulf. Finally hooked a ride downriver in some Frenchman's *pirogue*."

As Naylor talked, Heap turned to look at Charlotte again. She met his gaze, and his Adam's apple jumped like a cork on a string. His neck swelled up, and his face got red, and finally he grinned like a fool. His embarrassment was so acute she almost laughed.

But Naylor was looking at her again, too. His anger at Swain had receded; that other expression had returned to his face, so familiar to her. But somehow, this time, it was different. His youth, the melancholy look of his eyes, some underlying sensitivity—whatever it was, she did not feel the inevitable defiance, the old set of defenses rising up.

Swain spoke to Charlotte. "This is Owen Naylor and Heap. They owned the keel that went down." He paused. "Gentlemen . . . Charlotte Dumaine."

Naylor had not taken his eyes from her face. "I guess I knew," he said softly.

Swain looked from Naylor to Charlotte. There was a quizzical expression on his face. Then he asked Naylor: "Do you have a place to stay?"

"Not yet."

"I recommend Pepper Annie's Inn."

Pepper Annie spoke querulously from her dais. "Somebody's gotta pay. I ain't runnin' this place f'r my health."

Naylor looked at her. Then he fished a handful of coins from his pocket, still mixed with river silt. "Your sign outside says a picayune for a meal and a picayune for a room."

Annie accepted the coins, sniffed disgustedly, jerked a thumb at the kitchen. "Charlotte'll dip you up some gumbo."

48

Swain inclined his head at Charlotte. "Do you think Louis will be down today?"

"I doubt it," she said. "There's a race across the river."

"A pity. I'd hoped to see him." He shrugged. "Tell him I'm back. Staying at Connelly's Tavern." He bowed. "I'll take my leave."

He looked at Naylor, showing no humor, and turned to walk jauntily out the door, tapping his sword cane against his tight pants. Naylor watched him till he was gone.

"A coincidence," Charlotte said.

"No," Naylor said. "We were hunting him."

"Why should you suspect him of pushing your keel off?" she asked.

He looked at her with that utterly dour expression in his deep-socketed eyes. It made her wonder if he ever smiled. "We got our reasons," he said.

She felt a faint flush come to her cheeks. She turned and led them into the kitchen. It was a gloomy room, its ceiling beams black from the smoke of the fires. A brick fireplace ran across one side. Within its yawning mouth, iron kettles hung from sooty cranes, a pair of three-legged ovens stood nearly buried in the hot ashes, and a huge cut of beef was spitted above the open fire, dripping juice into the low flames. At the other side of the room was a long table, and behind it was a wooden sink draining directly into the river below.

Charlotte nodded at it. "Maybe you'd like to wash."

Naylor picked up the bar of homemade soap, reeking of ash lye, and found a frayed washrag. There was water in a wooden tub on one counter. Heap was still gaping at Charlotte. When she looked at him, he grinned foolishly once more, gulped, and turned away. She swung one of the kettles out on its crane and dipped gumbo onto a pair of plates.

49

"I've got to do the shopping," she said. "You'll find your room upstairs, at the end of the hall."

Naylor was drying his hands. It made the muscles of his back bunch and knot beneath the flimsy shirt. He put the towel aside and met her gaze again. "Thanks."

She put the plates down, wondering why he should irritate her so. On the surface there was nothing to differentiate him from the countless other boatmen she had known in her life. His clothes were of the roughest sort—a linsey-woolsey shirt that had been torn to shreds when he fell into the snags, tow-cloth trousers black with dirt and grease, moccasins with their toes worn out. He even smelled of the river, the rank and marshy odors of the bottomlands they had waded through. Yet there was something about him that sent a disturbance through her—an animal magnetism that looked out of his melancholy eyes, coming through all the roughness, the filth, the fatigue, and creeping against her like a subtle pressure. It angered her that she should be so affected. She went quickly to get the market basket, and turned to go out. But, as she stepped through the door, she could not help glancing back. He was still watching her.

Chapter Five

Charlotte always lingered as long as possible on her daily shopping trip to the town on the bluffs. Aside from the coach rides with Louis, it was the nearest she had ever gotten to the fairy-tale world of Natchez. Like a ragged urchin staring wistfully through the locked gate of a lovely garden in which rich children played, she drank in all the sights and the sounds and the smells of it. The square was gay with life and movement. Bazaars lined the plaza, their merchandise piled up under the arcades and out in the open. The air stank with rotten persimmons and trampled apricots and melons. She filled her basket with the fresh fruit for a picayune, spent a fip on some mullet sold by a Muskogee Indian, bought a dozen ears of corn from a farmer in from Washington. A black coach drawn by a lathered team cluttered recklessly through the crowded square, with a cloaked Creole galloping *àcheval* to one side and a Negro slave riding ahead to clear the way with his hoarse shouting. She stared after it till it was gone.

At last she had to return to the inn. She found the kitchen empty. Pepper Annie told her that Naylor and Heap were asleep in their room upstairs, exhausted by an all-night ride down the river. The rotten old building steamed with the oppressive heat of early summer, and her dress was soon sticking to her perspiring body. When she could bear it no more, she went upstairs for a bath in the wooden tub. The water was straight from the river and thick with silt, doing little good. She lay listlessly on her bed, waiting for the meager relief of evening.

She must have dozed, for she was awakened by Pepper Annie's raucous call. It was growing dark, and she could hear the murmur of voices and shouts of rough laughter downstairs. She put on a fresh cotton dress, brushed her hair, and descended to the kitchen. Looking through the door, she could see that the taproom was already beginning to fill up. The bar was lined with boatmen in their red shirts and shack bullies in tow-cloth pants, and at the tables were mulatto hawkers and a pair of gamblers in soiled frock coats and frayed nankeen trousers. Cane John was filling a plate with rice and oysters.

"Patroon in the black coat want this *jambalaya*," he said.

Charlotte drew some hot rice cakes from the oven, brushed ashes off with a turkey feather, and added them to the plate. Then she took it to the blanket-coated patroon seated in a corner.

"Some rye, too, Charlotte, with a chaser," he told her. "And none of your damn' river water. My bowels are so full of bottom sand now I feel like a loaded pool cue."

As Charlotte swung through the tables toward the bar, she saw the men turning to look at her, passing salacious comments behind their hands, laughing huskily. It made her skin crawl. No matter how long she had lived in it, she would never get used to it.

As she reached the bar, a fresh group of boatmen shoved through the door. She recognized old customers: a tall red-head named Wheeler who wore a steel hook for his right hand; a big-bellied keeler named Nicolas Fry who always donned a frayed green frock coat when he went ashore; a squat, saturnine cook they called Pandash.

Wheeler waved his hook at Charlotte. "Break out the Nongella, honey, we beat the old river again, and we're celebratin'. Been to half the taverns on Silver Street and we ain't rumsquaddled yet."

Pandash swayed drunkenly against the bar and put his elbow on it for support. Although he was barely taller than Charlotte, he was immensely broad. The cords of his neck spread into his shoulders like the thick roots of an oak, and the muscles stirred in sullen currents beneath his greasy red shirt. His eyelids drooped sleepily, as he tried to focus his gaze on Charlotte.

Nicolas Fry guffawed and shoved him roughly. "Where's all that Spanish fly now, Pandash. You was chock-full of brag and fight at the Big Black."

With the mention of the Big Black, Charlotte knew these men must be off Naylor's keel. She saw a little ripple run down Pandash's bearded cheek. Drunk as he was, she could see that the taunts were goading him.

"I thought that was all hot air," Wheeler mocked. "Horny as a goat right now. Charlotte Dumaine for Pandash this time."

Pandash made an ugly sound and started walking toward Charlotte, a wild shine wiping the glazed drunkenness from his eyes. She backed along the bar, realizing that they had probably been building up to this all afternoon. Pandash moved after her, flat-footed, shoulders swinging loosely. "This is Pandash, honey. You been makin' meat too long."

She backed into a man at the bar. He would not give way. Swinging a look at his flushed, grinning face, she tried to wheel around him. Nicolas Fry circled pompously onto her flank. Then Wheeler took up another position. She tried to dart between them. With a laughing shout, Pandash caught her arm and swung her against him.

"We come to share y're bed, Charlotte! Won't cost you a fip."

They were pressing in on all sides now, so close she couldn't move. The heat of their bodies enveloped her, reeking of sweat and filth and stale whisky—the old stench of Silver Street she knew so well. Gagging on it, she fought Pandash, but his strength was overwhelming. Laughing deep in his throat, he pinioned her arms, bending her back, his lips seeking hers.

"Damn you, Pandash . . . !"

The shot drowned her curse. She saw the raccoon-skin cap plucked from Pandash's head, as if by an unseen hand, whipped across the bar, and dropped. The deafening echoes seemed to stop all the sound in the room. Pandash's face was an inch from Charlotte's, mouth open foolishly in shock. Slowly, still holding her, he swung his head till he was looking toward the end of the room. Everybody else was staring that way, too. Charlotte knew what they were all looking at: Pepper Annie, on her shabby dais, with her huge Kentucky pistol in her hands. Blinking her rheumy eyes, peering at Pandash over the sea of heads, the old woman was reloading the gun.

"Let her go, Pandash!" she squalled. "Next time I'll shoot yer fanny off."

Nearsighted as she was, the old harridan had a lethal reputation for her accuracy. Half a dozen keelers were still plying the river with her bullet holes somewhere in their bodies. Charlotte could see this knowledge move palpably through Pandash's face. The planes of his bearded cheeks grew, tight and flat. He squinted his eyes almost shut, made a rough sound, and released Charlotte.

The other men spread away, still gaping at Pepper Annie. The old woman had the Kentucky pistol reloaded now. She swayed a little on the platform and put one hand on the table to steady herself. Pandash made an ugly shape with his mouth, spat at Charlotte's feet, then let his air out in a husky roar and wheeled around to hit the bar so hard the whole room shook.

"Gimme a drink, dammit. I got a thirst like a whole Mississippi gone dry."

Tension flowed out of the room. The men filled the bar again, laughing self-consciously, watching Charlotte from the corners of their eyes as she moved stiffly toward the rear of the room. Revulsion moved through her now like a brackish tide. She had her hands locked tightly in front of her and her lips compressed, and she refused to meet any of the eyes that followed her back.

Pepper Annie had subsided, stout billows overflowing her tawdry chair, one hand still covering the pistol on the table. She had been drinking port all afternoon and was as drunk as Pandash. Nearing the dais, Charlotte heard the old woman muttering to herself. "Damn keelers. I wouldn't have t' put up with yer. Be the richest madam on Girod Street. Look at that gal. Make a hundred dollars a day, a body like that. A thousand. But what? No. Got t' be pure. Got t' be lily white." She hiccoughed. "Dunno why I p'rtect 'er. Dunno why I keep 'em off 'er. Have the biggest house in the bizness. Gold mirrors and all. But what? No-o-o. Let her ol' aunt starve t' death. Got t' make like fancy, up on the hill. Poor, starvin', lovable ol' aunt, starvin' t' death."

Suddenly, on the stairway behind Annie, Charlotte saw Naylor. He was almost hidden in the shadows. His face was a featureless wedge, topped by the black mass of his hair. It stopped Charlotte, for an instant. How long had he been there? Had he seen what had happened with Pandash? She felt a flush heat her cheeks. Shame? Why should she feel shame in front of him?

She went through the kitchen door and outside onto the

porch that stood in the alley between Pepper Annie's Inn and the Natchez Bar next door. The darkness was still cottony with heat. She leaned against the wall, clothes sticking damply to her body. She began to tremble. She knew it was the reaction, but she couldn't stop it. Stupid. Stupid, she told herself, to let it affect her so. Why couldn't she be like other women on Silver Street? It didn't touch them. Some actually gloried in it. Some made a game of it. Some were calloused to it. But she could never seem to gain that indifference.

She had learned to erect those enigmatic defenses in front of the boatmen. She had gained a poise and a maturity that often made her appear older than she was. She could show the men an ivory mask that made her seem untouched by Silver Street, but underneath it was always the same— this sick reaction to ugliness, this seething need to escape, this poignant wish for a world where men were a little more than animals and a woman was a little more than a body for their use.

There was a sound at her side, and she saw Naylor's tall, slope-shouldered silhouette in the open door. She didn't want to talk with him. She wanted to be alone. She turned her head away.

"Can I do anything?" he said.

"No."

"It happens often like that?"

"What do you think?"

"I think I'd wanna get out of it."

"Maybe I will." She was talking despite herself.

"A man?"

"How else?"

"You love him?"

"Yes."

56

She walked to the porch rail, wanting him to go, angry that she had let him draw her out. Why should he bother her so?

"I'm sorry," he said. "Guess it's none of my business."

He moved to the rail beside her. The alley ran out to Silver Street, flaring torches silhouetting the constant flow of the crowds, and the noise was an endless babble.

"Hot night," he said. "Ain't this bad in Louisville till August."

His voice was soft, sympathetic. She turned to him. The sympathy was in his face, robbing it of that melancholy. He was smiling, and it made him seem younger. She knew why she had felt shame. He was unlike the other boatmen. There was a difference, a sensitivity. She was responding to it, losing her sense of antagonism.

"They talked a lot about you," he said. "I had a crazy picture."

Her lips grew thin. "I suppose so."

"You're different."

"How?"

"Way they talked, you belonged here." His voice grew husky. "You don't."

She saw understanding in his eyes, understanding of so many things that she couldn't explain to Annie or Swain or any of them, understanding of the needs in her, the hate of Silver Street, the dreams. It took the remnants of suspicion from her. It filled her with a need to know that understanding. In a whisper, she asked: "How can you tell?"

"My ma was a decent woman. She woulda hated this place like you do. You got that in your eyes."

She moistened her lips. "Your ma was a boatman's wife?"

"She ran away with Pa. Come from a fine Virginia family. I got a picture."

He unpinned a brooch from inside his shirt, opened it, showing a faded miniature, hair as black as his, lustrous and curling about a pale sensitive face with wide blue eyes that looked out on a world where gentleness and love came to a woman as naturally as sun and light, a world Charlotte had dreamed of since she was a little girl.

"How is it . . . to live like that?"

"She told me," he said. "Dimity and cotillions and women like angels on a cloud. She read Greek and played Mozart on a pianoforte. Tried to give me some o' that. Never got much beyond my ABCs. Guess I was too busy in the boat yards."

She had never shared a moment like this with a man. She had talked with them of life on the bluffs or in New Orleans, but they had never touched her so simply with so few words. All her hostility for this young man was gone. They were in a charmed circle. She was sharing with him something she had never shared before. They were both looking at the miniature, and it had drawn them together till their faces were inches apart. In the darkness, she could see the sensitive, sculptured crevice of his lips. The heat of his body stole against her, making her intensely aware of his nearness. He seemed to notice it at the same time. Their eyes lifted together, met.

"If I kissed you," he said, "would you think it was like Pandash?"

It broke the spell. She took a step backward, a sharp breath lifting her breasts high, but she wasn't angry. That surprised her. She felt shaken, unsure, standing on the brink of something with a dizzying drop at its edge. He was smiling, without mockery, just smiling. She remembered having wondered if he ever smiled.

"You sure you love him?" he asked.

She hesitated, then vehemently: "Yes." She wheeled and walked to the door. Her steps slowed. She stopped, just inside, and looked back. He was leaning against the rail, still smiling. She shook her head impatiently. "I do."

"You trying to convince me," he asked, "or yourself?"

Chapter Six

Naylor woke early the next morning. The fetid loft room was already steaming. He was still drugged with sleep, held down by an oppressive lassitude. He knew what it was. He had felt this intense defeat ever since the loss of his keel. After so many years with his whole being focused on one goal, it was like being cut adrift from life itself. The anger still came when he thought of his keel, but most of the time it was a vast emptiness at the very pit of him, an all-pervading apathy that left life without purpose or meaning.

Heap was still asleep, mouth gaping, snoring loudly. As Naylor dressed, he thought of last night. He and Heap had gone out on Silver Street, and what they had seen had left an imprint Naylor would never lose. He'd thought the Louisville waterfront was tough. It seemed like Sunday school now. Bred on the frontier, he had seen enough violence and brutality so that he was not easily shocked. But Silver Street seemed to contain a special brand of its own—as if all the bestiality and depravity of man had been gathered here, condensed, distilled, turned loose in the narrow network of alleys where men lost all humanity and fought and bred and wallowed like animals in the slime of a nascent world.

He could understand Charlotte's bitter need to escape. He didn't think he could stand Natchez-Under very long himself. How much worse it must be for a woman with her needs, her quivering attunement to life, her sensitivity—all the things he had seen in her face for that moment last night, behind the Silver Street mask.

He went downstairs rubbing sleep from his eyes and saw Cane John, serving grits and bacon to a blanket-coated patroon and a cadaverous commission merchant. They were already deep in an argument and gave no notice to Naylor; the commission merchant was pounding the table with a bony fist.

". . . And what good did your Mister Jefferson's Embargo do us? It didn't stop England from taking men off our ships, did it?"

"England's not completely wrong, Martin," the patroon said. "A lot of her seamen are jumping ship on this side. There's a dozen places in Boston right now that will forget them citizenship papers. Didn't you hear what they admitted about the *Constitution*? A hundred and forty-nine of her crew avowed British subjects. . . ."

"My brother wasn't a British subject. Taken right off his own ship when that damn *Leopard* attacked the *Chesapeake*. Some Limey snotty claiming he was a deserter from His Majesty's Navy."

"France is doing the same thing. Napoléon's confiscated hundreds of ships on the basis of his Milan decree."

"Now you're talking like a damned Tory!"

"And you're talking like a damned Federalist!"

The commission agent jumped to his feet, trembling with rage. "You shouldn't have said that, John. You can cancel that shipment of sugar. I'll send it north on a keel that doesn't stink like a British man-o'-war."

He turned to stalk out, while the patroon sat staring stonily at the table, his hands clenched together. Naylor looked on, a little amused, a little confused. The impressment of seamen was an old bone of contention; he had heard it chewed on for years in the Kentucky taverns. He had not become politically conscious too long ago, and, like

61

many on the frontier, his consciousness had been a provincial one. He had followed Henry Clay's career with lively interest and hoped the man would run for Congress next year, so he could vote for him. He had approved of Jefferson, until the Embargo had brought depression to the river. Even then he had realized that the Embargo was only one of a dozen economic factors at work. He had been aware of the shadowy threat of war on the horizon for the past years, but the issues seemed to become more and more involved, and his own struggle for existence had been too urgent to allow him much thought on the matter.

As the commission merchant stalked out, Naylor heard a sound on the stairs behind, and turned. It was Charlotte. A cottony dryness filled his mouth, and he became aware of the pulse pound at his temples. It was the same thing he had felt with his first sight of her the day before. He understood now Heap's salacious obsession with her, knew how she could become such a legend on the river. Her body would have been enough. She had stunning breasts, proud and high, and the bold columns of her thighs lent tantalizing shape to the sleazy skirt. A man wanted to sink his hands in the rust-red hair, massed in such silken abundance at her shoulders. Her eyes seemed to swim with the violet shadows of some inner fire. Perhaps the impact of her was a compound of all these things. Perhaps it was something less tangible—an essence of sensuality, a pure and poignant femaleness that struck a man with distinct shock, yet defied definition.

He moistened his lips. "Them picayunes. They cover breakfast, too?"

She did not smile. She showed him none of the softness, the reaching out he had seen last night. "You can have some grits, if you want."

Her cheap shoes clattered as she came down the stairs. Her scent crept against him as she passed, haunting as that of a tropical jungle after a rain. He followed her into the kitchen. From one of the iron kettles she ladled steaming grits. He sat down. His back was to her, but he could hear the silken rustle of her dress against her body. He had never been so acutely conscious of a woman. Even Evadne, with all the sense of shadowy unspoken things between them, had not made him feel so uncomfortable. Charlotte put the plate on the table, regarding him soberly.

He smiled at her. "Eat with me?"

"I'm not hungry."

She went back to the pot on the grate, pouring him a cup of bitter chicory coffee. She seemed withdrawn from him, back in her shell once more. That moment of kinship they had known last night was gone. He sensed that she was sorry she'd revealed so much of herself to him, and this was the reaction. Then she surprised him by speaking.

"You're pretty young to own a keel."

"I worked seven summers for it."

"No wonder you were so mad."

"Mad ain't the word exactly." His eyes went blank. "Like cutting a piece out of your heart."

"How did it go down?"

"Not enough power."

"A whole crew couldn't have saved it in those shoals."

"Maybe a steam engine could."

She turned. "A what?"

He looked up, surprised at himself. He hadn't been consciously thinking of Captain Abner. Yet it must have been hovering around in him somewhere, to come out so automatically. Now he was thinking of it, strongly, vividly, as if with a new discovery. "A steam engine," he said.

She brought the coffee to the table. "When I was twelve, some man named Evans built a hull in New Orleans. They shipped a steam engine for it from Philadelphia or somewhere. It's still down around New Orleans, running a sawmill."

"You mean it didn't work?"

"Did you expect it to?"

"I don't know." He regarded her closely. "Is Swain interested in steam?"

She lifted her shoulders, dropped them indifferently. "He's interested in about everything under the sun."

"I'm serious. Do you know for sure?"

"I don't know anything for sure," she said, "about Swain."

He did not answer. They were gazing at each other, and it was that silence between them again, that tension, building up like a pressure. He wanted to break it somehow; he couldn't find any words.

Then Cane John appeared in the kitchen door. "Looks lak *M'sieu* Reynaud comin' down the hill, missy," he said.

A startling change ran through her. She took a sharp breath, a flush running into her cheeks. For an instant her guard dropped. Her eyes began to sparkle, and she was like a little girl, breathless with excitement.

"Tell him to wait at the bar," she said. "I'll have to change, John." She rushed past the mulatto, still talking excitedly. "Give him some of that long cork claret. It's his favorite. Tell him I'll hurry. Keep him amused somehow. Those Cajun stories of yours. . . ."

As she hurried through the door, she almost collided with Heap. He jumped aside to let her by, gaping after her. His eyes shone like fish in a barrel, and his mouth hung wide open. Naylor looked blankly at the door, even after

Charlotte had disappeared. Finally he became aware of Heap. It was an effort to take his mind from Charlotte.

"You old fraud," he said.

Heap turned to him, blinked. "Huh?"

"The way you made them shapes with your hands."

Heap grinned sheepishly. "Wal . . . mebbe they was a little exaggerated."

"Talkin' like a reg'lar stud hoss. Like you was the only one even seen Charlotte Dumaine."

Heap rubbed his baldpate, looking ashamed. "I guess I was pullin' the long bow, chil'e. I guess I jist ain't made fer anything so fancy and furforraw." He looked up, eyes wide. "But who'd ever dream I'd git so close to the likes o' her? Who'd ever dream I'd be sleepin' in the same house, right acrost the hall? Even Danny Blackwell can't make a brag like that."

The man was one of the few people who could bring Naylor's humor to the surface. He looked so ridiculous— tall and gaunt, the nervous sweat turning his cheeks to varnished mahogany, fidgeting and squirming like an agitated turkey—that Naylor had to laugh. "Sit down and eat your grits," he said. "If you're a-goin' to make a brag, you got to have a full belly."

As Heap joined him, the humor left Naylor once more. He stared at the door, thinking of Charlotte again, trying to reconcile the breathless little-girl look with the ivory enigma of a few minutes before.

Chapter Seven

Charlotte tried to suppress her excitement as she dressed in her room. It wouldn't do to seem like a foolish child in front of Louis. Yet the drumming of her heart persisted. His arrival was one of the few things that could upset the poise and self-control her life on Silver Street had imposed. It was not only Louis himself—although he would have been exciting to any girl—but what he represented. For as soon as she had become old enough to recognize the filth and degradation and brutality of her surroundings, escape from Silver Street had been the basic need of her life.

She could take none of the usual channels; she had seen too many others travel those routes, and fail. The ones who married their own kind—the shack bullies and pimps and hawkers of the street—had merely traded one crib house for another; or the few who tried to escape by the river, considering themselves lucky enough to marry a boatman—and in two or three months got left behind in some other dreary river town by their improvident men, forced to turn back to the only trade they knew to make a living. There was only one way out of it, for Charlotte, and that was on the bluffs above. She knew what a symbol she had become on the river. It set her apart—in the minds of those fine gentlemen of Natchez above—made her a goal coveted in a different way than the other women of Natchez-Under. It was what had made her fight so dogged through the years—to keep herself untainted by Silver Street. There had been more than one offer, from up on the bluffs. She had thought she wanted to escape badly enough to accept a marriage of convenience, until Armand Dubois appeared, fifty-five, seamed, and spidery, worth a half million dollars. He had gagged her with his sly, senile advances, and she had realized there were some things she could not do. Then Jacques Devereux, handsome, reckless, became the dashing answer to Charlotte's dream, till she knew him better. It was common gossip on the bluffs that he would soon gamble away a huge patrimony. Their romance had been a childish storm of passionate protestations one day and violent quarreling the next. She had seen failure in such a mercurial match, and failure meant a return to Silver Street. But at last in Louis Reynaud she had known triumph.

She was dressed now in the filmy sarsenet Spanish Lou had helped her make from those patterns in *La belle assemblée*. She put on her topaz earrings, the only thing left of her mother's, slipped a muslin pelisse over gleaming bare shoulders, took a last look in the cracked mirror, and went downstairs.

Louis stood at the bar, sipping his beloved long cork claret, smoking a Spanish cigar. He was a tall, slim youth, dressed in the clothes that had become almost a uniform for the young Creoles—the long mauve tail coat, the striped trousers drawn tightly under the boot by an instep strap, the tall hat cocked to one side of his head. She stopped on the landing, saw his head turn, saw the change that always came over his face with his first sight of her. A faint flush stained his wax-pale cheeks; his jet-black eyes began to glitter. He came toward her quickly, swinging his sword cane, smiling eagerly.

"*Bon jour, ma foi.* I would have come yesterday, but business interfered. . . ."

She answered his smile, holding out her hand. He took it

and bent his sleek black head over it. He smelled vaguely of fine tobacco and good wine. As she tucked her hand under his arm and started toward the front, she saw Naylor, standing in the kitchen door, watching her go. It was like a cloud passing over the sun. For a moment all her breathless anticipation was gone.

The coach stood in the street, the coats of its matched bays gleaming like wet blood in the bright sun. It was a sumptuous vehicle, black-topped, paneled in a variety of handsome woods, its fittings shining brazenly in the early morning light. Louis helped her onto the step, and she climbed inside, settling with a luxurious sigh into the padded leather seat. When he was in, the coach jerked on its leather understraps and lunged forward. The crowds were already thick on Silver Street. A long line of black men was marching back toward the bluff, followed by an overseer with a coiled whip and a gold-chased pistol stuck into his belt. A fitful wind swept the stench of rot and decay through the window.

Charlotte saw a pinched look come to Louis's nostrils. She spoke hurriedly. "Swain was down yesterday. I think he was looking for you."

He smiled. "I saw him last night."

"Has he come back from New York with some new wild scheme?"

He nodded. "Very mysterious. Won't tell me yet what it's about. Trying to whet my appetite, I imagine."

She turned to him. "Louis, do you suppose he was really mixed up with Aaron Burr?"

"If you can believe all the stories about him"—Louis sighed—"he has been associated with everything from the discovery of the New World to John Law's Mississippi Bubble." He squeezed her hand, moving close. "But why are we talking about him, *chérie?* It seems a lifetime since I've had these precious moments with you. . . ."

He stopped as a wild screaming broke through the other babble outside. They were passing the Scarlet Lily, a teetering, two-story barrel house that stood on the corner of an alley bisecting Silver Street. A yellow-skinned hawker rushed from the door, ramming against the edge of the crowd. A red-shirted flatter followed him, a skinning knife in one fist. He caught the hawker in the crowd. The yellow-skinned man grabbed the flatter's knife arm with both hands to keep from getting stabbed. They tripped and fell in their struggle, rolling into the mud of the street. A woman stumbled from the Scarlet Lily, still screaming, a bottle in one hand. She backed up against the wall of the building, looking up at the sky and bawling at the top of her voice. "Somebody stop 'im, for God sakes! Benny wasn't doin' nothin'! Somebody stop 'im!"

The crowd spread away from the fight, making no attempt to check it. Louis saw the expression on Charlotte's face and called sharply for the coachman to pull around it. Then he yanked black curtains across the window. "We'll be out of it quickly, Charlotte. We'll be up on the bluffs in a few moments."

She leaned back, looking straight ahead, trying to shut the woman's raucous bawling from her mind. How could she tell Louis what it really meant to her? Not shock, as a person who had never known violence or degradation before would be shocked. She had seen things immeasurably worse—the beatings, the killings, the rioting boatmen.

Louis was talking, trying to take her mind off the scene, trying to help. She put her hand on his. "It's all right now, Louis."

"It will not mar our day?"

69

"Of course not." She looked straight ahead again, moistening her lips. "Your grandfather. How is he?"

He shook his head. "My dear, he is very low."

She leaned against him, feeling his whole body tighten.

"Louis, is it so terrible a thing to want? Your grandfather's had a full life. He's lived ten times as much as most of us. Adventure, riches, women. . . ."

He studied her face as he would study a child's, smiling softly, shaking his head. "Whenever I come down on Silver Street to get you, whenever I see Pepper Annie, whenever I stand a few minutes in the stench of that tavern and see the men who come in, I can understand how a woman like you should want so desperately to get away from it. When it is like that, Charlotte, it is not such a terrible thing to want."

She looked up at his face, his smiling, indulgent face with its jet-black eyes and its haughty nose and its sensitive mouth, and she knew he was wrong. She leaned back, looking out the window. It was a terrible thing. No matter what reasons a person had, it was a terrible thing to want a man to die. She couldn't help wanting it, knowing it would mean her escape—but she still knew how bad it was. Pepper Annie was right—like a couple of ghouls.

"Charlotte. What is it? You are so strange today."

She realized he was right. She was in a strange mood, thinking of things she rarely had before.

They left Silver Street and rattled down Market and through the square, where the fruit and the squashes and the melons lay heaped in the sun. They left this behind and rolled into jessamine-lined streets, passing the iron-balconied buildings, going by King's Tavern, where a group of Creole dandies stood gossiping and tapping sword canes against their legs. Then the town was behind, and they were on the road, the soft white loess worn down by years of

70

travel till the surface lay five feet beneath the surrounding country. The scent of orange trees was like wine. Charlotte drew it in on a deep breath that swelled the upper slopes of her breasts against the pelisse. She saw Louis's eyes on them, as he leaned toward her, one hand sliding up her bare arm.

"Louis. . . ."

"I cannot wait," he whispered. "It has been so long. It is like fire burning in me, Charlotte. You don't know how I dream of you. Your eyes haunt me. Your face is constantly before me. . . ."

His hand slid off her shoulder, caressing her hair, sensitive fingers touching her cheek, her neck. She leaned back, trying to find the pleasure she usually took in his ardent lovemaking. She had known so much violence and crudity and boorishness on Silver Street. The first time he had said these things to her was like a fairy tale come true. His lips sought hers; his body pressed her against the seat. She felt the blood begin to throb through her body. Her breasts tingled, and a trembling ran down her legs. But it did not come as willingly as before, and it seemed to fade. He was breathing heavily, his face flushed, murmuring passionate endearments as he kissed her.

She turned her head aside and pushed his demanding hands away. He kissed her on the brow, the cheek, the neck, his voice muffled against her hot flesh.

"Louis, not today."

"But I have not seen you for so long, you can keep me away no longer. . . ."

"Louis, you promised."

"Charlotte. . . ."

"You're hurting me!"

He sank back against the seat, anger making his face

71

sullen, pouting his lips like a child's. Then he tried to smile. "Always it is like this, *hein?* Forgive my passion, *ma petite.* It makes a boor of me."

"It's forgiven."

His dark brows pulled together in a quizzical frown. "Always before you made me laugh about it."

She took a deep breath, unable to understand the strange restlessness in her. She knew the streak of boyish sulkiness in Louis, knew what thoughtless reactions it brought, had carefully avoided rousing it in all their relationships. Why should she be so foolish now, when the end was so near? She turned to him, trying to smile. "Perhaps it's the heat, Louis. Did you bring a lunch today?"

He brightened. "*Grillades, estomac mulatre,* some of that Amontillado Grandfather had kept from the Spanish times here, fruits, nuts, Parmesan cheese . . . a feast to delight your heart, Charlotte. We must find some beautiful spot to dine in."

They rode to a place he knew on the river, where a trail led from the road to the palisades. Here, on the bluff overlooking the Mississippi, they had their picnic. Afterward they made love, but she could not respond fully, and he sensed it, and it spoiled the day. There was a strain between them as they rode back in the late afternoon. In vain she tried to decipher her mood. Was it truly the heat? These rides up into another world had always meant so much to her. She had always taken such delight in merely being with Louis. What was tainting it today?

Louis left her at the door of the inn, still confused and growing sulky. She stepped inside, and stopped. It was still early in the afternoon, with a pair of customers at the bar: Heap and Owen Naylor. Naylor's elbows were braced on the bar, bowing his shoulders, making them look even heavier and broader. The edges of his hair were banked, black and shaggy, against the gunstock color of his young neck.

She knew, suddenly, what had been wrong all afternoon. That animal magnetism was creeping against her again. She felt faintly sick, as if in anticipation of some forbidden excitement. It was a sensation that had come to her in a shadowy, nagging way in their previous meetings, but now it was fully formed, stark, primitive, almost frightening.

She had never questioned her feeling for Louis before. That's what had been so wonderful about him. Expecting to make compromises, willing to accept so much less than love, she had suddenly met a man who captivated her, as he did everyone else, who stirred her as she had never been stirred before. She had accepted it swiftly and naturally as love, had known no doubts. But now . . . ? A sudden anger ran through her. She was being a fool. She had known a thousand other river men, and they had meant nothing to her. How could one—young and penniless and moody—step in out of nowhere and affect her this way? She would let it go no further. She couldn't let it taint what she had with Louis.

She tried to get past him before he saw her, but he turned to look at her, as she reached the landing by the stairs. The shadows lay deeply in the hollows of his gaunt young face; his lips had a brooding shape.

"Louis Reynaud?" he said.

She stopped at the landing, felt her chin lift in some kind of defiance. "Yes," she said.

He smiled mockingly, raised his glass. "To the bride and groom."

Chapter Eight

Naylor continued to look up the stairs after Charlotte had disappeared. His palm was moist with sweat, against the glass.

Heap stirred restlessly beside him. "You got to quit that, hoss. You ain't got a chance."

"She's too good for that dandy, Heap."

Heap chuckled. "Jealous of him already."

Naylor turned moodily to the bar. "Maybe I am."

"Every keeler feels this way, fust time he sees her, chil'e. You got to realize, you're just one of a thousand, to her." He clapped Naylor on the back. "Few days on the river'll straighten you out. We got to start lookin' for a boat back."

"I'm staying here."

Heap stared blankly at him. Finally he shook his head. "You got it plumb sergiverous, chil'e."

Maybe I do, Naylor thought. *Maybe I got it so sergiverous I'll never get over it.*

Heap said he was going out to hunt a spot on a boat anyway, and Naylor was hardly aware of his leaving. He spent the rest of the afternoon in the taproom, waiting for Charlotte to reappear. The evening crowd was gathering when she finally came down, but Naylor got little chance to speak with her. She was kept busy serving and disappeared upstairs when things began to get rough around nine.

The next few days were no different. Naylor saw Louis Reynaud come twice for Charlotte, and Kenneth Swain accompanied him once. The rest of the time she seemed to be

74

deliberately avoiding Naylor. But once in a while, when she was serving, their glances met across the room, and there was something in her face that kept the torment stirring in him. The smoky things in her eyes, the pensive shadow on her face, the way her lips stirred and compressed and grew full—all so akin to the same things he had seen in Evadne. And Captain Abner'd told him Evadne was a woman he could have had.

On Friday morning he awoke before Heap, and went to the kitchen alone. Even Cane John was not yet up, and Naylor made his own breakfast out of cold grits and leftover coffee. He was just finishing when Charlotte entered through the doorway.

She halted abruptly, surprise turning her face blank. Without speaking, she crossed to the sink. "Heap said you'd gotten a job on a boat," she said.

"*He* did."

"What about you?"

"Maybe I'm not going."

She turned toward him. "You want to see New Orleans?"

"I want to stay here."

She studied him a moment. Her hair was like a tousled mass of rusty fire spilled over her shoulders. It made her flesh seem startlingly white. Her eyes were still puffy with sleep, and there was a petulant fullness to her lips that made her look like a little girl. A sudden need ran through him, painful as a knife thrust. He rose and crossed to her. He saw her whole body lift a little, grow rigid.

"Charlotte," he said, "it'll never last, with Louis. He's soft . . . he hasn't got any guts . . . he'll go down in the first shoals."

Her voice was mocking. "Plain talk, Mister Naylor."

75

"We've been sparring long enough."

Something hard entered her face. "Then I'll meet you on your own ground. Even if I wasn't in love with Louis, you wouldn't stand a chance. I know what I want . . . and you haven't got it."

"Then why are you afraid of me?"

"Afraid?"

"You've been avoiding me all week."

"I'd avoid Pandash, too."

"This isn't like Pandash. You know it isn't."

"Then what's it like?"

"Like nothing I've ever felt before . . . or you, either."

She stared at him a moment longer, trying to hold the mockery in her eyes, but she was breathing hard, with something more than anger. It lifted her breasts high, taut, and swollen-looking, and filled her face with a deep flush. She turned away sharply and crossed the room to the market basket. Then, swiftly, she moved to the alley door.

"Going up on the bluffs?"

She halted, with the door open. "An old friend of Pepper Annie's has a plantation downriver. He lets me get all the fruit I want from his groves."

"I'll go with you."

"No." She looked at him. "I'll go alone."

She slipped out the door, closing it definitely and finally behind her. He was stilled a moment, staring emptily after her, but the scent of her was still in the room and the memory of her heated nearness. It turned him wild and foolish, unleashing a youth and a recklessness that rarely reached the surface in him. He had seen through her mockery for a moment, had seen the same ferment in her that had been tormenting him all week. His breath left him in a husky rush, and he strode swiftly to the door, opening it, stepping out onto the side porch. He could see down the valley to the river. Charlotte had reached the water and was turning southward on the muddy beach. He left the porch and hurried down the alley.

In the shallows below the inn a snowy ibis was poking at the water with his yellow bill. The surface of the Mississippi was coffee-brown near shore, gleaming brass in mid-channel, white as milk on the opposite side. The forest on the opposite shore billowed up like smoke signals in the heat glaze, growing pale and shadowy as the eye followed it northward through the loops and coves of the river till at last the massed timber merged with the haze and became a sleeping vapor on the horizon.

Unaware of Naylor behind, Charlotte wound her way through a tangle of trumpet vines and willows at the southern tip of the mudflat forming Natchez-Under. Here, in a cove, was an old, rotting *pirogue* hollowed out of a cypress log that some river rat must have abandoned long ago. She dropped the basket in and pushed it into the water, then stepped aboard. As she moved amidships, taking up the paddle, Naylor burst from the tangle of undergrowth and ran into the shallows, giving the canoe a hard shove as he jumped aboard. It almost pitched Charlotte into the water.

She turned, grasping the thwart, her face contorted with anger. He took the paddle from her and dipped it deep, shooting the *pirogue* ahead with a powerful stroke. The recklessness was still in him, and he laughed at her. His teeth made an ivory-white flash in a dark young face, and his eyes sparkled with mischief.

"We're goin' clear to Cuba," he said. "I've got a chest of gold buried there. When we come back, it'll make Louis Reynaud look like a rag picker."

She had righted herself, and her eyes were blazing. "Turn around. Put me ashore."

He grinned impudently. "Make me."

She leaned toward him, hung there a moment, then settled back. Her lips were full and pouting with a petulant anger, and her eyes were almost closed.

"Too bad you don't have a gun," he said.

"I'd use it."

"I have no doubt."

He kept digging deep, sending the *pirogue* ahead so swiftly a wake bubbled up behind them. He looked like a ragged, grinning rogue, sitting high in the stern, his shaggy hair curling up as it grew damp with sweat. Finally she could hold her anger no longer before his impudence. She smiled grudgingly.

"You're impossible."

He leaned toward her, losing some of his humor. "Forget what I said in the kitchen. Maybe I was wrong. I just want to go downriver with you. It's as simple as that."

She settled back, studying him closely. Then she nodded. "All right. As simple as that."

The fretwork of spars and riggings that rose over the Natchez landing was behind them now. They were borne along by the current, past banks matted and tangled with tall palmettos and gay-colored papaws all hooked together with grapevines and draped with dim green Spanish moss. It was like being plunged into a pristine world, and Charlotte could not help succumbing to its mood. She leaned back, trailing her hand in the water, studying Naylor.

She had seen him watching her at the inn, throughout the week, but somehow it had not been an animal staring out of his face, as it was with so many of the boatmen. It was softened and altered subtly by the other things in him—

the youth, the strain of melancholy, the wry humor lying so deeply within him—and she knew that she need not fear him the way she would fear Pandash, or Fry, or the others. That wasn't what bothered her. It was that sick feeling of anticipation in her, like a child, reaching at forbidden candy. She should have made him turn back. But how? Again the anger. Why dramatize it? Maybe he did attract her. He was young and handsome, in a wild sort of way, but other men had attracted her, and none had ever compared with Louis, and none had broken through her defenses. She knew what she wanted out of life, and she was too close to getting it to play the fool now.

She lay back in the bow, watching Naylor from half-shut eyes. He rose and dipped rhythmically with the paddle, saying nothing. He was not watching her any more; his eyes were on the birds, clamoring and honking on the willow islets that swept past. It gave him a detachment that made her feel foolish. The sun was warm on her body, spreading a drowsy contentment through her, washing out the tensions of his presence.

They swung around a long bend, and the cove beneath Nassaur's plantation swept into view. She pointed it out, and Naylor turned the *pirogue* neatly into the bank. Above the beach the ground was matted with poke and trumpet flowers, and the orange trees on the bluff filled the air with a penetrating sweetness. She didn't think she had ever been so conscious of the forest perfume.

They were like a couple of kids, slipping in the wet grass and climbing up the steep bank with the aid of the twining vines. At the top he put the basket down and turned to catch her hands and swing her up beside him. Then he snapped loose a passion flower and twined it in her hair. Her cheeks flushed with exertion, her eyes sparkling, and she scooped up the basket and ran ahead. She pointed out the ripe fruit, and he climbed trees and tossed her down oranges and lemons and pomegranates to her. Then he opened a pomegranate for her, and they got the red juice all over their faces. He looked so funny and so wild she got a stomach ache from laughing. They wiped their faces clean with a cloth from the basket and started down to the banana trees Nassaur had transplanted from Cuba. A red and blue parakeet was following them, squawking comically, and a breeze had sprung up, damp with the smells of the river.

They reached a stand of trees on a slope looped with grapevines. He dropped the basket, catching her around the waist, lifting her into a great noose of a vine, then he gave her a push, and it swung high out over the slope with her. She grabbed at the vine on either side, giddy with the sensation of falling. But she did not fall. She came back at him in a swooping arc, and he caught her and pushed her again. She swung outward again, with the parakeet squawking at her from an orange tree.

"It's like a swing," she laughed. "Like a little girl's swing."

She surrendered to the childish abandonment of it, forgetting her strange moods, her apprehensions of a while ago. She had never felt so exuberant, so uninhibited, so free to give vent to a mood of happiness.

A groaning crack broke in on her giddy thoughts. It was the vine, breaking, spilling her out. She fell hard into the grass and rolled down the slope. She heard Naylor call her name before she stopped rolling. He was beside her before her head stopped spinning, fear in his eyes, his voice husky and trembling.

"Charlotte, I didn't mean for that to happen. . . ."

"I'm all right."

"If you're hurt. . . ."

"The grass is soft."

"Tell me you're not hurt!"

"I'm not, Owen, I'm not!"

"Are you sure . . . tell me . . . ?"

"Owen. . . ."

The jumble of words stopped abruptly, as they both realized how close they were, so close that her deep and shuddering breath lifted her young breasts against his chest. The contact seemed to release all the pressures that had been building up in her since he came. Like water from a broken dam, passion poured through her, and she lifted up to him as he came down to her.

It was all inchoate sensation after that. The glittering look of his eyes, cruel and tender at the same time, the sound of her passionate sobs, her lips opening widely beneath his bruising kisses, the rough calluses of his palms on her breasts. The wind made a roaring about her, and suddenly the parakeet's squawk ran through her head in a brilliant spasm of sound.

Sometime, sometime long afterward, she heard her voice. She was clinging to him, her white arms locked around his neck, her voice husky and pleading. "Take me away, Owen, take me away from Silver Street, anywhere, Owen, I'll go anywhere with you. . . ."

"Of course, honey. We'll go back to Louisville. I know the town. I'll get a job. A shipwright, maybe. . . ."

"A job?" With a great effort, she seemed to be swimming out of a delicious pool of concupiscence. She gazed up at him, trying to find a clear thought in her mind. She looked down at her body. It made a pale gleam against the vivid green of the grass. It came as a shock. She couldn't remember taking off her dress. She stirred, moved away from him. "A job?" she said again. The concupiscence was gone now.

"Of course," he said. "I'll have to support us somehow. We can get married up on the bluff. I saw a church there."

"Married?" Her voice was bitter as ashes. She found her dress crumpled on the grass and stood up. She felt shame and humiliation and acrid self-recrimination for her weakness.

He looked at her open-mouthed, unable to comprehend her mood. He got up, suddenly self-conscious as a little boy at his nakedness below the waist. He picked up his pants and jumped around ridiculously on one leg, trying to get them on.

"Charlotte," he said. "What is it?"

She had her dress pulled on over her head and twisted her body into it. "Nothing," she said. "Nothing."

He belted his pants about his shirt tails and wheeled to her, frowning intensely. He caught her arms. "There is something."

She twisted out of his arms, stepping back, her face drawn and bitter. "Do you think I've fought my whole life for this? A penniless boatman? A kid, without a dollar to his name?"

He tried to take her arms again. "Of course, you fought all your life. But you wouldn't have given in to me unless you really meant it. Can't you see, Charlotte . . . ?"

"See?" The words seemed torn from her, shrill and hysterical. "All I can see is I've been a damned fool!"

Chapter Nine

Charlotte had no clear knowledge of her trip back. She knew she reached the *pirogue* before he caught her, and shoved off, leaving him on the bank behind. She wore herself out paddling against the current and reached the cove so exhausted she had to kneel for a few moments in the beached boat, regaining her strength.

Reaction was still churning violently through her. She tried to strip away all the bitter anger and confusion and define what had really happened to her. This was what had been working at her ever since she had met him. They had been swept together this afternoon on a tide of simple animal attraction that had been pushing them and pressuring them from the beginning. It couldn't be anything else. She told herself it was the same as when had she given in to Louis. She was a healthy, vital young animal with a frank knowledge of her own desires. She had seen enough of Silver Street to know that passion could exist separate from love. That was what Naylor had touched in her, then. She was a fool to have given in—she didn't know yet exactly how or when it had happened—yet it didn't mean the end of everything.

She finally rose and stumbled up the trail toward Silver Street. She couldn't face the inn and Pepper Annie in her present state of mind. There was only one place where she could find a little understanding and sympathy. Spanish Lou had been her mother's friend in New Orleans.

Silver Street was already swarming with the evening

crowds. A half dozen new keels had docked during the afternoon. Their crews were wandering up and down the muddy road, gawking at the women who called to them from upstairs windows, dodging the heavy drays loaded with produce, reeling in and out of the deadfalls.

Pepe's voice rose shrilly above the babble. "You won't find nothing like her on Silver Street, keeler. She's foreign, keeler, foreign. Part Chinese, part Creole, part French, part Indian. . . ."

"Which part's French?"

Pepe saw Charlotte and let go of the keeler's arm, calling across the street: "When are you goin' to come to work for me, Charlotte? I got signed contracts."

A drunken flatter lurched out of a barrel house, making a grab for Charlotte. She eluded him, jaw clenched, and hurried on.

"A fip, a fip, that's all it costs, a fip, the biggest, loudest, shiniest watch in the world, Swiss movement, gentlemen, Swiss movement. . . ."

It all had a nightmarish quality for Charlotte in her tormented state, and she pushed her way blindly through the crowds, tearing free of pawing hands, heedless of the lewd comments. She reached the Scarlet Lily on the corner of Silver Street and a narrow alley.

Lou's door opened onto the landing above, and Charlotte knocked hurriedly. Spanish Lou answered it. She was in a faded wrapper, heavy-fleshed, immensely breasted, the striking contrast of jet-black hair and dead-white skin giving her dissolute face a first impression of fading beauty.

"Come in, *chica*. You look like you could use little sympathy or something. Pepper Annie she been shoot your fanny off again?"

Without answering, Charlotte walked into the fetid

room, smelling of cheap perfume and cheap whisky. She stopped at the window, staring down at the brawling crowds below without seeing them. "Will Sunday Bill bother us?" she asked.

"Hell, no." Lou spat disgustedly. "He must have get drunk and fall in the river again. I no see him in two day. What will she be, *chica,* absinthe or opium?"

"I don't feel like anything. You have one."

"Just the eye opener, ah?" There was a *clink* of glass, a muted gurgle, a long sigh. "Now, what makes the trouble? You look pale. Mussed up. Some bully feeling his grog?"

Charlotte pushed her tumbled hair off her face and went over to slump on the bed. She stared emptily at the floor, dredging the words up with difficulty. "Lou, what would you do, if you'd settled on one man, if he meant everything you'd dreamed about all your life, if you'd built everything around him . . . and then another one came along?"

Lou stood, holding her empty absinthe glass, frowning at the girl. "Is the one you love that count, honey. If the most rich he is, take him."

Charlotte's question came from the depths of her infinite confusion. "What is love, Lou?"

Lou was still gazing intently at Charlotte, and comprehension took the glaze from her big black eyes. "Not that kid?" she whispered. "Not that boy has been hang around Pepper Annie's with Heap."

Charlotte smiled mutely, an utter misery filling her eyes.

Lou put down the glass and went to her. "Don't be a fool, *chica.* He's no got a cent. Like all those other keelers. You ever see the wife of them boatmen? Their men gone half the year, drink and wench in some town down the river. Leave the wife behind to have the kids. Barefoot in some shack, having kids. One kid. Two kid. Three. Then what are you? Fat and ugly. Who loves fat and ugly? One day the man he go downriver and he don' come back. Then what are you? How you make the money? Right on the street. That's how." Lou paced the floor in her agitation. "How many of us get the chance? Only one I know of. In all these women down here, jus' one. Me. You know that, Charlotte? Fine man, big house, live like queen. So what I choose? Sunday Bill I choose. A boatman. Two dollar in his pocket and the sweet talk in his mouth. Marry in Pittsburgh. Drunk in Redstone. For a week, drunk. And what does Lou do? We got to eat, don't we? How you think I got started on the street? Take a look at me now. You want that? You want to be like Spanish Lou? Like Pepper Annie? Jesus! I got to have another drink. You want one?"

"No. You have it."

"Just an eye opener. Now don't be a fool, honey. Marry this boatman, you lose everything. If they don't make whore out of you one way, they do it other. You and me know is only one way off Silver Street. *¡Hijo de la chingada!* You got chance for heaven, don't take hell."

Charlotte lay back in the bed, trying to tell herself Lou was right. The babble of Silver Street swept in through the window and seemed to inundate her, all the sweating faces and the rolling eyes and the sly looks and the grimy hands reaching up and trying to pull her down into the muck and the depravity with them—till the pressure of her need to escape was like something ready to burst in her. She hardly heard the door open and was only vaguely aware of Sunday Bill, coming in. His face was puffy-looking, brambled with a three days' growth of beard. His clothes were streaked yellow with dried mud. He shambled to a chair, lowered himself into it, groaning heavily.

"Somebody musta spiked me drinks," he mumbled. "I woke up under the levee."

"Well, is about time, damn you," Lou said. "Which will she be, absinthe or opium?"

Bill closed his eyes. "I couldn't stand it now. You take one."

"Just an eye opener."

"I seen Louis Reynaud's coach in front of Pepper Annie's Inn," Bill said. "You better hike back there, Charlotte."

She sat up. "What?"

"Ain't you heard the news?"

"What news?"

"Louis has come down to get you, honey," Bill said. "Old Grandpa Reynaud finally died."

Chapter Ten

Naylor reached Natchez-Under an hour after Charlotte had left him on the river. It had taken him that much time to find his way up through the tangled jungle to one of the loess roads that led into the town. As he came down the shelving road that led from the bluffs onto Silver Street, he saw a coach forcing its way through the crowds. It was heavily curtained, and he could not see inside as it passed him, but he recognized it as Louis Reynaud's rig. It only made him more eager to see Charlotte again. He couldn't conceive of her going on her regular afternoon ride with Reynaud, so soon after what had happened. She was probably up in her room now, and Pepper Annie had sent the Creole away.

All the way back, Naylor had told himself that, if he could just see Charlotte again, could just talk to her when she was calmer, he could change her mind. Naturally she had been upset, probably the first time and all. But he knew, with youth's arrogant and unreasoning confidence, that she was *his* woman. It had been too pure, too searing to mean anything else. All the erotic memory of it still lay hotly in his mind—the satin-softness of her flesh in his hands, the rhythmic moans of her mounting passion, the wind roaring off the river, and the sudden spasm of the parakeet's squawk.

He had never known the need of a woman could come so violently to a man. It went right down to his very bones. It made him dizzy when he thought of her, hot all over, sick at his stomach. But it was more than the need of the flesh. As strong as their physical attraction was, there was more. Why couldn't she see that? Why couldn't it be as clean and bright and simple to her as it was to him?

In this mood he reached the inn, walking swiftly into the gloomy room. There was already a thin evening crowd at the bar, and a few tables at the back were occupied. Pepper Annie was ensconced on her tawdry dais. She leaned back in the chair, looking like a gross and frowsy doll, her face slack, her eyes glassy. There were three empty wine bottles on the floor, and the fruity reek of port filled the rear end of the room like a cloud. As Naylor hurried toward the stairs, Heap stood up.

"Did Charlotte come in?" Naylor asked.

Annie hiccoughed. "Damn' rights."

"You better ship out with me, hoss," Heap said. There was a strained look to his face. "Nash has a spot open on the keel."

"Where is she? Up in her room?"

"Damn' rights she come in." It left Annie in a bibulous squawk. She swung her head till her furry wattles quivered slackly, trying to focus her eyes, trying to find Naylor in the room. "In an' out, damn' bitch, leavin' 'er ole aunt . . . starve t' death in this damn' barrel house. . . . Lovable, sick, starvin' ole aunt. . . ."

A dark premonition ran through Naylor. "Heap . . . what's she yammerin' about?"

"Old Man Reynaud died, Owen. Louis come down f'r Charlotte. Took her up on the bluff. They're gittin' married as soon as they kin find a preacher."

For an instant there was utterly no response in Naylor. He seemed to hang in a vacuum. Then the bottom dropped out. He felt so sick he thought he would vomit. After that

came a wild, reasonless reaction that carried him in a rush
to the door. He stopped here, staring in a strained way at
the bluff. In the tawny haze he saw the coach struggle up
the last few feet of the shelving road, reaching the espla-
nade. It was silhouetted there, black against the pale sky.
Then the bluff seemed to swallow it.

Another reaction ran through Naylor, the impulse to run
up after her, plead with her, even to take her away from
Reynaud bodily. But he knew that was foolish. He knew
Charlotte's indurate core. She had made her choice.
Nothing he could say or do would change it now. He turned
back into the room. He walked suddenly to the table by
Heap, sinking into one of the chairs. His eyes were staring
emptily at a world lying shattered at his feet.

Annie made an effort to rise from the chair, failed miserably, and settled back with a long, wheezing protest. Her
eyes blinked like an owl's and spittle ran from her slack
mouth. She began talking to herself, the obscene cursing
gradually becoming incoherent as her multiple chins sank
against her chest and the glassiness again took possession of
her eyes. Then Naylor felt Heap's hand on his shoulder.

"You'll be comin' back upriver with me, won't you?
There's nothin' else to do."

It seemed a million years before Naylor could dredge the
words out. His voice sounded papery, dead. "I guess you're
right. There's nothing left to do."

So it started, minute by minute, foot by foot, mile by
mile—walking, all day long, walking. Your world was a
cleated runway eighteen inches wide, and you were fighting
with a twenty-foot pole with an iron tip at one end and a
button on the other and your shoulder was pinned to the
button and your toes curled around the cleats and the sweat

ran down your body. It was as if you fought the whole force of the giant river as you struggled to push the puny craft a few more feet against the current. You were one of a dozen men who stood in pairs at the bow and drove their poles into the bottom and walked sixty feet back to the stern and lifted your poles and jumped up to the top of the cargo box and scampered back to the bow again while your companions walked past you toward the stern in the runways below. The sun broiled you and the heat baked you and most of the time you were bent forward so far against the pull of the boat that you could grasp the cleats in front of you with your hands and you looked like a line of giant spiders crawling down the boat. All the time, that patroon, up on the cargo box, was bellowing at you: "Toss your poles! Down on 'em! Set your poles! Git a fire in your butts, damn you! Raise your poles! Head two! Up behind! Come on, you hosses . . . !"

That first noon they warped into the bank a few miles above Natchez and had their lunch of sowbelly and potatoes roasted in the dirt-filled firebox. Naylor sat slackly against the bole of a cypress, head thrown back, eyes closed, face turned old by the grooves of exhaustion so great it was pain. Heap sat beside him, squirming in sympathy. He'd known Naylor since he was a button and hated to see him go through this. Yet the upriver trip was the final test for a boatman. Compared with it, the trip down had been child's play. It was hard enough, going back, for an experienced boatman; for a new hand it was hell on earth.

"If you can't eat, chil'e, at least take a chaw of this garlic. We're in fever country now."

Naylor groaned, and turned his head aside from Heap's offering. Heap heard the crunch of feet in the sand and turned to see Pandash, approaching. Three of the present

91

crew had poled on Naylor's keel, but Heap was sorry Pandash had to be one of them.

"Look at the greenhorn," he said. "Goin' out like a light."

Heap looked up at the man's eyes, tinged a rancid yellow by the firelight. "Give him a chance, Pandash. He'll be doin' a jig with you every night after dinner."

Pandash looked contemptuously at Naylor, spat at their feet, and swaggered away toward the fire.

Naylor didn't jig that night. His hands were raw and bloody, and his shoulder was so sore he couldn't bear to move it. He was so played out he didn't even want to eat. He lay sprawled atop the cargo box, his breath passing through him with a shallow wheezing. Heap himself was worn out, but he heated some water in the firebox, and mashed up potatoes in it to make a gruel that he fed Naylor. Then he poured his ration of whisky on the boy's raw hands and rubbed hot tallow into his shoulder.

It hurt Heap to see the boy suffer so, but he knew what was inside Naylor hurt him more than anything the river could do. Heap had gotten only a hint of what lay between Charlotte and Naylor, but that had been enough. Naylor was no ordinary boatman, sleeping with a woman in every town, forgetting them as soon as he was gone. He rarely showed his emotions, keeping them scrupulously reserved within himself. Heap knew that, as young as he was, the boy was made for deep feelings, and what he had felt for Charlotte went deep. In this upriver journey, Naylor had sought escape from a hopeless situation. Perhaps the unending struggle and the physical misery would keep him occupied most of the time, but Heap knew that Charlotte would still be on his mind, a sick and bitter memory that would be a long time dying.

Heap wondered why it had to be that way. Why was a horse always torturing himself for something he couldn't have? That was the trouble with the world. Nobody was satisfied with his lot. Boatmen were always dreaming and yarning of the time they could quit the river and live in a fine house on the bluff, the dandies in the fine houses on the bluff coming down to Silver Street to wench and drink and try to forget their nagging wives and their mortgages and their gambling debts. Why couldn't they be like Heap? The river was enough for him. He had been born on it, and he would die on it. He had seen the first light of day on a broadhorn floating down from Redstone-Old Fort with George Rogers Clark. Heap's people and a handful of other settlers had stopped at the Falls of the Ohio, while Clark and his troops went on into history. All Heap could remember of his father was that he had once beaten Daniel Boone in a shooting match. He was a hunter and a farmer and raised his boys to be the same. But the boatman's horn had already begun to echo across the river, and the same frontier restlessness that had sent Heap's father downriver with Clark had sent Heap off on a keel when he was fifteen. Kentucky was still the "dark and bloody ground" in those years, and Heap had returned the next year to a town that had suffered a Shawnee attack. A dozen outlying farms had been burned out, a score of people killed, among them the farmer who had beaten Boone at a shooting match, and his wife, and the three sons who hadn't followed Heap onto the river. Heap couldn't go back to the farm, not him, not a child of the river, belched from one of those yellow whirlpools where the Ohio and the Mississippi meet, spawned with his fur on and his fangs in, half horse, half alligator, wearing his red feather in his hat and clicking his heels together and cock-a-doodle-doo.

Bayou Pierre. Grand Gulf. Palmyra. Walnut Hills. Going north. Fighting every minute, fighting a great sluggish brown giant that cut a piece out of your heart for every foot you gained. Zadoc Cramer had it.

Yazoo River, 3 miles below 103. Above and below the mouth is a large willow beach. Keep rather nearest the right-hand shore in passing.

No. 103—My Wife's Island—9 miles below lies below a right point—channel left side. The right pass may be gone in floods, but it is much the nearest, but not so safe.

Zadoc Cramer had it. But he didn't tell of the pain and the misery and the sweat and the blood and the backbreaking toil it took to pass each point as it came up in his dry, informative little book. He didn't tell of the times they reached a stretch where the river ran too deep in the channel to pole, and they had to hug the bank and bushwhack, each man in turn standing in the bow and grasping an overhanging branch or a clump of brush and walking aft. The first night after they did that, Naylor's hands were so raw and bloody he couldn't hold his plate. Heap rubbed them with lard and gunpowder and lay awake while the moon rose, listening to the boy's groaning in pain as he slept. Sometimes, with no bottom for their poles, the bank was too high for bushwhacking, and they had to cordelle. They got the cable out, six hundred feet of two-inch rope attached to the stub mast on the cargo box and running through the bridle that kept the boat from swinging. Twelve men on the bank were at the end of that cable, fighting their way through the brush and the swamps and the deadfalls, the sun frying their brains and the mosquitoes feasting on their flesh. Half the time the pull was so great they had to loop the rope around their waists and squeeze their guts out to keep the boat moving. One day the heat and the incredible strain of it killed one of them. He simply collapsed and fell into the mud with the cable still wound about his waist. They tied him into a tarpaulin and buried him in the river, and went on.

That night Naylor vomited what little he tried to eat, and then lay on his belly, face buried in the dirt so the rest of the crew wouldn't hear his sobs of exhaustion. It twisted Heap's guts to see the boy in such misery, and he tried to persuade Naylor to desert and beat his way inland to the Trace. But the youth refused.

"If I'm a-goin' to die, it's a-goin' to be on the river."

Seary's Island. Grand Lake. Island Number 89. Spanish Moss Bend. The slap of bare feet against wet cleats and Captain Nash's shouted orders and the sun rising from the dawn-shrouded timber on the east bank and the panthers screaming out in the canebrakes. Gradually, slowly, with the amazing recuperative powers and adaptability of youth, Naylor was hardening to it. Calluses were forming on his hands, and they did not bleed as much now. The lobster red was gone from his torso, and he was turning the bronze black of polished mahogany. He ate ravenously now, and he actually seemed to be gaining weight on the atrocious diet, but the constant bending and twisting had stripped every ounce of surplus flesh from him, and all the gain was sheer muscle. His belly was corrugated like a washboard. When he strained at the poles, ridges of muscle ran like quicksilver across his back. Heap had seen it happen in others. In a few short weeks the incredible hardships had robbed him of what was left of his youth and had given him a kind of manhood that could be found nowhere else in the world. Sooner or later, before they reached Louisville, the river would have its own way of testing that manhood.

At the Devil's Race Ground, thirty-five days out of Natchez, it took them the best part of the day to pole the three miles, fighting a forest of snags and the torrential force of the boiling current. They were too exhausted to go farther, and beached the boat above the rapids. The half-drowned crew gathered around the keg of Monongahela chained at the rear of the cargo box, clamoring for their traditional fillee after a bout with the river. Each man took his cupful neat, then dipped another cupful of river water up for a chaser. Naylor still was not used to the muck-filled water, and stared at his cup with a grimace.

"Don't let it settle, hoss," Heap told him. "The sand scours your bowels."

The youth drank it, almost gagging, and Heap took the cup for his drink. The rapids had kept him wet all day, bringing on his ague, and even the heat of the whisky couldn't ease the ache in his joints. He went over to the fire, rubbing his arms. The men were gathered around, shivering and cursing. Naylor sprawled flat beside Heap, head thrown back, eyes closed, face drawn and haggard, but the vitality of youth brought recovery to him soon. As darkness swallowed the surrounding timber, he sat up, moving nearer to the fire to dry his clothes. Pandash passed them, spitting great chunks of salt pork over the flames. He glanced at Naylor, his eyes sullen and heavy-lidded, then went back to the keel for the potatoes.

The pork juice hissed and spat like an angry cat in the fire. Pandash returned with the sack of potatoes and dumped them carelessly in his Dutch oven. A man named Crib took up his fiddle and began scraping at it, singing the boatman's song.

Oh, the keeler is a right bright hoss,
Nobody is the keeler's boss,
The keelers dance and the keelers sing,
A boatman does 'most anything. . . .

They wolfed their food silently, dribbling meat juice on their shirts and wiping greasy hands on their pants, and finally going to the river to wash off the molasses. Heap stuck his face underwater and came up, spewing and snorting like a bull alligator.

Naylor grinned affectionately at the sinewy buffoon. "I guess it's long past time I should thank you, Heap."

On his knees by the river's edge, Heap squinted up at Naylor. "What fer, hoss?"

"For keepin' me alive. I don't think I'd've made it without you."

Heap wiped mucky water from his chin. "Don't git sentimental," he said. "It embarrasses me."

Naylor chuckled. "Maybe you'd rather have me boot you in the river."

Heap chortled. "Gittin' rough now. Few days on a pole, button thinks he's a real 'gator."

Naylor put his foot against the man's rump and, with a whoop, gave a heave. It spilled Heap off his knees, face first into the water. He got to his feet, sputtering and cursing, and lunged at Naylor. The youth turned to run, with Heap after him. Laughing, he shouted: "Gittin' old, Heap! Can't even keep up with a button."

With a shout, Heap launched himself in a dive, tackling Naylor and spilling him into the river. They rolled free of each other and came to their hands and knees in the water. Naylor was laughing again, and Heap couldn't help but join in. "Damn you," he said. "I ain't that young any more.

Mebbe I oughta tell the patroon you can handle two poles."

Naylor helped him up, spitting muck and chuckling. "I'm sorry. I wasn't thinkin' of your ague."

"Ague be damned," Heap said. "I had plenty of animal spirits a few years back. Next time try 'em out on a 'gator." He didn't really care, though. The comradeship of it warmed Heap, as they walked back to camp. It was good to see Naylor feeling good again. He hadn't seen so much humor in the youth since they'd met Charlotte.

They dried off at the fire, slapping irritably at the mosquitoes that had begun swarming out of the willows. Naylor looked disgustedly at his hands. All the calluses had been torn to pieces by the day's savage battle on the poles, and his palms were raw and bleeding again. "Time like this, I think Captain Abner was right. A man's a fool to break his heart on the poles this way."

Heap frowned at him. "That don't sound like a keeler."

"A man don't have to kill hisself just 'cause the river's in his blood, Heap. The more of this I see, the more I think a steam engine ain't such a crazy dream, after all."

Heap shook his head. He had always thought Captain Abner a little touched—any man had to be, tinkering with those damned rods and teapots and talking about a boat going upriver without any polers.

Pandash passed them, making an outrageous clatter as he collected dirty dishes. He was but five feet away when he pulled his red shirt out to scratch a bite on his belly. There was a hole in the tail, the shape of a triangle. Heap and Naylor stared at it blankly. Then Heap saw rage leap into Naylor's face, pure and wild and completely uncontrollable. With an inarticulate sound, Naylor lunged at Pandash, swinging him around, grabbing the front of his shirt in both hands. "You!"

Off balance, Pandash tore at his hands, half shouting: "You crazy? What the hell you yelling about?"

In his rage, Naylor jerked the man back and forth. "My boat, Pandash, I'm yellin' about who pushed off my boat."

Pandash tried to tear free. "I didn't touch your boat."

Still grappling the man, Naylor yanked from his pocket the triangular piece of red wool he had saved from the keel. He flung it on the ground. "I found that on the binding strake."

Pandash stopped struggling, looking down at it. Every other man in the circle glanced at the piece of wool, then at the triangular hole in Pandash's shirt. Pandash's eyes shuttled across their faces, filled for a moment with a rat-like guilt. Then his expression changed, became sly, cunning. With a sudden jerk he pulled free.

Naylor was looking at the man who had destroyed a dream. He leaped after Pandash before the man could set himself. With a sound of utter fury he smashed him across the face. Pandash staggered backward, and Naylor followed, hitting him again, giving him no chance to recover, venting all the rage and defeat and bitterness of weeks in the blows. Dazed, half blind, Pandash threw himself against Naylor, grappling him. They staggered across the sandy beach, and then tripped and fell, rolling into the shallows like a couple of alligators, kicking and roaring and slugging.

Pandash tried to roll on top, but Naylor caught him by the hair and surged up high, throwing his weight across the man. It put Pandash under, and Naylor straddled his body, holding the panicked, thrashing man under for a full minute. Then he jerked his head out of water. "You didn't do it for yourself, Pandash. Who was in on it?"

Gasping and sputtering, Pandash coughed out the words: "I didn't push your damn' keel off. . . ."

Before he could finish, Naylor jammed his head under again. Pandash went into a spasm, trying to get free, but Naylor rode him like a log, holding him under. The men gathered along the shore, not knowing exactly how to treat this. It had not followed the traditional pattern, with the ritual of taunts and boasts preceding the battle. It had erupted on them with a sudden fury, and they still didn't understand all the ramifications. Heap did. He ran up and down the bank, shouting advice to Naylor, laughing and cursing Pandash.

Naylor jerked the soggy head up again. "Who was in on it, Pandash? Who paid you?"

Pandash was half drowned, retching and writhing. "I didn't . . . god damn you . . . I didn't. . . ."

Naylor shoved him under again. After a minute his body seemed to erupt in a great spasm. Naylor had all he could do to hold him under. Finally Pandash's struggles subsided, and Naylor dragged him out of the water, pulling his head till it lay on the beach, the chin an inch from the edge of the river. Sprawled across the sodden body, still holding the hair, Naylor gasped: "Who, Pandash?"

The man was half conscious, sobbing and mewling like a baby. His words were barely coherent, gurgling with the water that flowed from his slack mouth. "The hell with you. . . ."

Naylor started to drag his head back under. Pandash fought, but he was too weak to stop Naylor. At the last moment, with his head going under, he sobbed: "All right. . . . All right."

Naylor yanked his head back onto the beach. Pandash lay limp and beaten for a moment, retching miserably. Then, coughing up water, he spoke the name. "Kenneth Swain."

Chapter Eleven

Far down the river—by Zadoc Cramer's calculations five hundred and eighteen miles down the river from the Devil's Race Ground—was the house. It had been Gaspar Reynaud's house, built in 1781, when he had grown rich off sugar and indigo in New Orleans and had moved up out of the fever and the heat to the cool bluffs south of Natchez. It was a Creole house, built high on brick piers, with broad screened galleries that looked out through a jungle of orange and palmetto trees to the tawny river a hundred feet below. It was here that Louis Reynaud had brought Charlotte the day after Gaspar Reynaud had died.

That had been over a month ago, a strange, illusory time for Charlotte, curiously unreal and out of focus. Not that it hadn't fulfilled the wildest fancies she had woven for herself on Silver Street. Perhaps that was the very thing that made it seem so unreal, as if she had been floating languidly through a perfumed dream of luxury and ease and richness and elegance—and passion—for now that she was his wife Louis had exceeded every promise his suave and ardent courtship had ever given her. Amoral as a young animal, she had followed him with uninhibited curiosity down the secret labyrinths of love. It had really blotted out the memory of Owen Naylor, although her feelings about him were still in a tangled confusion. Steeped in the wonder and excitement of her new life, she was in no condition even to think much about him, and there was truly no chance, during the first weeks, for much introspection about her past. Louis was a gay and charming companion, keeping her in a state of constant delight with his intimate little dinners by candlelight and surprise trips to St. Catherine's Creek and picnics along the river and shopping tours in town.

At last Louis got a call from his lawyer in Natchez, concerning the probate of the will, and had to go in for a conference. Knowing it would be a long meeting, he advised Charlotte to stay behind. He left at eleven that morning while she was still in bed. She had breakfast before arising, the Creole breakfast of black coffee, *grillades,* and *pain perdu.* Then she bathed and had the maid do up her hair, and dressed in a light dimity. It was afternoon when she went downstairs. She stopped a moment in the entrance hall with the subdued movement and soft talk of the servants whispering through the rooms. It gave her the sense of sudden loneliness. She walked into the parlor and stopped at a window, looking through the wavy opalescent glass toward the river.

She turned deliberately and looked at the sumptuous elegance of the room. The French hand-blocked wallpaper, the gold-framed mirrors, the wine damask hangings, the crystal pendants dripping like ice from silver candle sconces. As much pleasure as she took from it all, she knew it was merely the surface symbol of what Louis had given her. Beyond the glittering house, the opulent living, the money, the security, lay the intrinsic value of her escape. She was beginning to partake of the decency, the respectability, the simple dignity she had sought for so long.

She was lifted from her thoughts by the sound of a carriage rattling in the drive outside. She wondered why Louis had returned so soon, and went into the entrance hall. Angelique was already at the front door. She was Charlotte's personal maid, a twenty-three-year-old octoroon with skin the color of *café au lait*. As the girl opened the door, Charlotte saw that it was not one of their coaches by the steps. It was a rental hack from town, and climbing out of it was Kenneth Swain.

He was impeccably tailored as usual. His stock was white as snow, his bottle-green morning coat untouched by the dust of the road. There was not a single wrinkle in his striped *toile de lin* waistcoat, and his Hussar boots had a polish that reflected the gallery steps like a mirror. He swept off his beaver hat as he saw her and bowed from the waist. His perfectly groomed hair was tawny as a lion's coat. His eyes were the same color, almost golden, and kindling with bright little lights as he straightened to look at her.

"Charlotte, you look radiant as the sun this morning. Which only befits the most beautiful woman in Natchez."

His wry charm had never failed to lift her spirits. "Louis and I have both missed you, Kenneth. You should have come sooner."

Smiling, he came up the steps and stopped before her. His pale, aristocratic face was unlined save for the grooves on either side of his lips. It was a characteristic that enhanced rather than marred his handsomeness for a woman. It somehow hinted at past suffering.

"We can sit on the gallery," Charlotte said. She spoke to Angelique. "Mister Swain is partial to that West India rum. And perhaps some baba cake."

They took chairs. He carefully leaned his sword cane against the rail. It was always with him.

"Louis is in town, Kenneth. He should be back for dinner. We'd be delighted to have you stay."

"I'm sorry," he said. "I'll have to miss him. I have an appointment at three."

"Always some mysterious business. What is it now? Are you taking up where Burr left off?"

"Something far more heinous, *madame*."

She gave a pleased laugh. "I didn't really know what a blackguard you were till I came up on the bluffs. Louis says the slaves all hide in the sugar house when you come. They make little dolls that look like you and stick pins into them."

He bowed his head. "I am fulfilled."

"And this new scheme?"

He took out a gold-chased snuffbox. "At present, I am in negotiations to get full possession of the Mississippi River."

She laughed again, tilting her head back. "Swain, you're wonderful."

He took a pinch of snuff. "My dreams of empire amuse you, *madame?*"

As she started to answer, a wave of giddiness swept through her. Then it was nausea, turning her face white, bending her forward. Swain rose swiftly, coming to her side.

"Here, I've made you ill, with all this talk of business."

She was bent over an arm of the chair, holding a hand over her mouth, thinking she would vomit. She could hear Swain, calling the maid. Then the nausea faded, leaving her weak and shaken. Angelique came running from the door, and Sanite Dede, the mulatto housekeeper, and a pair of kitchen servants. Charlotte was sweating heavily now, with her dimity clinging like paste to her body. When Swain saw that she was not recovered, he said: "It might be fever, Charlotte. They'd better get you upstairs to bed. I'll go for the doctor in town."

She was too weak to protest. It was all she could do to gain the upstairs bedroom with their help. Angelique undressed her. Once in bed, however, she felt better. The

nausea was gone, and she was not perspiring as much. In an hour Dr. Dumont arrived. He was a bustling little Frenchman, bald as an egg, with a pepper-and-salt goatee and waxed mustaches and a vigorous bedside manner. He examined her, asking many questions. Then he sat up straight, pulling at his beard.

"Aside from these other symptoms, what else do you feel? Your breasts tingle? Feel heavier?"

"I'd noticed it," she said. "But I thought it was. . . ."

At her hesitation, his eyes twinkled. "Love?" he asked. "In a way, *madame*, it is. You are going to have a baby."

Chapter Twelve

Kenneth Swain awoke near noon, on the morning after he had been to see Charlotte. He had quarters on the second floor of Connelly's Tavern, overlooking Canal Street, a block from the bluffs. The rooms were already stifling with the unbearable August heat. His bedclothes were sodden, and he rose and stepped out of them, calling his man. Dominique came running from the other room with a towel to dry him off.

"Do you realize, Dominique, that you are attending the most scrofulous blackguard this city has probably ever seen?"

The Negro showed a blaze of ivory teeth in his coal black face. *"Bou zou, miche."*

"It's been quite a strain, living up to my father's magnificent infamy, but I feel that at last I am worthy to stand humbly in his black-hearted shadow."

"Dieu sait, mo pas conne, miche."

It was their morning custom to prattle on like this although Dominique spoke only the French-Negro patois they called gumbo, understood little of what Swain said, and Swain had never mastered gumbo and so could not understand Dominique.

"You understand, Dominique, that I am descended from the very Carter Swain who drew up the plans of West Point that Benedict Arnold tried to sell to the British."

"Zaffaire Cabritt ça pas zaffaire Mouton."

"Exactly. And when Father was hanged, I was thrown

out into the world, a mere child forced to make his way with his sly wit and his nimble fingers. I'll have the scarlet weskit and then the bottle-green coat with the round cuffs."

"Oui, miche."

Brushed, groomed, and curried like a Thoroughbred horse, Swain descended to the taproom. He joined a pair of Creole cronies, had eggs, coffee, hoecakes, grits, and lingered over coffee to learn the latest gossip from King's Tavern and Silver Street, then proceeded outside.

On the steps he paused, glancing again at the cuffs of his shirt. Were they beginning to look frayed? His sardonic humor left him for a moment, as he remembered all the other times he had stood on some steps, or some street corner, looking at his frayed cuffs, just before the big turn of the cards—and how that turn had always never quite come off. Suddenly all the pretense and the guile and the charlatanism of his life seemed to back up in his throat like the rancid taste of bile, gagging him.

He moved slowly down the steps, trying to shake off the mood. Perhaps part of it came from seeing Charlotte yesterday. How could a woman like that choose such a shallow vessel as Louis? He had charm, true enough, and was handsome as the devil. But Charlotte needed so much more: fire and depth and savagery. Swain shook his head. Louis had offered her both love and escape from Silver Street, a devastating combination. Swain had seen how desperate was her need for that escape and knew he was not yet ready to offer it. How could she know how spurious and deceptive Louis's offering was? A few hundred thousand did not make a man truly rich. A bad cotton crop, a market recession, a political shift—and he was wiped out. The only true escape from the things Charlotte hated lay in power. It was a lesson Swain had learned from his own life. The visionaries like Burr had taught him that, and his education had been completed in the glittering vistas opened for him by Livingston and the other financiers he had met in the East last year. Where Burr had failed, he would succeed. If only Charlotte had waited . . . ah, well, love was like cards. A man's worst mistake was in tipping his hand at the wrong time. There were tides in a man's life. Swain had learned to swim with them. They were changing now, and, when he was carried inward on the top of the crest, Charlotte would still be there . . . in the meantime.

A sumptuous coach clattered by on Canal, mud spattered across the armorial cipher on its cherrywood door. A glimpse of a face turned toward him, creamy flesh and damp red lips, Antoinette Carreau, widowed and wanton. He tipped his hat, smiling sardonically, and she opened her fan across her face. That had been savory last night. If there must be a meantime, it was good to fill it with such pleasant dalliance.

Reluctantly Swain turned down into the sweltering misery of Silver Street. It was going full blast already, the air filled with the familiar babble of yellow-skinned hawkers and the husky shouts of boatmen and the shrill voices of squabbling women. Charlotte's aunt stood in the door of her inn, hands on her hips, surveying the mob disgustedly. Her dyed hair straggled mop-like from beneath a hat of white whalebone and paper flowers. Swain lifted his cane in salute.

"I wager you miss your niece, Annie."

"Not f'r long, Mister Swain. High sassiety. Charlotte promised. Soon's the honeymoon's over, I'll be right up there with the rest o' them Creole pukes." Pepper Annie hawked and spat. "And if she don't send f'r me soon, I'll go up m'self."

He grimaced and turned down the landing, seeking the

wharf master. He found the man collecting duties from a barge captain out of Louisville.

"Right on time," the wharf master told Swain. "Sooner or later that friend of yours will show up."

"Montgomery was the name."

"There's some new flats at the north end. A young man on one, with his wife. Don't look like farmers."

Swain found them at the end of the half-moon landing. Near the bow of the flat stood a tall, spare man in his thirties wearing worn nankeen breeches and a linsey-woolsey shirt. Recognizing John Montgomery, Swain hurried forward. Montgomery greeted him with his usual New England reserve. He had a long, pale face, the thin lips shaped into careful composure. There was something narrow and watchful about the gray eyes that disturbed Swain. He asked how the trip went.

"I took a million calculations," Montgomery said. "The spots where coal might be found, the best landings for wood, the channels that would give trouble. I know my findings will convince Fulton. We'll be building that steamboat at Pittsburgh by next spring."

"Capital. I've been gathering backers here. Some of the biggest names in the country. Warwick, Nassaur, Reynaud. I've used the utmost discretion."

"We have nothing to hide."

"On the contrary, my dear Montgomery. You don't realize what a tiger you have by the tail."

"Fulton has all the patents. Nobody can build a steamboat without his license."

"He has patents to specific machinery," Swain said. "He hasn't been able to contest this man French on his high-pressure engine, has he? And there's a Captain Abner in Louisville, working on some kind of horizontal cylinder.

With proper financing, he'll have a boat on the river."

Montgomery's lips adopted the pursed, Puritan look Swain remembered so well. "I heard about him at Louisville. It seems he has a friend named Owen Naylor, who owned the keel that brought you here."

"That's right."

"I understand the keel went down at the Big Black."

"Correct again."

"Was Naylor, by any chance, planning to finance Captain Abner?"

The suspicion in Montgomery's eyes made Swain suddenly wary. "How would I know?"

"We encountered a keel at Chickasaw Bluffs under the command of a Captain Nash," Montgomery said. He was watching Swain closely. "This Owen Naylor was aboard. I didn't talk to him, but I heard the story from some of the crew. They told me Naylor and a keeler named Pandash had fought at the Devil's Race Ground. It appears that Pandash pushed Naylor's keel into the shoals at the Big Black. Pandash said you had paid him to do it."

Swain's face went pale. "The man's insane."

Montgomery's voice trembled faintly, in his righteous anger. "Did you honestly fear Captain Abner's competition that much?"

Swain tried to regain his cloak of irony. "It's easy to see, my dear Montgomery, that you have little understanding of the river. This Pandash has an old grudge against me. . . ."

"I'm going to place this whole matter before Fulton and Livingston. I'm sure they will wish to sever connections with you immediately."

Swain thought fast. "And lose Governor Claiborne's support?"

"What?"

110

"I've just come back from seeing Claiborne in New Orleans," Swain said loftily. "I have a letter promising that he will put a petition before the Territorial Legislature of Orleans, granting our company the exclusive monopoly of steam on the river." Swain leaned toward the man, eyes beginning to glow. "Do you realize what that means, Montgomery? Enough of our steamboats on the Mississippi and we'll control the shipping of half a nation. Do you know how many millions of dollars go through New Orleans annually? Do you know what that could do to the company . . . in the way of riches, of power, of . . . ?"

"You're talking like a fanatic."

Swain drew himself up, feeling the heated flush on his cheeks. His eyes grew hooded, his face wooden. "A word from me could reverse Claiborne's decision. I'm sure Chancellor Livingston would be glad to hear that you put your faith in rumors rather than results."

For a moment he saw Montgomery's reserve break, a confusion darkening the chilly gray eyes. Swain knew the man's fear of the crusty old Livingston's wrath.

"Swain," the man said. "We're in a legitimate enterprise. If we fight competition, it will be in a legitimate way. We won't stand for violence."

"Who spoke of violence? You come across a boatman with a grudge and you jump to conclusions."

Before Montgomery could answer, they were interrupted by a commotion farther down the wharf. Dominique came running through the gangs of keelers.

"*Miche, miche,* Louis Reynaud, *épée, épée.* . . ."

The black man reached him, panting and gasping, eyes rolling like white marbles in his head. When Swain could decipher his bizarre mixture of gumbo, French, and broken English, he discovered that Louis Reynaud was going to have an affair of honor south of town.

"I must go now," he told Montgomery. "But before I leave, I will make one thing clear. I won't be treated like a poor relation. According to my contract, my acquisition of Claiborne already gives me more shares in your company than you can ever dream of obtaining. Shall we forget the twisted lies you heard, or shall I tell Governor Claiborne the deal is off?"

It was painful for Montgomery to bend an inch. His lips compressed, pride made a stiff mask of his face, but finally he said: "Very well. But if I find. . . ."

"Tut, tut, my dear fellow. Tell your grandmother to go suck eggs."

In the hack Dominique had brought from Connelly's Tavern, Swain gave way to his own disgust with Montgomery. It was a pity he had to be saddled with a man of such narrow vision, an engineer, unable to see beyond his cogs and his wheels, having no conception of the true vastness of the project in which he was involved. Couldn't the clod realize that in such a stupendous undertaking, ordinary measures would not suffice?

They rode up onto the bluff and followed St. Catherine's Street into one of the loess roads that led into the dense woods south of town. There was a clearing overlooking the river, a favorite dueling spot for the young Creole blades. A group of men was already gathered in the open ground.

Swain recognized Louis, facing Pierre Coquille. Both of them were in their shirt sleeves, faces pale and wooden. Between them stood Dr. Dumont, still wearing his rumpled coat, and Achille Cambre, holding a pair of naked rapiers. Swain got out of the hack, and hurried to the group.

"Kenneth," Louis said stiffly, "I am glad you came. It would have been awkward to have the doctor as my second."

Swain slipped out of his coat, handing it and his cane to Dominique. "You know you can always count on me, my friend."

"Everything is in order," Dumont said gravely. "Only to choose the weapons."

Cambre held out the rapiers, and Coquille took first choice. Louis took the remaining weapon, stepping back, testing its give, flexing his legs. Cambre took his position on Coquille's side, and Dumont joined Swain. The contestants advanced to face each other, and Swain spoke to the doctor in a low voice. "What was it?"

Dumont shrugged resignedly. "Some remark Coquille made in the café. I personally didn't consider it an insult. He merely asked if Madame Reynaud liked the bluff breezes better than the heat she would have been suffering on Silver Street. Louis is too jumpy."

"You know how hotheaded he is," Swain said.

"He'll have to cool down, then," Dumont muttered. "He certainly went into it with his eyes open. If he is going to read things into every comment about Madame Reynaud, he will be fighting every man in Natchez."

"*En garde, m'sieu.*"

"*Gardez vous, m'sieu.*"

The sunlight ran like quicksilver down the slim rapier blades as they touched. For a moment the two stood motionless there, facing each other, left hands high behind. Then Louis disengaged and attacked. Coquille dropped his point to parry. Louis feinted and thrust. Coquille executed a brilliant double parry and a riposte. Louis had to retreat.

In the lull between the clashing of their blades, Swain said: "I'm glad it wasn't the fever, with Madame Reynaud yesterday."

"Yes." Dr. Dumont kept his eyes on the fencers. "Fortunate."

"Is it to be a child, Doctor?"

"Professional ethics, Swain?"

"My humble apologies, Doctor."

Coquille's advance was accompanied by a swift beating of his front foot. Swain followed along with the other second, Achille Cambre, watching each execution judiciously. They were both brilliant fencers, evincing great technical skill, each thrust and parry timed perfectly, as blinding and deadly, if it connected, as the strike of a snake. Finally Coquille made the mistake of giving Louis an invitation in tierce. Louis responded with his triple feint. Like the zigzag of lightning, his blade flashed through the second and third positions, feinting to Coquille's side, his knee, with Coquille's desperate parries always an instant behind.

"Touché."

Louis recovered and stepped back. The fencers stood four feet apart, their swords pointed to the ground, with the stain of blood already spilling over Coquille's sleeve. Swain followed Dr. Dumont out. It was the right of the seconds to effect a reconciliation after first blood. This was met with such strict observance among the Creoles that it took but a nod from each duelist to end the affair. Swain looked at Louis, saw him nod, and knew a return of his cynicism for the tradition governing these affairs—the *code duelle* developed in New Orleans by the Creoles and still adhered to so rigidly by the young *chacalatas* of Natchez.

Swain had been taught in a different school; he had spent half a lifetime in the *sale d'armes* along Exchange Alley in New Orleans, learning the art of *épée* from Pepe Luigi, that infamous Italian who had nothing but contempt for a man who ignored a duel, knowing a touch would settle

114

the offense. Safe within the confines of his *code duello,* Louis looked like a brilliant fencer. Swain always wondered how the youth would fare if he knew his life hung in the balance. . . .

The young Creole had come in his own coach, and Swain joined him, while Dominique took the hired hack back to town. Louis looked moodily out the window as they rattled along the loess road.

"Montgomery arrived today," Swain said. "I gave him your name. He was quite impressed."

"Who?"

"Fulton's engineer. He said their subscription list was almost filled. I'd suggest you make your decision in time for him to take your name back with him. It would be a shame to lose out on such a handsome investment."

Louis frowned out the window, without answering. Swain glanced closely at him, then smiled. "Forgive me. I thought you might want your mind taken off the duel. But I can see you're still thinking of it. You can be proud of yourself today, Louis. Your *deuxième intention* had him completely mystified."

"I should have run him through," Louis muttered.

"Why didn't you?"

Louis glanced at him.

Swain laughed deprecatingly. "Never mind, Louis. Only I wish you wouldn't advertise your triple feint that way by shifting just before you lunge."

"I know," Louis said irritably. "The French school."

Swain twirled his gold-headed cane. "I only tell you as a friend, Louis. As Pepe Luigi says, it is not our opponents, but our own bad habits that will one day kill us."

Chapter Thirteen

Charlotte was having coffee on the gallery when Louis got home that afternoon about four. He was in a strange, distracted mood. He let her pour him some coffee, and then sat brooding in a cane chair without drinking it. She thought it was the heat; it had made her irritable and restless all day. She tried to lift his spirits with small talk, asking whom he had seen in town. He told her he had been with Swain. The man had told Louis jokingly what Pepper Annie had said about coming up to the Reynaud house. It bothered Charlotte. She had promised Annie she could come and live with them when the honeymoon was over. Louis had agreed to it more than once before their marriage. Now, when Charlotte pressed the point, he rose from his chair and paced the gallery, scowling like a little boy.

"*Sacré*, I know I promised. But we are not settled yet. Give us a little more time."

"It's been over a month. We've got to do it sooner or later, Louis. I'm not blind to what the old lady is. But she did bring me up, and I owe her this much. You'll just keep putting it off."

"I won't. But there are so many other things. You have wanted a party. Would you desire Pepper Annie among the guests?"

She bit her lip. "That's another thing you've been putting off. Are you ashamed of your wife, Louis?"

All the sulkiness left him. He came to her, taking her in his arms. "*Chérie*, how can you say that? You are my prize, my triumph. Any man in Natchez would give his soul to possess what I have. Only my selfishness made me put it off. I wanted to keep you to myself as long as possible. If you want, we shall make the guest list today."

"And Pepper Annie?"

"After the party. It is my word."

She realized he was putting her off again, realized he had brought up the party only to divert her mind from the old woman, but she had to make a choice. She knew his reluctance about the party had come from more than the desire to have her to himself. He faced the same misgivings that she did. How would they accept her, the Charlevoix, the Mooneys, the Devereux, all the other fine families on the bluff? It was a test that would set the pattern for her whole future life up here. To tell the truth, she had been as reluctant as Louis to meet that test, but she knew it had to be faced. For the parties and cotillions, the balls and the celebrations, and the endless visiting were a big part of the life on the bluff, and anyone who did not move in that circle was a veritable outcast. So she had won half a victory, and she forgot Pepper Annie for the present.

Having restored his good humor, having gained even that much ground, she was afraid to tell him about the baby. She knew too well what his reaction would be. It was something neither of them had expected. They had taken every precaution against it. Louis had given her the excuse that they were still young, that they should drink deeply of this wondrous thing that had been given them before settling down to the responsibilities of children. But she sensed that in reality he did not want the child at all. His life had been too gay and irresponsible, and he shuddered at the thought of the fetters fatherhood might place upon him. In a way she could not blame him. She hardly knew what her own reactions were. It was still too strange, too big, too new. Although she had never thought of herself as a mother, she wanted to be happy with the child. But there were her deep misgivings about Louis's reaction, and that other apprehension, deep down inside of her, shadowy and somehow almost frightening. It had been almost the first question that had come to her after Dr. Dumont broke the news, and it had stayed with her ever since. She tried again to put it out of her mind, tried to tell herself that her only real worry was Louis, and she would break the news to him in a calmer moment, when she'd had time to prepare him.

The excitement of preparation soon left her no time to dwell on her apprehensions. When Louis saw what a delighted interest she was taking in the thousand and one details, he turned much of it over to her. Sanite Dede, the Reynaud housekeeper, was a free woman of color from Santo Domingo, tall, statuesque, in her early thirties with a skin the color of stained ivory. Up to now she had shown nothing but a thinly veiled resentment which Charlotte could not understand, but the menu had to be discussed, so Charlotte went into the cavernous kitchen with its mingled odors of onions and thyme and okra and bay leaf. She made a few halting suggestions, hoping to prod Sanite Dede into some reaction. For a while the haughty, high cheek boned face was set in the mask of sullen reserve Charlotte had come to know, but finally the opaque eyes kindled with mocking little lights, and the woman smiled maliciously.

"Ah, no, *madame. Jambalaya* is only for the *canaille,* the rabble. Let us say instead *daube glacé.* It was always a favorite with the old man. Then it could be *macaroni au fromage gratte* and *gumbo Zhebes* . . . one does not have to wait till Holy Thursday for that . . . and for the dessert we could begin with angel's food cake . . . not with your open kettlc sugar, *madame* . . . they make it white as snow in the city now."

After that came the wine lists, the flower arrangements, the musicians, and the gowns. There was a mulatto seamstress in Natchez, *Madame* Perier, who had gained such a reputation that appointments had to be made a month in advance, but the Reynaud name bore weight, and within a day she was at the house.

"I like the silver chambray. In *La belle assemblée.* . . ."

"*Sacré, madame,* what you want wiz a fashion magazine? A woman like you do not follow style, you create it. I am not fit some French spinster three thousand mile across the sea. I am fit a woman with the bust most *magnifique* in all Louisiana. It should be this French net over imperial satin, *madame.* Can you not see how it will focus attention on the breast? The *décolleté,* the diamond waist, the simple sleeves. . . ."

The evening of the tenth was sultry and humid, with very little breeze coming up off the river to relieve the oppressive heat. Charlotte lingered over her bath and luxuriated in the fluttering attentions of the excited Angelique. *Madame* Perier had insisted on a hair dress to go with the gown—the hair brought tightly from the roots behind and twisted in a cable knot on the left side, the ends formed in falling ringlets on the left. But at the last moment Charlotte decided, much to Angelique's horror, that it was too affected: she let her hair hang loosely and full and had Angelique brush it for fifteen minutes. Then she donned the emerald necklace linked with dead gold that Louis had given her for the occasion, spent ten minutes choosing a perfume, and finally went downstairs at exactly eight o'clock.

Louis was waiting in the parlor, an ashtray already filled

with the smoked butts of his cheroots. She paused in the doorway, taking an excited pleasure in the way his head suddenly lifted, eyes widening. The rooms were open, revealing a dozen chandeliers that mounted three hundred candles, the jeweled prisms of their countless crystal pendants multiplied the light into a million glittering shafts, all seeming to find their focus on Charlotte. It made gleaming alabaster of her bared shoulders and the seductive upper slopes of her proud breasts. It shimmered wetly against the satin of her dress that clung so daringly to the curves of her body. It gave her eyes a jeweled glow and burned against her hair like a cascade of restless fire.

Louis rose and came quickly to her. *"Ma foi,"* he murmured. "You are a dream. What an occasion this will be. You'll capture all of Natchez, *chérie.*"

She couldn't help a pleased smile. He bent over her hand with the charming gallantry that still made a delightful occasion of their most mundane relationships. He escorted her like a queen to a chair and offered her a drink. She took port, sipping it. Through the dining room door she could see Juba, standing beside one of the gleaming pier tables—a six-foot black recruited from the field workers only last month, resplendent in his green livery—proudly arranging a dish of salami that stood beside the gelatins and salads and endless layers of angel's food cake. Other servants added to the sense of subdued excitement, padding through the back room and whispering in doorways. For a while Louis kept Charlotte delightfully entertained with the repartée and gay chit-chat at which he was such a master, but time began to bear against them, and by eight-thirty the small talk had worn thin.

Sanite Dede appeared, freshening the flowers banked in riotous profusion in the silver epergnes centered on the

120

great mahogany table. Her smoldering eyes met Charlotte's, then she turned to look at Louis. She wheeled and left the room, cotton skirt plastered against the sinuous movement of her feline buttocks. Louis frowned after her, then stood sharply, throwing the rest of his cheroot at the fireplace. "Why do these fine ones always pride themselves on such bad manners?" he said. "I swear that I will never be late again to another party."

"Have another cheroot," she said.

As he stopped by the silver-inlaid cigar box, there was the rattle of a coach from outside. It made Charlotte jump, and she realized how nervous she was. She rose, and they both went toward the door in the entrance hall. A footman was already opening the door. Kenneth Swain came in and gave the man his cloak, his hat, his cane. He had outdone his usual impeccable elegance. His shirt was dark blue and cutaway, the basket buttons winking like brazen coins in the soft light. He stopped before Charlotte. For once his reactions were not veiled. A distinct flush ran into his chiseled features, and his eyes kindled with tawny lights. He bowed low over her hand.

"I had always accounted you a remarkably beautiful woman, *madame*. Tonight you put the angels to shame."

The mixture of ironic humor and sincere admiration in his voice made her cheeks glow. "Flawless, Kenneth, delightful. But I hope it ends the formalities. I know it will be that West India rum for him, Louis."

Louis smiled and went to pour the rum. "What is this new fantasy I hear, Kenneth? Your father and Benedict Arnold?"

Swain pulled his razor-creased pants up a precise three inches and took a seat. "I will not be responsible for the scurrilous rumors mongered in the marketplace by my enemies."

"It's no use, Kenneth," Charlotte said. "Juba unmasked you the other day. He told me the true story of your father."

Swain's brows raised. "Ah?"

"Anthony Swain, one of those privateers flying the flag of Cartagena, wanted for enough piracy and murder to hang a dozen men, sneaking into New Orleans for an affair with an exiled Italian countess."

"Charlotte," Louis said.

She tilted her head back, laughing. "Don't be an old hen, Louis. If other people didn't spread these fantastic rumors, I think he'd do it himself."

"She was French," Swain said. "And she wasn't exiled."

They all laughed at that. Then Louis and Swain got into a discussion of steam on the river again. Louis had told Charlotte about the investment in the steamboat company that Swain wanted him to make. It seemed a little risky to her, but Swain had letters from Robert Fulton and Chancellor Livingston and a dozen other eminent men, plus a host of imposing figures concerning the profit made on the *Clermont* during her first year of operation on the Hudson. Charlotte tried to maintain her interest, but she saw that it was after nine. Louis glanced at the candles, seeing how they had burned down. He ran a finger around the inside of his collar.

"This heat. It's stifling."

The hoof beats of a horse outside made them all look sharply toward the door. Juba answered the knock, taking a note from another Negro, bringing it in to Louis. The young man read it, his face turning wooden.

"An apology from Charlevoix," he said stiffly. "His wife is ailing." He crumpled the note, lips compressed, and threw it into the fireplace.

Swain cleared his throat. "Ah, well. No great loss."

Charlotte could not bear to meet the heat quietly any longer. She rose, walking to the window. The satin clung with perspiration against her flesh. She could hear the whispering servants in the other room again. She felt breathless—suffocated. Swain made an attempt at conversation. Louis answered him curtly, frowning at Charlotte, brushing a hand nervously across his sleek black hair. Finally there was the clatter of a coach outside.

"Another note?" Louis asked angrily.

But it wasn't. It was Martin Mooney, the commission merchant, with his new bride, who had been Celestine Lamont, daughter of one of the finest Creole families on the bluff. Mooney was a square keg of a man, dressed in simple broadcloth, with ruddy jowls and twinkling blue eyes.

"The seamstress was tardy with Celestine's new dress," he said. He paused, as if waiting for something, then glanced at his bride. She was a wraith of a girl with huge eyes and a petulant underlip. She looked at the floor, stammering something barely coherent. "*Oui* . . . late was the dress . . . so foolish. . . ."

Charlotte saw then how tightly Martin had been holding her. The men gathered near the fireplace, firing up cigars, talking. Celestine took the chair Charlotte offered and sat, silent and owl-eyed as a child overwhelmed by her elders. Charlotte made an attempt at conversation, but it was like prying at a clam to get any answer from the girl. The heat pressed against Charlotte with an almost unbearable weight. All the men had their handkerchiefs out, mopping their brows. There was another note of apology. Another. It was almost ten o'clock. Charlotte's fists were closed so tightly the nails dug into her palms. Then a party of three arrived. Captain George Maddox who ran the biggest fleet of keels on the river with his prim New England wife, whose pursed lips and gimlet eyes reflected suspicion and distrust of everything in this country. Their companion was Harold Warwick, whose family ran back to the first English settlers in the section.

Hannah Maddox joined Celestine. There was another attempt at conversation, dying in the heat. The room was thick with cigar smoke. Charlotte felt a sudden start of nausea and called quickly for Juba to fan the room. When Charlotte did not think she could stand it another minute, Jacques Devereux arrived. A tall, young man, proud scion of the finest of Creole families, he had obviously been drinking earlier in the evening. His face was flushed; the devil sparkled in his eyes.

"*Sacrebleu,* how sorry I am to be so late. Our coach she had the wheel break an' this little *fille* was so anxious to have the early arrive, too. . . ."

This little *fille* was Antoinette Carreau, notorious young widow of the late Armand Carreau, who had scandalized Natchez with her escapades and was known throughout the town now as Devereux's mistress. Charlotte felt a thin anger at Devereux churn up the nausea in her stomach again. Antoinette gazed at her in brazen defiance, a relish of the situation in her slack-lipped smile. Charlotte clenched her teeth, fighting to keep her anger from her icy voice.

"I thought you were bringing Celestine's sister, Jacques."

The young man waved his hand flippantly. "Heat too much for her. Sends her regrets. You all know Antoinette."

The men murmured greetings. Antoinette's bold eyes swung across them till she met Swain's gaze. He bowed gallantly. "*Madame.*"

She smiled secretively. "*M'sieu.*"

Charlotte had recovered herself, introducing the widow

to those women who hadn't met her. Celestine reacted in complete confusion. Mrs. Maddox nodded coldly, without speaking. The tension was broken by Juba, with another pair of notes. Louis handed them to Charlotte without comment. She read, tight-lipped, then turned to the group. "It seems Madame D'Artaguette has been seized with a sudden recurrence of her malaria, and the Fossats have been suddenly called out of town."

Juba whispered something to Louis, who said: "The Rouquettes will not be here, either."

"I think there is no use waiting longer," Charlotte said. "Shall we dine?"

Coughing uncomfortably, grouping themselves self-consciously behind Louis and Charlotte, they moved into the dining room. They seated themselves at the head of the long table, occupying only ten of the fifty seats. The muffled movement and restrained breathing was like the rustling of ghosts in a tomb. Sanite Dede moved silently through the shadowy background, directing the serving. Louis made a few attempts at conversation, then lapsed into helpless silence. Charlotte could see the wrath growing in him, till the ridge of white flesh about his compressed lips was dead white. She made no attempt to talk. She understood it now. She realized what was happening, and it left her with a rage of her own, like a core of ice at the pit of her stomach.

At first she hadn't been able to understand why any of them came, when the rest of the town had made such an obvious decision concerning the evening, but now their motives were becoming clear. Out of his friendship for Louis, Mooney had apparently forced his young bride to come against her will. Curiosity had brought the Maddoxes, simple vindictive morbid curiosity on the part of Hannah

Maddox with her turkey-gobbler neck and her eyes darting over the room like a bird's, assimilating every juicy item of gossip that she could disseminate to her Yankee cronies the next day. Harold Warwick, titular head of the Tory faction in Natchez, was one of the major shippers along the river and had long handled the Reynaud cane and cotton and could not risk losing such a lucrative account. A bachelor, his political ambitions among the Tories still forced upon him at least a surface display of morality, and he had never been able to afford an overt alliance with the women of Silver Street, but now, with Charlotte under the dubious sanction of the Reynaud name, he could afford an open look at the wanton Louis had brought up from the dens of vice in Natchez-Under. Charlotte could see it in the flush on his face and the furtive glances he cast her way when he thought she was not looking.

"The *bouillabaisse* is superb, *Madame* Reynaud."

"Is it, Swain?"

"Yes." Maddox cleared his throat. "Do I detect a touch of that long cork claret Louis prizes so?"

"I wouldn't know."

Then came the silence again, the discreet coughing behind napkins, the tinkle of silver. Sanite Dede entered to oversee the serving of the entrée—turkey and goose and chicken and venison and wild hog that had been cooked for fifty people. Heaped upon the table, it made a travesty of the pitifully small gathering. The housekeeper looked once at Louis, then turned her eyes to Charlotte. The opacity left them for a moment, and they glowed with a malicious vindication.

"How will the cane be this year, Louis?"

"I don't know. I leave that up to Gayarre."

"Well . . . he's a good man."

Louis picked at his food, features pale and set. Hannah Maddox bent over her plate, eyes darting bird-like across the faces. Then Charlotte heard a commotion at the front door. Angelique came running into the room.

"Madame, your aunt. . . ."

Before Charlotte could rise, Pepper Annie appeared at the entrance way. Like a figure from some nightmare, she lurched against a *jardinière,* almost upsetting it. Her hair dangled in a tousled mat from beneath a tilted chip hat; her cloak was crumpled and stained. She blinked rheumy eyes at the room, seeking to adjust to the glittering collection of a hundred crystal pendants on the chandelier.

"Charlotte? You here?"

Surprise and anger flushed Charlotte's face, and her first impulse lifted her half out of the chair. Then she sank back, realizing that whatever she did would be too late. She stared emptily at her aunt, gripped in a strange helplessness, as if she were bound to the chair and powerless to stop this. But Louis reacted. His chair made a shriek as he shoved it back and walked in quick strides to the old woman. He caught her arm, trying to jerk her out of the doorway. "Will you go upstairs. You're in no shape to come here."

"Upstairs, hell," Annie said. She swayed drunkenly, squinting nearsightedly at Charlotte. "That you? I heard about the party. I thought it'd be as good a time as any. You been puttin' me off long enough."

Louis jerked at her, voice growing shrill. "Annie . . . !"

The old woman pulled away with all her gross weight. The cloak ripped off, and Louis was left holding it, while Annie lurched into the room. She caught at the back of a chair to keep from falling. Swaying there, she blinked at Charlotte.

"Why didn'tcha sent for me like you promised? Ashamed

of yer old aunt now? Think I was a hair-lip idjit or somethin'. Keepin' me down there in the muck while you was eatin' high on the hog up here. Think you can put on airs. Fergit yer old aunt. Let her starve to death."

The thought made her begin to sniffle with drunken self-pity. She reached for the Chinese shawl to wipe her nose, furry lips parting in surprise when she couldn't find it. Then she became aware of Hannah Maddox gaping at her. "Take a good look." Annie spat. "Git a lot of juicy little tidbits to take back t' yer sewin' circle. Be sure an' tell 'em about your husband, too. Tell 'em about that little octoroon he keeps at the Blue Lily down at Natchez-Under. Tell 'em how he ain't tussled you in bed these last five years."

Hannah Maddox went dead white. She turned to stare at her husband, all the pursed primness of her face wiped away by shock. Maddox's face was crimson. He stood up, breathing in quick little gasps. He sounded strangled. "Hannah, we will go."

Warwick pulled back his chair. "I will also take my leave, *Madame* Reynaud."

Annie cackled. She slumped into the chair, sodden with drink. "Watcher 'fraid of, Warwick? I'm gonna pop off 'bout the boots next? Harold Warwick, pure as snow, gonna sell Natchez back t' the British someday, gonna be guv'ner, gabblin' like a preacher up here 'bout the sin an' the muck below the bluffs."

"Madame!" Warwick said sharply.

"Sneakin' down after dark f'r Giselle an' her boots. Five dollars more f'r high heel boots. . . ."

Warwick stared at Annie while the helpless fury blazed like bonfires in his eyes. Then, with an inarticulate sound, he wheeled and stalked out of the room. Louis stood a foot behind Annie, still holding the cloak. The damage had been wrought, and he made no further effort to stop her. He was white and trembling, his eyes fixed on Mooney, as the man rose and helped his shocked bride to her feet.

Annie saw Jacques Devereux looking at her. "Whatcha gapin' at?" she sneered. "I'll shoot y'r fanny off."

Antoinette Carreau broke out laughing. She leaned back with her mouth wide open. It rang though the house with a brazen hysteria. Jacques tried to stop her, but couldn't. Tears were running down her cheeks, and her whole body shook. Her words were hardly recognizable through the laughter. "You better go back to Silver Street, Charlotte, honey. You'll be mighty lonely up here."

Charlotte sat rigidly, sick at her stomach.

Pepper Annie slumped into a chair. Spittle formed on her furry lips. Her eyes were glazed with drunkenness. Her head began to nod, and she put her arms on the table. "Shoot yer fanny off," she mumbled. Her head fell forward on her arms.

Jacques finally got Antoinette quieted, and led her out. The only sounds were the soft sputter of the candles and Pepper Annie's stertorous breathing. Charlotte turned slowly to look at Louis, where he stood behind the old woman's chair. Beneath the sharp ridge of his cheek bones, his flesh looked like wax. He was trembling violently with a rage he could no longer repress. "I could have expected this. Bringing a bitch like you up off Silver Street. . . ."

"Louis!" Swain's sharp voice cut the young man off.

Louis turned toward him, face contorted. Then, with a strangled curse, he whirled and ran from the room. Dimly Charlotte heard him tear open the front door, heard him shout to Juba for a horse. Slowly, like someone in a dream, Charlotte turned back to Swain. She was trembling now, sick and trembling, and she thought she was going to faint.

Swiftly he came around the table. "Perhaps you'd like to lie down," he said.

He pulled the chair back, half lifted her to her feet. A shudder ran through her frame. She swayed against him, giddy, nauseated, unable to stop the violent trembling of her body. He held her tightly. "You must forgive him, Charlotte. He didn't mean it."

The sickness passed; the shuddering died down. She held her face pressed tightly against his chest for a moment, gaining control. "It's not him I blame, Kenneth."

"Say the word. I'll present my *cartel* to every family in Natchez that didn't come."

She looked up, a smile twitching spastically at her lips. "I know you would. And run them all through, too, but it wouldn't do any good. We both know why they did this. The Maddoxes and the Mooneys spoiled the plan by coming. The town wanted to put me in my place once and for all, didn't it? To humiliate me so deeply I should never ask for their friendship again. Why else would they wait till the last minute with their notes? They knew what it would be, left alone, with all the food on the table, the wine opened, the servants waiting."

"The proud *chacalatas*," Swain said acidly. "A bunch of barbarians."

"They haven't beaten me, Kenneth." Her chin lifted, her eyes hardened, her face became the ivory enigma she had showed every boatman in Natchez-Under. "I made my choice. They can't make me go back to Silver Street."

"You're sure you're all right?"

"Perfectly. I'd appreciate it if you'd go after Louis. Keep him out of trouble, but let him get good and drunk. I think he needs it."

He bowed over her hand. Then he let Juba help him into

his cloak, set his beaver hat jauntily on his tawny head, and took his leave. She watched his tall, gallant figure swing through the door, then turned to look at Annie. The old woman's head was buried in her arms on the table, and she was snoring peacefully. Charlotte told Angelique to show Annie to a room when she awoke, then started up the stairs. The servants stood banked up in the doorways, watching her go, frightened and subdued. As soon as she was out of their sight, she heard their whispering voices break out, sweeping through the house like the scampering of a hundred rats. She let her shoulders droop, and lost the mask of defiance she had showed Swain. She had been rejected completely by the people of Louis's world, and it gave her a sense of bitter defeat, a bleak foreboding of the months ahead. Nausea was setting in now. She knew a part of it came from this evening, but the other part was the baby. The thought made her defeat fade before the old apprehension. The question that had been with her, actually, since she had first learned she was to have a baby. Would it be the child of Louis Reynaud—or of Owen Naylor?

Chapter Fourteen

The first heavy rain came to Louisville in early October that year. Evadne Archer heard it start, as she stood in the open kitchen door of the Red Feather Inn. It made a sodden sound against the layer of decaying leaves banked up against the log building, a sodden, dripping sound, miserable as a crying baby in the night. She shivered, because it meant the beginning of winter with the cold and the sun gone. Somehow, as often happened in these moments when loneliness stole upon her, she thought of Owen Naylor. His leaving had left her with a strange sense of loss, a loneliness she could not define. For her feelings were vague and indefinable concerning him. A thousand times she had tried to go back and pick up the cobwebby threads of the thing that had stood between them.

She knew that part of it was his pure animal magnetism. She had seen other women drawn by it, had watched more than one married woman look at him on the street longer than she should, had known two girls for certain who'd been tumbled in the hay by the boy, with nothing but luck or the time of the month to keep them from begetting. She had felt her own attraction for him growing during that year since her husband's death, but it had been a smoky, tenuous thing, and she had not seen enough of him for it to develop. He had been like a slave in those boat yards, working every waking hour to keep his mother alive and make something extra for his boat.

Whenever she did see him, there seemed so much to

keep them apart. The age gap alone made it a treacherous relationship, and his strange nature that kept him so veiled to her. Once in a great while she thought he recognized the vague reaching out in her. Then he would withdraw again, into his dream of a boat and a river where a woman couldn't seem to follow. How could she express something she wasn't sure of herself, when all of that stood between them?

The bear grease was popping in the floating wick lamp, and she shut the door to keep the wind from blowing out the flame. She should know better than to let these thoughts possess her, after her life with Saul. He had showed her the best a woman could expect from a man, and she should be grateful for it and not allow herself to waste her day in romantic dreaming like a silly young girl. She had been sixteen when she married Saul, a plain one, then, not ripening into her sulky beauty till much later, and the boys calling at the Kitteridge cabin in Pittsburgh had all been for her sisters. So Saul was the first, and the only one. Never a romantic, knowing little of love, raised to the tradition of the frontier where the cruel struggle for mere existence smothered any indulgence in frivolous romance and molded into most women an eminently practical attitude toward marriage, Evadne had accepted Saul as quietly and fatalistically as she accepted the rest of her life's pattern, and she had never regretted it. Saul had been decent enough to her. It had been a blow to him when he learned he couldn't have children, but he had accepted that in his plodding, phlegmatic way, and life had gone on. Perhaps she was little more than a chattel, helping him fourteen hours a day in the tavern they bought in Louisville, but that was no different than the lives of most of the other women, and her talks and comparison with those same women gave her no case to expect any more from him in bed. Apparently God had made it that way, the men to be no more than animals and the women nothing but receptacles, knowing only the barest taste of what it might be like. Three times a week, regular as clockwork, Saul crawled on, sometimes bearded and unwashed and fetid as a boar in its nest, taking his satisfaction and rolling off to begin his snoring, while she lay awake with the unslaked desire he had but faintly aroused, fading and dying out again. Yet, when she thought of Owen Naylor, with that melancholy shadow lying on his face, it made her wonder.

She shook her head irritably. She was getting as bad as Moll, lapsing into sentimental foolishness like this. She brushed her black hair back from her heat-flushed face and bent to give the haunch of venison a last turn. Then she swung the spit out and forked the meat off onto a platter, cutting a dozen thick slices and putting them on a tray. To this, she added the crusty corn dodgers, brushing off the gray ash with a turkey feather.

She carried it out into the taproom, jammed with men driven in by the rain, filled with the smell of sweat and tobacco, dampened wool and whisky. The usual quartet of townsmen had captured the choice space before the roaring fire and were holding the tails of their coats up to warm their hams while they carried on their heated discussion of politics. England was getting her usual share of fire and brimstone, Clay was being deified, and the town barber was putting Madison in his place.

"Look at his queue, sir, look at his queue. How can the country ever retain her dignity when her President has a pipe stem sticking out the back of his neck? It should have been Dagget, by all the odds. Have you ever seen his queue? Big as your fist, sir, big as your fist. He would have had

England in her place within a week."

Beyond them, the lusty talk of the boatmen filled the room. "I told that 'gator I wouldn't go down on the pole for him even if he was Danny Blackwell hisself . . . and that with the bow no more'n five foot from the sawyer."

She set the tray on the end of the bar, and Moll came to get it. A boatman leaned out to pinch the barmaid's meaty hip as she wobbled by, and Moll whistled at him through her harelip. As Evadne started to turn back into the kitchen, a pair of newcomers pushed the door open. They closed it behind them and halted, water dripping off their buckskins and puddling the puncheon floor. Evadne felt the breath clog up in her throat as she recognized Heap and Owen Naylor.

The change in Naylor was a distinct shock to her. He seemed taller, broader, thirty pounds heavier. It was as if he had left a boy and returned a man. His neck was cambered like the trunk of a young oak, its thick cords and muscles spreading downward in searching roots to give his shoulders a slope and a thickness they had not possessed before. He even stood differently, feet spread a little, as if seeking balance on a yawing keel. The somber expression was still on his face, with the bony brow casting his eyes into shadow so that they regarded a person like coals burning faintly in the depths of a hearth. As his gaze swung across the room and met hers, she felt all those strange and shadowy things that had stood between them rush through her again. She walked through the crowd to him, smiling her welcome, speaking throatily. "Welcome home, Owen."

He answered her smile—a thing he had not done too often before—and it made him look younger again. "Good to be home, Evadne."

They were silent, gazing at each other. This was the inarticulateness of the frontier, the Spartan code of life that impressed such rigid bonds on any expression of emotion. She felt the necessity of making the welcome more significant, of saying something else, but she could find no adequate words. The smile left her; the pouting shape was on her lips again, giving her face the hint of sullenness. "Come into the kitchen. We got venison and ashcake and plenty of red top in the cellar."

Heap slapped the greasy buckskin of his thigh. "Well, that do take the rag off the bush. I been in this place a heap o' times, but I never got an invite to the kitchen before."

She turned and led them into the kitchen. Naylor dragged a chair and sprawled into it with his wet feet to the fire. All the tension left his body instantly, and he was relaxed as a sleeping cat. She sliced some venison for them and shoveled some corn dodgers from the coals. She set them on the table, standing a few inches from him. The nearness brought a sudden breathlessness to her. "Upriver keel brought us news of your wreck, Owen. I'm sorry."

He nodded soberly, without answering, his eyes half closed as he stared into the fire.

"Looks like you poled your way back up," she added.

"And fought his way," Heap said enthusiastically. "Look at the red turkey feather in his hat. Had to lick every man jack of the crew before we reached New Madrid, every bully of the town from there to Louisville."

"Not quite," Naylor said.

She set Heap's plate before him. "What now? Down the river again in spring?"

Heap took a monumental bite of venison, added a chaw of dodger, and answered with his mouth stuffed. "Not him. Owen's goin' to build hisself a steamboat." Heap watched her face expectantly, but she showed no surprise.

Naylor's bare head was wet with rain. The impulse ran through Evadne to reach out and touch its glossy surface. "Steam must be in the air," she said. "A man passed through here on a flat a while back. Montgomery, I think. Claimed he was going to build a steamboat for Robert Fulton in Pittsburgh."

While Naylor ate, he told her of the fight with Pandash, and how Pandash had finally admitted that Swain was behind the sinking of Naylor's keel. "They thought I was going to back Captain Abner with the money I got out of that cargo, Evadne."

She could see what it signified to him. The fact that they would go to such lengths to keep another steamboat off the river suddenly gave the idea of steam a new importance. "Is that what convinced you?"

"Part of it. I never laughed at Captain Abner, but I guess I didn't really believe in his engine any more'n the rest of you. I guess each man has to learn for himself, Evadne. I learned. On that upriver trip I learned. Cut your heart out, piece by piece. Shrivel your soul up. If it doesn't kill you, it does everything else. I used to wonder why them boatmen went so wild when they got ashore. Now I know. I got the river in my blood. If there wasn't any other way, I suppose I'd go back. But there is another way. I'm sure of it now. And I'm a-goin' to do it."

That was a long speech for Naylor. She knew it would take deep excitement to make him reveal himself so fully. She had seen the same look to him during those last frantic days when he'd been finishing the keel, fulfilling a dream that had burned in him for years. She folded her hands, looking at him with half-closed eyes. "I'm sure you will, Owen."

He glanced at her, the unusual play of expression across

his face suddenly stilled. A new thought brushed shadows into his eyes, and he seemed to be searching her face with his look. Then he turned and began eating again. After their meal they emptied a bottle of homemade whisky between them, showing no effects. Naylor had learned how to drink like a man, too. They were dead tired, just in off the keel, with sixteen hours of poling behind them, and she showed them to an upstairs room. They lay down in the bunks without undressing, pulling the single blanket carelessly across their bodies. Heap was snoring before she left the room. She blew out the candle and shut the door behind her and leaned against it. She could still see Naylor's face, with the melancholy shadows lying like soot in its gaunt hollows. She could feel the nipples of her breasts swelling and growing hard as nubs, and she moved her arm up and pressed it tightly, almost savagely, against them.

Naylor and Heap went out to find Captain Abner the next day. He usually waited for calls on his service as Falls pilot in the Ivory Bill, one of the meaner taverns near the downriver end of the Louisville waterfront. It was a squalid log building, reeking of mud, getting none of the townsmen's trade as did Evadne's inn. On the wall above its bar were the dozen stuffed woodpecker heads that some naturalist named Audubon had gathered and then donated to the place in payment of a bill. Their scarlet crests were faded to a tawdry pink and their bills shone like old ivory in the gloom. Captain Abner occupied a table at the rear, his whole corner thick with the fruity reek of his peach brandy. As much as he drank, however, he never seemed to get drunk. He was delighted at their return and got up to do a tipsy jig when he heard Naylor wanted to build a steamboat.

"I've got almost four months' wages saved up, Captain,"

Naylor told him. "It's enough for a start, ain't it?"

Captain Abner frowned judiciously at his peach bottle. "Might pay for the boiler. What about the hull?"

"I'll go back to work in the boat yards. Make the money there to pay for the rest of the machinery, build the hull in my time off."

The old man sucked his lips in over toothless gums till they looked like the puckered edges of a purse. "You're really serious."

Heap chuckled. "Crazy is the word."

Captain Abner whirled on him. The cords in his neck stood out white as string, and the furry seams of his face deepened with indignation. "You're the one that's crazy. All of you scoffing fools that don't see the millennium when it's before your eyes. Do you realize they've been working with steam since before the time of Christ? The physician, Hero, wrote about it in Alexandria." Captain Abner jumped to his feet, red-rimmed eyes feverish with excitement. "Roger Bacon was describing it in the Thirteenth century. In Sixteen Fifteen, Solomon de Caus published his book on hydraulics. . . ."

"Captain, why don't you show him the model?"

Captain Abner whirled to stare at Naylor. Then, gnawing on his mustache, he turned and shambled out of the inn, followed by the two men. His shagbark cabin lay outside of town, a miserable shack with a rawhide door and a cat and clay chimney. He lit a floating wick lamp made of clay and bear grease, and the uncertain light bloomed up over the ten-foot skiff set on horses at the back of the room. At the stern was a frame built to accommodate the two-foot paddle wheel. The boiler was made from a ten-gallon cast-iron pot with the head soldered on. The cylinder was wood, strongly hooped.

"When did you decide a stern wheel was better?" Naylor asked.

"Ain't a matter of being better." Captain Abner got a greasy rag and began wiping rust and grime from the confusing maze of steam pipes and connecting rods that ran between engine and paddle wheel. "I heard Fulton was bringing suit against all them Eastern builders that are making side-wheel boats. But when I moved the wheel to the rear, I couldn't work out a decent system for converting the upright motion of the piston to a horizontal motion for the wheel. I finally laid the cylinder down and used a direct connection. Should've done that in the first place. Fitch was experimenting with a horizontal cylinder twenty years ago."

After he had cleaned and adjusted the engine, they helped him drag the skiff out through the woods to Grayson's Lake. With the boat on the beach, they hunted for suitable lengths of dry wood. Then they drew water into the boiler, stoked the brick firebox, and made a blaze with flint and steel and tinder. The steam began to mount, and the safety valve started to chatter. Heap watched wide-eyed as a child with a new toy.

Captain Abner took his seat in the waist, Heap in the bow, and Naylor shoved off. As they slid into the water, the safety valve let out an ear-splitting shriek. Heap jumped to his feet, almost upsetting the boat. "Look out, she's a-goin' to blow up!"

Smoke belched from the sooty stack, and the seams of the boiler began to spread. Captain Abner opened the throttle. The safety valve was still shrieking as the piston creaked in the cylinder, the connecting rods clattered, the stern wheel gave a jerk. Heap sat down again, gripping the thwarts tightly, his face shining with apprehension. The engine was shuddering and clanking wildly, and Naylor thought it would tear itself apart. As the piston reached the end of its stroke, the valves opened, exhausting the steam with a deafening report. Again Heap stood up, shouting frantically: "Godlemighty, Cap'n, let us off this foolish contrapshun afore she blows all to hell!"

Captain Abner seemed unaware of him. He sat bent over the panting, clattering engine, listening to every sound, nodding and smiling at the hiss of steam, frowning at a new rattle, adjusting connections and working the throttle delicately, talking to the engine as if it were human. "Take it easy, hoss . . . leak a little steam . . . the ol' captain don't mind. Quit shakin' that pitman, damn you. I tightened those screws. Now, now, don't spit, I wasn't really riled. . . ."

The hissing crash of exploding steam drowned him out. The boiler was panting visibly with the opening and closing of valves, its seams leaking steam and water like a sieve. There was a perceptible pause at the end of each stroke, so that the boat went forward by leaps and jumps. A rain of soot and sparks descended on them each time a new cloud of smoke belched from the swaying chimney. Heap had seated himself again, half hidden by billowing smoke, gaping in awe at the roaring, clanging, shuddering little engine that was driving them through the water at the fearsome rate of four miles an hour.

"Put some flues inside the boiler," Captain Abner shouted at Naylor. "Makes fifty percent more steam than the old one. Gas and smoke hits the head, comes clear back to the firebox through them flues. . . ."

A deafening explosion drowned the captain's voice. Naylor had the sense of metal whistling by his head, inches away. The engine went wild, shuddering and clanking and screaming like a thing gone mad. Captain Abner shouted at Naylor to damp down the fires, and he grabbed the bucket and scooped up water, throwing it into the firebox. The flames died with a gigantic hiss, and the safety valve went on shrieking. Finally the unearthly noises subsided. The wheel had stopped turning. The piston gave a last groan and quit. They were drifting placidly, with steam hissing from the boiler joints in quiet little tendrils.

"Busted connecting rod," Captain Abner said. "Always these little mechanical difficulties."

Heap was leaning forward in the bow, sweat making his face shine like polished saddle leather. As his fear subsided, Naylor saw the dazed wonder grow in his eyes. Heap's voice left him in a whisper. "I got nine rows of jaw teeth, roar like a 'gator, and I do love the wimen, but I never thought I'd clap my peepers on anythin' like this. She really goes, doesn't she? That little engine really pushes her."

"Now do you think we're crazy?" Naylor asked.

"Maybe you are," Heap said. "But if it's this excitin', I want to be crazy, too. How'd you like another partner in your steamboat?"

That was how they started. Heap had his wages saved up, too, and Captain Abner had a little nest egg. There was no smithy or foundry in Louisville capable of building the engine he wanted, so they agreed to let the captain go to Pittsburgh with the money and get the engine there. Both Heap and Naylor would go to work in the boat yard and send him more money as he needed it. They saw Captain Abner off on an upriver keel the next day. That same night, after their shift in the boat yard, they went into the timber north of town and started building the ways for their boat on the bank of the Ohio. On Sunday, with a full day off, they started into the forest before dawn, hunting the tree for their keel. Naylor wanted no splicing on this member. The boat would be as long as the tallest straight trunk they could find.

They found their tree and felled it and cleaned off the limbs and squared the butt with a saw. It took them all that day and most of the next week, working after their day in the boat yards, to strip the bark, rough it out, and shape it up. Then they borrowed Evadne's wagon mare and hauled the keel, a hundred and twenty feet of it, to the ways on the riverbank. Poling the keelboat upriver had conditioned Naylor to incredible labor, but they were actually putting in more time here than they had on the upriver trip, laboring from dawn till dusk in the boat yards, then working on their hull by torchlight until midnight and after.

Through October and November they kept at it, with the fox grapes turning blue along the runs and the gums turning red as blood in the bottoms and their leaves whispering off and spreading a tanning yard scent through the forest. They worked in a miserable rain. They worked in a wind that snapped branches off in the forest like the distant crack of rifle shots. They worked on misty Sunday mornings with the skunk smell making a fermented cider of the thin air and on black weekday nights that were growing so cold not even the great horned owl came to groan in the oaks above them. They saw little of Evadne, although she did some sewing for them and brought them hot rum and meals while they were working. Then in December the first snow came, a storm so bad they had to leave the work and hurry to shelter. They had been staying at Captain Abner's cabin, but the town was nearer, and they sought protection from the driven snow in the Red Feather Inn. Evadne invited them back into the kitchen, giving them their dinner. Heap pulled his chair up to the fire after eating and fell asleep there. Naylor remained at the table, numb with exhaustion, staring blankly ahead of him.

He finally felt Evadne's quiet gaze upon him and turned to meet it. A smoky light came into her half-closed eyes. He had a sense of that same, disturbing thing once more growing between them. Awareness of her came more acutely. She did nothing to enhance her looks. Her dark hair was worn in a severe style, parted in the center and drawn back tightly to a bun at the nape of her neck. A man had to look carefully to see any definition to her body beneath the formless muslin blouse, the voluminous wool skirts. But now the firelight gave form to that half-hidden shape, outlining the heavy roundness of her breasts with definite shadows, burning softly against the luxuriant swell of her hips. It was the subdued and unawakened beauty of a lush maturity, hinting at fires yet unlighted.

"You'll kill yourself," she said, "if you keep this up."

He drew in a weary breath. "It's the only way we'll get the boat built, Evadne."

"I never saw a man like you, Owen." She moved closer. Her clothing made a soft rustle against her body. "You were the same way with that keelboat. When you get started on something like this, it's like you was living in another world."

He didn't answer.

She was a foot away now. The smoky light made her underlip look full and pouting and vividly red. There was something intensely sensuous about it. "Why try to go on to the cabin in this storm?" she said. "Heap can sleep by the fire here. You can have the bunk in the loft room."

He nodded dully. There was a wholesome glow to her bare forearms. They were strong-looking, with a satiny texture to the white flesh. Her voice sounded odd.

"Why don't you go upstairs, Owen?"

He got to his feet with great effort, bidding her good night, dragging himself upstairs. The brick chimney was built up one side of the loft room and kept it comfortably warm. He undressed and crawled into bed. Despite his weariness, he kept remembering that sensuous look on Evadne's face. It did not hold his thoughts to her, however. It made him think of another face, a shadowy face, framed by a tumbling mass of rust-red hair, with uptilted eyes and oblique shadows under the cheek bones. He rolled over restlessly. The hell with that. He couldn't let it keep coming back to him. It was behind him. He would never see her again. He might as well accept it.

He tossed and turned, trying to put it from his mind. But the desire grew, becoming more than a desire for Charlotte—making him realize how long he had been a celibate—becoming desire for *woman*, poignant, trenchant, unbearable. Then he heard the door open, and close. He heard the soft shuffle of feet approach his bed. He heard the breathing, soft and husky, in the utter darkness. After a long while he asked: "Evadne?"

Chapter Fifteen

It was a new year when Danny Blackwell got back to Louisville. It was January 12, 1810, with ice still inches thick on the river, creaking against the keels in Bear Grass Creek, lying in a scummy crust on the levee. Blackwell had a blanket poncho-style underneath his bearskin coat and a wool sweater beneath that, and still he was cold. His knees ached and his feet were numb and his face was raw as sandpaper. He had walked all the way up from Natchez.

He'd hung around there for a month, trying to get an upriver keel, but summer was slack time, with a dozen patroons for every keel, and the owners didn't have to take a man who'd just lost his boat, no matter what the circumstances. So finally Blackwell had been forced to take the route used by all boatmen who couldn't get an upriver keel, the route he had bragged he would never have to take—the Natchez Trace. It had been a walk he would never forget, a thousand miles of it, alone most of the time, with the illimitable forest stretching before and behind, the tangled canopy of its foliage blotting out the sun so that a man walked in perpetual shadow. The great bald cypress standing with their knees sunk in oxbow lakes, choked with seed moss so iridescent it shone like green fire in the endless twilight; the great oaks with their butts dripping moss and moisture and half buried in the decaying heaps of leaves that had fallen through countless centuries; the sycamores hung with grapevines that looped down into the trail like the nooses of giant gallows.

On the Tombigbee it was the mosquitoes, biting Blackwell till he was so swollen and horrible the Indians ran from him in fright. At the Tennessee it was the Black Vomit, a month in the shack of that half-breed squaw, swimming in sweat, so sick he wanted to die, never knowing from one minute to the next whether the Indians would scalp him or save him. South of Duck River it had been the Hell Holes, seventy-five miles of bog and swamp, where the quicksand got you if the cottonmouths didn't. It had gotten the keeler who traveled with Blackwell from Colbert's Ferry, screaming and sobbing and cursing while he sank into the bog, with Blackwell unable to save him. And the silence, all the time the silence, pressing in on a man like a suffocating weight, filling him with a loneliness so great he started talking to himself, shouting down the endless lanes of timber, going out of his head sometimes in his fight with the swamps.

Blackwell now turned down the Louisville waterfront to the Ivory Bill. He stopped a moment before the door, his primitive ego shrinking from what he knew would be inside. But there would be drink and warmth and companionship, too, and he needed that after four months of hell. The place was crowded with boatmen. He found Wheeler's face in the crowd, and the man saw him and whooped like a crane and rushed for him. In an instant a dozen more were around him, Furgeson and Wheeler and Nicolas Fry, shouting and clapping him on the back.

"We figgered maybe you were afraid to come back, Danny," Furgeson said. "I never thought I'd see the day when you lost a keel!"

"I didn't lose no keel," Blackwell said.

Furgeson's eyes widened in surprise. He was a big, red-headed man, half a head taller than Blackwell, twenty pounds heavier. But the savage anger in Blackwell's face brought an insidious fear to the redhead's eyes.

"Maybe you'd like to come up to taw?" Blackwell said.

"Take it easy, Danny. I didn't mean it that way. We all know it wasn't your fault."

"Let's have a drink," Wheeler said. "Wash the Trace out of your guts."

Blackwell wheeled on him, snarling. "I didn't come up the Trace."

"Awright, awright. So you didn't come up the Trace."

"Let's have that drink anyway," Nicolas Fry said. "Town hasn't been the same with you away, Danny. Haven't had a riot in months."

It mollified Blackwell somewhat. He swaggered to the bar, pulling a handful of piasters from his pocket and throwing them down. "I got these in N'yawlins," he said. "I caught me a fifty-foot cottonmouth at Natchez and rode it down the river. Laid every woman in the swamp with one hand while I drank all the Nongeela in town with the other. Then I met Jean Lafitte, bit off both his ears, found a thousand piasters in each one, hired me a special packet to bring me home."

It was a big brag, really, for the miserable time he'd had. The piasters had come from that keeler who'd been sucked down in the Hell Holes. He'd tossed Blackwell his money belt in the hope they could use it as a rope to pull him out, but it hadn't been long enough.

The boatmen were willing to accept any brag as long as the drinks went with it, and they crowded around Blackwell asking for more. Blackwell hadn't eaten all day and was roaring drunk on his third cup. Soon all of them were rum-soaked, and the next natural step was the women.

A dozen of them started up the levee to the miserable

shacks outside town. They passed the woodchopper's hut and farther on caught a glimpse of a half-built boat in a clearing near the river. They passed it in a swaggering, shouting group. Nicolas Fry was so drunk he had to hang onto Blackwell to keep from falling.

"Little different from the Trace, uh, Danny? No wimen on the Trace, eh?"

"I told you I didn't come up the Trace."

"How else could you?"—stumbling, hiccoughing—"Wheeler said they wouldn't give you no keel in Natchez, after losin' Naylor's. . . ."

"Damn you!" Blackwell swung a vicious blow at Fry. It knocked the man rolling, and Blackwell ran after him, shouting in rage. "I didn't lose no keel, and I didn't come up the Trace."

Fry dodged a kick and rolled to his hands and knees, fear shining in his eyes. He looked from side to side like a cornered rat, seeking some way to divert Blackwell. "Why waste y'r stren'th on me, Danny, when you got bigger game in the woods? What about Naylor's steamboat?"

The name stopped Blackwell. "Naylor?"

Fry was on his toes, eyes bright, ready to dodge if Blackwell lunged again. "You saw it in that clearing. Nobody's there now, though. Captain Abner claims the steamboat'll put us keelers out o' business."

Blackwell swayed on his feet, mind inflamed with drink and rage. Naylor's name seemed to give focus to all the vicious need of release that had been building up in him for so long. The hell of the Trace had only intensified the bitterness and frustration of his failure this year, and Naylor had been at the bottom of the failure, hadn't he? A kid like that didn't have no right owning a keel. It had been a jinx boat from the beginning. Like pus from a rotten wound, something seemed to burst within him, filling him with a raging need to exorcise his defeat in an orgy of destruction. His hoarse bawl rang through the forest. "Nobody's going to put Danny Blackwell out of a job!"

Shouting and yelling, glad for anything to divert Blackwell's killing rage from them, the boatmen joined him in a rush down the trail. They were all wild drunk. Fry tripped and fell a half a dozen times. Wheeler ran full tilt into a tree and knocked himself out. They broke into the woodchopper's hut and found some axes, then ran in a hooting, howling mob to where the steamboat hull sat on its ways. Face flushed, shaggy blond mane swinging down over his eyes, Blackwell jumped to a thwart, swinging his axe high and screaming like a berserker. "Tear it apart! Nobody's gonna put us out of a job. When we get through, there won't be one god-damn' stick left of Owen Naylor's god-damn' steamboat!"

Chapter Sixteen

February was a magnificent month in Natchez. It came in a fierce, pagan rush of color and brilliance. The fogs and chills of January were swept away by a blazing sun that brought a china-blue brightness to the sky. The ground was mantled with new green shoots—the live oaks turned branch tips up in new life—the moss that had hung on the cypress like gray cerements throughout the winter was showing a shadowy green rebirth. Beneath the bluffs, the ancient river was stirring and grumbling at its banks, as if gathering strength to bear the torrent of spring floodwater that would soon come shouting down from the north.

Charlotte could enjoy little of it. She was big with her child now, and her confinement was only weeks away. The disastrous party in August had thrown Louis completely off balance. He had stayed away three days, and had finally returned with a monumental hangover and a terrible temper. She had given him a few more days to get over it, then told him about the baby. He'd evinced surprise, shock, resentment—all the things she had expected. But he surprised her by settling down soon and making a valiant effort to accept it.

They both realized the limited course their social life would run now; the party had taught them that. Louis could still mingle with his male friends in the taverns and coffeehouses of town, but Charlotte would not be accepted by their families. It put a deep taint on their lives. They avoided town, but there were still drives along the river and picnics at St. Catherine's Creek and visits from Swain who enlivened their evenings with his ironic wit and easy camaraderie. When he was not there, Charlotte played endless games of *écarté* with Louis and Pepper Annie.

Louis also tried to take an interest in the plantation, spending many days in the cane fields with their half-breed manager, Gayarre. But Charlotte could see what a strain the pressures of boredom and loneliness were beginning to put on Louis. And there was Annie. He had made every effort to accept her, but she was completely incongruous with the rest of the household, a travesty to any outsider who might have happened in, a mockery to Louis, a constant reminder of that night when he had been so completely severed from the circle he had known all his life. By April, his resistance was beginning to wear thin, and he started spending more and more time in town.

Charlotte's mother had taught her to read and write when she was a child, but her ten years with Annie had given her little cause to practice either. Now, with her confinement upon her, and Louis's growing absences leaving time heavy on her hands, she found herself turning to reading again. Gaspar Reynaud had collected a fine library, and they still took two newspapers. On the last Saturday afternoon in April, Juba came back from town with their weekly packet of the Louisiana *Courier*, and Charlotte settled herself on the gallery, wrapped in a heavy cloak, to read them. She was laboring over a front-page article when Annie came out, setting a bottle of port on the table and lowering her amplitude into a cane chair.

Charlotte rattled the paper. "It says here the President's wife uses snuff."

Annie took a deep drink of wine. "Spanish Lou used to snuff, before she took up opium."

"What's non-intercourse?"

"How the hell should I know?"

"I'll ask Louis tonight. He's been helping me. Such a fine education. Two years in France and all those tutors here."

"Two years polin' a keel woulda done him more good."

"It says here that President Madison did something about non-intercourse with England and everybody thought our trouble was over, but a man named Canning did something else, and now it's all a mess again."

"We'll have a war yet," Annie said. "Louis in the fields?"

"No. He went to town again. He gets so restless."

"I know why he goes." Annie sniffed, took another drink. "Ever since that night. Old Pepper Annie. Spoiled it f'r ya, didn' I? Come up right in the middle of y'r party, drunk an' slobberin'." She began to sniffle, pulling her Chinese shawl around to wipe her nose. "Spoilin' my little Charlotte's party. Worked so hard t' git off Silver Street, all her life she worked, then some old bitch comes up and busts in." Her face shone with tears of self-pity, and she was snuffling loudly. "Some old bitch, drunk as a keeler, blowin' her top about Maddox and his octoroon and Warwick and his boots. . . ."

"Annie, please. It was all over before you came. How many times do I have to tell you? They'd only come to gawk."

The old woman wiped at her eyes. "I really ain't all bad, am I, honey? Drunk most o' the time, ugly as sin, cussin' like a Kentucky boatman. I can't help it, can I?"

"You're what Silver Street made you, Annie. Both of us are."

"But you tried to change, at least. I never even put up a fight. Jist drift with the river, drink all the likker, what an old wreck. . . ."

She broke off as Charlotte gasped sharply. Face contorted with a spasm of pain, she doubled over. Annie gaped at her, then grabbed her arm. "Y'r time come?"

"I don't know." Charlotte could barely speak. The agony seemed to tear her apart. She heard Annie calling to the servants. Juba and Sanite Dede and Angelique came running. Then the pain was past, leaving her weak and shaken. Still bent over, she heard Annie's voice. "Juba, you ride for the doctor. Dede, git back in the kitchen and have some water bilin'. Angelique, he'p me git this girl upstairs."

With the pain gone, Charlotte needed little help to climb the stairs. She lay down in her bed, while Annie sagged into a chair, sending Angelique after her port. The maid came back up with the bottle, and the old woman took a long pull. Angelique sat on the bed, worry lining her young face. Charlotte could hear the whispering of servants downstairs, the shuffle of their feet. She realized this was just the beginning and knew a growing dread of what was to come. The sunlight filtered like golden meal through the windows, casting deep shadows behind the damask hangings of the bed. Time seemed to drag, and a listlessness stole over her. Then the agony came again, like hands tearing at her insides. It sucked the breath from her, doubled her over. She heard Annie lurch out of the chair, felt the old woman pulling on her arm.

"Git up now, honey. Walk around. . . ."

"Madame," Angelique pleaded. "She no can walk. Can't you see, she hurt, she hurt. . . ."

"Leave me be," Annie said querulously, shaking off Angelique. "Think I ain't seen a million babies come? Charlotte honey, git up. Annie'll take care of you. Walk around. Time passes quicker that way."

The pain was gone again, and she rose, weak, panting, to

154

walk around the room with Annie. The smell of port on the old woman's breath was sickly sweet, and she swayed now and then, eyes turning foggy. Charlotte saw Angelique, gaping at them, and it struck her suddenly what a ludicrous picture they must make staggering about the room—one so swollen she couldn't see her feet, the other so drunk she was liable to topple any minute. Charlotte couldn't help laughing. It sounded shrill, hysterical. Annie blinked at her, then grinned foolishly.

When the pain came again, Charlotte clutched at her aunt. Pepper Annie swayed and almost fell. If Angelique hadn't come running, they would both have pitched to the floor.

The afternoon passed like that, growing more unreal, more nightmarish as the pain increased, filled with endless walking, with the sight of Annie's slack, furry face, with sweating and crying out and struggling.

It was almost dark when Juba returned, his face shining with perspiration. He said Dr. Dumont was across the river, tending to a man wounded in a duel, but was expected back in an hour. Juba had left word with his wife, and she had promised the doctor would come as soon as he returned. But he had not arrived by nightfall. Charlotte was too exhausted with the spasms of pain to walk any more, and lay suddenly on the bed, soaked with perspiration. Annie sprawled on the squab sofa, muttering thickly to herself. "Said he was comin' in an hour. Seems more like midnight. Damn these pill peddlers anyway."

"Annie!" screamed Charlotte. "Annie!"

It was worse than ever this time. She didn't think she could stand it. Thunderclaps of pain rocked her body, and she couldn't help screaming. Pepper Annie lurched to her feet, catching at the rolled back of the sofa to keep from falling. "Looks like we can't wait for Dumont," she mumbled.

"Annie, stop it somehow. I can't stand it any more. Annie, please stop it."

"I get Mammy Lolo," Angelique said.

"None o' them black wimen," Annie said drunkenly. She tore off her shawl, staggering to the bed. Hanging onto one of the posts, she swayed heavily, trying to focus her eyes. "Git me a gallon o' black coffee. I can't deliver the little bastard if I can't even see him."

Angelique was horrified. "You can't do. Not when you lak this. You can't do. . . ."

"The hell I can't," Annie bawled. "I been a midwife more times than you et breakfast. Now git me some coffee, damn you, I got to sober up."

"You can't do. . . ."

"I'll shoot yer fanny off!"

Angelique scampered out of the room. The agony had passed again, leaving Charlotte so weak she could not move. Fear lay like a leaden weight at the pit of her, clogging the breath in her throat. She saw Annie drunkenly rolling up her sleeves. Her forearms were muscular as a man's. Then the agony came again, and Charlotte could hear herself cry out. After that it kept coming so fast she had little consciousness of anything else, only the pain that ran in great spasms through her body, doubling her up, tearing sounds from her that no longer seemed human. The rest of it was broken glimpses of Annie, gulping black coffee, of Angelique, bending over her and crying, of Sanite Dede, standing back against the wall, enigmatic and untouched, of Annie's voice breaking through her spasmodic outcries.

"Git me more coffee now. Things are beginnin' to clear

up . . . Dede, we'll need something to cut the cord. How about them scissors? Keep y'r knees up, Charlotte. That's all right, honey. Pepper Annie's here now."

Then the agony came again, a black wall of it, blotting out everything. She didn't know how long it lasted during the final session. When it was finally over, she lay in an exhaustion so complete she couldn't find the will to move, to think. She heard a slapping sound, a squall. She opened her eyes to see Annie, holding the baby up by its heels, red and wriggling, seamed little face contorted with its bawling.

"Annie," she said. "Annie. . . ."

"It's all right, honey. Just close y'r peepers now. It ain't quite over yet. Gimme them scissors, Dede."

There was more whispering movement about her, a giggle from some great distance. Then the rushing sound of footsteps, and she looked up to see Dr. Dumont bending over her, face flushed, collar awry.

"*Madame,* my deepest apologies. Some fool Americans dueling across the river. I had to perform an amputation. Complications. The man would have died if I'd left."

Charlotte knew a sudden fear. "Doctor, my baby . . . ?"

He smiled, patting her shoulder. "Safe and sound. Your aunt did a magnificent job. You have been delivered of a baby girl, *Madame* Reynaud."

They brought the child for her to see, wrapped in a soft white blanket. Only the face was visible, red as a beet, seamed like a satchel. Charlotte felt happy tears fill the corners of her eyes, and she held out her arms. Tenderly Annie put the warm bundle down beside her. While she was holding it, there was another rush of feet on the stairs, and Louis burst in. His eyes were shining brightly, his face looked strangely loose and wild. He ran to the bedside and dropped to his knees, staring open-mouthed at the child for an instant, then bending to Charlotte.

"*Ma foi,* forgive me, what a fool I am, to be away when this was going on, can you ever forgive me? I had no idea. Somebody told me Juba had been looking for the doctor. If you only knew the fear I had."

She could smell brandy on his breath. But the feeling of the child, her warm child, in the crook of her arm, filled her with warmth, a happiness akin to nothing she had known before, and she could not blame Louis for anything. She smiled at him, eyes still filmed with tears, and she saw relief flood his face. Then he was looking at the baby again.

"A girl," he whispered. "They tell me it is a girl."

"I'm sorry it isn't a boy."

"What is the difference? It is our child. We were going to call her Denise, if it was a girl, remember?"

"It's a beautiful name."

"A beautiful child. Look at that hair, already. Look at those eyes. Every man on the bluff will fall under her spell. I wish Grandfather were here to see her."

He started to touch her with a fingertip, then pulled back. He made helpless motions with his hands, eyes wide with wonder. She could see how completely he was captivated. It was something she had hoped and prayed for but never quite expected. Pepper Annie bent over the child, chuckling softly.

"She looks like you already, Louis."

Just those few words. An inevitable comment at such a time. Yet it wiped all the warmth and happiness from Charlotte, filling her with a sudden dark portent. She turned to look at the red little face, her voice a hollow echo in the room. "Does she?"

Chapter Seventeen

Louis Reynaud was the epitome of his time, his place, his class. His parents had died when he was eight. His grandfather had taken him into the house on the bluff, to grow up in that unique patriarchal agrarianism that was the culture of the Creole planter, with its cornerstones of honor, hospitality, punctilio, and gracious living. His education had been one of modes and manners rather than information and enlightenment. He had a flair for languages, and it was about all he retained of the tutoring imposed on him during his boyhood. His two years in Paris had taught him to drink, fence, and play *écarté,* and little more. Upon his return, he had fallen comfortably into the unique mold of Natchez—the curious mixture of the elegant and the vulgar so peculiar to the town—strolling and drawling in the sun-drenched streets, dueling and chaffering for slaves, chivalrously courting the secluded Creole beauties on the bluff and rutting like a young stud among the women of Natchez-Under, betting on the horse races and gambling all night in the coffee houses, attending the constant round of parties and cotillions that were such an integral part of the traditional hospitality. So the young *chacalata* developed—rich and idle, pampered at home and catered to in town, his every whim immediately satisfied, finding no cause to put a curb on his temper or his appetites. It left a man who responded to most of life on the emotional level, a man who found little time or inclination for reflective thought.

Thus Louis had little understanding of the subtle change

the baby had wrought in his personality. When he did try to explore it, to analyze the strange new emotions the child brought, the sources evaded him. All he knew was the child touched a new depth in him, giving him an appreciation of home and family he had never felt before. For those first few weeks after the birth, it was enough. The wonder and the novelty of fatherhood held him to the hearth. He was surprised that he had to make no effort to adapt himself, that he could resign himself to the confinement of their simple life, taking renewed interest in the plantation, going back to the evenings of *écarté* with Pepper Annie and Charlotte, helping his wife with her reading again, taking endless delight in the baby.

If their life had been more normal, the change might have had a chance to take root, to give him the maturity and the balance he so sorely needed. But there were too many things at work; he was cut off in too many ways from the life he had known. Every day, by a dozen channels, it was brought to his attention. The last week in May he kept overhearing the house servants whispering of the grand cotillion to be held at the Villiers' plantation. On the first Saturday evening of June he and Charlotte took one of their drives and passed the Mooney house, blazing with lights and ringing to the laughter and gay voices of a hundred guests. Swain was the only one who visited them, and, when he left for a month in New Orleans, they felt like exiles cut off from the world. Thus, after the first flush of pleasure in his fatherhood, the first enthusiasm of his new-found paternalism, the pressures began to exert themselves against Louis once more. The enjoyment he found in the baby was not enough to stem the growing restlessness in him. He became short-tempered with the tensions of confinement, fought with Annie, quarreled with Charlotte.

With June, the summer heat was upon them. The sky was never blue. It was bleached muslin in the morning, naked steel at noon, a blazing furnace at sunset. When there were clouds, they lay like burning banners across the horizon, crimson and yellow and purple, of hues so vivid it hurt the eyes to look at them. The sun's merciless heat constantly sucked moisture from the land, and the steam rose from the bottoms and bayous till the whole world seemed on fire. The nights brought no relief. They slept naked and uncovered on a mosquito-netted tester bed, awakening in the morning as drained and listless as when they retired.

One evening early in July, Louis came downstairs from a futile attempt to nap. It was humid and sultry, and, although he had just bathed, his clothes clung to him. He heard soft footsteps in the hall and turned to see Sanite Dede, coming down its dark chasm from the kitchen. Louis had been fifteen when she had come to the house, a daughter of one of the field servants who had been brought over from Santo Domingo. Her intelligence and her strange influence among the servants had given her eminence in the household while she was still young. Gaspar Reynaud had made her his housekeeper while Louis was away in Paris. In her early thirties now, she had a primitive beauty to her body, with its high, cone-shaped breasts, its hollow-cheeked flanks. She halted by the pier mirror, her enigmatic face gleaming like polished ivory in the gloom.

"Jacques Devereux he give birthday party at his house tonight. Last year you give it for him."

Louis ran his fingers around the inside of his wilted collar. "You don't have to remind me."

She stepped closer, and the pungent scent of her flowed against him, the wild, musky reek of a savage thing not long from the jungle. "When you gonna git rid o' her?" She

161

looked at the parlor behind him. "When you gonna laugh again an' sing again an' have this house fulla your old friends again . . . ?"

"Sanite, will you stop it?"

Her face tilted up, and her voice was barely a whisper. "When you gonna come to me again?"

For a moment he did not answer. Their husky breathing was the only sound in the gloomy hall. Then he spoke in a savage undertone, intensely conscious of the parlor's proximity behind him.

"How many times do I have to tell you? That's over. It's got to be. We can't possibly have it again."

Her nostrils fluttered like those of a spooked horse. She looked beyond him at the parlor door, and the feral glow of her eyes became a smoldering resentment. Then, without a sound, she turned and went back down the hall. The humidity plastered her cotton dress wetly against her body. Her buttocks were completely defined, moving sinuously beneath the slither of cloth.

He hunted for a handkerchief, and wiped the sweat from his face. Then, reluctantly, he went to the parlor door, stopping there. Charlotte sat on one of the settees by an open window, fanning herself. Her gray-blue eyes were heavy-lidded with listlessness, and the masses of her red hair curled against a cameo-pale face, damp with perspiration.

"What was it in the hall?" she asked.

"Sanite Dede," he said. "Something about supper."

"Tell her to make it light. I don't think any of us have much appetite."

Angelique stood by the mantel of African marble, holding the baby. Louis went to her, the sight of the squinting, pawing little bundle lifting him momentarily from his depression. He let her curl tiny fingers around his thumb, gurgling and chuckling.

"Look how strong she is, Charlotte. I'll bet she could hang on if I lifted her up."

Charlotte smiled. "Don't you dare."

He took Denise from the maid's arm and walked her around the room. Then he sat on the floor and played with her while Charlotte looked on indulgently.

"What would the gay blades down at the Café Lafayette think of you now?"

"They would think I had gone mad," he said. "And I wouldn't care. I tell them about Denise all the time. They call me Papa Louis now."

Finally it was time for the baby's nap, and he reluctantly gave her up to Angelique. With the cooing, gurgling child gone, a depression settled on him again. He wandered across the room, pouring a drink, tasting it, putting it down. Juba appeared, telling him Gayarre wished to see him. Louis nodded, and in a moment their manager entered. He was a tall, narrow-shouldered half-breed, son of a Kentucky boatman and a Choctaw squaw.

"I wonder what you did about the cane, Mister Reynaud. Go much longer in this heat, we won't have any crop."

"I haven't been to town yet. I'll let you know."

"It can't wait, Mister Reynaud. I told you we'd run into this if we sold them field hands."

Charlotte turned in her chair. "What's happening?"

Louis waved his hand impatiently. "Never mind."

"I want to know."

Gayarre glanced hesitantly at Louis. Lips compressed, Louis said nothing. Gayarre twisted his straw hat in gnarled fingers, muttering: "This is the worst summer we've had in years, *Madame* Reynaud. We got to git water up from the river, and we can't do it by irrigation. It's got to come bucket by bucket."

"How many blacks do you need?"

"We sold off a hunnert. That'd turn the trick."

Charlotte's eyes widened.

Louis knew what she was thinking. A hundred blacks at five hundred apiece would mean fifty thousand dollars. Louis spoke testily to Gayarre. "I told you I'd take care of it as soon as I got into town. Now I wish you wouldn't come to the house and bother *Madame* Reynaud with these problems."

Color stained Gayarre's Indian cheek bones. He turned and shambled from the room.

Charlotte was looking at Louis. "Why did you sell the hands?"

"It was a complete waste," Louis said. "They were just lying around."

"Your grandfather obviously had a reason for them. Now you'll have to get them back."

"I will. I will." Louis paced to his inlaid cigar box, snapping open the lid. He was conscious of Charlotte, still watching him, and looked up impatiently. "Everything will be all right. Must we quarrel over it?"

She leaned back in the settee. "I'm sorry, Louis. It must be the heat. I don't think I can bear it much longer. Why don't we take a drive to Saint Catherine's Creek?"

He bit off the end of the cheroot, licked down the wrapping, leaned over a candle, and sucked flame into the slender cigar. "It will be so crowded," he said.

"You mean all your friends will be there?"

He sent her a sullen glance. "That's what I mean."

She was silent for a moment, staring at him. The acrid smell of *perique* tobacco filtered across the room. "You mean you're ashamed of your wife?"

His teeth clamped savagely against the cheroot. "Do you want to face them? Do you really want to go?" His voice was acid.

For a moment her eyes sparkled with anger. Then her lids fluttered, dropped. "No," she said in a subdued voice, "you're right. Let's just go for a ride, then."

"A ride, a ride. It's all we do."

"We've got to do something, Louis. It's been weeks now, with this weather. I'll go crazy if I have to stay in this house any longer. . . ."

"You'll go crazy? What about me? I've been just as close to it all. Sweltering in those fields all day. The stupid card games at night. Those endless rides to nowhere. That old witch from Natchez-Under getting drunk every evening. . . ."

Charlotte sat straight, eyes blazing. "Why don't you leave, then? Why don't you run from it, just like you do everything else? Go back to your coffee houses and your fine Creole friends!"

He felt a hot rush of anger flush his face. In the same moment, Pepper Annie appeared at the door. She had a tawdry wrapper pulled around her shapeless tub of a body. From behind the straggling vegetation of her hair, drink-glazed eyes blinked at Louis. She held up a half-full wine bottle, swaying against the door frame. "Tell them sonabitches inna kitchen t' stay outta my port."

It was the last straw. With a savage look at Charlotte, Louis wheeled and stalked from the room. Without even getting his hat and coat, he went out to the stables. While the boy saddled his favorite mare, he paced back and forth through the sawdust and hay. How had his marriage come to this? It was so completely different from what he had envisioned when he was courting Charlotte. He had never dreamed but what she would meet complete acceptance up here. After all, hadn't every man on the bluff tried to court her, at one time or another? He had expected resistance from the women of the fine families, but he had been confident that the Reynaud name and Charlotte's dazzling beauty would overcome all opposition. How had it disintegrated into this so soon—living like monks, cut off from the world he had known, trapped in the house with that incredible travesty of an aunt? He felt baffled and completely helpless before it.

As though trouble with Charlotte wasn't enough, now this thing about the field hands had to come up. He knew Gayarre was right. He shouldn't have sold those hands, but he'd needed the money to pay off his gambling debts. Now where could he borrow to get the hands back? He couldn't put another loan on the house. There were two mortgages already, with the payments long overdue. The other planters were having the same problem with the heat, and their hands and funds would be tied up. He had a frantic sense of impotence, of being pushed farther and farther into a corner with no way out. The need to escape it all was like something crawling in his stomach. He mounted Jet and put her into a gallop past the rear of the house. He saw a figure, standing motionless on the gallery, watching him go. Light came in a diffused channel from the window, gleaming like ivory against bare arms, silhouetting the savage grace of Sanite Dede.

Louis did not return that night, or the next. Charlotte was not surprised. She had seen the tensions building up and knew this would happen sooner or later. It was a disillusioning realization, yet she could do nothing but accept it.

She woke early, the second morning, and had breakfast on the gallery. Sanite Dede served, bare feet whispering over the cypress planks.

"*Maître* not come down this morning, *madame?*"

Charlotte glanced up at the woman. Dede's face was a tawny mask, but the eyes held a vindictive gleam. The woman knew Louis had not returned. "Why do you resent me, Sanite?"

"Resent, *madame?*"

"Would hate be a better word?"

The woman's face did not change. A flicker of expression ran through her eyes, and then the lids drooped to veil them. Without answering, she wheeled and slithered into the shadowy depths of the entrance hall. She closed the door behind her soundlessly. The effect was much more sinister than if she had slammed it.

Charlotte leaned back, her appetite gone. Was she to meet acceptance on no level up here? She was so steeped in her bleak mood that she did not hear Angelique approach with the baby. She looked up, startled, and then had to smile faintly, because Angelique was one of the few who had shown her genuine affection. She took the child, baring her breast for her feeding. Looking down at the little fingers, pawing at her white flesh, she sank into her depression again. No matter how much she loved Denise, no matter what pleasure she took in her, there was hardly a time when she could hold her or look at her without the dark question coming to her mind, making her search the pink little face for some similarity to Owen Naylor. A hundred times over she had tried to tell herself how foolish it was. The chances were a hundred to one in favor of it being Louis's child. Dr. Dumont knew of the precautions she and Louis had taken against a child, and had warned them how dubious they

167

were at best. He had not seemed a bit surprised that they had failed. If any feature of Owen's was going to appear, it would have become evident by now. Yet, despite the endless arguments she made against it, she couldn't help looking into the face.

It left her more depressed than ever, as she finished the nursing, and gave the child back to Angelique. The maid took Denise inside, and Charlotte sat looking listlessly out through the grove of pecans and oaks toward the yellow river. Finally the rattle of a coach pervaded the humid silence, and a hired hack from town appeared on the drive. Kenneth Swain stepped down from the door, tall, tawny-haired, impeccably tailored as ever. She knew a lift of pleasure at the sight of him, and went to meet him at the head of the steps. He bowed low.

"*Madame,* how do you manage to look so ravishing in all this heat?"

She answered his smile. "I know how I look, Swain. But thank you for being so gallant anyway."

He came up the steps and stopped before her. "Not all gallantry, Charlotte."

There was no smile on his face as he said it. She had seen the searching look in his eyes before, with the faint crevices like crow tracks at their tips. He had been one of their few links with the outside world, and she had always taken enjoyment from his friendship. But once in a while she was given the sense of treading on thin ice in their relationship; there was something beneath his ironic mask that disturbed her. She did not want to see it today. She was in no mood to cope with anything deeper than light badinage.

"I'm glad you came today, Kenneth. I need a lift."

He followed her, and she felt his distinct effort to respond to her mood. "I do magic tricks, and can juggle six oranges at a time."'

She seated herself, trying to smile. "Louis met a man from Bordeaux in town last week. An agent commissioned by Napoléon to find the lost Dauphin. The man had just been to Louisville, checking into the rumors about some naturalist named Audubon."

Swain pulled his trousers up two inches, seating himself. "Ah?"

"The man said Audubon couldn't be the Dauphin. He didn't have the deformed ear." She was looking at Swain's ears as she said it, unable to keep the smile from her lips.

He bowed his head. "I, too, saw the man from Bordeaux, if that's what you're thinking. He assured himself that I was neither the lost Dauphin nor the illegitimate son of Benedict Arnold and a New York procuress named Molly Forrest."

It made her laugh, as this game always did. "Keep it up, Kenneth. I need cheering so badly."

He leaned toward her. "Then for once, Charlotte, I must fail you."

She saw that he was holding three pieces of paper out to her. They were *bons assignats* to Swain, signed by Louis, totaling more than ten thousand dollars. After studying each one carefully, Charlotte looked up at Swain. He rose, pacing to the gallery rail, his back to her. "I'm not one to bear tales. You know that. But I feel very close to you and Louis. I know it isn't the Creole way to include the wife in on business affairs. But I also know how much this escape from Silver Street means to you, and I think it's time you understood how things are going, before they all come down about your ears."

Her voice sounded brittle. "He lost this much last night?"

"And the night before. Devereux and Coquille won about the same amount from him as I did. Louis was drunk, playing foolishly. I tried to get him away, but I couldn't."

"Tell me the truth, Kenneth. Did Louis go on these debaucheries before we were married?"

He hesitated, then he shook his head. "No. He drank and gambled as much as the other young Creoles, but he could always handle it. He's gone wild lately. I think it's some kind of outlet for him, Charlotte, some kind of escape."

Charlotte bowed her head. "I suppose I have to face it, Swain. I didn't see it till after we were married. There's a weakness in Louis. He's never had to face any real problems before. And now, every time things get too much for him, he runs."

"What do you suppose it was these last two days? He was wilder than I've ever seen him."

She rose, her face going tight. "Gayarre told us the cane was dying. We had to have a hundred blacks to save it. Fifty thousand dollars, Kenneth."

His eyes narrowed. "For your own sake, Charlotte, you'd better go and find out just how bad this is."

François Preval was Louis's cousin and had been the Reynaud lawyer for the last thirty years. He and his wife had been the only two in the whole Creole circle who had shown Charlotte any respect or friendship, and she was very fond of them. In such a patriarchal culture as that of Natchez, it was *passé* for the women to pry into their husbands' business affairs. But balanced against his rigid tradition was Preval's disapproval of Louis's idleness and irresponsibility. It was what finally swayed him to reveal the mess to Charlotte. He paced his office, a spry little man, archaic queue twitching with each jerk of his narrow skull. Swain had accompanied Charlotte, and it was worse than either of them had anticipated. All the bank accounts were overdrawn; there were two mortgages on the property, both behind in the payments; there were a dozen bills outstanding for the shipping of last year's cotton and cane and other services.

"Louis came to me last night, ordered me to get another loan for the blacks to save his cane," Preval said. "I told him how impossible it was. There is nowhere we can turn. It must have been what sent him so wild."

Charlotte had to take a seat. The bottom seemed gone from her stomach. Her hands were clammy and chill, the roof of her mouth felt dry. Suddenly she seemed to hear the babble of Silver Street again, echoing through her head in cacophonous mockery. She felt a fear of it surge up in her, a repugnance stronger than ever before. When she had been a part of Natchez-Under, fighting to escape, her idea of what she would find up here had been warped, fanciful, a vision seen through a veil. But now she had tasted it. Now she knew too well what a return to Silver Street meant. Decency. Cleanliness. Gentility. Respect. They had been merely words before, half-formed concepts to be longed for as a child would yearn for images in a dream. But now they had become reality. In these last months they had become far more tangible, more important than the jewels, the servants, the handsome coaches, the big house she had woven into her fancies on Silver Street.

"I warned Gaspar not to put the whole estate in the boy's hands," Preval said. "But the old man loved Louis so. And Louis had quit most of his carousing during the last years, convincing us he was growing up. . . ."

Charlotte's first sick reaction left her. Now came a surge

171

of angry rebellion. She could not give up so easily. There must be some way out. She straightened in the chair, little muscles taut and strained about her mouth. "Suppose we sell out?"

Preval nodded. "It is the only thing left to you. But it is no solution."

"The Reynaud plantation is the finest on the bluff," Swain said. "Coveted by half the planters in Natchez."

Preval turned to him. "And when they find out it is a forced sale, they will wait till you have to put it on the auction block, and get it for half the price they'd pay in a normal market."

"Suppose we sell before anybody finds out how bad off we are?" Charlotte asked.

Preval was dubious. "There's a slim chance. You'd have to move fast. Get hold of Louis somehow before he gives his position away, if he hasn't already done that. Fabricate some story that could cover your real reason for selling."

She rose, too restless to sit still. "Would we have anything after the debts were paid?"

Preval sat down at the desk, riffling through papers, adding figures quickly. He asked Swain how much Louis had lost during these last two nights. Then he sat back, quill in hand. "As nearly as I come out, assuming that you get the true worth of the property, you should have ten or fifteen thousand left after all your creditors are taken care of."

She sat down again. "Not much, is it?"

"It merely presents you with a new problem," Preval said. "If you live off the capital, it would be gone in two or three years. With such a small sum, there is no investment that would give a big enough return to maintain you."

"How about a stock that would pay fifty percent on

the principal?" Swain asked.

Both Preval and Charlotte looked up sharply. Then Charlotte frowned at Swain.

"Are you talking about the steamboat again?"

Swain nodded. "Montgomery is getting ready to lay the keel at Pittsburgh."

Preval shook his head. "There are enough wild schemes here, if *Madame* Reynaud wanted to throw away her money."

"Would a man as eminent as Chancellor Livingston put all his time and money into a wild scheme?" Swain asked. "Would the river men be so afraid of it unless they thought it could succeed?"

"Afraid?"

Swain turned to Charlotte. "That boy Naylor tried to build a steamboat in Louisville last year. Blackwell and his crew went on a rampage and wrecked it completely."

The reminder of Naylor shadowed her face. But the main issue was too urgent to let her dwell on it.

Swain began to pace now. "The Ohio Steamboat Navigation Company has a proposition for incorporation before the Indiana Legislature right now, Charlotte. They'll have a capitalization of fifty thousand dollars to start with. You'd be getting anywhere from fifty to a hundred percent on your investment the first year."

Preval was aghast. "How can you arrive at such incredible figures? A keelboat owner is doing well to make ten percent."

"Simple arithmetic," Swain said. "A hundred and fifty tons of cargo at five dollars a hundredweight. That's fifteen thousand gross a trip. Three weeks downriver and six weeks up. That's ten trips a year. Even after wharf duties, insurance, wages for the crew, commissions, repairs, payments

173

to the patentees and officers, you'll have a capital surplus of well over a hundred thousand. What would this mean to a stockholder, Preval, owning over twenty-five percent of the shares?"

Charlotte saw Preval's eyes grow wide. "Your figures are unassailable, *m'sieu.* But they are all based on the ability of the boat."

"If you'd stood beside me in the *Clermont* during that trip to Albany, you would have no more doubts about the boat, Preval. Where poling takes four to five months to get upriver, steam will make it in six weeks. We stand on the threshold of a new era."

Swain took a sheaf of papers from his pockets—letters from Livingston, Fulton, Claiborne, copies of their petitions to various legislatures, their patents, plans of the boat and the engine, commitments from several important men in New Orleans and Natchez who wanted to buy stock. Charlotte had never seen Swain so enthusiastic. His eyes glowed; his cynical reserve left him completely as he talked. It was contagious. Charlotte felt her heart begin to thud with a strange new excitement. Swain had talked to both Louis and her before about this, but she had dismissed it as simply another of his fantastic stories. Now, with all the facts and figures and documents before her, she realized it was true, and she could see Preval's mounting interest. She knew how much it would take to impress the shrewd, conservative little man so deeply.

Why not, then? Charlotte was of the river. She knew enough about cargoes and rates, about the millions of dollars of shipping that passed through New Orleans annually. If Preval accepted Swain's figures, they were certainly valid. It all rested on the boat itself, then. The possibilities of it, sweeping in on her, made her suddenly too restless to sit

174

still. She rose, pacing across the room, her eyes sparkling.

Swain stood still, smiling sardonically. "I think the fever has finally got you, Charlotte. All you have to do now is convince Louis."

On the morning of August 2nd, Louis was awakened by the distant murmur of voices. Pain shot through his head as he sought to open his eyes, and he sank back into the pillow. He had but a foggy memory of the last two days and nights. A drunken card game at the Café Lafayette—Swain in it somehow—then a trip to Nassau's place, a gay bachelor who had a plantation downriver. More cards, more drinking. Women. Louis couldn't even remember if he'd slept with one. Finally, squinting at the pain, he tried to open his eyes again. He had a foggy vision of damask hangings, half drawn, a *girandole,* sending out eye-shattering reflections, a *bibliotheque* of Circassian walnut, housing a fine collection of leather-bound books, and, standing by the squab sofa in a corner, Charlotte.

He came up on one elbow in surprise. It made him sick at his stomach, and he hung his head. When it passed, he looked at her again. He knew where he was now. His face flushed with embarrassment.

"Don't worry," Charlotte said thinly. "Jacques let me in the back way. His family doesn't know. The harlot from Silver Street won't humiliate you again."

He flushed more deeply. "I wasn't thinking of that."

"Weren't you?"

"You don't have to come after me like I was a child or something."

"This time I did, Louis. I've been hunting high and low for you. Jacques is bringing you a suit of his. You'll put it on and come with me."

Jacques Devereux entered, carrying the clothes, obviously embarrassed by the whole situation. It was humiliating enough for Louis to have her come after him like this, and under any other circumstances he would have refused to go with her. But a scene in front of Jacques would only make it worse. A servant brought up coffee, strong and black, and he drank three cups as he shaved and washed and finally put on the suit. Then Jacques let them out the back way, where Charlotte had a coach waiting. Charlotte sat stiffly in the corner till they were well away from the Devereux plantation, rattling down the loess road toward the river. At last Louis could stand it no longer. His voice was bitterly sarcastic.

"Are you going to make me suffer now?"

"Don't be like that," she said. "I've had my anger. If you'd have been there when I first discovered why you did this, we might have had a scene. But now it's over. We must go on from here."

He stared at her blankly. "What's over?"

"I've been to Preval. He's told me the whole story."

As he grasped fully what she meant, a hot anger ran through him that she should have pried, an impulse of the old childish rebellion. But it wouldn't last now. His defiance seemed to crumble before the overwhelming defeat of what Charlotte knew. He lowered his aching head into his hands. "I guess I went crazy, Charlotte. I was looking at my own ruin, and I couldn't face it." He turned his head from side to side, fingers digging into his glossy-black hair. His voice was tortured. "What's happened to everything? To me. To our marriage. It started out with so much. Even with the baby, there was so much. When Denise came, something changed in me. The *bon vivant,* the rakehell. I don't understand it yet, but I know I loved the baby, I loved you twice as much for having one. I wanted to be such a good father, such a good husband. And now"—he made a helpless gesture with one hand—"all this."

She spoke calmly. "I think we were both children when we married, Louis. We didn't understand what we were getting into. We had a lot of illusions about marriage, expected it to solve all our problems, hand everything to us on a silver platter. Maybe all those illusions have to be shattered, one by one, before we grow up."

He looked at her, his face pale and distraught. "But what will we do now?"

"There's one way out, if you have the courage to take it."

Hope came into his eyes. He caught her hand. "Anything. I swear, I'll try again, Charlotte. No more of these debaucheries. If we can only salvage something, I'll fight for it with you."

The ivory reserve left her face; she smiled softly at him. "Then let's start."

She showed him the investment figures Preval had made out for her, how it would be impossible to get a living off the interest they might expect in real estate or cotton or shipping or any other investment. Then she told him about the steamboat. Swain had talked to him about it before, quoting the same figures she possessed now, but Louis had never really listened, considering it another one of Swain's fantastic schemes, thinking that, if he got a little extra money, he might invest it merely for the sake of Swain's friendship. He was surprised, now, to see that both Preval and Charlotte seemed convinced. The discussion lasted till they reached the house. They gave Juba their wraps and retired to the living room. Louis was feeling steadier now, and began pacing in front of the fireplace.

"You say cotton speculation is risky. How can it be riskier than putting the last money we have into something completely new, untried, in a company fifteen hundred miles away?"

"Naturally we wouldn't put the money in so blindly," she said. "I want to talk with those engineers, to see the boat they're building."

"What about the baby?"

"We'll take her. Babies are being born every day on those flatboats, being brought a thousand miles down the river without any trouble at all."

He circled the room. "Oh, no, not Denise."

"You know the only way either of us would be willing to invest that money is to go north and see this. Would you want to leave the baby here?"

"No, of course not. It makes the whole thing out of the question."

His circling had brought him back toward her. The moiré skirt whispered across her thighs as she rose. He stopped, three feet from her. There was a new expression on her face. Tawny shadows lay in a wedge-like stain beneath the exotic cheek bones. The lids had crept together over her eyes, giving them a slumberous look. Her lips were damp and shimmering and intensely red.

"I've thought this thing through a hundred times, Louis." Her voice was hardly more than a whisper. "I wouldn't suggest taking the baby on such a trip if there was any other way out. But Preval has convinced me this is the *only* way."

She had stopped, inches from him. The scent of her brushed him, the perfume of passion, he could look down and see the nubile swelling of her breasts, filling him with a sense of all the rest of her satiny concupiscence, beneath the clinging dress, and he knew what she was doing. This was *her* last resort. She was fighting with the only weapon a woman had left when all else failed. Before their marriage it had made him give her a hundred promises. Now he knew it would make him give her another, despite himself, and he would have to keep this one. His palms began to sweat. The blood made a throbbing in his temples. It had always been this way. She aroused a desire in him no other woman could match. It was what would bind him to her, no matter what else strove to tear them apart.

Her whole body lifted against him, hot, silken, demanding. His arms went about her and his mouth sought hers and her lips flared beneath the kiss. His hand found her breast, a heavy cushion of flesh that burned through the moiré of the bodice. She moaned and threw her head back. Her hair came loose and spilled in a rusty torrent over his hand, hiding it completely. Her eyes were closed and her lips were parted and her teeth were clenched and white and pointed and savage.

"Louis . . . take me upstairs."

Chapter Eighteen

In three days Preval had found them a buyer: Harold Warwick, the Tory who had long wanted to branch out into planting. A shipper, his funds were not tied up in slaves and cane that needed water, and he could raise enough cash to swing the deal within a week. It took some juggling on Preval's part to keep Louis's true position from leaking out, but the contracts were signed before the facts became known. Preval had told Warwick simply that Louis had a chance for a prime investment in the East.

The story soon circulated through Natchez, and was accepted. To most, it signified a triumph for the Creoles, indicating that their ostracism of Charlotte had taken its desired effect. Everyone knew how hateful the whole situation had been to Louis and took this as his effort to escape it. After the mortgages, bills, and gambling debts were paid off, it left them a little over fourteen thousand dollars. Preval got passage for them on an upriver keel, carrying a consignment of coffee and rum for Henri Villiers, one of the big Creole shippers of Natchez.

Pepper Annie said she was too old for such a trip, and returned to her tavern on Silver Street. She had been growing more restless and quarrelsome around the house every day, and Charlotte believed the old woman was secretly glad to return to the old life. Despite her complaining, the inn gave Annie enough to live on, and Charlotte knew she would be all right.

All the slaves had been sold with the plantation, save for

Angelique, whom Charlotte had kept as a personal maid, and Sanite Dede, who was a free woman of color and could not be sold. On the day of departure, all the other slaves crowded along the gallery and around the steps of the house, wringing Louis's hand, crying openly, bestowing pathetic little gifts and voodoo charms upon him to ward off the Imp of Death and other evil spirits. Charlotte's regret and sense of defeat were tempered by all the unhappiness she had known here. She looked forward to the trip as a chance for a new start.

The coach rattled down the drive, with the Negroes running beside it and shouting and calling. But one did not follow. One stood alone at the end of the gallery, watching them go. It was the last thing Charlotte saw. Sanite Dede, standing like a pale yellow statue on the gallery, the hate smoldering in the feline eyes as she watched them go.

That was the end, and the beginning. The beginning of endless days filled with the curses of the boatmen, sweating at their poles, living in a cramped eight-by-twelve cabin at the stern of the cargo box. There were two other male passengers, a rich farmer from Wheeling and a commission merchant from Pittsburgh. They played endless games of brag and *écarté* and twenty-one atop the cargo box with Louis and Swain, while Charlotte and Angelique sweltered in the heat beneath a hide shade the patroon had rigged for them. Charlotte had been afraid of what the confinement and boredom would do to Louis. After the first few days she could see the strain it was making on him. But it was a new adventure for all of them, and Swain helped immensely. He was an experienced traveler, knowing a hundred different ways to alleviate the monotony and trials of such a journey. The baby gave them little trouble. She seemed to thrive on it, developing a voracious appetite, knowing fine health.

The August nights were sultry, filled with the booming of frogs, the piping of insects. The shore forests were coal black, even when the moon turned the river white as milk. They were awakened by panthers, screaming back in the brakes, and great black bats blundering through the canes overhead.

At Walnut Hills they saw corn fifteen feet high and cotton stalks taller than a man's head. At New Madrid they saw produce rotting on the levee for want of a keel to take it down, and bales of cotton that had been piled there for weeks, waiting to be shipped. It convinced Charlotte more than ever of the need for steam on the river. On the 1st of October they reached the boiling yellow whirlpools at the meeting of the Ohio and the Mississippi. At Fort Massac, they passed a keel from Louisville and were told that Owen Naylor was building another steamboat, at Louisville. It came with an abrupt impact to Charlotte. It was in no way a renewal of her thoughts about Naylor. How could it be, with the baby as a constant reminder? But the baby was her only concern in relation to Naylor.

It was November before they reached the Falls of the Ohio, and autumn mist lay like snow over the forested banks about Shippingport. The town was on the Kentucky side just below the foot of the Falls, and the keels made a landing to take on a pilot. The waterfront looked cleaner than Natchez. Charlotte saw an imposing flour mill, several log warehouses, a boat yard filled with the *clap* of hammers and *hum* of saws, a whole line of boys pulling hemp at the ropewalk. The plank was dropped, and the patroon told them they could stretch their legs, if they wanted, while he went ashore to find the pilot. Charlotte and Louis and Swain followed him onto the landing. Used to the languor of the South, it seemed to Charlotte that everyone else was in a rush. The waterfront commerce swept by in an urgent tide—knots of boatmen, swaggering along the muddy levee, boys from the ropewalk, shouldering by with their coils of hemp, farmers from upriver flats, gawking at the fine brick houses behind the landing. Most of them seemed headed in one direction, toward a rapidly gathering crowd at the head of the landing, just in front of the flour mill. Farther upriver a scarf of black smoke hung against the tawny autumn sky.

"What is it?" Swain asked one of the boys of the rope-walk. "A fire in Louisville?"

"No, mister. That's the new steamboat Owen Naylor built. They been waitin' for a rise to take her through the Falls. Looks like they're goin' to chance it today."

Charlotte felt suddenly breathless. Her eyes met Swain's for a moment. He didn't seem to notice the strange, stiff expression of her face. He had turned again to stare upriver.

They had reached the crowd in front of the flour mill now. The smoke was growing blacker against the sky. Beside Charlotte stood an old river man, chewing on his pipe and scowling fiercely at the smoke.

"She won't get through the Falls," he said. "Ain't fitten to have a fool contraption on the river what belches and coughs like a man with the Black Vomit."

The belching smoke seemed to be moving away from shore, past the mid-river islands, into Indian Chute. The crowd milled about Charlotte, all craning for a first glimpse of the boat. Finally it came into view, already in the channel. Haze and the great distance gave the craft an unreal look.

"It's just a keelboat with a smokestack," Charlotte said.

"Naylor's crazy, puttin' all that machinery on deck," the old river man said. "Whole thing's so top-heavy she'll capsize first big blow. Only a four-foot draft. . . ."

"She'd drag her keel if she was any deeper," Charlotte said.

"Where you a-goin' to put the cargo, then?" the man asked querulously. "And that damn' high-pressure engine. Listen to the steam blow off. Think it was a whole battery of sixteen pounders."

Charlotte could hear it now, even over the roar of the rapids. The steam exhausted regularly into the air with the clap of a heavy gun; the sound accompanied the boat down the river like the slow roll of a steady cannonade. The ten-mile current was carrying the craft rapidly through the chute now. It had passed the uppermost islands and was fully in view.

As Charlotte had said, it was no more than a big keelboat, perhaps a hundred and twenty feet long. In place of a keel's cargo box was a long cabin, starting sixteen feet back of the bow and extending to within ten feet of the stern. Perhaps a third of the way back, the sides of the cabin were open, exposing the engines to view. Just abaft the hatch, leading from the forecastle to the upper deck, the boiler was laid horizontally on deck, with the open firebox at its rear casting a ruddy glow over the figures of engineer and fireman. The single stack shot up through the roof of the cabin and twenty feet into the air. It belched mushrooms of black smoke and showered sparks on every side. A few feet in front of it was the wheelhouse, set on the hurricane deck formed by the roof of the main cabin. Charlotte realized she was squinting in a vain effort to distinguish the figures there. Could one be Naylor?

As the boat neared Rock Island, near the lower end of the rapids, even the rush of water and the crash of escaping steam could not hide the hideous clanking and clattering of machinery. The boat seemed to advance by leaps and jumps, lurching forward with each revolution of the paddle wheel at its stern, shaking and shuddering with the strain of overworked machinery. A deep disappointment filled Louis's patrician face.

"Is this what we came so far to see? It looks like a burlesque on Dante's *Inferno*."

"Don't judge our steamboat by this," Swain said. "It's a travesty."

Charlotte did not share their concern. She was looking at the faces around her. She saw awe in the gaping mouths, wonder in the staring eyes, and she began to share that awe herself. They were seeing something they had thought would never happen—steam on the river. It might be in its crudest, most experimental form, clattering and showering sparks like some mythical monster, but it was here. They were no longer on the threshold of that new era Swain had talked about; they had stepped through the door, and they were face to face with it.

"He'd better take a sheer," Swain said. "She'll ram Rock Island."

Unaccountably the boat had turned in toward the island. Fifty feet ahead of its plunging bow the white water boiled to froth around the lethal reefs. A figure ran from the engine room, cupping his hands to shout at the wheelhouse. The wheelhouse door was flung open, and another man came out onto the hurricane deck, shouting at the man below. The man on the lower deck turned and ran back into the engine room. Flames were licking out of the firebox and across the deck. Both men in the engine room were fighting the fire frantically now.

"Why doesn't he turn it?" Swain said sharply. "He can still bring it about. They'll smash on those rocks. . . ."

Then the sound: it was like a giant thunderclap. It

185

seemed to rock Charlotte's head, deafening her for a moment, and then she could hear the echoes, rolling back and forth across the river. At the same time a gout of flame shot skyward from the boat. Its upperworks seemed torn apart and spewed in a hundred pieces out over the river. Charlotte saw the smokestack, stamped blackly against the sky, bent like a hairpin. It struck the water with a splash, an angry hiss of red-hot metal, and sank beneath the surface. A second grinding crash filled the air as the boat ran head-on into Rock Island. A vast cloud of black smoke was piling up to obscure the boat. The pilot house was barely visible on what was left of the hurricane deck, tilted to one side like a crazily cocked hat. Two figures staggered from its shattered shell, hanging to the edge of the hurricane deck and dropping down to the main deck.

The boat was hard aground on the island now, heeling over with a grinding of braces and a crackling of smaller lumber. Crimson flames shot up from the bowels of the engine room, adding more smoke to the pall that hung over the boat. With the first shock gone, everybody started running. Men streamed past Charlotte, heading toward the landing. A dozen keels and *pirogues* and skiffs were being pushed off, filled with rescuers. A doctor ran past, his collar flapping, a black bag in one hand. A horseman clattered by, heading back into town, shouting someone's name. A bell began to peal, its brazen *clang* rising over the distant crackle of flames and the shouts of the crowd.

Charlotte felt Louis's hand on her arm, pulling her back. She realized she had started for one of the skiffs.

"We've got to do something," she said. "We can't just stand here."

Swain sent her a strange look, then smiled. "What can you do that half the town can't? There are already a score of

186

boats on the way, Charlotte."

She saw that skiffs and keels from Louisville at the upper end of the Falls were already pushing into all three of the channels. She stood on the very edge of the levee, still restrained by Louis's hand, filled with a sense of terrible helplessness.

A pair of skiffs from Shippingport were the first to reach the burning boat. They landed on the near side of Rock Island, and half a dozen men ran across the barren strip of rocky land to the other side. Two of the steamboat crew had managed to jump off the smashed bow onto the island. Others had been thrown out into the channel or had dived off later. Charlotte could see their heads, bobbing like black corks in the foamy rapids. They saw the Shippingport men on the island and swam toward them. The first one reached a reef, clung to it, battered by the torrential force of the rushing water. The men from the skiffs threw him a line and hauled him in. They did the same with three others who reached the reefs. Then they hawled them back to the skiffs and pulled for the shore.

They made a landing above town, hidden by timber and the flour mill. But wagons had already gone up there to haul them back, and soon the first one appeared with its load of dripping, smoke-blackened men. The doctor ran to meet the wagon, and the crowd eddied after him.

Charlotte saw one of the victims helped down, a paunchy white-headed man, smoke and soot grimed into the million wrinkles of his seamed face. The doctor began cutting his burned coat away, and someone in the crowd shouted at him: "What happened, Cap'n Abner?"

Captain Abner winced as the doctor tore a sleeve off. "Damn' sparks caught in the packing," he said. He coughed huskily, squinting his eyes in pain. "Fire burned one of the tiller ropes. Owen lost control. She swung into the island. Damn it, Doc. Take it easy."

"What exploded?"

Captain Abner coughed again before he could answer. "While we was fighting the fire, the safety valve jammed. She got too much pressure up. Must have blown off a weak boiler plate."

They were helping another man out of the wagon now. He was tall, gaunt, narrow enough to take a bath in a musket barrel. His forehead was a bald and shining dome, and the white of his eyes gleamed like marble in his black face. It took Charlotte a moment to recognize Heap.

Some of the Louisville keels had landed, and the new additions to the crowd separated Charlotte from Louis and Swain. She took the chance to hurry to Heap. He gaped at her in amazement, apparently still half dazed.

"Miss Charlotte, what're you doin' here?"

"We're on our way to Pittsburgh, Heap. You're all right, aren't you?"

"Blast came up behind the pilot house. Aside from a few splinters in my behind, I'm whole as hog side. . . ."

"And Owen, Heap? Owen . . . ?"

"He wasn't hurt. They brought him back in the skiffs with us. He made sure the rest of the crew was all right. Then he took off up the river."

"Why, Heap? What on earth . . . ?"

The man settled onto his moccasined heels, scrubbing at the black grime on his face. "Owen's like some animal when he gits hurt. Jist hankers to run off and lick his wounds alone. You won't ever know what he put in that boat. A year of it. Eighteen hours a day. Seven days a week. Bad enough when them keelers wrecked our first hull. . . ."

"We heard about that," Charlotte said.

188

Heap spat cinders. "Owen hunted 'em three days without sleepin'. Would've kilt every one. But they'd gone up the river, huntin' more wimen and more likker. Owen disappeared finally. I didn't see him again for nigh onter two weeks. Don't know where he was. Come back lookin' like some varmint, been sleepin' in a cave. I think it's the same today. Only a heap worse. A big heap worse."

She grasped his arm. "He won't do anything crazy."

He smiled at her. " 'Tain't that bad. Mebbe Owen's got some dark corners in him you 'n' me'll never understand. But he'll be back sooner or later."

Louis came elbowing his way irritably through the crowd. "Charlotte, what are you doing? Captain Fletcher's found his pilot. We're going to shove off."

Reluctantly she said good bye to Heap and went with Louis to board the keel. Earlier in the year, Captain Fletcher might have stayed a few hours to satisfy his passengers' curiosity about the wreck, but they were racing against time now. Winter was too close, and Fletcher didn't want to take the chance of ice catching him before he reached Pittsburgh. Indian Chute was crowded with craft, and the steamboat was still burning furiously, filling the air with a pall of smoke and soot. It was obviously a total loss, burned to the gunwales already, its shattered hull settling deeper and deeper into the river. There was enough water in the middle chute so the keel could take it without trouble.

Standing with Swain and Louis atop the cargo box, Charlotte looked toward the dark timber on shore, thinking of Owen Naylor back in there somewhere, alone, licking his wounds. It filled her with an intense reluctance to leave, yet what could be gained by staying? She didn't know. She only knew that whatever she felt wasn't identifiable—was as fragmentary, as incomplete as the moment of ecstasy from which it sprang. She had seen the same thing in Annie, in Lou, in a dozen others. She was coming to believe that every woman had something like it in her past—a broken thread, something she had lost before really finding it. She could not return to it any more than she could return to Silver Street. She felt Swain watching her closely, eyes squinted in speculation. "What's the matter, Charlotte?"

"Nothing." With a great effort, she turned her face upriver. "I'll be all right when this is behind us."

Chapter Nineteen

For weeks Naylor stayed in the dog-run cabin his family had put up, abandoned since the death of his mother. He had wandered there after the wreck, hardly knowing where he was going, hardly caring. He was sunk in a great apathy. He didn't seem to have the power to think, to move. He sat most of the time in the doorway, staring blankly into the autumn forest, knowing the miserable bitterness of abysmal defeat. When he got hungry, he fished, or hunted berries, or found a stray hen. He had little appetite for any food. Sometimes he wondered what made him put forth the effort to sustain his body.

He understood all this, in himself. It had happened before, after the boatmen had wrecked the first hull. It was the other extreme of the tremendous creative effort he had put out during the last year. Working ten hours a day, seven days a week in the boat yards to pay for the rest of the machinery and the fittings and the millwork necessary on the larger members of the craft, walking out to the ways every evening and putting in six or eight more hours of grueling labor on the steamboat, pouring every ounce of energy and strength and thought and concentration into their dream. This was the other side of the coin, the letdown after those incredible labors, the reaction to the smashing of the dream that had kept them going almost beyond human endurance.

Finally hunger and the growing chill of winter drove him back to the company of his fellows. He found Abner and Heap staying in the captain's cabin, as dejected and apathetic as he. For a week they mourned around the shack, playing somber games of old sledge, talking little. Once Captain Abner made some beer from the honey locust pods off the tree outside his cabin, and they got drunk and started talking big about another boat. The captain had a dozen ideas for improving the safety valve so it wouldn't jam again and sheathing the tiller ropes in metal boxes so they wouldn't burn. But when they woke up the next morning, they knew it had all been bravado. None of them could face the thought of another year such as they had put in.

When the snow came, Naylor made his first trip back to the Red Feather Inn. Evadne's pleasure at his return was almost pathetic, breaking through her usual passive reserve and bringing her into his arms with tears on her face. She gave him his first decent meal in weeks, and then they went upstairs to the bed they had shared often this past year. It was one of the threads of his life he could pick up unbroken. For what they had was a comfortable, tacit thing, requiring little explanation between them. Her love was like her beauty—rich, opulent, something of the mother earth. He knew she did not take men this indiscriminately, and thus sensed that at the back of her mind must be the thought of marriage. Yet she had never mentioned it. Perhaps it was due to the deep strain of fatalism in her nature, making her accept most of life as it was given, without asking more. Or perhaps she recognized the confusion in him that would have made any mention of marriage futile. In many ways she satisfied him. It wasn't the soaring, burning thing he had known with Charlotte, but it was a full current of satisfaction that could run to the end of a man's life.

More and more he realized his obligation to her. She had

given herself completely to him. He should do so with her. He wanted to. More than once he'd been on the brink of it. Knowing what it would mean to Evadne, he had the poignant wish that he could offer marriage sincerely, honestly, without reservations. Then he would be seized by the deep restlessness, the doubts, the confusion. It was what held him back. He knew what it was. He didn't talk about it with Evadne, didn't even want to think about it himself, but he knew what it was. He couldn't give himself to a marriage with that still in him. He knew Evadne would accept him, however he came to her, whatever he gave, but it might hurt her too much in the end. It was as though he would be offering her something that wasn't his to give and could be withdrawn cruelly at some future time by a force completely outside himself. He wouldn't do that; he couldn't go to her that way till all the doubts and the restlessness were burned out of him for good.

So the old year wore out, with a cold wind whipping the waterfront and the boat yards deserted and the taverns filled with men devoting themselves to cards, whisky, and politics. The war spirit was rising on the frontier, where the recession was attributed to the British blockade, and a man was called a Federalist only as a deadly insult. Clay was fulminating in the Senate, and the papers were printing his speeches.

"Sirs, is the time never to arrive when we may manage our own affairs without fear of insulting his Britannic Majesty? I trust I shall not be presumptuous when I state that I verily believe that the militia of Kentucky are alone competent to place Montreal and Upper Canada at your feet." That was 1810, when the American Navy had twelve vessels, and the English Navy had eight hundred.

Napoléon had rescinded his Decrees restricting American commerce, and Madison had announced that, if England did not similarly rescind her onerous Orders in Council, we would have to revive the non-intercourse measure against her. But England had more experience than Madison with the wily French emperor and upheld her Orders in Council, saying that Napoléon no more intended to stop his blockade on American shipping than he intended to stop the war.

Naylor heard it all, sitting in the taproom, sometimes taking a part in the arguments. The ice had come, locking the river for five weeks, and a man was like a ground hog in his hole. On the 5th of February it began to break up, and the nights were filled with the creaking and groaning of the great white giant striving to snap its chains. Two keels were crushed in Bear Grass Creek on the 10th, and by the 16th chunks as big as a house were moving downstream. On March 2nd, 1811, Madison declared that non-intercourse was resumed as to England; the Tories and the Federalists said it simply meant the United States had fallen into Napoléon's trap and was joining Napoléon against England. On the same date the commons turned green in Louisville.

That was the beginning of a strange spring. During the earlier months the rivers were in unprecedented flood, overflowing the levees and inundating the waterfronts, bringing an epidemic of fever and sickness. A magnificent comet illuminated the heavens for weeks, robbing the night of its rightful blackness and casting a weird twilight over the land. An inexplicable migration of squirrels came from the north. In tens of thousands they swept through the Indiana forests and poured into the Ohio. Some reached the opposite shore, but most of them drowned and thousands of their lifeless bodies choked the river, floating downstream. It filled the towns with a spirit of wonder and foreboding and only seemed to intensify the restlessness growing in Naylor. He spent much of his time at a front table of the Red Feather, sometimes with companions, sometimes alone, looking out the window and watching the keels pass every day. He knew what it would be, knew the hell a man consigned himself to when he took a pole on one of those boats. He would be a fool to do it. Yet it was pulling at him.

Through March and April he resisted the pull, going on lone hunting trips that lasted for weeks, working now and then in the boat yards to pay his keep at the inn, unable to settle down to anything. Then, one afternoon in May, he was sitting at the front table when the packet from Pittsburgh docked in Bear Grass Creek and the passengers disembarked and walked toward the inn. A mulatto maid carrying a black-haired baby followed a handsomely dressed gentleman and lady. The lady was Charlotte. The complete shock of it brought Naylor to his feet, emptying his mind of all thought in that first instant, leaving only reaction.

Charlotte stopped just inside, accustoming her eyes to the gloom. He stared blankly at her, waiting for her to see him, his hands closed into fists. Her dress hat of black satin, turned up in front, made a striking contrast to the exotic cameo of her face with its gray-blue eyes, its vivid red mouth. The picture of her brought the past back to Naylor in a poignant rush. It was as if he had never left her. His mouth felt dry and cottony, and the blood was pounding through his body; his mind was no longer empty; it swam with a hundred bittersweet memories, a thousand inchoate thoughts.

Her hands were hidden in an immense beaver muff. Holding it against the front of her sable coat, she let her gaze slowly circle the room until it reached him. She showed no surprise.

"Owen. You look quite shocked."

He could hardly trust himself to speak. "I suppose it's just that this is the last place I expected to see you."

"We passed through last year on our way to Pittsburgh. Just in time to see your unfortunate accident with the steamboat. Didn't Heap say anything?"

"No," Naylor said, and knew why Heap hadn't told him. The man must have been reluctant to add more turmoil to the bitterness of his defeat over the boat.

Charlotte was smiling, but it was an utterly composed smile, giving her face that quiet aloofness, and yet, beneath it, in the sparkle of her eyes, in the shadowy change of expression that kept subtly altering the shape of her lips, was a hint of the tempestuousness that always lay at the core of her. She half turned to the man beside her.

"Louis, you remember Owen Naylor."

Louis Reynaud tilted his head amiably at Naylor. "To be sure. Allow me to express my regrets about your steamboat, *m'sieu*. You were very lucky to get out alive."

Naylor acknowledged it with a nod, and, as it brought others besides Charlotte again to his awareness, it also seemed to lessen the shock and poignant impact of seeing her. He knew a renewal of the bitterness and sense of betrayal he had first felt upon losing her to Louis. Somehow it steadied him, giving him a better command of himself.

"We've come for a purpose, Owen," Charlotte said. "Is there anywhere a little more private?"

He said stiffly: "How about the kitchen?"

They both nodded, and he led them back through the taproom, wondering what could possibly be on Charlotte's mind. Evadne was at the sink, running gray-white meal for bread through a doeskin sifter and mixing it with water and precious salt and maple syrup. Naylor introduced them, and Evadne nodded pleasantly at Louis, wiping meal-powdered hands on her soiled apron. Then her eyes met Charlotte's. The women stared at each other for a moment, utterly without humor on their faces. Then Evadne smiled.

"I'll warm some milk for the baby," she said. "She looks like she's wakin' up." It drew Naylor's eyes to the child again. Black-haired, pink-cheeked, a beautiful little doll of a baby, Charlotte's baby, Louis's baby. The bitterness deepened in Naylor.

Louis pulled back one of the rude chairs for his wife, and she took a seat at the table. The heat of the room caused her to throw her cloak back, revealing the sage-green gown with its brocaded stripes. Naylor saw that the baby hadn't pulled her down. The stays lifted her breasts high into the bodice, riper, more arrogant than ever. He raised his eyes to hers. She was smiling ironically now, as if with her own secret knowledge of what was going on in him. It suddenly made him angry.

"You'll have something to drink," he said abruptly.

"If you have any long cork claret, my husband will be your lifelong friend," Charlotte said.

"We have," Evadne told them. "I'll get it from the bar."

Louis pulled aside the tails of his dove-gray morning coat and took a seat, leaning back with a sigh. His hands were slim and soft as a woman's. He'd probably never done a lick of work in his life. Yet Naylor had to admit he was handsome enough in a sensitive, aristocratic way. His hair was glossy black as a wet beaver pelt; his eyes flashed brilliantly whenever they moved; his slightest motion held the unconscious grace of a master fencer.

"Do you plan to build another steamboat, *m'sieu?*" he asked.

The milk was beginning to simmer, and Naylor took it

off the grate, finding a mug to put it in. "I guess not," he said. "We used up all we had to get that one on the water."

Charlotte leaned forward, her elbows on the table. "What if you didn't have to work in the boat yards to earn the money first, Owen? What if you had the machinery right now, and a full crew of shipwrights to work on the hull for you?" she asked. He frowned at her, feeling another thin rush of anger at her. She saw it, and continued. "I'm not mocking you, Owen. Louis and I came north to invest fourteen thousand dollars in the Ohio Steamboat Navigation Company. We've spent all last winter at Pittsburgh, watching them build that boat beneath Boyd's Hill."

Louis smiled. "It's true. My wife spent so much time with those shipwrights and engineers I think she could build a steamboat herself. And this book by Oliver Evans, *An Abortion of the Young Steam Engineer's Guide* . . ."—Louis grimaced—"she quotes it in her sleep, *verbatim*."

Naylor looked for some sign of suspicion, of antagonism in the man's pale face, yet saw nothing but good humor. It convinced Naylor that Louis had no inkling of what had happened between him and Charlotte.

"I'm certain Fulton won't be successful," Charlotte said. "Montgomery's the engineer, still thinking in deep water terms. All his shipwrights and mechanics are from the East Coast. They're simply building another *Clermont*. A huge engine. Cylinder thirty-four inches in diameter. And still she only develops ten pounds of steam to the square inch. Much too weak to drive such a heavy hull against any current. Putting the engine upright in the hull, she'll need a twelve-foot draft to contain it. Do you think a hold that deep will get up the Mississippi in low water?"

Naylor gazed at her wide-eyed, amazed at her grasp of

things it had taken him all these years to learn.

"Isn't that right?" she asked. "How much water does a keelboat draw?"

"Two feet."

"Fully loaded. And even a keel drags its bottom on some of the runs. How much draft did your steamboat have?"

"Hardly three feet."

"That's what I mean, Owen. You had the right idea. All you really did was put an engine on a big keelboat. I tried to convince Montgomery of his mistake. But they all thought I was crazy. Even Louis. . . ."

"*Ma foi,* please. . . ."

"You did, Louis. You know how long I had to argue with you."

He laughed indulgently. "Very well, I admit it. Even Swain could not understand it."

Naylor glanced at him. "Swain?"

"Kenneth Swain," Louis said. "The Natchez agent for the Ohio Steamboat Navigation Company." Louis chuckled to himself. "I have never seen him so shocked as when Charlotte told him we had decided not to invest in his boat, after all."

Naylor was silent, with his own bleak thoughts of Swain. Charlotte leaned toward him. Some of the composure had left her. In her flushed cheeks, her sparkling eyes, he could see a reflection of the same burning enthusiasm that had gripped him at the height of his dreaming and planning about the boat. "You were on the right track, Owen. I've talked with Oliver Evans up in Pittsburgh. He says a high-pressure engine is the only kind for a riverboat. He says he can build one that doesn't weigh as much as the balance wheel on Fulton's engine. . . ."

Naylor nodded. "Captain Abner claims those low-pressure engines go up to eighty or ninety tons. Ours didn't weigh ten. And it had five times the power. . . ."

He broke off, realizing how fast he had been talking. As he settled back, Louis chuckled again. "I know how you feel, *m'sieu*. I still find it amazing that a woman can know so much about such things."

"Will you do it?" Charlotte asked. She was like a different woman now. She made motions with the hands as she talked, and her eyes danced excitedly. It was a hint of the ferment and the tempestuousness that lay behind her usual composure. "We'll form a corporation, just like Fulton and Livingston. We'll all be shareholders. With so few of us the profits would be much greater."

It seemed insane to him, unreal. It was hard to think clearly. The revived hope and enthusiasm were still with him. After what they had gone through before, it would be child's play to build a boat under those circumstances. But there was so much more to it than building a boat.

He rose from his chair, his face growing dour and somber as he looked at Charlotte. The shape of her body beneath the brocaded dress was curved, provocative. Every time he looked at her, it was like a renewed heat spreading rawly through his body. It gave him a hint of the dangerous complications that could so easily arise if he agreed to build the boat under these conditions. The play of expression had left her face now; the glimpse of tempestuousness was again hidden beneath the Silver Street mask. It was hard to believe she was only twenty. She had such extreme poise, such command of herself. He had seen it before. It was something Silver Street had done to her. But it seemed even greater now, as if, in her child and her marriage, she had gained a new level of maturity.

"Are you afraid?" she asked.

He knew what she meant. It was a question excluding Louis. He would put a different interpretation on it than Naylor. It was a direct challenge. Suddenly Naylor felt a swift anger. In Charlotte was still the trenchant need for a security that would keep her away from Silver Street, a need driving her till she was quite willing to go through with this, to use him, knowing fully that what had happened before might happen again. It made her seem hard and ruthless to him—perhaps that was what he had mistaken for a greater maturity—completely ignoring the feelings of someone else, riding roughshod over anything or anyone that clashed with this need of hers. But with his anger came something else. He had a chance within his grasp, the biggest and best chance he'd had so far, perhaps the last chance. He felt the flush of a deep excitement such as he had not known since the day of launching their last boat. It broiled through him and gnawed at him and filled him with a willingness to overlook other consequences, too. Perhaps he and Charlotte were the same in that respect. They both had a dream, and it was bigger than they were.

He wheeled around the room, gripped in the growing excitement of it. He saw Evadne, standing in the shadowed doorway leading to the bar, holding the bottle of claret. No telling how long she had been there, listening, waiting. He could see, in her face, a partial grasp of the undercurrents running through this room. She couldn't know what Charlotte meant to him; he had never told her. But she had a feeling for the hidden implications of life. It made her eyes veiled, her lips petulant, as she watched him. He felt she didn't want him to do it, but that couldn't stop him. He wheeled back to Charlotte. "All right. Let's build a boat."

Naylor went out to tell Heap and Captain Abner that afternoon. They were jubilant, wanted to start work right away. They looked up a lawyer named Howard Twist on Market Street—eyes like saber points and a nose that twitched when money was mentioned—and he drew up the contract between the three men and the Reynauds. Louis and Charlotte were to hold sixty percent of the stock in the company, while Naylor, Heap, and Captain Abner retained the other forty percent. Naylor realized the danger implicit in such an arrangement. He didn't like to think of Charlotte, with her tempestuousness, her stubbornness, her driven needs, having a majority vote in the management of the boat, but she would not give in. Her argument was that their salaries as captain, pilot, and engineer compensated them for the difference in stock held, and they finally had to accept it.

With the contracts signed, Charlotte deposited the money in the bank and had a letter of credit drawn up for the amount Captain Abner needed to get the machinery in Pittsburgh. Before he left, however, she went over every detail of the engine with him, amazing them once more with her grasp of mechanics. Part of it was the technical knowledge she had picked up in the last months—but another part stemmed from a common sense application of principles she had absorbed without even knowing it during her girlhood on the river. She insisted the boilerplates be three-eighths instead of the three-sixteenths the captain had specified. She argued him into a wooden pitman because Evans had told her its resilience suited it to withstand shocks better than cast iron. She vetoed open brick fireboxes and insisted on iron doors to make them watertight. Sometimes Captain Abner stubbornly held to his ideas, but mostly he reluctantly admitted Charlotte was right. Finally, on June 1st, he took a packet to Pittsburgh.

In the meantime, Naylor had been at the mill, contracting for the keel and keelson, the knightheads and other heavy timbers. Then he began hiring his crew. It was the busy season for building, and in order to get any men at all he had to pay higher than the boat yards offered, and he still had to scrape the bottom of the barrel, taking men like Indian Thompson, a half-Shawnee who drank on the job and had a wicked reputation for brawling. Naylor was still short-handed when he began erecting the ways on the river, three miles above town. An hour after they started, Little Ike appeared in the clearing. He was an ex-keeler who had lost his right arm to an alligator at Spanish Moss Bend. It had left him unfit for keel work, and he had to content himself with odd jobs about town. He was a scrounging, defeated little man, not much over five feet tall, his legs so bowed they would fit fine around a hogshead. He wore a greasy red-wool shirt and a pair of rawhide leggings, with a battered copy of Zadoc Cramer sticking out of the pocket.

"I heard you was having a hard time getting hands, Owen," he said.

Naylor tried not to look at the empty red sleeve. He knew the boat yards would have nothing to do with the man. Ike saw his dubious expression.

"I could do all the little jobs," he pleaded. "I'd even take half wages. I can hammer good as anybody, some hand holds the treenails."

A grin broke slowly over Naylor's face; he went to Ike and put his arm around the bowlegged man's shoulders and started walking with him toward the ways. "Let's start hammerin', then."

They got the ways knocked together that week. On the afternoon that Naylor started his crew to shaping the timbers in the sawpits, the Reynaud coach clattered into the clearing, stopping beside the shagbark cabin that had been built by the ways.

Naylor walked over to meet them, sweat pasting his damp shirt to the quilting of muscles in his broad back. Louis stepped out of the coach and helped Charlotte down, followed by Angelique, carrying the baby.

Louis smiled amiably at Naylor. "We thought we'd bring Denise out to show her the boat she will soon be taking down the river."

Charlotte was in a good humor and smiled indulgently. "You'd think he was the mother, the way he spoils that baby."

"It is my one weakness," Louis said. He took the baby girl from the maid's arms, pulling the blanket from the cherubic face. The look in his eyes was almost worship.

It surprised Naylor. He had always considered Louis typical of the young Creole blades he had known—gay and charming on the surface, basically selfish, spoiled, pampered, incapable of any deep and lasting emotion. Yet the man seemed completely wrapped up with the baby. "She's a cute little bug," he observed. "How old is she?"

"A little over fourteen months."

It brought the baby into sharp focus for Naylor. It struck him as strange that he had not given it more consideration before, but the intense consciousness of Charlotte that first night had kept him from dwelling much on anything else, and since then the thousand and one details of getting the boat started had crowded other considerations from his mind. Fourteen months. Like a fool, he realized he was counting back, and stopped himself. But the sick premonition remained in him. His gaze moved slowly to Charlotte. Her eyes were close lidded and watchful, and her face was inscrutable.

"Look how she clings to my fingers." Louis chuckled. "I wager I could hold her up."

Angelique grinned. "*Maître* . . . don' you dare."

"Let us see the boat," Louis announced. "Denise, want to see the men sawing the boat?"

The baby cooed and gurgled. Louis marched off toward the sawpits, with Angelique behind. In a moment the cabin hid them.

Charlotte was still watching Naylor. "Did you count back carefully, Owen?" Sarcasm made her voice ugly.

He was breathing heavily. "Charlotte," he said, "I've got a right to know."

Her face was stiff and pale. The sarcasm left her voice. "I don't know," she said. "I honestly don't know whether Denise is your baby or not."

His weight settled heavily onto his heels. He saw the subdued torture in her eyes and knew what misery it must have caused her all this time. When she spoke again, the torture was in her voice. "I keep looking at her face," she said. "For your eyes, your mouth, your jaw, some sign. I can't see it, Owen. Can you?"

The last came like a plea. It took all the antagonism from between them. They were simply two lost people searching for the same answer.

"No," he said. "It can't be."

Her eyes widened. "You don't want it to be?"

"That'd be cruel. What kind of start would that give the kid?"

She took a ragged breath. "You're right. We should be thankful. If there was any of you in her, it would have showed up by now." A faint relief softened her face. "It's settled, then."

"Not all of it."

The harsh note of his voice brought her chin up. She stood that way, the antagonism vibrating between them again. Finally she said: "You're talking about us now. That's settled, too. It's got to be. We're different people now. We can't go back."

"Charlotte," he said, "why did you do it?"

Her voice was low, strained. "Because I loved him, Owen. I loved him before you came, and I love him now. What you and I had wasn't love."

He caught her by the arms, speaking savagely. "Now you're lying to yourself as well as me!" He could feel the satiny softness of her flesh through the fabric of her carrick. It seemed to burn his palms. For a moment he thought he saw response in her. Then her lips compressed, strongly and deliberately, and she twisted free of his grasp, taking a step backward. Her voice was thin and bitter. "I told you, Owen. I love Louis. This boat is the only thing we can have between us."

Chapter Twenty

All the way home Charlotte sat silently in a corner of the coach they had hired. Louis was beside her, occupied with the baby, and did not notice her mood. Charlotte's face was no longer the expressionless mask. That had only been for Naylor. She couldn't let him see the doubts and confusions in her. It was the one thing she had feared, coming back. It had been a hard decision to make. Watching the *New Orleans* take shape through the winter months, talking with Montgomery and his principal shipwrights, pouring over the plans for the engine and hull, gradually realizing how completely unsuited the boat was for the river—she had known a gnawing sense of defeat. Always, at the back of her mind, had been the thought of Naylor's boat. Investing in it, she realized, would be an even greater gamble than that Swain had offered, but the alternative was an incredible return to Silver Street, or its counterpart, and, from what she had learned, she still had enough faith in steam to take the gamble.

Obviously Naylor thought that in her decision to return to Louisville she had disregarded the treacherous complications that might arise, but in that he had been wrong. Her love was for Louis. She hadn't been lying when she told Naylor that. She looked at Denise—pink-cheeked, black-headed, cooing and gurgling in Louis's lap—and a flood of tenderness welled up. Somehow it gave her strength. She was a married woman now with a child, with all the obligations that implied. That was the final answer to all her questions and all her doubts.

They had rented a one-story brick house on Market, simply furnished with hooked rugs on the floor and plain, solid furniture. After the Reynaud mansion it seemed barren and cramped, but Louis made no complaint. Throughout their long river journey and the winter stay at Pittsburgh he had made a valiant attempt to face up to their circumstances. They had their spats, and he sulked once in a while, but in the main he gave no evidence of reversion to the complete childishness with which he had met every crisis in Natchez.

During the weeks after their arrival at Louisville, he continued in his effort, staying in the house with the baby, playing *écarté* with Angelique, studying the boat plans with Charlotte. Soon he was wandering down to the Red Feather Inn for an after-dinner drink. His wit and charm gained him *entrée* to the circle of armchair politicians who occupied the taproom every evening, and soon the inn became his club. Charlotte could not object. It seemed to lift his spirits immensely, gave him something to occupy his time, and he always came home sober. She was sure he realized the gravity of their situation and would not take a chance on ruining them again. To insure it, she only allowed him pin money for his drinks and made him promise not to gamble.

At first, wanting to see Naylor as little as possible, she tried to stay away from the boat, but her interest was too intense to remain aloof long. A week after the building started, the news from New Orleans concerning the Fulton monopoly made her go down to the ways. There was much precedent behind Fulton's request for a monopoly. Four States had given Fitch such a charter for the exclusive use of steam on their rivers as early as 1787. Fulton himself was running his *Clermont* under a twenty-year monopoly granted him by New York. Fulton and Livingston, through their

Ohio Steamboat Navigation Company, had petitioned Kentucky, Ohio, Tennessee, Upper Louisiana Territory, and the Territory of Orleans for a similar monopoly on the Ohio and the Mississippi. Only the Territory of Orleans had reacted favorably, and now the Kentucky papers carried the confirmation that the Territory of Orleans, on April 29th, 1811, had granted the Fulton-Livingston group their desired charter. Charlotte knew what a blow it was to their plans and wanted to discuss it immediately with Naylor and Heap.

Louis was already at the Red Feather, and Charlotte took the hired coach alone to the ways. The driver pulled up by the shagbark cabin, and Charlotte saw Naylor, sweating over a timber in one of the sawpits with a pair of his shipwrights. As she stepped from the coach, Heap came to meet her.

"Did you hear that Orleans gave Fulton his monopoly?" she asked.

He nodded, scratching irritably through his grease-blackened buckskin shirt. "We heard this morning. Is it really as bad as Owen thinks?"

"It's pretty bad," she said.

"The grant only goes to the borders of Orleans Territory. That leaves the river clear down to Natchez."

"Which means nothing," she told him. "Most of the shipping on the river passes through New Orleans. If we can't go there, it will cut our profits to nothing. This grant might give Fulton a chance of getting charters from other cities. He could control the whole river."

"Cuss these lice." Heap reached under his shirt, scratching vigorously. "Breed in that damn' sawdust." He brought one out, crushing it between thumb and forefinger, then dropping it to the ground. "Captain Abner said

209

somethin' about Fulton's boat comin' up to taw."

She knew Heap meant the specifications contained in the grant of monopoly. It was their only hope. Chancellor Livingston's first New York charter had been revoked due to his failure to build a boat within the time limits set, and Charlotte had heard there was a minimum speed requirement in the Orleans charter. "I think the boat has to go four miles an hour against the current to retain their rights," she said.

Heap grinned. "Way you was talking, Montgomery won't even be able to start his boat ag'in' the current, much less make four miles."

"I just hope I'm right," Charlotte said. She saw him fish out a twist of garlic. "Heap, must you?"

"You saw what happened this spring, Miss Charlotte. Half the waterfront down with the Black Vomit. Not ol' Heap." He popped the garlic into his mouth.

"Then we shall continue our discussion," she said, "another time."

She walked past the ways to the first sawpit. Naylor and his men had finished shaping the timber and were hoisting it from the pit. Naylor was shirtless, dripping sweat. The movement of muscles ran like quicksilver beneath the surface of his wet back. There was an animal sensuality about it that struck her with distinct impact. She felt her defenses rise, turning her face tight and wooden. She couldn't let him see that he had any effect on her. He would see it as a weakening, a relenting, and would take advantage of it.

"I wanted to get your reaction to the monopoly grant," she said.

His face was stiff, reserved, but there was a dark watchfulness to his somber eyes. "Nothing much we can do except go on. I'd appreciate it if you'd write Captain Abner a letter, get his ideas on it. I'm not much at spelling."

"I'll do that. I'm also going to see Twist this afternoon, at four. He has some ideas on the legal side of it. Would you like to sit in?"

"I'll be there."

She turned her attention to the timber. "Isn't that pine?" she asked.

"That's right."

"You specified oak, six by six, for the ribs."

He took a tired breath and ran a hand through his black hair, curly and damp with sweat. "We started with oak. But the natural crooks kept splitting out."

Charlotte told him there was plenty more in the forest. He said he couldn't waste any more of his crew hunting farther out in the woods. She said she wanted oak. He told her she was asking him to do something on fifteen thousand dollars that Montgomery was using thirty-six thousand for. They were working against time and had to cut corners. She told him cutting corners was exactly why they had lost the boat last time. If the boilerplates had been three-sixteenths of an inch thicker, the boiler might have held till they got the safety valve fixed. It grew into a furious argument. Finally, in a rage, Naylor told her he would get the oak, but she shouldn't blame him if they ran out of money halfway through the job.

That was the beginning. She couldn't stay away after that. She was down early and late, arguing with him on a hundred points. She wanted one-by-sixes instead of the two-by-sixes he was putting on as bottom planks; she insisted the seams be butted square instead of the clinker work he'd put down to the bilge strake; she found Indian Thompson drinking on the job and fired him while Naylor was at the mill. Their fights became the topic of every taproom in town.

It lasted that way through June, with the heat adding its pressure to grueling labor and fraying everybody's nerves. On the first Monday in June, Charlotte got to the ways early. The sun was already blistering the men, drenching them with sweat, frying the juice right out of them. Naylor was at the stern, stripped to the waist, shouting in a hoarse voice. He sounded mad, and Heap told Charlotte a bad day had begun.

The treenails had started it, splitting strakes out at the end. Then the shoring collapsed and let down the stern, smashing three bulkheads and a pair of knees. It had taken them hours to repair it, and one of Naylor's best shipwrights had broken an arm in the process. Another man had to take him to town in a wagon, and it left Naylor shorthanded. Now, as a last straw, the bottom planking was warping away from its oakum.

Charlotte knew it would be the worst thing she could do to clash with Naylor on a day like this and tried to avoid him, walking out toward the river. But as she passed the bow, she saw the rake. It stopped her.

In a moment she heard the *crunch* of boots in the sawdust behind her. It was Naylor. A fine film of sawdust gave a silvery sheen to his sunburned face. His eyes were sunk deeply in his skull with fatigue, red-rimmed and feverish-looking. She knew she shouldn't speak, but it was something she had to stop before they went any further. "You specified a sixty-degree rake in the bow."

His mouth turned gray about the edges. "Don't start in again. I can't make it today."

"We've got to settle this," she said. "You promised sixty degrees."

"It didn't work out. You'd lose thirty tons of cargo."

"That's hard to believe, Owen."

"It'd need so many more bow timbers you wouldn't get a barrel within twenty feet of the stem."

"Half your landings won't have any levees. You can't slide up on a beach with a cutwater like a brig."

"It's got as much rake as any keel I ever built."

"A keel has a dozen poles to maneuver it," she said.

"We've got an engine worth a hundred polers."

"I didn't put up my money to see you make the same mistakes as Montgomery."

"I can't change it now."

"You can, Owen."

"You'll lose too much time again. We'll have to rip off all the strakes and shape a new stem knee. . . ."

"Do what's necessary."

"I been building boats since I was fourteen!" he shouted. "You think you can come up here and know everything in three months that took me ten years to learn?"

"Either put more rake in the bow, or I'll cut your funds off."

"You won't have to. You can find yourself another builder!"

White-faced, trembling with fury, he turned from her and stalked down the boat, past every man in the gaping crew, forgetting his shirt where it hung on the stern, stamping shirtless out of the clearing and into the forest. Charlotte watched him go, steeped in a rage of her own. She saw all the men watching her, now, and called to them in a shaking voice. "Get back to work . . . all of you!"

Heap took off his raccoon-skin cap, rubbing his shining pate. "A-feared you won't be able to do much with 'em, Charlotte, without Owen."

A helpless impotence swept her. Too furious to discuss it with him further, she hurried to the coach, ordering the driver home. Louis was not there, and Angelique was playing with the baby in the yard. Charlotte paced the living room, striving to calm herself. She had been right. She knew she had. Naylor was a stupid, stubborn fool. How could she ever have thought she was attracted to him? He was everything she hated, stinking of sweat and river mud and tavern whisky, shouting at her like a village idiot in front of those men, too proud to give in to a woman even though he knew she was right.

She was too upset to eat dinner. Angelique put the baby to bed, finally retired herself. Louis was not at home when Charlotte finally went to bed. It did not worry her. He had come in often after she was asleep, to spend the next morning regaling her with a lively account of the violent arguments in the taproom of the Red Feather or the Ivory Bill. Her mind was still in a turmoil about Naylor when she finally fell asleep.

She was awakened by Angelique in the morning. The maid told her that Louis was sleeping on the couch. She dressed and went into the living room to find him sitting up. His clothes were rumpled, his glossy black hair down over his brow, his eyes bloodshot and puffy-looking. The guilty look of them sent an ominous portent through her. She had to force the story from him. But once she pried the beginnings loose, it came in the boyish flood of contrition and self-recrimination to which she had become accustomed in Natchez.

It seemed that Swain had arrived in Louisville the evening before, had invited him to dinner and a friendly game of cards in the taproom. At first there had been no money involved. But others had entered the game—there had been drinking—money appeared. Louis had gotten too drunk to remember much after that.

"But you had no money," Charlotte said. "Just the few dollars I gave you."

He shook his head miserably from side to side. "I must have signed checks. I seem to remember. . . ."

"Louis." It filled her with a cloying sense of horror. "How much did you sign away?"

"I'm not sure," he said, holding his head in his hands. "One . . . two . . . three thousand."

She began to pace the room, her face taut and pale with anger. "Swain, Swain. He always claimed he was such a scoundrel. I never believed him."

"Don't blame him. . . ."

"Are you blind, Louis? Can't you see what he's done? We may not have enough to finish the boat now. They must have sent him down here on purpose for this." She stopped, eyes stormy. "He hasn't won yet. We'll simply stop payment on your checks."

He raised his head, his face pale with outrage. "How can you do that? Half a dozen men hold them. It was on my honor as a gentleman. Who would ever accept my word again? How could I show my face outside the door?"

Without even bothering to answer him, she hurried to get a wrap and left the house. The bank was only a few blocks away. Its doors were already open, and Kenneth Swain was just emerging. He stopped when he saw her, tipping his hat, his tawny mane shimmering in the bright sunlight.

She halted before him, speaking in a trembling voice. "Swain, how could you do this? Trying to ruin us. . . ."

"Hardly, Charlotte. Ruin was the very thing I kept you from in Natchez, if you will remember."

"Only so we could invest our money in your company."

"And you still can," he said. "I would be happy to forget Louis's debt, if you would but return with me to Pittsburgh. You did me immense harm when you backed out on your agreement to invest in the Fulton Company. You were the biggest prize I could bring them. It wasn't only the money. The Reynaud name linked to the steamboat would have smoothed the way for us in Louisiana as little else could."

"Are you saying you did this out of spite?"

"Hardly out of personal spite, Charlotte. Your steamboat constitutes a definite threat to our monopoly of the lower river. You can be sure we will do all in our power to stop it."

"Even if it means smashing your best friend? You're unspeakable, Swain!"

"*Madame.*" He tilted his head ironically. "Perhaps, when you learn how unspeakable, you will return to me on your knees." He was smiling, but his eyes were bright and blank as silver coins. "It's useless going into the bank, Charlotte. You can't stop payment now. You established too admirable a credit here. This is a gambling town, my dear. The bank honored Louis's checks without question."

Speechless with fury, she left him and went inside. He had told her the truth. Their account was down over five thousand dollars, paid out to the half dozen men who had cashed Louis's notes this morning. When the manager had realized how many were drawing on the account, he'd started to send a messenger to the Reynaud house, but it had been too late.

Swain was standing by the door when she came out again. There was an expectant look to his face, and she knew he hoped she would give in now. She stopped but a moment before him, her voice brittle and venomous. "I'm not on my knees yet, Swain. Before this is over, it may be *you* who comes crawling to *me*."

Then she went on down the street, skirts swinging, rage blazing like twin strawberry marks in her cheeks. Louis was still in the parlor, on the settee, sulkily drinking some coffee Angelique had made for him. Charlotte sat in a chair facing him, folding her hands in her lap, her face white now and set woodenly with the decision she had formed. It was an all-too-familiar scene. When Louis saw her icy calm, the slack contrition began once more to come into his face.

"Don't bother going into your act again," she said. "It doesn't do any good to apologize, to be sorry, to make all those wild promises about never doing it again. You've just about finished us, Louis. There's only one chance left."

He gaped at her blankly. "What's that?"

She moistened her lips. "You've got to sign the rest of the money over to me."

Chapter Twenty-One

Naylor woke up in Evadne's bed the next morning. He had gotten drunk yesterday evening, after his fight with Charlotte. He could remember some kind of brawl on the waterfront and falling into the river, and a lot of singing and wandering blindly from one tavern to the next, dripping wet. His head ached, and there was a foul taste in his mouth. Evadne came in with breakfast and clean clothes. While he dressed and downed a pint of black coffee, she told him about Louis.

Louisville was still not a large enough town to hold its secrets long. Everybody on the waterfront knew of Louis's all-night card game. His loss was reported at anywhere from five to twenty thousand. The Reynauds had been to the bank, closeted for an hour with the manager, and it was now rumored that Louis had put everything in Charlotte's name. It swept all the antagonism for Charlotte out of Naylor. His first impulse was to get his hands on Swain. He knew a savage desire to beat the man within an inch of his life. Evadne calmed him down and talked him out of it. They had no proof. There had been others in the game besides Swain. Naylor knew she was right. He finished eating and went up to the Reynaud house. Louis was in, but would not come to the door. Angelique told Naylor that Charlotte was at the ways.

Entering the clearing by the river, Naylor saw the crew first, milling about the boat and arguing among themselves. When they saw him, most of the talk stopped. The coach stood by the cabin, and beside it Charlotte was walking with Heap. Naylor stopped before them. Charlotte's pale, drawn face told him how serious it was.

"I thought you might need me," he said.

She came to him, her eyes grave. "Owen . . . I'm sorry about yesterday."

"It doesn't seem important now, does it?"

She shook her head. Then she went on to tell him exactly what had happened. With what Louis had lost added to the amounts already paid out, they had less than three thousand dollars left.

"That might take us halfway through," he said.

"Then what?"

"We'll have to lay off the crew. Me 'n' Heap'll finish it."

"Can you?"

"On one condition."

She took a deep breath. "I know what it is," she said. Her lips compressed, as if in some decision. Then she said: "I realize what a load this will put on you. I also realize how my interference upset things, even if I thought I was right. I'll agree to your condition. If you'll go ahead, I won't interfere any more."

So they began once more. The first thing Naylor did—with Swain still in town—was to give every man on his crew a pistol, stack a dozen rifles at hand within the cabin, and set a twenty-four hour watch on the boat. Heap and Naylor were up before dawn every day, studying the plans by a hog-fat candle in the little cabin by the ways, sawing and riving and chopping and carting by flaring torchlight. It was the old absorption, the old frenzy, like a force from without entering Naylor's body and his mind and cutting him loose from the ordinary considerations of life. He ate his meals while he worked, got by for weeks at a time on four hours' sleep a night, didn't even take time out to shave. His beard grew like a sooty bramble into the hollows beneath his angular cheek bones, and his eyes became feverish and sunken in his head. He began to lose weight and grow jumpy as a wild animal.

"I knew an artist oncet," Heap told him. "Paintin' that pitcher for weeks at a time without eatin' or sleepin' or changin' clothes. Like some demon got a holt on him. You better git Evadne to wash them britches. You stink like a varmint's cave."

Naylor saw little of Louis. For a man of his pride, reared in the patriarchal culture of the Creoles where a man was king and the women were completely dependent upon his every whim, putting everything in Charlotte's name was the most humiliating thing that could have happened. Charlotte had admitted to Naylor that the only thing that finally brought Louis to his knees was the baby. Charlotte had been forced to use Louis's love for the child as a weapon, painting an ugly picture of what would happen to Denise if they failed now.

Louis could not return to the circle of friends he had developed in the taverns; apparently he could not face the jeering of the wags or the hidden smirks and patronizing of the other men. The few times Owen saw him, the man's old gaiety and charm seemed pitifully subdued.

Then it was the end of August, and Charlotte told Naylor their money had run out. He made the announcement to the crew the next morning, offering shares in the company to whomever would stay. But these men had grown up in the tradition of keelboating, and had little faith in steam. They spent a few minutes talking and muttering among themselves, and then began to drift out of the clearing. It was their answer. Naylor watched them go, till only two men remained by the boat: Heap and Little Ike. Both Heap and Naylor stared in surprise at Ike. The man spat.

"Hell, Owen. You give me a job when no other boat builder would. I can't back out on you now."

Naylor had to grin, and he clapped Ike on the back. But as he turned back to the boat, his humor faded. He had little hope, now, of finishing the boat before the *New Orleans* was in the water. An hour after they started work, a lone figure wandered into the clearing. It was Indian Thompson, the half-Shawnee Charlotte had fired for drinking. His greasy sable-black hair was queued at the base of his neck, and his hatchet face might have been hacked from a narrow piece of dark mahogany. Around his neck, hung on a rawhide thong, was the inevitable skinning knife, glittering wickedly in the bright August sun.

"I heard you was offering shares," he said. "I thought you might want me back."

Naylor was hesitant. He knew Thompson had run with Blackwell's gang off and on, and he didn't trust the man. But he needed help desperately. "No more drinking on the job?"

"No more drinking on the job," Thompson said.

"All right," Naylor said. "You can start on the forecastle scantlings."

So that was his crew—a one-armed derelict, a renegade half-breed, and an aging keeler who chewed garlic and rubbed bear grease into his elbows every hour to ease the misery of his ague. The work went with painful slowness that first day, compared to the buzzing activity with which the full crew had filled the clearing. They labored till long after dark and then had a meager dinner of hog side and hominy. The others turned in, while Naylor took the first watch on the boat. As had been customary these last weeks, he saw that every rifle stacked just within the door was loaded and primed. He also stuck a pair of loaded pistols into his belt—massive .48 caliber Kentucky pieces, full-stocked and brass-butted, with a red violin finish to their woodwork. A man who got one of their balls through him would never be the same again.

He walked a hundred yards down to the river and watched the moon rise, spreading its lemon-yellow light over the placid surface of the Ohio. The night was filled with summer sounds, the shrill flutes of the crickets and the 'cello booming of bullfrogs and the sighing hum of gnats in the willow thickets. It took all the tensions of the day from Naylor, relaxing him. Then Charlotte came to his mind. The driving labors on the boat had kept him from thinking of her much—although whenever he saw her, she struck him anew with poignant impact. How could he keep feeling this way, when she had shown him such complete rejection? She seemed content with Louis, despite his weaknesses.

A sound behind him broke into his thoughts. It was a faint noise, like the crackle of underbrush. He could see nothing. There was a rush of running feet, and a mass of shadowy figures broke from timber, heading toward the boat. Knowing what it was now, he ran toward them.

"Heap!" he bawled. "Turn out! Ike, Thompson, turn out!"

He held his fire till he had a figure fairly before him. He shot for the middle of the nearest shadowy shape, and the man shouted and pitched onto his face. He tried to hit the next man beyond, but missed him completely. Then, with both pistols empty, he heard the stutter of feet on his right flank. A man came bursting from timber, club upraised. When he was five feet away, Naylor recognized Furgeson, a big red-headed keeler who ran with Blackwell. Naylor checked his headlong rush for an instant, flinging one of his heavy pistols fully into Furgeson's face. The man reeled back, clapping hands to his face, and then twisted around and fell.

The raiders were swarming over the hull now, light from a dozen torches throwing their contorted faces into lurid relief. As Naylor plunged toward them, he saw the cabin door flung open. Indian Thompson was the first out, the wicked skinning knife already in hand. Ike was behind him, a pistol in his single fist. Then Naylor saw Heap sinking to one knee in the doorway, bringing the first loaded rifle to his shoulder.

This was the man whose father had beat Daniel Boone in a shooting match, and, when he fired, something went down. His first shot picked a man off the deck and pitched him onto the ground. As Heap dropped the rifle and snatched up a second from the stack, Naylor reached the boat, scrambling up the stocks. The first thing he saw on deck was a man in the waist, chopping a hole in the planking so his companion could drop a torch into the hold. Naylor knew the boat would be finished if a fire started down there.

The axe man wheeled to meet Naylor as he rushed. Naylor lunged dangerously close, feinting the man into striking, dodging the blow. As the axe bit into the deck, Naylor wheeled back and threw himself into the man. It knocked him against his partner.

While they struggled to regain balance, Naylor tore the axe from the man's hand and swung. The flat of its blade hit the man's head with a sharp crack. He dropped like a stone. The other man flung his torch at Naylor.

It struck Naylor in the face. He heard himself scream, and staggered backward, blinded, still gripping the axe. The tramping rush of feet was all about him and hands clawed at him and his head rocked to a blow. Bawling like a berserker, he tore free and swung the axe in a wild arc. He felt the flat of the blade strike a man's head, felling him like a poled ox—saw the ash handle club a second man across the neck, dropping him to hands and knees—saw the edge of the blade bite deeply into a third's upper arm and come away, dripping blood. Then he was pinioned from behind, and a contorted face burgeoned up in front of him, a knife flashing above his head.

Before it could strike, Little Ike rushed against the man, clubbing him to his knees with an empty pistol. At the same time the hands pinioning Naylor were jerked free, and he half wheeled to see Indian Thompson burying his skinning knife into the man's back. Naylor shouted recklessly and turned and led them in a rush down the deck. Heap was still keeping up his cool fire from the door of the shack. The whip-like *crack* of his rifle beat steadily into the babble of shouting and the clatter of running feet. Two of his victims lay face down on deck, soaking the planks with their blood; a third was crawling toward the gunwales, hugging a shattered arm to his body. The others who had climbed onto the boat were forsaking their exposed position and dropping off onto the larboard side.

Illuminated by their own torches, intent on setting their fires and dodging Heap's devastating fusillade, they were totally unprepared for Naylor's rush from the shadows amidships. He ran to the gunwales and dropped off in their midst, with Ike and Thompson right behind.

A man wheeled, dropping his torch and jerking up a pistol. Before he could fire, Thompson's bloody skinning knife flashed past Naylor, burying itself in the man's side. He doubled over, dropping his pistol.

Naylor charged into another man, swinging the axe as he

brought up his pistol. The blade cut through his upper arm like butter. Blood spurted and the pistol dropped from nerveless fingers and the man fell back with a blood-curdling yell. It only lasted another moment, a brief, savage battle under the hull and among the shorings, with Naylor swinging the lethal axe and Thompson scooping up a dropped pistol to shoot a man in the face. Then the remaining raiders broke and ran for timber, dropping their torches all the way across the clearing.

The sudden quiet was almost painful. The whole battle had lasted but a few minutes, coming and going with the fury of a summer storm. One of the raiders was sitting on the ground two feet away, trying to pull Thompson's knife out of him. Another up by the bow groaned and rolled over, holding his head. A third was plodding blindly and mechanically toward the timber, still holding his shattered arm against his body.

"Jesus!" a man on deck said. "Somebody come and stop me from bleeding to death. For Chris' sake, somebody come and stop me. . . ."

All this Naylor saw and heard in an instant, with the sickness of reaction rushing through him and making his whole body tremble. But Indian Thompson was already running along the stocks, kicking the dropped torches away from the boat. Naylor realized that the pine-pitch reek of smoke filling the air came from more than those torches. Heap ran around the stern, cradling a rifle in the crook of his elbow.

"That was one helluva shootin' match!" he shouted. "Is it all over now?"

"Not yet," Naylor said. "Is there another fire on the other side?"

"I didn't see any."

Smoke swept against Naylor, making him cough. Eyes watering, he clambered onto the deck. Then he saw where it was coming from. Although they had decked it over tightly, one of the raiders had managed to tear loose a hatch. The smoke was filtering from the rectangular opening like a sinister scarf. Even as Naylor saw it, the scarf thickened and billowed out and grew black as coal.

"Get the buckets!" Naylor shouted. "She's burning in the hold!"

They had put a dozen buckets of water in the ways for just such an emergency. The three men formed a line and passed them up to Naylor. It was a bitter, half-hour battle. After the buckets were empty, Ike and Thompson and Heap ran to the river for more water, while Naylor dropped into the hold, choking and coughing in the smoke, chopping away smoldering embers with his axe, ripping off his shirt to hold them with as he threw them out.

When it was over, Naylor crawled on his hands and knees to the deck and sprawled flat on the hot planks. He lay there for a few moments, too exhausted to move. Tears from his watering eyes made a grimy white network of streaks through the charcoal blackening his face. He was swept with successive paroxysms of coughing. He vomited up all he had in his belly and still kept retching. Finally he got the smoke out of his lungs, and the sickness passed.

He climbed off the boat and got the loaded rifle Heap had put down against the shoring. Then, without a word, he turned and walked across the clearing. Heap and the other men watched blankly. Naylor had taken but a dozen steps when a horseman appeared from the timber, cantering to him. It was Dr. Fellows, from town.

"I set a broken arm in the Red Feather," he said. "The man told me there'd been a bad fight up here."

Naylor jerked his head at the half dozen raiders still crouched or sprawled about the hull, too badly wounded to move. "You got some business," he said.

"What about you, man? Where are you going?"

"To get Swain," Naylor said.

Naylor didn't find Swain. He spent an hour searching the waterfront, looking into the taverns and inns and deadfalls, before he discovered at the Ivory Bill that the man had taken a packet for Pittsburgh the day before. It did little to weaken Naylor's conviction that Swain had instigated the raid that night, but his rage was cooled, and he finally returned to the boat.

He found more townspeople in the clearing. Two of the raiders had been dead when the doctor reached them, and there was doubt about a third. Naylor tried to get one of the wounded keelers to tell him the true source of the raid, but the man wouldn't talk. They got them all into wagons and headed back to town, leaving Naylor and his men alone once more. They climbed into the boat and assessed the damage. Bulkheads would have to be repaired, a dozen knees, most of the larboard strakes, and some decking. It would have been a minor thing for a full crew; short-handed as they were, it was a major setback.

Charlotte came down the morning after the raid. Naylor showed her what had burned, told her how long it would take them to repair the damage. She inspected it with tight lips and a pale face. Naylor could see her definite effort to keep from giving them advice. She did admit sharing his opinion that Swain had been behind it.

The next day they were working in the charred hold when the Reynaud coach once more clattered into the clearing. But this time it was Louis, and he was alone. He spent a lot of time inspecting the damage, looking over the boat. Naylor could see he had something on his mind. At last, with obvious effort, he spoke. "Charlotte tells me this was almost the last straw that broke the camel's back. You are up against the wall. I . . . that is . . . perhaps it is time"—he shook his head, letting it out in an exasperated gust—"I would like to do something."

Naylor was amazed. He could not help looking at Louis's hands. Louis turned them palms up, soft and pale as a woman's.

"I know," he said. "I have never done a day's work in my life." He lifted his chin defiantly. "But a man can adapt. After all, this is my boat, too. . . ."

Naylor grinned at him. Although this was the man who had stood between himself and Charlotte, he had never been able actually to dislike Louis. He knew what a sacrifice of pride and of lifelong attitudes this meant to a Creole. He wondered whether it was due to pressure from Charlotte, or from shame, or from a simple realization in Louis that he had come to a turning point in his life and would have to change his ways. "All right," Naylor said. "You can buck for Thompson on those new 'midships timbers in the pits."

Louis tried valiantly to keep up with the half-breed, but the sedentary living of the last years had left him soft as a baby. In an hour his hands were raw and bleeding, and he was too exhausted to continue. Naylor tried to give him an easier job, cleaning out the charred and burned timbers they chopped from the hold. They were all tired and irritable and grimed with charcoal, and Louis couldn't seem to keep out of the way. Finally he bumped into Heap and dropped an armload of trash all over Naylor.

"Damn it, Louis," Naylor said. "Can't you pick up your feet?"

The young man grew livid. "*M'sieu* . . . I have run men through for less than that."

"I'm boss on this job and I'll cuss you out when I have to."

Louis was trembling. "Don't you understand? I have offered you my cartel."

"If you're talking about a duel, the hell with it. We don't have time for that."

Louis was aghast. "Don't have time . . . ?"

"Either git back to work or git out of our hair, Louis."

"*M'sieu,*" Louis said, "I wouldn't take that kind of talk from a pig."

Pale and trembling, Louis stalked to the coach. Naylor watched him go, surprised that he felt little anger.

He saw Charlotte a couple of days later, and she said Louis was still sulking about the house. In Natchez his pride could have been restored on the field of honor, but the raw frontier attitudes with which he had been forced to cope this last year had completely upset his values, leaving him baffled and unable to adjust. A week later, however, Louis came back.

"I will not apologize, *m'sieu.*"

"Forget it, Louis. We're all jumpy as cats. This thing is like a million pounds on our backs."

"I still want to help somehow."

"I may cuss you out again."

"Perhaps I will understand better, this time."

"Then git on some decent duds. Those frills won't do."

That time Louis lasted three days. They were painful days, to both him and Naylor, for Naylor was given a picture of someone so rigidly molded by a tradition and a culture that it was almost impossible for a man of his emotional instability and adolescent attitudes to change.

The effect of this last year had only made it worse. Charlotte's gradual assumption of authority in their household had apparently undermined Louis's initiative and confidence. He avoided responsibility and often had trouble making small decisions in his work. He wasn't strong enough for the heavy work, had no mechanical aptitude, and lacked the patience for the joining and fitting and other lighter work. The others had tried to make him one of them, but he was too conscious of his failure at job after job.

At the end of those three days, Louis fell off the boat and wrenched his back. The doctor bound him up and put him to bed. He stayed there two weeks. Even after he got up and around, he did not return to the boat and made it plain that he could not stoop over to pick up things. It might have been true; it might have been his excuse. Either way, it had represented his attempt to conform, and his failure.

With autumn setting in, Naylor began to worry about Captain Abner. The man was overdue, and there had been no word of him. October waned, with the broom sedge turning brown in the fields and the gums by the river flushing red as turkey wattles and the hickories turning to gold on the ridges. Ringtail raccoons waddled through the forest, heavy with fat stored for the coming winter, and the spotted rattlers and the copper snakes began to hole up. All night long the leaves whispered down about the shagbark cabin, the nuts rattled against the roof, and pigeons feasted on the fallen acorns that stippled the clearing. Then the pigeons were gone, and a man could look up through a lacework of remaining leaves and see the sky that a month ago had been hidden by the dense green foliage. Captain Abner arrived then, with all his machinery aboard a keel.

He brought with him the discouraging news that the *New*

Orleans had been ready for launching when he left Pittsburgh. Those last weeks were the worst, working against the coming winter and the discouraging realization that they were losing the race. They set up sharers to hoist the heavy boiler aboard, laying it on longitudinal timbers amidships. On the 28th of October they started assembling the engine. They worked late into the evening, setting up torches to see by. They were all haggard and snappy with exhaustion.

Naylor was helping Captain Abner bolt the pitman to its eccentric on the paddle wheel. He thought he heard a distant gunshot and raised his head, staring off at the shadow-pocketed timber. The sound came again, louder, echoing through the forest. The others stopped their work, raising their heads. There was a glow silhouetting the trees now, turning the sky above the river an unearthly pink.

Panic varnished Thompson's eyes. "Must be that comet again."

His voice was drowned by the next explosion of sound. It made them all jump, crackling and banging through the forest, its echoes multiplying till the timber was alive with shocking sound. The glow grew brighter over the river timber. It was hard to separate echoes from the original sound now. The whole forest seemed to be rocking with the deafening thunderclaps.

"It's the comet!" Ike yelled, turning and running for timber. "It's the end of the world . . . !"

Captain Abner looked blankly at Naylor, then scrambled off the boat, running toward the river. Naylor followed him. They stood on the bank and saw it coming majestically around the bend. The bright glow came from sparks shooting out of her single stack and falling in a shower all about the boat. It cast a weird red illumination over the whole craft, revealing her clearly to Naylor.

She looked to be about a hundred and fifty feet long, with three times the freeboard of their boat. Her hull was sky-blue, carrying a pair of cabins fore and aft, with masts and a bowsprit like a schooner. Her upright engine rose like a steeple high above the gunwales, with the arched hog frame and the beam clearly visible.

"The *New Orleans*?" Naylor queried.

Captain Abner nodded, his face lined with defeat. The buckets of her sidewheels kicking up a dirty froth of water, the steamboat passed down the river toward Louisville, escaping steam still crashing through the forest, echoing and reëchoing like a giant cannonade. Ike and Thompson had crept back to the edge of the forest, watching the boat disappear. Although Heap and Captain Abner had told them what a boat looked like under steam, they had been really unprepared for such a display; ignorant and illiterate, they were as awed and frightened as primitive man with his first sight of fire.

Dispiritedly the men walked back to their craft. They stood around, looking at it, their faces slack with fatigue and discouragement.

"Let's turn in," Naylor said. "Don't seem like much use in all this hurry, now."

Naylor was awakened the next morning by the clatter of a coach in the clearing. He pulled on his pants and stepped to the door. The driver had pulled the team to a halt by the stern, their nostrils steaming in the crisp air. The first man to step out was Kenneth Swain. Naylor grabbed a pistol off the shelf and went out toward him in long, savage strides, heedless of the cold.

"Swain," he said, "I'll give you one minute to get out of here."

Swain looked quizzically at the gun. "Just time enough to introduce you to your arch rival. Mister Naylor, this is John Montgomery, engineer and builder of the first steamboat on Western waters."

Naylor looked at the second man, alighting from the coach. He was tall, narrow, dressed in a drab nankeen suit under his heavy cloak. He had a pale New England face, sharp-jawed, bony-cheeked, with gray eyes that fastened like leeches on Naylor's face. "Do you treat all your visitors so rudely?" he asked.

Naylor was looking at Swain. "I just don't want another burning."

"You had a fire?" Swain asked.

"A bunch of keelers raided us. Convenient for you, leaving the day before."

Irritation sent a shadowy flutter of muscle through Montgomery's cheeks. He glanced sharply at Swain. The other man turned blindly to him. "I've observed the growing resentment against steam among the boatmen," Swain said. "It would behoove us to keep a sharp eye out ourselves."

Montgomery's lips grew pursed and gray-looking. He looked at Naylor. "Young man, I will admit we are rivals. But why should the Ohio Steamboat Navigation Company stoop to anything besides the most legitimate procedure, when we have every legal weapon under the sun with which to stop you the minute you put that boat in the water?"

Captain Abner had reached them by now, putting a restraining hand on Naylor's arm. "You don't need to be this way with Montgomery, boy. From what I saw in Pittsburgh, he's all right." He grinned slyly at Montgomery. "Mebbe you'd like to see what a real steamboat's like."

Reluctantly Naylor allowed them aboard. He watched

Swain like a hawk, hand on his pistol all the time. Montgomery was interested in the engine more than anything else. He expressed surprise at the horizontal cylinder. The friction of the piston would eat out the walls in no time. He studied the direct connection carefully. The pitman would never stand the steam. He spent long minutes over the valve gear, shaking his head. When the inspection was finished, Montgomery took his leave, inviting them to come down and see the *New Orleans* before it went over the Falls. As the coach clattered out of the clearing, Naylor saw a faint smile on Captain Abner's face.

"See him studyin' them valves?" the old man asked. "Lookin' fer patent infringements, that's what. I changed 'em from slide to poppet, and not a bolt in the whole gear he can lay claim to. They ain't got as many legal weapons as he'd like to think."

That evening they went down to the levee. Charlotte met them there, and they all went aboard the *New Orleans*. It was immediately obvious that John Montgomery was not of the river. Naylor could stand in one spot and see a dozen of the mistakes Charlotte had mentioned. Over twenty feet long, so big it had to be set in masonry, the boiler's massive size and weight affected the flotation of the ship. The engine had an elephantine clumsiness compared with the one Captain Abner had built. The flywheel alone must have weighed as much as the whole engine aboard Naylor's boat. The air pump and condenser, the oversize tubes necessary to conduct the low-pressure steam, the heavy hog frame required to support the upright machinery—all only added more poundage to an already overweight assembly.

The safety valve, Montgomery told them, was set to blow off at twelve pounds—hardly a quarter of the pressure Captain Abner used at normal cruising speed. In all, Montgomery was trying to drive a boat twice as heavy as Naylor's with an engine developing less than a fourth the power.

Naylor and Abner and the others retired to the Red Feather and spent the rest of the evening exposing the *New Orleans*'s weaknesses. Charlotte sat quietly, saying little. Everything they had seen was her triumph and her justification.

The next morning they returned to work with renewed fervor. They were now convinced that the *New Orleans* had little chance of returning upriver against the current, and, if she couldn't fulfill the stipulations in the monopoly grant, it would void the charter and leave the river open. Their hopes were further raised when the *New Orleans* couldn't get over the Falls. There was plenty of water for the keels and flats going through Indian Chute daily, but the steamboat, with its twelve-foot draft, could not risk it at this shallow stage. Finally, to bolster his failing prestige along the river, Montgomery took on passengers for a trip back to Cincinnati. It was a triumph for Naylor and put him into a veritable frenzy to launch his boat before the *New Orleans* could get through the Falls. In the last week of November, Montgomery returned, but the water was still not deep enough, and the *New Orleans* once more tied up at the levee, waiting for the freshet that would allow her to pass through.

That night Cripple Alice came to the ways. She had been one of Momma Pelugia's girls till last year when Danny Blackwell had beaten her up in one of his drunken orgies, and now all she could do was peddle cakes and fruit along the waterfront. Naylor was cementing in the last bricks of the after firebox when he saw Alice, standing by one of the flaring torches, shivering in her patched carrick, her neck held in its perpetual, twisted position.

"Why don't you go into the cabin?" he said. "Heap has some hot coffee."

"I got somethin' t' tell ya," she said. Naylor climbed over the side and went to her. There was a bitter look to her drawn face; her voice trembled with an old rancor. "Blackwell just brought a keel in from New Orleans. I seen 'im with Swain at the Ivory Bill."

Naylor felt an old rancor of his own. "We'll keep a double watch tonight."

"I can't let Danny do this, Owen. He's done enough bad things. You been good to me, and I can't let him do this to you."

"Do what?"

"Furgeson came to Momma Pelugia's tonight. He's one of Blackwell's men. He got drunk, and he talked. He said Swain knows you're about ready to launch. They're afraid you'll git over the Falls before the *New Orleans*. Swain hired Blackwell to stop you. Blackwell has two crews and a pair of keels. They're goin' to run you on the rocks when you go through the Falls."

By now the others had gathered around them. Naylor turned to Captain Abner. He could see the cocky gleam in the man's eyes and guessed what was in his mind. "How near done are we, Abner?"

"Near enough," Captain Abner said. "I say we get the jump on 'em. I say we launch her tonight."

Naylor went into town to tell Charlotte and Louis. With their money gone, they had been forced to accept Evadne's invitation to eat at the Red Feather, although their lease on the Market Street house did not expire till January. Naylor found them in the sitting room at the house, playing *écarté*. Even Louis showed excitement, when he told them the situation. They agreed to pack and be at the boat as soon as possible. Then Naylor went down to the Red Feather Inn, and the thing he dreaded.

There were a few drinkers at the bar, the usual group of townsmen arguing politics about the taproom fire. Moll was nodding over the fire in the kitchen. That meant Evadne was upstairs in her sitting room. He went up the stairs slowly, saw the yellow streak of light under her door. He knocked, and her voice bade him enter.

She sat in a rocker by the bed, darning the holes in a pair of his socks. Her hair was parted in the middle and drawn back tightly. It made a glossy black crown for her head, shimmering like a wet pelt in the lamplight. She put the darning needles aside, and a glow of pleasure came to her face, robbing it of its sulkiness.

"Owen," she said. "I hardly expected you."

There was a breathless expectancy in her voice, a subdued hope. His driven labors on the boat had left him little time for her. It had been weeks since they had known any intimacy. In the simple earthiness of their relationship, he had never felt awkward with her before.

She rose to meet him. She knew how close they were to finishing the boat, and now, with her intuition for the undercurrents of a moment, she sensed the reason for his visit. Her body settled, and the shadows seemed to deepen in the hollows of her face.

"You're done," she said.

He felt helpless, inarticulate. "Evadne. . . ."

"You're going."

"Yes," he said. "We're launching her tonight."

The glow went out of her eyes. They were wide and lost-looking, filled with a hopeless hurt. Naylor had seen the same look in the eyes of a hound dog, left by its master. He went to her and took her in his arms. "Evadne . . . we'll be back."

She put her face close against his chest. A deep shudder ran through her body. "You're going," she said, "with her."

Chapter Twenty-Two

The son of an itinerant English millwright, Captain Abner had been molded in the tradition of constant tinkering and unquenchable curiosity that seemed such an integral part of those early experimenters in steam. He had grown up in the grimy workshops of the blacksmiths who built the mine engines for Boulton and Watt; his baby toys had been wrenches and steam pipes and condensers. When he was fourteen, his father had migrated to America, apprenticing Abner to a mill owner in New York. Upon his father's death a few years later, Abner had begun his wandering life.

At Philadelphia, he had helped Fitch in his tortured experiments with the steamboat, had watched the man discard the horizontal cylinder because it leaked, had seen Fitch, in August of 1787 launch the first steamboat in America. Financial difficulties and ill health and public apathy had combined to prevent Fitch from following up his first success, and the completion of his dream was retarded until Fulton brought it to fruition ten years later. Fulton's success was merely the culmination of scores of mechanics and inventors in a dozen countries for a hundred years, and Abner was one of those tinkerers.

Like Fitch and Rumsey and Stevens in America during the last thirty years, Captain Abner had been defeated by a combination of circumstances. He had lacked the contacts and financing of Fulton. Engine after engine had broken down because of faulty workmanship or crude parts. He had been hooted at by the people of a dozen towns and

stoned by the boys of countless villages. The dream had laid
dormant for years at a time while he contented himself with
repairing mill engines in Pittsburgh or piloting keels over
the Falls of the Ohio, but finally the pieces had come together. In Naylor's tremendous vitality and drive he had
found the elements with which to hew success.

It didn't matter to him now—as he stood in the torch-lit
clearing on the Ohio—that Fulton had beaten him to it in
New York or that Montgomery would have the honor of the
first boat on the river. His triumph was too complete. Even
his earlier failures with Naylor had no significance. They
had profited by those failures. Both the engine and the hull
were an improvement over the boat that had blown up. He
knew an abiding faith that this boat would get them through
the Falls and clear down the river to New Orleans.

The *clap* of hammers echoed out into timber as Ike and
Thompson removed the shoring, allowing the boat to rest
altogether on her cradle. Then Heap began rubbing bear
grease on the ways, and Ike carefully removed the keel
blocks. They were still at it when the Reynaud coach rattled into the clearing. Louis and Naylor were first to
alight, helping Charlotte down, then Angelique, carrying
the baby.

"It's all set," Captain Abner called. "All we gotta do is
give it a push."

Charlotte's eyes sparkled with subdued excitement.
"Aren't you going to christen it?"

"We haven't got any time to spare," Naylor said.

"At least let's give it a name," Charlotte said. "We've
talked it over so much before. The last I remember we had
pretty well agreed on *Kentucky*."

Captain Abner looked around at Heap and the other
men. They nodded, and he grinned. "So be it. Make like

the first taste of water in champagne. From now on, it's the *Kentucky*."

"You 'n' me better go aboard," Naylor told Captain Abner. "We'll need the rest ashore for the ways and the hawser."

The two of them climbed the pole ladder to the deck, and walked toward the forecastle. Here Captain Abner asked: "You tell Evadne good bye?"

A strange look came into Naylor's face, then he nodded. "The Reynauds picked me up. Evadne didn't want to come out."

He left it at that, but Captain Abner could guess why. The parting was painful enough for Evadne, and she had never been one to expose her griefs to the public. Captain Abner turned to look at the men below him.

"Down dog shores!" he called.

Reacting to the time-honored signal, Heap removed the triggers, and Ike and Thompson knocked out the shores. The ship groaned on the shipways, began to slide down the tracks. Slowly, majestically it slipped into the water. Naylor and the captain braced themselves against the forecastle as the hull gave a sudden violent lurch, rocking on its beam ends. Then it settled into the water.

They threw the lines ashore and warped it back against the beach. Then they ran the gangplank off the bow and began loading their things aboard. Most of the Reynauds' belongings had been packed into a couple of trunks and a few boxes. Evadne had sent with the coach what supplies she could spare from the Red Feather—five barrels of flour and meal, a dozen rashers of bacon, a half dozen hams. The men had little to add save the arms stacked in the cabin and the extra clothing. While Naylor and Captain Abner got all this aboard, the others started gathering fuel. They sawed up all the shorings and the lumber in the ways and gathered the countless pieces of scrap from the sawpits. With the cargo loaded, Naylor and Captain Abner joined them, and they spent three hours felling timber, chopping and sawing it into proper lengths, loading it into the fuel cribs. It was almost dawn when they had enough, and the whole crew was drenched in sweat and completely spent from their labors.

Heap and Naylor climbed to the pilot house while Indian Thompson and Little Ike stoked the firebox. Captain Abner bent lovingly over his engine, tightening a crosshead guide here, adjusting the lifter on an exhaust valve there, tinkering and testing while Ike and Thompson pumped steam into the boiler and stoked the fireboxes.

Charlotte stood by the port gunwale, watching him. Her cheeks were flushed and her eyes sparkled with subdued excitement. Naylor came down the forecastle stairs from the wheelhouse and stood beside her a moment. Captain Abner knew what lay between them, but now there was no sense of the tension or strain they had shown during the building of the boat. It was as if the moment wiped all the dark turmoil from their lives and they could join together in this triumph. But Captain Abner wondered how it would be when they got underway. They would be weeks in the close confinement of the boat, brought together constantly, day and night, with no escape.

Smoke was beginning to belch from the tall stack now, and steam was up. As the safety valve began to spit and clatter, Captain Abner told Naylor they were ready. Naylor gave the order, and Ike and Thompson scampered to throw off the lines. Then Naylor climbed to the wheelhouse. The big bell jangled for dead slow ahead. Captain Abner cupped his hand lovingly around the throttle and eased it open.

There was a *clank* of gears. The whole boat seemed to cough, to wheeze, to shudder. The escape pipes sighed gustily. Then the pitmans quivered and jerked into motion. A shudder ran through the stern wheel, and it started her revolution, picking up the first bucket of water. The river began to ruffle at the bilge and boil away in a frothy wake behind the turning wheel.

Charlotte's voice was barely audible above the *clank* and *crash* of gears, the *squeak* of crosshead guides, the deafening explosion of escaping steam. "Captain . . . it's moving."

He lifted his grease-smeared face to look at her. Her eyes were wide and shining, almost awed. He laughed at her in triumph, then saw Heap, leaning out of the wheelhouse, a grin fit to split his shiny cheeks in two. Captain Abner raised a fist to Heap, and the man yelled something he couldn't hear. Then Abner bent back to his engines, clucking over them like a mother hen, losing awareness of their passage downriver. "That's the way, gal. Easy on that port exhaust now. Damn that lifter. Not enough pressure? Maybe a little wad o' steam."

Sending its crashing echoes across the river like a cannonade, showering sparks like a Roman candle from its stack, giving a visible lurch ahead at the end of each stroke of the piston, the *Kentucky* swept down the Ohio into the growing light of a pearly dawn. Bear Grass Creek came in sight, with the *New Orleans* anchored at a levee among the other boats. It was light enough to see the figures appearing on deck, awakened by the giant handclaps of steam that had become audible while the *Kentucky* was still miles away. Front doors of the taverns along the waterfront began opening, and men gathered in little knots on the levee. Then a man emerged from the Ivory Bill, his shouts striking the thin morning air like the distant bark of a dog. He

243

headed for the anchorage, gathering men along the levee as he ran, until a full score were galloping after him. The *Kentucky* was near enough now for Captain Abner to see the red feather in the leader's cap. "Blackwell," he breathed.

The gang clambered aboard a pair of keels in Bear Grass Creek, tossing their poles, pushing off. Naylor had seen them from the wheelhouse, and the bell jangled for full ahead. Captain Abner eased his throttle wider. The deafening crash of escaping steam came faster. The clanking and banging of gears gained crescendo. Like a pair of sinister sharks, the keelboats nosed out into the river after the *Kentucky*.

Heap came hurriedly down the forecastle stairs. "Falls ahead. Ike had better take over the engine."

"Jist watch that safety valve," Captain Abner told Ike. "If she starts screamin', ease your throttle back."

He turned and scrambled up the stairs. Heap and Thompson already knew their duties. They broke out the keel poles Naylor had put aboard and ran toward the bow. Naylor was at the wheel, peering through the dawn at the water frothing over the reefs ahead. "I never saw anything go so fast," he said. "One point off and them reefs will slice us like butter."

"It's all or nothing now," Captain Abner told him.

He glanced out the window and saw that the lead keel was closing the distance between them, but the men were breaking their hearts on the poles, and they couldn't keep that up forever.

The roar of the rapids joined the clank and crash of the engines now, and Captain Abner could see the reefs before Goose Island, looming up on their larboard. The boat had begun to rock and pitch and suddenly lurched ahead with surprising speed. They had been going about four knots an hour under steam; now, in the space of a few seconds, the swift current was driving them three times as fast. Ahead of them was a keel stranded on the stony flank of Goose Island, being battered to bits by the savage current. Foam parted from a jagged line of black rocks on their larboard.

"A point to the starb'rd!" Captain Abner shouted. "Then a point back. You've got a hidden reef twenty yards beyond."

Naylor swung the wheel, and the *Kentucky* took a sheer, with the reef flashing past a foot from their gunwale. Another swing and the boat wheeled back, kicking its stern up like a saucy wench at the unseen rocks waiting to eat the bottom out.

"That's one the *New Orleans* couldn't've danced over!" Captain Abner shouted. "Now take this eddy on the bilge and she'll sheer around the rock beyond."

Naylor swung the wheel a point, driving the *Kentucky* at an angle into the water boiling around the point of a reef. The eddy caught them up and swung them out, causing them to wheel smoothly as a gull around the gigantic saw-toothed rock below the reef. There was a clear stretch and then another eddy that Naylor calculated to a nicety. Beyond that Goose Island appeared on the larboard, black, ominous.

"Channel's too narrow to wheel 'er through here," Captain Abner said. "Two points to the starb'rd o' Goose Island and hold 'er in 'er marks, no matter what." He leaned from the window, cupping his hands and shouting: "She's in 'er marks! It's up to you now!"

He couldn't be sure that Heap and Thompson heard him above the rush of water and crashing of gears, but they had been over the Falls a hundred times and knew what was necessary. They took their stance at the gunwales, poles tossed, like spearmen waiting to strike. The boat rocked and pitched wildly as it shot into the chute. Spray hung like shredded lace over the bow, sometimes spitting so high it hit the men on deck.

A reef suddenly appeared on the larboard, threatening to rip the bilge strakes stem to stern. Captain Abner saw Naylor start to jerk the wheel, then check himself, face taut. With consummate skill, Heap drove his pole at the reef. Iron squealed against stone. It was as if he merely touched the rock, tossing his pole high before he turned the boat too far to the larboard. The gunwale slid by the reef with inches to spare. A jagged line of rocks leaped at them from the starboard, the very reef Naylor would have driven them on had he turned the wheel.

It was Thompson's turn this time. The *Kentucky* took a sheer as the man drove home, but he held fast too long. There was the squeal of iron, and the pole was torn from his hands. He had to drop to his knees to keep from being pulled overboard with the pole.

"Heap!" Captain Abner bawled. "Head one on the larb'rd!"

Heap turned and saw Thompson down. He ran to the larboard and went down on his pole just in time. The boat took a sheer, rocks flashing past its gunwale with inches to spare. It yawed through the last twenty yards of the chute like a shying horse, then straightened out and shot into the wide mouth of the channel. The jagged shape of Rock Island leaped out of the foam on their larboard. A reef appeared on the same side, like a gnashing fang. Naylor started to swing the wheel.

"In 'er marks!" Captain Abner shouted.

"But that reef . . . ?"

"You've got enough leeway. Dead ahead."

Naylor's knuckles grew white as he held it steady. Through streaks of clear water they could both see the black rocks passing beneath the hull. It seemed impossible that the boat could get over them, but Captain Abner knew his soundings at this stage. The reef was four feet beneath the surface, and the *Kentucky* drew barely three feet with an empty bottom. Naylor watched in fascinated horror as the last of the rocks flashed beneath them.

"That's another one that'd take a bite outta the *New Orleans*," Captain Abner cackled.

The *Kentucky* pitched and yawed her way through the last wild stretch of Indian Chute, with Naylor fighting the wheel and Captain Abner shouting himself hoarse at the men below. The rapids gave them a final lusty kick, and then the boat shot into quiet water, settling perceptibly.

Captain Abner turned a greasy, flushed face to Naylor. "You're free now. Just hold her dead ahead. I'll give you a wad of steam that'll blow us clear down to New Madrid."

He scrambled down the forecastle stairs. The first keel was just shooting from the rapids behind them. Ike stood with his hand glued to the throttle.

"Thank God you come down," he said. "She's goin' to blow us up, I swear."

Grinning impishly, Captain Abner ducked into the engine room, grabbing the throttle as the man gladly relinquished it. "She ain't even started to talk yet, son," he said.

Head cocked, listening to every telltale knock and clatter of the engine, Captain Abner eased the throttle to full ahead. The clank and crash of gears rose to a wild crescendo. The whole boat shuddered and shook, picking up speed with a perceptible lurch. The safety valve let off a piercing scream. For once, Captain Abner ignored it, watching the boilerplates carefully, eyes darting along the pumping pitman to the panting inlet valves. "Where are them keels?" he shouted.

"On our tail," Ike answered.

"Gainin'?"

"No."

"Droppin' back?"

"No."

The boilerplates were red-hot now, beginning to expand and contract visibly. He could not take his eyes off the engine for a second. It was the crucial moment. "Give 'er some o' them pine knots," he yelled.

The firebox door banged open. Ike stoked the blazing maw with a dozen pitchy knots. The blaze roared up, spitting and cracking wildly. Captain Abner shifted to emergency ahead. A new shudder ran through the whole boat. The thrashing of the wheel seemed fit to tear them apart. The boiler was panting and groaning with the strain of expanding pressure. "Now?" he shouted.

"They're droppin' behind!" Ike squalled.

Captain Abner held on till he saw steam begin to hiss from the boilerplate joints. Then he eased the throttle back. The safety valve was like a thing gone mad, hurting his ears with its incessant, ear-splitting shriek, but he couldn't help risking a glance backward now. The keels were swiftly dropping astern. The men had broken their hearts on the poles. They were crouched in the catwalks or leaning against the cargo boxes in exhaustion. Blackwell stood on the cargo box of the nearest boat, every line of his broad figure depicting a raging defeat. Foot by foot, the *Kentucky* was pulling away from them.

Captain Abner saw Charlotte, standing by the cabin door with Louis, where they had taken refuge during the run through the Falls. The wind whipped her cheeks pink, and her chin was lifted in triumph. Captain Abner saw Naylor, leaning out of the wheelhouse. He was gazing astern, toward the Louisville waterfront, hidden behind the islands. The *New Orleans* was there, lying impotently at anchor. With an impudent grin, Naylor lifted his hand and thumbed his nose at the invisible boat.

Chapter Twenty-Three

To the people of Kentucky, 1811 was the *annus mirabilis*—a year of strange and miraculous occurrences. There had been the unprecedented floods in the spring, swelling the rivers from bluff to bluff and leaving great sickness in their wake; the comet had filled the heavens with its glory and cast its weird twilight over the forest; the migration of squirrels had swept southward through the land; and the first steamboat came down the river. The settlers along the Ohio had heard that such a craft was being built in Louisville, but they had scoffed at it and were completely unprepared for its appearance. What happened at Hendersonville was typical.

The *Kentucky* reached the town on the evening of the third day out of Louisville. It was already dark when they neared the hamlet, sparks shooting from their stack in a great shower, the cannonade of exploding steam rolling back and forth between the riverbanks like gigantic gunfire. When they made the landing, they found half a dozen townsmen on their knees in the main street of the village, praying to the Almighty. The children had run to hide in the forest and wouldn't come out for an hour. The town drunk had thrown himself in the river and didn't emerge till he was stone sober, swearing he would never touch another drop.

Below Hendersonville it was an autumn river—a river winding between the mist-hung walls of a dawn forest that echoed to the screams of great cats and the shuddering migration of bison that were never seen. They steamed by creeks that shouted down from the hills like schoolboys at play—Deer Creek and Windy Creek and Crooked Creek and a hundred others without a name. They passed countless islands that loomed out of a fog-shrouded morning or swept into view around a black-wooded bend—Diamond Island, Straight Island, Slim Island, Wabash Island—all the way to Shawneetown where a tribe of Indians had once lived and now only their burial mounds remained. Here the cañon-like shores receded, and the prairie stretched endlessly into the distance, flat, treeless, filled with a tomb-like silence and matted with the gray-yellow hue of dying grass.

Heap was pilot now, for Captain Abner had never been down the river. Naylor spent many of his daylight hours in the wheelhouse, spelling the keeler on the wheel. In those long watches, with Heap silently studying Zadoc Cramer or marking the channels, Naylor's thought often returned to Evadne, and her words would come back to him: *"You're going . . . with her."* It was typical of Evadne, that she should never have mentioned her intuition of the true relationship between Naylor and Charlotte. He wondered how long she had known it. Perhaps it had begun with her first meeting of Charlotte, lying there all that time since, a pain, a torture. It filled him with a poignant sense of her loss and her loneliness, yet he was helpless to change it.

This was only one of the things that seemed to taint the triumph of the downriver trip for Naylor. Often, standing at the wheel, he could see Louis appear on deck, Denise in his arms, walking the deck with her, pointing out things ashore, taking his endless delight in her cooing and babbling. Every time he saw the baby, Naylor was filled anew with dark confusion. He and Charlotte had agreed that, for the child's sake, they had to stop questioning, they had to assume that

Denise was Louis's, but it did not seem sufficient. More than once he felt a trenchant jealousy of Louis. It seemed a bitter irony that he should be forced to stand by and watch another assert the rights of fatherhood that might be his. Yet how could he be sure? He always had to fall back on the same, final conclusion: For the child's sake, it had to be this way.

As busy as he was, Naylor could not avoid constant contact with Charlotte. His duties took him all over the ship, and he had to meet or pass her a hundred times a day. It was like a tension building up in him till he could feel the muscles crawl across his shoulders every time he went down the forecastle stairs.

Shawneetown was the first landing after Hendersonville, and after dinner the crew went ashore for wood. They felled and chopped a full cord. After the wood was carried aboard, Naylor went back for their axes and saws. He was returning, in sight of the boat, when a figure on the beach astern caught his eye. It was Charlotte, sable cloak wrapped tightly about her against the wintry chill. She heard him on the sand and turned. The moon planted wedge-like shadows beneath her exotic cheek bones, made her lips look almost black. He stopped three feet from her, and they did not speak for a moment. The first flush of the new adventure was gone from between them. The old tensions had returned; the old turmoil was coming back to him.

"I wanted to stretch my legs," she said.

He didn't answer for a moment. He knew he should leave, knew it would be better. Yet she held him. It was the conflict she always brought. He had been able to lose himself in the grueling labors of building the boat; that had obviated many of the insidious complications of such proximity as they had known in the town. Now that was over, and it was all coming into focus again. He moved toward her, almost against his will.

"Maybe your husband wouldn't like it," he said. "Being out here alone with the captain."

Her body stiffened. "Louis is not by nature a suspicious man."

"Maybe he's too busy with his own troubles to notice."

"Notice what?"

"What any man with eyes could see."

"All he can see is that we fight whenever we meet."

"Why do you think that is, Charlotte?"

Her lips parted, almost in surprise. Then he could see anger dance to the surface of her eyes. "Owen," she said, "why does it have to be this way? No matter what happened between us, no matter what you felt before or what you feel now, I'm a married woman, with a husband and a child. That changes everything. Why can't you accept it and go on from there?"

Some of his hostility, his sense of conflict faded. He knew she was right, had known it a long time. He was being a fool. He couldn't go on forever acting like a child with the sulk. He shook his head, grinning ruefully at the ground. "You're right, Charlotte. Man's a fool to butt his head against a stone wall."

Her anger was gone now. There was a softness in her face, to the shape of her lips he had not often seen. "It's been hard on both of us, Owen. Maybe we had some of what happened at Natchez still left in us and just had to get it out of our systems. But now it's done. We'll go on from here as friends. Tell me we will."

He was warmed by a sense of kinship, something apart from the passion, the burning need he had known. He wanted to forget his antagonism, his hopeless desire, his sense of loss—wanted sincerely to go ahead with her on this new basis. It was the only logical, adult way they could accept each other. He had been stupid to resist it so long. He could see it with his mind—if only he could see it with his emotions.

"I allow it's somethin' that just takes time," he said. He took a long, deep breath. "I'll try, believe me I will."

She smiled reassuringly and started to reach out to touch his arm. A shaft of light checked her motion, coming from an opened door aboard the boat and falling across the water in a shimmering yellow path. Louis's slim silhouette appeared in the doorway.

"Charlotte?"

Her voice sounded surprisingly calm. "Why don't you come and walk with me, Louis? It's a beautiful night."

He seemed to hesitate, then turned down the deck to the gangplank. As he approached Naylor, he smiled uncertainly. "I wish I could help with the wood." He put a hand to his back.

"I know," Naylor said.

"Do you still think Blackwell's behind us?"

"Most likely."

"At least I can take a watch."

"It would help. How about midnight till four?"

Louis nodded, still smiling. Naylor turned from them, crossed the gangplank to the boat. Here he could not help but look again. They were walking down the beach, arm in arm. His hand began to ache. He looked down at it. Only then did he realize he had been gripping the axe handle so tightly his knuckles shone whitely through the flesh. . . .

Past Shawneetown even the grass was gone from the prairie. The Indians had burned it over in their fall roundup of game, leaving nothing but charred and blackened earth. All the long islands, so clamorous with birds earlier in the year, were empty and silent now. They passed through Big Chain, where Naylor's father had been battered to death on the rocks. An autumn mist lay like deep snow on the earth, hiding the confluence of the Mississippi and the Ohio. It was here, groping through the mist, that they ran aground on a sandbar not noted in Zadoc Cramer. They were going half speed ahead and the *Kentucky* slid blandly over the bar to its very amidships before it ground to a halt and settled itself like a stubborn old maid in her rocker.

If they'd had a cargo, they might have unloaded and floated it off. But they were empty. It looked like the river was rising, and they waited two days for that, but not enough water moved in to lift it. Then they had to go ashore and cut timber for a pair of shears and rig a makeshift capstan.

They erected the shears on either side of the boat, jamming them deeply into the sand, and attached lines from them to the capstan aboard, and walked it off like a grasshopper. It took three more days of sweating and laboring and cursing over the capstan to do it, moving the boat inches at a time, staring upriver every minute for the dreaded sight of Blackwell. He had not appeared by the time they were finished.

Then it was the Mississippi's vast current washing against them like a chalk-gray wall. With the bell ringing for full ahead, the *Kentucky* plunged like a rearing stallion into the broiling backwash, sending its cannonade of exploding steam defiantly across the turbulent waters to the distant shore. On their starboard was their first sight of the Louisiana Purchase, a high, bold bank topped with oak and hickory that massed blackly beneath the bare white branches of the lofty sycamores.

On the evening of December 15th, they reached New Madrid, sprawled like a slattern on the shallow plain only a few feet above the Mississippi, its muddy streets running haphazardly back among dilapidated houses, a rotting church, a row of log stores and taverns. A gaping crowd gathered along the waterfront to watch them warp the *Kentucky* against the levee. The townspeople began to shout derisively.

"Jist look at that ondacious thing, hosses! How do they ever figger to git such a contraption fernenst the river?"

A bellicose patroon stood on the cargo box of his boat and spat brown tobacco juice on the *Kentucky*'s deck. "Looks like a pregnant keel to me. They jist planted them top-works on deck and couldn't stop 'em from growin'."

This drew a shout of laughter from the crowd, and someone else called: "*Kentucky*, they name 'er! Should be *Mississippi Mud*, allus sinkin' to the bottom."

Captain Abner gave out with a sudden wad of steam. The ear-splitting shriek of the safety valve drowned the man's shouting. The crowd eddied backward frantically, fear on their faces. Captain Abner poked his greasy face from the engine room.

"That's better. You oughtta show a little more respect for the first steamboat on the Mississippi."

Naylor stepped out on the boiler deck, gesturing at the baled cotton stacked on the wharf. "Who owns the freight?"

A stooped, narrow-faced man in a broad-brimmed straw hat disengaged himself from the crowd. "It's mine. These air keels ain't got the room, but they say there's one hailing from Pittsburgh in a week with enough bottom."

"And it'll take a month more to reach New Orleans," Naylor said. "We'll do it in a third of that time and give you half rates."

The planter shook his head. "Think I'd trust my year's crop to a devil's contraption like that?"

This drew another derisive hooting from the crowd, and some wag shouted: "Better tie a hawse around her bilge, Cap'n! She'll shake herself to pieces!"

Undaunted, Naylor and Heap went ashore and tried to find other freight. They finally turned up a planter with three hundred bales of late cotton who was desperate for a shipper, but it was inland, and it would take at least two days to get the cotton to New Madrid. Naylor knew they couldn't wait that long and told the group of his decision over dinner. Charlotte disagreed with him.

"At half price, that's still over two thousand dollars' worth of freight," she said. "You know how badly we need that money. We don't even have wharf duty for New Orleans."

"It's too big a risk. I'm surprised Blackwell hasn't caught up with us already."

"The fact that he hasn't proves he gave up."

Naylor shook his head. Most of the nights since they'd left Louisville had been cloudy and moonless, and the snag-filled river would have been too dangerous for Blackwell to run. The fact that he hadn't shown up yet merely indicated to Naylor that the man had been held to the normal running time between Louisville and New Madrid, which was between ten days and two weeks. But the steamboat itself, after the delay at Big Chain, was over ten days out of Louisville. If Blackwell still followed, he was dangerously close. "We can't take the chance," Naylor said.

"We've got to. Arriving in New Orleans with freight will be our final proof."

It was a return to their violent arguments over building the boat. They were both standing, Charlotte's cheeks flushed, Naylor's face gaunt with anger. "Getting to New Orleans will be proof enough," he said.

"Maybe the rest of us feel differently. That two thousand dollars. . . ."

"Will just put you another two thousand further away from Silver Street!"

Louis came to his feet. "*M'sieu,* you have no right."

"I have every right." Naylor turned savagely to Louis. There was a flashing change of light against the surface of his eyes. They turned green as jade. "If I have to put every move I make to a vote of the company, you better get a new captain."

He turned and walked out of the cabin. He was trembling. How could she make him so mad? A man he would have knocked down. Maybe that was it. Times like this he wondered how in hell he'd ever been attracted to her. She seemed cold and ruthless to him, right on the brink of Silver Street now, so afraid of being thrown back into it that she'd risk the boat and the whole crew for a couple of thousand dollars. He climbed to the boiler deck, pacing up and down. He wasn't aware of the silvery beauty of the river under the light of the first moon they'd seen since Shawneetown.

After a while Louis appeared at the hatch and came up beside Naylor. "We have discussed it, *mon ami.* The men uphold you. The captain's word should be law. If Charlotte keeps constantly contesting your authority this way, we shall have nothing but chaos." He sighed. "I wish you two could get along. Sometimes I think you almost hate each other."

Naylor tried to get himself under control. He went downstairs with Louis, still tense. Charlotte had left the main cabin, but the others were still there, finishing their meal by flaring hog-fat candles. With the moon out for the first time in a week and the possibility that their delay had allowed Blackwell to close the gap, Naylor felt that extra precautions were necessary. He sent Ike to a point a mile north of the boat, to high land from which the river could be seen several miles beyond. If Blackwell was sighted, Ike was to shoot off his gun. The shots would be heard aboard the *Kentucky*, giving them time to fire their engines before Blackwell reached them. A running man could beat the keels in such a distance, and Ike would be aboard the steamboat before it shoved off.

Naylor took first watch aboard the *Kentucky*. He built a low flame in the fireboxes to keep the water hot. It would cut the delay of getting up steam.

He didn't know how many hours passed. He was kept busy regulating the fires. Once they got too high, and the safety valve started blowing off. He had to damp down and start over again, but to his mind this was the crucial night, and the extra work was justified. Several hours after midnight he was going forward to wake Thompson and Heap to take over the watch when he heard the sound of footsteps on the larboard. He crossed to that side and saw Charlotte, standing by the engine guards, her sable coat over a nightdress. He halted a few feet from her, and they gazed at each other without speaking.

Finally he said: "Restless?"

Her voice was distinctly hostile. "I couldn't sleep."

"Maybe you didn't let off all of your steam."

She studied his face without answering a moment. At last the stiff line of her lips relented, becoming a pout. "Owen," she said, "I thought you were going to try."

He moved closer. "I did. If you'd given me a chance, maybe it would have been different." He looked at her face, her soft white face. His voice grew husky. "Or maybe i⸍

259

wouldn't. Maybe it wouldn't be different no matter how hard I try."

A disturbance ran in changing shadows across her face. She took a sharp breath and started to speak. Then she checked herself, lips compressed, but the breath had parted the edges of her sable cloak, giving him a shadowy hint of her body beneath, swelling into her flimsy nightdress. It was like a tantalizing glimpse of passion. It seemed to release all his savage need of her that he'd been building up through the long months. He had been resisting it too long, and now there was no more strength left to him. It bore against him like an unbearable pressure, and reaction came in a thoughtless rush. He pulled her roughly against him. The bruising contact made her gasp, and he didn't know whether it was with pleasure or pain. She fought him for a moment with all the violence and savagery of Silver Street. He welcomed it, pinning her in his arms, bending her back as she struggled. Her head turned from side to side, but he finally found her lips. She tore an arm free and raked his face with her nails. Burning pain ran down his cheek, and then the blood flowed between their lips, thick and salty. She moaned, arched like a bow in his arms. There was a roaring in his head, and his pulses hammered through him till his whole body trembled. Then she got her other hand free, placed both palms against his chest, forcing herself back. He tried to hold her, but she was crying now.

Moonlight made silver streaks of the tears on her flushed cheeks, and she was pleading with him like a little child. "Don't, Owen. . . . Don't. Please. . . ."

He released her, and she stepped back. They were both breathing heavily. He could see the helplessness. Then, before he could speak, a distant cracking sound came down the river.

She saw the widening of his eyes. Her voice was trembling, breathless. "Owen . . . what is it?"

He did not answer. For a moment he couldn't subdue the passion in him, couldn't tear his attention from her. Then the sound came a second time, distinct as the snap of a whip in the night. He knew what it was now, and he could avoid it no longer.

"It's Ike's gun," he said. "Blackwell's coming."

It took but a moment before the *Kentucky* was shaking and clattering with the pound of running feet and the hoarse yelling of men and the clank and clatter of iron on iron. With Naylor's first shouts of warning, the men rolled out of their bunks in the open forecastle, pulling on trousers and running, blind with sleep, for the engine room and the fireboxes. Thompson yanked the iron door of Number One open, cursed as the hot handle burned his hand, blinked with surprise as he saw the banked fire inside. Captain Abner ducked into the engine room, holding his pants up with one hand, waving at Naylor with the other.

"Let about thirty gallons out of the biler. It'll give us quicker steam."

Louis ran up from the stern, pulling tight kerseymere trousers on under his nightshirt. Naylor told him to mount to the wheelhouse and call out with his first glimpse of Blackwell. Running for the boiler, Naylor passed Charl again. His eyes met hers, and he was filled with a poignant torture of having found something and seeing it torn from him all in the same moment.

It took him a few minutes to drain the boiler, firemen sweating over their boxes and Charl standing by with his head cocked, listening to the knocking and clanking. Then Louis warning from the wheelhouse. For a few minutes nothing was visible on the moon-silvered river. Then they slid into the view of those on deck, black and sinister as surfacing alligators, a pair of keelboats bearing down on the *Kentucky.*

"Heap!" Naylor shouted. "Take your rifle up to the wheelhouse. If we cast off before they reach us, you can have the wheel. If we don't, you can use your gun."

Heap left the after firebox and got a gun, his shot pouch, and powder horn from the forecastle, then ascended the stairs. Captain Abner went back to his engine, cocking an ear to the clicking and groaning of the heating boiler.

"How long?" Naylor asked.

"Five minutes," Captain Abner said.

They could see Ike now, running down the bank toward the levee. He fired his gun once more, and the barking of a dozen dogs answered him from town. Lights were beginning to bloom at windows in the houses ashore. The door of the Shawnee tavern was thrust open, and the bartender came out in a nightcap. The keels and flats on either side of the *Kentucky* began to creak as their crews came awake. Ike staggered aboard and flopped face down on deck, sucking in air like a bellows, so exhausted he couldn't move.

"Cast off your bowlines!" Naylor ordered.

Thompson deserted the forward firebox and ran to the ̀ow. The after firebox was a blazing inferno, but Naylor ̀ tossing in fresh pine knots. The pitch spat at him and ̀*the* engine room with a syrupy reek. Naylor watched Abner anxiously.

̀er minute and they'll be in range!" Heap called.

̀ur fire!" Naylor said.

̀ a knocking from within the boiler, a hiss of ̀g groan from the red-hot plates. Then the

̀n to chatter. Captain Abner cupped his

hand around the bright throttle, grinning toothlessly at Naylor. "Cast off our stern lines."

Thompson answered Naylor's shout running astern. The keels were clearly visible now only a few hundred yards away, sliding lubricously down the broad and placid river. The crews were bent so far against their poles that they looked like giant crabs, crawling down the catwalks. Then the safety valve let out its first ear-splitting shriek.

With a triumphant cackle, Captain Abner opened his throttle. Heap's rifle was pulled from the wheelhouse window. A clank of gears shook the engine. The *Kentucky* shuddered from stem to stern. The escape pipes emitted their first gusty sigh. Then the *Kentucky* began backing majestically from the levee. The shrieking valve and the crash of escaping steam drew more people from the taverns and houses ashore. By the time the steamboat had cleared the other craft of the waterfront, there was a sizable crowd on the levee.

As yet Captain Abner had devised no effective reversing gear. As they slid out into the river, with the keels so close they could hear the shouts of the straining crew, he had to throttle down and work his valve levers manually to reverse. The thrust of high-pressure steam against the valve faces made it a dangerous, laborious task. Working frantically over the greasy rods, he burned his hands more than once, jerking them away with a curse. Charlotte stood at the corner of the after cabin, tensely watching. Every time her glance crossed Naylor's, he could see her eyes fill with a tortured remembrance.

Then, just as Captain Abner got his wheel reversed, it happened. There was a deafening, gigantic rumble, seeming to come from the air, the river, the very bowels of the earth. The boat pitched up as if tossed by a giant hand. Naylor was thrown across the engine room into Charlotte, pinning her against the wall of the cabin. Held there an instant by the savage yawing of the boat, his mind registered a crazy kaleidoscope of pictures. The buildings on shore, the crowd, the keels and flats at the landing—all rocking crazily as within the frame of a jarred painting. The ground was suddenly parting at the south end of the levee to form a gigantic fissure that literally swallowed a dozen people, the fissure running like an immense snake back into town. Buildings slid off into it, people disappearing into its black maw, arms flailing. A whole section of the levee farther down caved into the water. A crew of Blackwell's keelers pitched off their boat as it tilted up on its beam ends. The chocolate waters of the river rushed through a dozen gaps in the levee and swirled waist-high about what was left of the panic-stricken crowd.

All this occurred in but an instant, with the terrifying rumble filling Naylor's head, blotting out all other sounds. Then the first oceanic wave struck the *Kentucky*. The mud-stained waters smashed in over the thwarts, lifting the boat on its beam ends, flooding waist-high across the deck. Naylor and Charlotte would have been pitched overboard save for the engine guards. They were hurled against the iron braces like rag dolls. Naylor gasped with pain as he was doubled over the guard, clawing frantically at Charlotte to keep her from being torn away. With a crazy sense of the boat's pitching and settling beneath him, he saw the gigantic wave sweep on toward the town. The keels and flats at the levee were lifted into the air, flung up on the bank like toys, smashed to kindling.

What was left of the crowd had already begun to run back toward the town, panic-stricken. The wave inundated the levee, overtaking them. A dozen running people disappeared beneath the first onslaught of hungry waters. The awesome rumble kept on, rolling over the river like the drums of doom. Lightning ripped jagged streaks through the black sky, casting flashes of noonday brilliance over the scene.

Charlotte was hanging desperately to the guard, struggling against the suck and pull of receding waters. She didn't seem to see Naylor. There was a loose, wild look to her face, and her mouth was open in a cry that was obliterated by the ghastly rumbling. "Denise!" she screamed. "Denise . . . !"

Fighting to keep her footing on the shuddering, yawing deck, Charlotte floundered toward the rear cabin. The tremendous shock of the whole thing had blotted all ability to reason from Naylor's mind. He followed his first impulse, plunging after Charlotte. Angelique swung open the cabin door, fighting the insane roll of the boat, her face dead white with fear. The first immense rumbling seemed to be dying out, and Naylor could hear the maid's scream above its hollow boom.

"What is it? What is it?"

"Must be an earthquake!" he bawled at her. "Get back inside!"

He caught at Charlotte, shoving her into the door. Before they got it shut, another one of the huge ground swells reached them. It blotted out the opposite shore. It seemed to rise above the top-works of the boat. With a deafening rush of sound, it swept over them.

Again the *Kentucky* was lifted into the air. Naylor had the inchoate sense of the roar of water all about him. On the outboard side, he was smashed against the cabin with stunning force, then torn free again by the boiling fury of the tidal wave. Water and mud filled his mouth, and he doubled over in a paroxysm of coughing, fighting to get air. At the same time he lost all contact with the deck and knew in a moment of wild panic that he was being swept overboard. Then something hooked him under the armpit. The force of the water tore at his body, striving to pull him away. The boat tilted violently the other way, yawing toward the starboard. There was a scream of wood, a rending of timbers.

Naylor fought to get his head above the water and débris that swept across the deck. Coughing up silt, half blinded with nausea, he saw that it was Charlotte, holding him. She had one arm around the doorframe, the other hooked under his armpit. Her clothes were plastered to her body, and her hair was down over her face in a sodden, dripping mass. She was sobbing with the painful effort of holding onto him against the wild force of the receding wave. He sagged against the door, braced against the pitching of the deck, too drained to speak or move, and he saw what had happened.

The first immense ground swell had swept them halfway to the levee, the second half had completed the job. Only the greater size and weight of the *Kentucky* had kept it from being carried over the top of the levee and smashed to kindling with the other boats. Now it was grinding up against the inundated wharf, yawing back and forth in the vicious suck of crosscurrents left in the wake of the wave.

"Inside," Naylor gasped. "Keep the door shut."

He pushed Charlotte into the cabin, pulling the door closed behind her. It was a terrible choice to make. If the boat foundered, Charlotte, Angelique, and Denise would be trapped in there, but they would be swept overboard on deck, and that was sure death. He staggered back toward the open engine room. Through the guards he could see that the second tidal wave was receding from the town now.

Under the blinding illumination of crackling lightning, he saw heads bobbing in the dirty sea. A man was holding a baby high as he sought a foothold in the chest-high water inundating the main street. Half a dozen others had been swept onto the roof of a building and were still clinging there as the river receded.

The earth itself was still shaking and trembling, new fissures appearing every instant. North of town a fifty-foot bluff slid off into the river, and a whole stand of timber had been felled as if by a giant's scythe. Out in the river another ground swell was heaving up.

Naylor knew there was only one chance left to save the boat. Reaching the engine room, he shouted at the pilot house. "Heap! Round-to! Head her head on into that next one!"

Louis poked his head from the wheelhouse window. His black hair was down over his wild eyes; there was blood on his face. "Heap's unconscious! That first wave threw him against the wall!"

"Then do it yourself! Turn the wheel all the way to starb'rd!"

Louis gaped at him, then disappeared. As Naylor whirled into the engine room, he saw Captain Abner on his hands and knees, half drowned, coughing and gagging. Little Ike was almost buried in a pile of wood, apparently knocked unconscious, the débris sweeping him back and forth in a foot of water.

"Fire's out in Number One," Captain Abner gasped. "Door was open when that fust wave hit us."

"I'll check Number Two," Naylor said. "Try to get some pressure. It's our only chance."

He staggered to the forward firebox. The iron door was dogged shut. He tore it open and saw a fire still going inside. Giving fervent thanks to Charlotte's insistence on these watertight doors, he groped for more wood. It was wet, but there was enough fire inside to dry it out and get it burning. The receding rush of the second wave carried them, rolling and pitching, away from the levee, but a hurried glance outboard told Naylor that the third gigantic wave was bearing down on them with awesome speed.

"You've got a fire!" Naylor shouted at the captain. "What can you do?"

Captain Abner was hanging to the guards with one arm, trying to keep his feet. As he eased his throttle back, there was a gusty sigh from the escape pipes. "We've still got a head!" he shouted. "Fill your box!"

Naylor threw a last load of pine knots into the blaze, slamming the door shut on their angry spitting and popping. Then he ran back to the engine room. There was but an instant left.

Captain Abner pointed to the safety valve. "Your belt! Tie it down!"

Naylor stripped off his belt and lashed the safety valve. At the same time, Captain Abner got a makeshift billet of wood from the débris. He jammed it between the rocker arm and the inlet-valve lifter, opening his throttle wide. There was a wild clash and clang of gears, rising to a screaming crescendo under the sudden head of steam. The boat lurched suddenly ahead, coming around, gaining speed. With its bowhead on toward the middle of the river, the third ground swell hit them.

Naylor hooked one arm around the guards and caught hold of Little Ike's hair at the same time. The *Kentucky* leaped like a pitching horse. A torrent of water rushed through the open forecastle and swept over the boiler, drowning Naylor in a spray of mud and silt.

Clinging desperately to the unconscious Ike's hair, he fought to get his head into open air. The boat yawed back and forth, and his feet were swept from beneath him. The arm he had hooked on the guard was almost torn from its socket by his outswinging weight. Choking, gasping, he sought a foothold on the slippery deck. Then they were beyond the crest and sliding down into the trough.

The water receded, swirling around his waist, dropping to his knees. Drifting wood from the fuel cribs piled up against his legs. Captain Abner came out of the water, sputtering and shaking his head like a cocker spaniel. The red-hot boiler was hissing and its plates were panting visibly under a tremendous head of steam. The safety valve was chattering like a monkey.

Captain Abner pointed at it, gasping. "Loose that valve before she blows us to kingdom come!"

As Captain Abner stumbled over to knock his billet from under the rocker arm, Naylor let go of Ike and ran to the engine, tearing his belt off the safety valve. It let out a banshee scream, shooting a miniature geyser of white steam into the air. Captain Abner eased his throttle back, and the crash and clank of gears lost crescendo. The yawing of the boat kept lifting its stern up, and the wheel thrashed and thumped at empty air, threatening to twist the boat apart.

Thompson staggered into the engine room from the stern. "Got knocked into the paddle box," he gasped. "Half those buckets were smashed when we hit the levee."

"They'll still push us," Naylor said. "Tie Ike to something here. Then look at Number Two."

With a fireman to help Captain Abner, Naylor staggered across the deck and fought his way up the forecastle stairs. Another wave was forming out in the river, and he couldn't trust Louis too far with the wheel. Again the terrifying rumble of shifting earth boiled up about him, blotting out all other sound. From the advantages of his height on the pitching boiler deck, he saw great masses of land torn off the bluffs and hurled into the river. Houses ashore were crumbling like matchwood, and half of New Madrid had been swallowed by the river.

Heap lay sprawled on the wheelhouse floor, unconscious. Seeing his white face and inert body, Naylor knew a sharp fear for his old friend, but he had time to do nothing more than drag Heap into a corner, wedging him there so he wouldn't be pitched out the door with the next wave.

Louis had lashed himself to the wheel with a length of rope. There was an exalted look to his face as he stared wildly at the river. "Another one!" he shouted.

Then the ghastly rumble of the earth blotted out his voice. Naylor staggered to the wheel, pulling it two points to the starboard to meet the oncoming wave. It was an awe-inspiring sight, from this height. For a moment, under the blinding illumination of crackling lightning, they could see the opposite shore, quivering and shaking as a new shock tore at it. Then it was hidden by the crest of the advancing wave.

Both men stared at the rising water with strained faces. Naylor knew the bell was useless and leaned out the window, waving his arms frantically. Captain Abner was in the waist, watching for the signal. He darted back into his engine room. Naylor knew the safety valve would be tied down, that billet would be thrust between arm and lifter again, that the throttle would be pulled wide.

The boat began to shudder violently beneath the sudden thrashing of the damaged wheel. It picked up speed perceptibly, lurching and shaking, smoke pouring from the stack and showering cinders and sparks into the wheelhouse.

Then the wave struck them. The bow lifted high, and Naylor was slammed against the rear wall. Tons of water smashed over the thwarts. The boat shuddered and thumped with the force of its impact. Spray filled the wheelhouse windows, blotting out everything. The *Kentucky* pitched and tossed, and Naylor almost tumbled out the door. Dazed and battered, he caught the frame and held on. Beneath him he could see muddy water swirling across the main deck. Then they were sliding down into the trough.

"To the starb'rd!" Naylor bawled. "You'll capsize us!"

Louis fought with the wheel. The boat answered suddenly, sliding into the bottom of the trough on its beam ends. The wave swept over the levee behind them like a chocolate wall. It obliterated everything but rooftops and the church steeple in the first blocks of New Madrid. Then it seemed to settle against the ground and recede back to the levee, leaving wreckage and destruction in its wake. The roar of the quake had subsided once more to a muted, intermittent rumble. The ground swells forming in the river were not so big, and the *Kentucky* took the next one with less water over the deck. It gave Naylor the first moment's respite he'd had since reaching the wheelhouse. He dropped to one knee beside Heap. The man was still slack, motionless, a pitiful collection of bony elbows and knobby knees jackknifed against the corner. Was he breathing? Fear was like a sickness in Naylor's stomach. Why did it take a moment like this to make you realize what someone really meant to you?

"He can't be dead. He can't be."

"He hit his head," Louis said. His face was white with anxiety. "What about Denise?"

"In the cabin with the women. Maybe you better check. Lash that wheel."

As Louis untied himself, lashed the wheel, and left the wheelhouse, the boat began pitching heavily again. Naylor knew he should be on the wheel himself, but he couldn't leave Heap. He had never felt so helpless. He pulled the man's head up and felt blood. He shook him gently, face tense.

"Heap, come out of it, hoss. Heap. . . ."

The man stirred, groaned. His eyes fluttered. Naylor sank back in relief.

"Damn you," he said. "You scared hell outta me."

Heap shook his head, groaning. " 'Gator's tit, what kinda shoal we run onto?"

"Earthquake," Naylor said hurriedly. "You all right now?"

Heap nodded, dragging himself to a sitting position. Naylor rose and took the wheel. Another ground swell was already lifting her bow, and Naylor battled to hold the boat steady.

The *Kentucky* bucked and fought like a wild horse, but this one was smaller, and the boat rode over its crest without shipping much water. Heap gained his feet, leaning on the windowsill, gazing in awe at the scene of devastation. All about them the earth-stained water looked red as blood. The moon, shining fitfully through the clouds, showed the river to be choked with débris. An empty keel floated past them, upturned. Whole masses of uprooted trees swept against the boat, their boughs snagging the paddle buckets, scraping along the planking. The water boiled and bubbled like a cauldron, and every new trembling of the earth sent choppy crosscurrents across its disturbed surface to make the boat yaw and sheer. Another ground swell came at them, and Naylor rang for full ahead and got a ragged burst of speed out of the laboring engines to ride over its crest.

But she was answering sluggishly to the wheel. She didn't seem to have any freeboard left, and it was a growing battle to turn her. In the next moment Naylor found out why. Thompson appeared at the door, dripping water like a drowned rat.

"She's busted her seams. We better do somethin' quick."

"Those ground swells ain't so big," Naylor told Heap. "Can you take over?"

Heap nodded, and Naylor accompanied Thompson to the main deck. Ike had regained consciousness and was stoking Number Two. The engine gasped and labored. The boiler was red-hot and panting, visibly expanding and contracting with each opening and closing of the valves. A joint had already parted, emitting sly little gusts of steam, and Captain Abner was jamming a wooden wedge into the opening.

"She can't stand it much longer, Owen. Somethin's goin' to blow."

"Dead slow ahead, then. Just enough steam to give us steerageway."

He passed to the stern, fighting the pitch and yaw of the boat. A mass of uprooted trees struck the boat, the branches almost sweeping him from the deck. He and Thompson had to hug the cabin wall, fighting off clawing branches. Louis stood in the door of the after cabin, face strained and white. Naylor called to him.

"Everything all right?"

He nodded.

Naylor passed him and reached the after hatch, opening it and looking in. The dirty, silt-thickened water was already a foot up the knees. He got down to it and crawled through the sodden timbers. There were no big holes, or they would have foundered in a matter of minutes. The grinding and smashing against the levee had wrenched open her seams and torn caulking loose in countless places and the seepage would soon be out of hand. He pulled off his shirt and began tearing it into strips, jamming them into what openings he could find, calling to Thompson for the pumps at the same time. Louis poked his head into the hatch, and Naylor sent him to Heap with word to find a landing where they wouldn't be caught if another shock should create the huge ground swells again. Then Thompson returned with the first manual pump, and they set to work.

Chapter Twenty-Four

In many places south of New Madrid, there was no bank left. The river had rushed over it to inundate the bottomlands for miles into the interior. Where the trees had not been uprooted by flood or earthquake, the water had swept in among them to lie dank and black beneath their branches. Whole hillsides had caved into the river, or had been split into seemingly bottomless fissures. They passed several bluffs still standing, but new shocks were still shaking the land, and, every time one came, huge slices of clay slid off into the water. Afraid of being caught beneath a cave-in, they finally had to settle for an isolated oak poking its topmost branches out of the river. It stood in what had once been bottomland, but now a half mile of water stood between the tree and the nearest dry land. If another oceanic swell caught them here, there would at least be no shore to get smashed against, and they might stand a chance of getting away.

Throwing their bowline on the tree, the whole crew joined Naylor and Thompson in the fight against the river. It was a bitterly discouraging battle. Every time they got one joint filled with oakum, they found ten more letting the river in. It seemed she had burst every seam in her hull. It was almost impossible to locate some of the openings, working underwater all the time. The pumpers labored in shifts till they collapsed with exhaustion. It was dawn before they began to make any headway. There was still seepage, but they had reached their limit. They pumped her as dry as they could, and then took to their bunks in a stupor.

They woke near noon with new tremors shaking the earth and disturbing the river. Naylor inspected the hull and found little seepage left. The water had swelled the fresh caulking, and the holes were plugged. Now the paddle wheel had to be fixed. They found the heavy iron shaft bent, the pitman broken, most of the iron straps on the wheel buckets torn loose and lost, half the buckets themselves smashed beyond repair.

As they were looking at the mess, a hail reached them from out on the river. It was a man and a woman in a skiff, their faces haggard with fear and exhaustion, their clothes caked with mud. As the skiff bumped against the side of the boat, Naylor could see that the woman was clinging to the man, hiding her face against him, sobbing over and over again: " 'Tis the end of the world . . . there be nothing left on the face of the earth, not even a bury hole for a body to die proper in. . . ."

The man's face was upturned, pleading. "I wonder could we come aboard. My wife's been put in such a bearm by this terrible thing. There jist don't seem no place left to go."

They helped the pitiful couple aboard, and Charlotte and Angelique took the woman into the cabin for a change of clothing and something to eat. Naylor got the man a pair of his extra jeans and a dry shirt and asked him about New Madrid.

"Dropped right down to the center of the earth," the man said. "Half of it gone clear to hell, I swear. Must have been our sinnin'. Mary did rag me for not goin' to church last Sunday."

"Is there anywhere we can get some ironwork done, get some planks and timbers?" Naylor asked him.

The man allowed there was a blacksmith shop left at the east end of town, but he couldn't be sure if the smith was still around. They were afraid to move the *Kentucky* any more, for fear the wheel would tear itself completely off, so Naylor loaded the bent paddle shaft into the skiff and took Heap with him back to town.

They found a scene of utter desolation. The waterfront was completely inundated, the streets for blocks into town five feet deep with water. They rowed in over where the levee had been, fending off wrecked boats and chairs and tables that had floated out of open windows. They picked up a miserable, shivering hound dog who was trapped on the first roof. There were other boats being rowed in and out of the buildings, seeking victims of the catastrophe. Everyone they saw looked dazed and fear-ridden. They finally grounded on high land and found a trail leading to the smithy, back of town. A hundred feet behind the smithy, the ground had opened in a huge fissure, fifteen feet across, running northeast out of sight. The smith was in the back of his building, trying to throw up some makeshift quarters for a dozen people who had fled there from the flooded town. He was a huge, heavy-muscled man named Harris, the seams of his primitive face grimed with the soot of his trade. When Naylor told him what they needed, he cursed roundly.

"How in hell can you ask for something like that now? Seems like the whole damn' town has come down on me. They've already et me out of house and home."

"What are you going to do?" Naylor asked. "You can't stay here. These quakes keep coming all the time."

"Think I don't know that?"

"Would you do the work I need if we give passage out of here to you and all these people with you?"

The man scowled, rubbing a callused finger through two days' growth of bristles. "It's that newfangled contraption, ain't it? That steamboat." He frowned, bit his underlip, then swore: "Hell, I guess anything beats being swallowed by the earth."

While he went to work, they collected the timbers they needed from the wrecked buildings, then took the load back to the boat. One of the families at the smithy wouldn't go, fearing the smoke-belching monster, but the others were pathetically eager to escape the doomed town. They loaded themselves into a pair of skiffs, and followed Naylor. Charlotte was waiting at the bow when Naylor brought his skiff against the thwarts. Her face was tight-lipped, hollow-eyed.

"We can't take any more people," she said. "A dozen came while you were gone."

"I made a promise to the smith," Naylor said. "It's the only way we could get our wheel going again."

She glanced once more at the bedraggled wretches, climbing aboard, then turned away from him, walking aft. The wait was nerve-racking. Through the night the river was lit by the torches of more and more refugees from the town coming aboard. The cabins were crowded, and the newcomers had to bed down on deck. The night was filled with the wailing of babies and the frightened murmur of sleepless men and women. And the earth kept on shaking.

One man said he had counted sixty-three separate shocks already, another claimed it was over a hundred. The river was covered with débris, uprooted trees, wrecked boats, house roofs, veritable islands of entangled foliage that kept bumping the boat and scraping against her thwarts all night long.

The smith came down the next day with the straightened paddle shaft and the new strap irons. The crew had already fashioned most of the buckets they needed, pinning them together with treenails where they couldn't use iron. They put the huge wheel together on the after deck, and then made shears to hoist it in place. They worked half the night to get it in place. But that wasn't the end of it.

Captain Abner had been inside the boiler, trying to clean out the silt brought in during their fight with the river. He found a flue collapsed from the abnormal pressure brought on by jamming the billet under the rocker arm and tying the safety valve down. He and Harris had to tear it out and return to New Madrid to forge a new one. With their limited materials and primitive working conditions, it was an almost impossible feat. It took endless ingenuity and patience. For two days, Captain Abner and the smith traveled between town and boat, cutting and trying, fitting and joining, failing, starting all over again. It was a harrowing wait, with the refugees still floating down the river and coming aboard, the food running low, the earth constantly shaking and trembling.

Then it was night again, with the torches winking out on the river and sending their light across the water in flickering yellow streamers. They were eating a meager dinner when something heavy thumped against the *Kentucky*. Naylor left the main cabin and went to the larboard gunwale. A makeshift raft had come athwart the boat. A half dozen people were huddled on the wet logs, and one bearded man held a pine-knot torch above his head.

"Kin we board ye?" he asked. "We heard ye was takin' on passengers."

Naylor saw Charlotte appear at the doorway of her cabin. Holding her soiled skirts, she moved out through the crowd of people bedded down on the deck. A baby set up a dismal wailing as she picked her way through the huddled figures and tried to step over the heaps of belongings, coming toward Naylor. She stopped before him, her face tense and brittle, her eyes burning feverishly.

"You can't take them aboard," she said.

"You want them to die out on the river?"

"Harris said the Black Vomit's broken out in town, Owen. I won't expose Denise to that."

"It'll only be a little while longer. . . ."

"While these people pour in on us like rats?" Her voice broke. "I've given all my clothes away. Our own food's almost gone. We'll never get through if we keep taking them on like this. . . ."

"I thought so," he said. "Are you sure it's Denise worrying you . . . or Silver Street?"

The feverish glow in Charlotte's eyes was brightened by a sharp anger. She started to speak hotly, then checked herself. She strove to hold his gaze, but her eyes fluttered with a guilt she could not veil. She bit her lip, lowering her face, eyes growing heavy-lidded and sullen. "Damn you," she said.

She turned, picking up her skirts. She stumbled, getting through the packed people bedded down on deck. Her shoulders were held tightly together, and her head was bowed. He was abruptly disgusted with himself. It was like he'd given her a foul blow. She'd been through hell and she was near the breaking point and he didn't have any right. He went after her and stopped her by the wall of the cabin, speaking in a low voice so the others couldn't hear.

"I'm sorry, Charlotte. It was a helluva thing to say."

She stood with her face turned away, eyes squinted shut. Her voice sounded squeezed from her. "Forget it."

"I can't. I'm apologizing. I'm asking you to forgive me."

She looked up at him. Tears streaked her grimy cheeks.

She tried to smile, a tight little grimace, and shook her head from side to side. "You did nothing to forgive. You told me the truth."

"Maybe you can't help it," he said.

She put her forehead against his chest and took a long and shuddering breath. "Maybe I can't," she said in a dismal voice. She clutched at his elbows, as if for strength, and lifted her face to his again. Biting her lip, she released him and turned and picked her way through the people to the gunwale and the raft. One foot against the thwart, she held out a hand. "Come aboard," she said. "There's a fire in the boiler room to warm you."

A woman was the first to take her hand and clamber onto the boat. As Charlotte turned to take a child from the next woman's arms, her eyes met Naylor's. He grinned at her broadly. She brushed a mass of curling hair off her damp face, and smiled back. He went to help her.

Before he reached her, he became aware of the sound echoing down the river. At first he thought it was the rumble of another quake. Someone whimpered like a lost dog, and a baby began to cry. One by one the fear-ridden people turned to look off into the night. Captain Abner came from the engine room, the pine-knot torch in his hand casting its smoky yellow light over the wonder and disbelief in his furrowed face.

"Owen," he said. "You know what that is?"

The sound was distinguishable to Naylor now, like the measured crash of a distant cannon, its echoes sending a shivering chorus across the river and over the broken land. Suddenly one of the women aboard the *Kentucky* screamed: "It's another quake! I can't stand another quake, Josh! I can't take it! I can't stand another quake, Josh . . . !"

She began running down the deck, stumbling over other

passengers, with her bearded husband following and shouting at her. More babies began to squall and cry. A hard-shell Baptist preacher got to his feet and started ranting: "It appears this yere's the day o' jedgment, the day o' jedgment . . . hah, Armageddon, Sodom and Gomorrah, Lot's wife . . . hah, you look behind you once too often, you miserable sinners been a-stealin' and a-covetin' and a-fornicatin' too long, too long . . . hah, and now the Lord's done sent his day of wrath, his avengin' angel . . . hah, right down to smite yew . . . hah. . . ."

It was a crazy cacophony of the shouting man and the crying women and the bawling babies and that endless thunderclap of sound echoing back and forth between the riverbanks. The sky began to brighten over the tops of the trees northward, a pink glow that looked like the reaction of a fire.

"New Madrid's burnin'!" someone shouted.

"It ain't the town. It's the comet again."

Heap moved out to stand beside Naylor. "Shall we tell 'em what it is?"

"They wouldn't believe us," Naylor said.

The glow grew brighter and brighter till the whole sky seemed afire. The people had joined the preacher now, and the shouting and wailing and crying was an insane babble of sound. Charlotte stood beside Naylor, her face set and pale as she stared at the awe-inspiring sight. The sharp detonations were growing so loud they hurt Naylor's ears now, punctuating the wild cries and shouting from the *Kentucky*.

Then, coming majestically around the bend, the boat hove into view. The bright glow came from the sparks shooting upward from her single stack and falling in a shower all about her. The wailing and shouting died about Naylor as the people realized it was another steamboat.

"The *New Orleans*," Heap said. There was a bitter defeat in his voice.

Naylor's shoulders sagged with his own despair. Then he shook his head angrily. "Get that boat horn and signal her. There's plenty more people that have to get out of here."

Captain Abner got the tin horn and started blowing. The passengers rose to their feet, shouting and calling, a different note to their voices now. But the deafening thunderclaps from the escape pipes of the *New Orleans* apparently drowned their noise, for they got no answer from the other boat.

"Light more torches!" Naylor shouted.

He went to the fuel cribs himself, handing out pine knots and lengths of pitchy wood. The people grabbed them up, lighting them off Captain Abner's torch, waving them frantically back and forth. Still there was no answer.

Shooting sparks like a burning house, making the night hideous with her exploding volley of escaping steam, the *New Orleans* moved on down the river and finally disappeared behind a distant cape. Naylor watched blankly as the glow faded on the horizon and the detonation of escaping steam died out in the distance. Finally there was no light and no sound save that of the torches, spitting impotently into the blackness of the vast and inimical night.

Chapter Twenty-Five

Louisiana Gazette and Advertiser
January 13, 1812

The steamboat *New Orleans* from Pittsburgh arrived here Friday evening last. The captain reports she has been under way not more than 259 hours from Pittsburgh to this place which gives about eight miles an hour. She was built in Pittsburgh by the Ohio Steamboat Company, under the patent granted to Messrs. Livingston & Fulton in New York. She is intended as a regular trader between this and Natchez, and will, it is generally believed, meet the most sanguine expectations of the company.

Kenneth Swain put the paper down and leaned back against his pillows with a contented sigh. He was in bed in his apartment on Conti Street, listening to the sleepy morning sounds of New Orleans come through his open windows, the squeal of high-wheeled carts and the clatter of carriage wheels in the narrow streets and the musical chant of the fish peddlers. It was comforting to have reached such a haven after the harrowing events of the downriver trip.

Here, with new shocks coming hourly, cliffs caving into the river, the banks changing constantly, they had been afraid to tie up at night. They had groped their way southward using the bright moonlight when they could, traveling by torches when the moon waned. Just after reaching the turbulent Mississippi, they had seen torches ashore and thought it was some settler in need of help. But when they had come in, they were met by the spears and arrows of fear-mad Shawnees who thought the smoke-belching steamboat was merely another manifestation of the awesome quake. Fifty miles farther, answering more torchlight and pitiful calls from an island, they had been met by a swarm of river pirates, desperate and starving after the quake. Only the superior speed of steam had saved them. New Madrid had been inundated and deserted, and they hadn't tried to land. Below the town they again had seen torches at night, but had been afraid to go ashore after their previous experiences.

The rest of the journey had been a nightmare. The pilot had lost his way a hundred times. Zadoc Cramer's NAVIGATOR was little help. Half the landmarks in the book had been changed or swept away. Huge slices of the Chickasaw Bluffs had caved into the river, completely changing the soundings for miles. The Devil's Race Ground was a madness of new snags and sawyers and boiling white water, and the boat was almost wrecked half a dozen times.

All the way down, Swain had known his growing dread over Charlotte. They had seen no sign of the *Kentucky*. He knew what a triumph this would mean to their company, but somehow, the chance that Charlotte was lost took the bottom out of any triumph. It left him indifferent to the fanfare of their reception on arriving at New Orleans, left him depressed during the following days, unable to enjoy the delights of the lurid town, waiting anxiously for some word of the *Kentucky*.

"Dominique. Do I smell coffee?"

"*Café au lait, miche.*"

The answer came from the kitchen, and in a moment

Dominique entered with the coffee and hot milk. He poured a cup half and half, grinning broadly. Swain accepted it, falling into their morning game with an effort.

"A proper drink, Dominique, for the most notorious reprobate, the direst blackguard, the unholiest cockatrice this town has ever seen."

"Oui, miche."

"Do you know when I first saw New Orleans, Dominique?"

"Dieu sait, miche."

"When father was made emperor, he had to remove the stain of the bar sinister from his escutcheon. He put up quite a proper front, married Josephine, disowned all his illegitimate progeny. My brother and I had to flee France to the New World. Here he took the name of Jean Lafitte, and I. . . ."

A knock on the door stopped him. Grinning broadly, Dominique passed through the parlor, admitting Toby Garret. He was a sober, intense young man from the office of Edward Livingston—brother of Chancellor Livingston—who was handling all the legal affairs of the steamboat company in New Orleans. Swain greeted him with a wave.

"Have a seat in the parlor while I dress. Must be something important to have you out this early."

"Quite important," Toby said. "The *Kentucky* has landed."

Swain stared blankly at him, then went to the door, still in his bathrobe. "Tell me . . . Charlotte Reynaud . . . ?"

"She's aboard. They all are. Apparently they were those torches you saw south of Madrid."

A sense of relief, sharp, almost painful, flooded Swain. His depression was swept away, and his feeling rose on wings of cynical wit, like champagne bubbling in his mind.

How strange, he thought, a hundred women along the river, a thousand, and only the most unobtainable one of all could touch him this way. Then he smiled wryly. Perhaps she was not so unobtainable. He had seen the insidious change that was taking place in Louis, up in Kentucky.

Toby was prattling on, telling Swain that the *Kentucky* had taken a load of refugees as far as Natchez. One of the people was a cousin of Nassaur and had talked him into shipping a sizable cargo of cotton on the steamboat.

"What are we planning?" Swain asked.

"Livingston is out of town," Toby said. "But he left instructions with me in case the *Kentucky* got through. Judge Pine has issued a writ of seizure. The sheriff will be serving it in a few minutes. I thought you'd like to go along."

"Indeed," Swain said, "I would."

New Orleans was a city of tile roofs and brick walls and narrow streets, lying in the waist of land between the Mississippi and Lake Pontchartrain. The river was a bronze scimitar, shimmering in the hot noon sun, and the waterfront followed its crescent curve for almost two miles. Just below the willow-crowned levee, the seemingly endless line of boats creaked and sawed at their hawsers, moored to the heavy timbers imbedded in the *batture*—blunt-prowed trading brigs from Europe and coasting craft from New England and clumsy Indiamen from the Antilles, countless keels and flats and barges and broadhorns from upriver as far north as St. Louis and Pittsburgh.

The *New Orleans* was anchored just above the Place d'Armes, the open square that fronted on the river. Montgomery was waiting here for them, with Marshal Silas Hamer, Sheriff George Finley, and a pair of constables. The marshal was a tall, stoop-shouldered man with drooping mustaches and a jaundiced color to his sunken cheeks.

Sheriff Finley had fiery-red hair and a substantial paunch and ruddy bulldog jowls.

"If all is in readiness," Toby said, "we might as well proceed."

The whole waterfront seethed with constant activity, swarming with a polyglot mixture of boatmen and roustabouts, slaves and merchants, clerks and seamen. Half-naked Portuguese argued shrilly with blond Dutchmen they couldn't understand; ant-like lines of Negroes wound forever over the levee bent almost double beneath their cotton bales and barrels of whisky and salt; knots of elegantly dressed merchants haggled with bearded keelboat patroons; hordes of buckskin-clad Kentuckians slept and argued and brawled and played cards on the decks of their flats and keels. The movement and babble and stench of it could be matched by no town along the river. Montgomery's thin nostrils pinched in at the noisome odors, and a Puritan disapproval tightened his lips. As the sheriff and Toby and the others drew ahead, Montgomery turned to Swain.

"I've been wanting to talk with you," he said. "Ever since I've arrived, I've been hearing nothing but fantastic rumors about you, Swain. The son of an Italian countess, the lost Dauphin, the brother of that pirate, Jean Lafitte. And now this business about you and Aaron Burr."

"Burr was nothing but a maligned philanthropist seeking surcease from political disillusionment in some Western haven."

"He was an arch-traitor, trying to sell half the Mississippi Valley to Spain," Montgomery said angrily. "We can't be associated with such a scandal, Swain. If it came out that one of the officers in our company was connected with Burr, it would ruin our chances here. The public is still scoffing at steam. We are beset by enemies on every side.

We got this monopoly grant by the barest margin."

"Through my influence with Claiborne."

"You're not going to hold that over my head again," Montgomery said. "I've already written Chancellor Livingston. . . ."

"Which you did before, with as little result. If you have proof of these wild accusations, produce it."

Montgomery was white about the lips. "I'm going to get proof, one way or the other. It would save you embarrassment to resign now."

"As a mere engineer, with a few paltry shares in the company, your request bears little weight with me," Swain said. "What about Naylor now? Might he not jump port?"

Montgomery could not accept the shift immediately. His hands opened and closed; he looked away, tight-lipped and pale with suppressed anger. Finally, in a stiff voice, he said: "How can he jump port? If you'd let me handle it. . . ."

"It will take far more than a court order and a constable to subdue Naylor. If you'd let me handle it. . . ."

"I forbid you, Swain!" Montgomery's voice lashed at him like a whip. "I told you we would handle this legally. I still suspect you of hiring those keelers to burn Naylor's hull up in Louisville. I won't have any more of your violence, Swain, I. . . ."

"Tut, tut, my dear fellow. Tell your grandmother to go suck eggs."

Swain took an immense delight in the rage that swept into Montgomery's face. He was saved the man's further wrath by the fact that they had reached the *Kentucky*, moored to the levee between a row of keels on one side and a high-pooped Indiaman on the other. Toby and the officers were already tramping across the gangplank. Montgomery turned to follow them, still speechless with rage.

Swain saw Heap standing on the boiler deck by the pilot house. At the same moment, Naylor stepped from the forecastle. The effects of the harrowing downriver voyage were stamped on him like a brand. His eyes were sunken deeply into his head, red-rimmed, feverish-looking, with the cheek bones running in startlingly white ridges against the flesh. There were open sores around his neck where the filthy, grease-blackened shirt of rawhide had rubbed him raw. Tension lay in the crow-track crevices at the corners of his eyes, the tiny ridges of muscle about his compressed lips. Naylor was at the end of a long rope, and Swain wondered if this new blow would not push him beyond control. The thought made Swain's slender swordsman's fingers toy with the head of his cane, as Naylor walked toward them. There was a rank hostility in the young man's face, as their eyes met.

"Greetings, my young cock," Swain said. "May I express my felicitations upon your safe arrival, and inquire after the health of the Reynauds?"

"They're ashore, hunting an apartment," Naylor said. "What's your business?"

Swain looked across the empty decks. "And your cargo? I understand you had seven hundred bales of Nassaur cotton."

"That's ashore, too," Naylor said. "I asked you what's your business."

Swain inclined his head at the officers. "Perhaps Marshal Hamer can explain."

The marshal unfolded a manila-backed document, cleared his throat, and began to read:

District Court of the U.S. for the Louisiana District. The President of the United States to the Marshal of

Louisiana District or his lawful deputy, Greetings:

You are hereby commanded to take Owen Naylor into custody and hold him to bail in the sum of five thousand dollars, that he be and appear in a District Court of the United States, for the Louisiana District, to be holden at the City of New Orleans on the third Monday of February next to answer to the complaint of Edward R. Livingston, John Montgomery, Robert Fulton, and Chancellor Livingston. . . .

Naylor's face turned dark with anger. "You mean I'm under arrest?"

Marshal Hamer nodded. "And the boat is to be impounded."

A rush of insupportable rage stamped itself on Naylor's face. His eyes flashed to Swain, green as a cat's. Then he lunged. Swain jumped backward, hand closing about the hilt of his sword cane. Before he could whip the blade free, Sheriff Finley's bulk interposed itself between them. The sheriff moved with blinding speed for such a heavy man, throwing his shoulder into Naylor. It spun Naylor around, back flat against the forecastle. The deputies jumped to each side, grabbing Naylor's arms. He struggled a moment against them, wheezing like a winded stallion.

"Take it easy, son," Finley panted. "You don't want a count of assault against you, too."

The three of them knew their business and finally Naylor subsided against the wall, staring balefully at Swain. There was no depth to Swain's eyes as he met Naylor's gaze. They had a blank, silvery surface, like a pair of coins winking in the sun. His smile made wounds of the two grooves bracketing his mouth, and his pale fingers twirled the head of his sword cane.

"A pity, Sheriff," he said. "That you had to interfere."

The two most imposing buildings in New Orleans were
the jail and the church. They stood side by side, facing the
Place d'Armes and the river. The building that contained
the jail had been erected during the Spanish rule there and
was still called the Cabildo. Its flat roof was lined with
squat wine jars in which yucca plants grew, their leaves
etched against the sky in a jagged and savage contrast to the
pristine silhouettes of the twin cathedral towers next door.
Pigeons clicked their red claws against its crumbling tiles,
and the wide arches across the front were cool with a shade
seldom touched by the sun. It was to this building that
Naylor was escorted. Swain and Montgomery took their
leave at the door, and Sheriff Finley accompanied him to
the clerk's office where he was to be put on the books.

Captain Abner and Heap had hurried to find the
Reynauds as soon as Naylor had left the boat. While he was
being booked, they all showed up—Heap, Abner, Charlotte,
Louis, and a lawyer named Charles Thibodaux, a tall, keen-
faced Creole who had studied law with Preval in Natchez
and was a good friend of Louis Reynaud's. Cambre also
came, the commission merchant to whom their cargo of
cotton had been consigned, a shrewd little man in a handsome lemon-yellow frock coat and the long pantaloons
Wellington had introduced during his peninsular campaigns.

"I understand the bond is five thousand dollars,"
Thibodaux told Sheriff Finley. "Will *M'sieu* Cambre's
check be acceptable?"

Finley nodded. "Everybody knows Mister Cambre."

As Cambre walked to the desk, accepting the clerk's
quill, Naylor frowned questioningly at Charlotte.

"The shipping payments on the cotton came to six thousand, four hundred dollars," she explained. "This will be taken out of it."

They found the judge in his chambers, and he signed the release without any question. Then they were all out on the street again. Naylor shook his head, grinning ruefully. "That's the quickest trip to jail I've ever made."

"You aren't clear yet," Thibodaux told them. He went on to explain that the boat had been impounded, and the cargo might be, too. Cambre would have to stop payment on the check if that happened, as he had taken a chance on paying for freight subject to court seizure. However, the cotton was destined for New York, and Thibodaux suggested that Cambre try to find an empty hold in which he could ship it out tonight. The court would have no jurisdiction over it on the high seas. Cambre agreed, shook hands all around, and departed. After that, the whole group of them went down Chartres Street to see the apartment Charlotte and Louis had taken.

It was a handsome place, occupying the whole upper floor of a two-story building overlooking the street. An arched carriageway ran along one side of the house to a flagged courtyard in the rear. The vestibule was floored in black-and-white marble; the doors were resplendent with carvings of Phoebus and his chariots; the staircase curled upward in a breathless spiral with no sign of support. Upstairs, three large drawing rooms opened into each other with sliding doors, and a porch, enclosed in wavy, opalescent glass, looked out over the courtyard below. Compared with the dismal waterfront taverns it looked like a palace, but it was one of the cheaper places in the French Quarter, and Cambre had secured it for the Reynauds at a surprisingly low rent. Dismally Naylor and Heap and Captain Abner seated themselves on the brass-inlaid chairs of the main drawing room. They were still dazed by Livingston's move. They had never quite believed in the monopoly's power. The legality of it was still so open to question. All the other river states north of Orleans Territory had attacked it so bitterly that Naylor had never dreamed it would have such force. They had all seen Fulton's failure in his suits over patent rights to the engine and thought they would meet the same thing in the area of the monopoly.

The most any of them had expected was a warning by Swain and Montgomery that could not be backed up. Even the lawyer, Twist, in Louisville, had advised them that the *New Orleans* would have to fulfill the speed and time specifications of the grant before the Fulton interests could invoke their power of seizure.

Thibodaux supported this reasoning in part. The seizure of the boat had precedent in New York, but it had only been recently established and was frowned on by many jurists as too great an extension of territorial powers. The district judge of New Orleans was of this opinion. Thibodaux was confident that, if they could get a hearing before him, the seizure would be reversed, and they would be allowed to clear port and operate outside the jurisdiction of the monopoly while the case was in litigation.

It was the one hope they had, and they proceeded to make plans for the wait. If Cambre got the cotton shipped before it was impounded, the remainder of the freight payment would give them all enough to live on till the hearing came up in the third week of February.

"You're all welcome to stay here," Louis told Naylor. "The sheriff won't let you keep quarters aboard ship."

Naylor shook his head. "I want to keep an eye on her,

anyway. We'll take rooms in one of those waterfront taverns across the levee."

Charlotte was at the door when they left. Naylor could not help looking at her. The harrowing trip downriver and the crowd of refugees aboard had given them no chance to meet each other alone again. He doubted if it would have done any good. He realized the barriers were up. She would give him no chance to repeat what had happened just before the earthquake. Her eyes, her face gave him no hint of her feelings now. He had a painful sense of his need for her— and of the gulf between them.

There was nothing to do after that but wait. The crew got quarters in a tavern called the Red Cock, directly across from the steamboat. From the windows they could see the constable who had been put aboard the *Kentucky*. The next day Cambre brought them the news that the cotton was safely on its way, and the remaining fourteen hundred was on deposit in their name at the Planter's Bank.

All the crew was recuperating from the physical effects of the trip. They ate heavily and slept long. The sores Naylor had contracted from going too long without a change of clothes were beginning to heal. He was gaining back his weight, his vitality, but recovery was only physical. He grew increasingly restless in the confinement of their rooms, becoming more morose and surly by the day. He knew it wasn't just the waiting. It was the consciousness of Charlotte—so near, yet so far—working against him like a growing pressure. All the unfulfilled, unexpressed needs she had aroused in him this last year were like a dull pain, throbbing insistently somewhere deep inside him. He couldn't help thinking of her, yet each thought was torture. A dozen times he left the Red Cock, filled with the over-

whelming impulse to see her, and every time he stopped before he reached Chartres Street, knowing how useless it
was. Whatever he may have uncovered in her just before the
earthquake had been but a momentary weakening. Whatever it may have meant to her, she was denying it now. He
felt, whenever they met, they were antagonists again. It was
a conflict that would seek its own release, sooner or later.
So they waited, while it ate at him, gnawed at him, festered
in him. . . .

Knowing the growing resentment of the boatmen against
steam, Naylor had posted a watch over the *Kentucky*. Each
man of the crew took four hours, day and night, at the
window from which they could see the steamboat. A pair of
Heap's rifles, loaded and primed, stood in the corner. They
let the whole waterfront know it, and the boatmen took a
healthy sheer around the *Kentucky* whenever they passed
her going down the levee.

On the 20th of January they had been there a week,
sweating it out. Naylor's watch ended at six that evening.
He hadn't been able to sit in the chair five minutes out of
the whole four hours, and he paced across the room to
where Thompson was napping.

"Your watch," he said, shaking the man.

Thompson rolled over, only half awake. "The hell with
it," he mumbled.

Naylor shook him angrily. "Do I have to drag you out?"

"Nobody drags me," Thompson said. He flung out an
arm, trying to roll over and go to sleep. His hand struck
Naylor painfully across the ribs. Naylor caught it and
heaved him out of bed.

"God dammit," he said. "It's your watch!"

Thompson struck the floor and slid halfway across the
room under the impetus of Naylor's pull. The half-breed

rolled like a cat, fully awake in that instant, and came to his feet. The skinning knife, always dangling about his neck by its thong, leaped into his hand, and he lunged at Naylor. Heap jumped from his chair and slid it across the room. It took Thompson's legs from under him before he could reach Naylor. Ike kicked the knife from the half-breed's hand, and Heap leaped over and sat on his head. Holding the kicking, squalling man down, Heap shouted at Naylor: "Damn it, hoss, why take it out on us? Either git that woman or throw yourself a drink."

Naylor swayed back and forth, his face bleak and savage. Then with an inarticulate sound he turned blindly and lurched out the door. He went downstairs and ordered a bottle of rotgut whisky. He had it half empty when he became aware of Heap and Ike and Thompson, bellied up to the bar beside him.

"Cap'n Abner's watchin' the boat," Heap said.

Solemnly Naylor passed the bottle to him. It went down the line and came back again. They emptied it, and a second, and a third. Then a big keeler in the corner said the *Kentucky* looked like a Girod Street whore with a carbuncle on her rump. Naylor whipped the keeler, and a shack bully, and then a big flatter got him down, and Heap had to hit the man over the head with a chair to keep him from gouging Naylor's eyes out. There were a dozen men in the fight, and they smashed every stick of furniture in the Red Cock.

After a while Naylor found himself outside, his clothes half torn off, spitting teeth and blood. He sat down against the building and held his head. It was night now, and Tchoupitoulas was going full blast. Gangs of boatmen wandered by, yelling and laughing, heedless of him. Heap came out, shirtless, and sat down beside him, groaning, happily.

"Ain't had such a frolic since the bear got loose in the Red Feather." He squinted at Naylor. "Feel better?"

Naylor shook his head. Heap offered him a twist of garlic. Naylor made a disgusted sound and turned his face away. Heap chuckled and began to chew on it himself.

Indian Thompson walked through the door and stopped, blinking around. "Somebody turn on the lights."

"You got hit on the head," Heap said. "Sid down."

Thompson groped his way to the wall and slid down, still blinking. Little Ike came to the door. He was chuckling to himself. His pants had been torn off, and there was a knife gash in his thigh from hip to knee. He leaned against the door, wiping the blood off his leg and looking at his fingers and chuckling all the time.

"Dammit," he said. "Dammit."

Heap chewed complacently on his garlic. "Well," he said, "a man's just got to have a frolic once in a while."

The waiting began again: four hours on, four hours off, watching the boat, sweating it out. The next afternoon Captain Abner got the *Daily Gazette* and found the notice in it.

For Natchez, the steamboat *New Orleans* will leave this post on Thursday, 23d inst.

Naylor and his crew were in the crowd on the levee that saw the boat off. To the familiar shrieking of the safety valve and the clank and clatter of machinery, it nosed out into the river, belching smoke pompously and churning up a froth of yellow water with the paddlewheel. As he headed away amid the cheers of the crowd and the shouts of keelers along the Faubourg Ste. Marie, Heap let out a contemptuous snicker.

"She ain't a-goin' very fast."

"Three knots at best," Captain Abner said. "I'll wager that's all she can make. I'll bet a year's wages she don't git past Natchez."

The *New Orleans* didn't. They got the word two weeks later. The current, even in the comparatively calm stretch below Natchez, had almost proven too much for the steamboat. It had never gotten over three or four knots an hour. Its deep bottom dragged in the shallows, and its low-pressure motor just did not have the power to conquer the stiffening current of the Mississippi. Its performance had fallen so far below expectations that even Montgomery and the other officers of the Fulton company had to admit they would not try to go on to Louisville.

It was a day of jubilation for Naylor and the others. Thibodaux prepared a petition for the legislature, contending that, by this failure to live up to the specifications of the grant, the Fulton interests had lost title to their monopoly. Everyone was so confident of victory that they planned a party at the Reynaud apartment to celebrate.

Naylor knew a deep reluctance to see Charlotte again, to intensify the painful turmoil of his feelings. Yet, with this excuse to go, he couldn't refuse. All their clothes had been in rags, and they'd already bought new suits all around. They were the first store-bought clothes Naylor had ever owned. He felt stiff and awkward in the double-breasted tailcoat, the tight kerseymere pantaloons. Captain Abner still clung to his ancient frock coat, frowsy as it was, although he had gotten a new pair of linsey-woolsey trousers.

They all agreed that someone should stay and watch the boat, so they drew straws, and it fell to Thompson and Little Ike. The rest of them picked up Cambre, who had also been invited, at his apartment on Canal Street. Then they headed down the waterfront toward the Place d'Armes.

Naylor had already fallen under the town's subtle spell. It was unlike any other place he had known; even Natchez seemed cramped and provincial beside New Orleans. There was an intensely foreign flavor to its vivid swirl of color, its exotic crowds, its medley of sounds. The streets seemed thronged with blanketed Indians and garlanded Creoles and trappers in buckskin and laughing mulatto girls. Ebony slaves slipped from grilled doorways, baskets balanced on their heads, piled high with purple figs or snowy washing. A Choctaw squaw caught Naylor's arm, blowing cascarilla smoke in his face from her pipe and offering him river water for a picayune a gallon. The smell of trampled fruit hung like syrup in the air, and the chant of the peddlers was never still.

Heap shoved an elbow in Naylor's ribs, chuckling to himself. "Look at that gal make meat, hoss."

He was leering at a quadroon who wound her way through the crowds, white cotton shirt plastered against the sinuous movement of her hips. The only thing she wore of any color was the madras handkerchief on her head, tied so that seven peaks pointed heavenward.

Cambre smiled at Heap. "She is a free woman of color, *mon ami*. They are often so beautiful. In the early days they were attracting so many men that the Creole belles became alarmed. They pressed Governor Miro to pass an edict forbidding any free woman of color to wear jewelry or silks or plumes. In a sort of defiance, the free women adopted that *tignon* on their head. It has become a symbol of that class."

Heap licked his lips. "Makes me wanna rub the velvet off with my horns."

Cambre smiled wisely. "That could be arranged."

They had reached the Place d'Armes when Captain Abner touched Naylor's arm. Naylor glanced at him, saw that he was looking behind them. Through the swirling crowds, Naylor saw a beaver cap with a red feather in its top. It seemed to bob over the sea of heads like a miniature red-sailed boat. Then it was closer and the hair beneath it became visible—a shaggy blond mane, burned a dozen taffy hues by the sun—and finally the face, with the scars making a chalky pattern over the primitive cheek bones.

"Blackwell," Naylor breathed.

It stopped all of them. Beside Blackwell walked Pandash, broad as two men, grease blackening his rawhide leggings, straw and gutter filth staining his red wool shirt.

A mulatto slipped by Blackwell, carrying a basket of rice cakes balanced on her head. While Pandash filched a cake from the basket, Blackwell pinched her on a buttock. She wheeled toward them, swearing in gumbo, and Blackwell's coarse guffaw roared out above the babble of street sounds.

"They follerin' us?" Heap asked.

"If they are, they're tryin' hard to act like they ain't," Captain Abner answered.

"They don't seem to see us," Naylor said. "Let's go on a piece."

They moved into the crowds of the square. The wind came from the river here, and the lanterns swayed and creaked on their hooks above the plank sidewalks. Facing the Cabildo were the pillories. A mulatto sat dejectedly in one, hands imprisoned, a crudely printed sign on his back.

My name is Taro.
I stole a pig from Monsieur Demand,
and have been sentenced to twenty lashes
and five days exposure in the pillories.

His face was already plastered with grapes and tomatoes pitched at him by a gang of screaming urchins. The crowds passed about him heedless of his misery. The cries of his tormentors faded in the babble behind as Naylor and the other two elbowed their way through a crowd of drunken flatters. Naylor risked a glance behind and could not see Blackwell or Pandash. He caught Captain Abner and Heap, pulling them quickly into a coffee stand. The old Nego woman in charge gabbled at them in gumbo.

"Bo zou, miche. Calas tout chaud? Estomac mulatre?"

Naylor pointed out coffee and rice cakes. Before she could hand them to him, there was an eddy in the mob and Blackwell and Pandash elbowed their way free. They were in a hurry, peering intently through the crowd. They both caught sight of Naylor by the coffee stand, and stopped suddenly, unable to veil their surprise.

Then Blackwell recovered himself. He moved closer, in the swaggering, indolent walk that made the muscles stir beneath his shirt like the shift and ripple of river currents. Pandash trailed him, eyes fixed balefully on Naylor.

"How's the steamboat cap'n?" Blackwell asked. His grin was lazy and malicious. "We thought mebbe one o' them holes had swallowed you up by New Madrid."

"You mean you hoped," Naylor said.

"We hoped."

"Last I saw o' you," Heap said, "you was pitchin' off one o' them keels."

"I swum ashore."

"And walked down the Trace?"

Blackwell's sly humor left him. "I never walked the Trace."

"Stay away from the boat," Naylor said.

"Why shouldn't I?" Blackwell asked. "From what I

hear, it'll rot at the levee."

"We can look right out on the *Kentucky*," Naylor told him. "There's a man at the window twenty-four hours a day. He's got a loaded gun."

"He must get right tired," Blackwell said. He looked at Pandash. "Let's shove off, hoss. I can't stand the stink o' steam any longer."

With a mocking grin at Naylor, he wheeled and swaggered into the crowd. Pandash hesitated a moment, still looking balefully at Naylor. Then he turned and followed the other man.

Captain Abner sucked thoughtfully on his toothless gums, then glanced at Naylor. "Don't bust your biler."

Dourly Naylor watched Blackwell disappear into the crowd. "He always did make me build a mighty head of steam."

"They certainly seemed to be following you," Cambre said.

Naylor frowned. "I don't like it."

They went on to the apartment without talking much, each occupied with the troubled thoughts Blackwell had brought. Louis and Charlotte met them at the door. Charlotte had recuperated from the terrible downriver voyage, gaining back lost weight, no longer bearing the feverish look. *En route,* she had given all her extra clothes to the refugees from the quake and had been forced to buy new gowns in New Orleans. This one was sky-blue satin, fitted to make the most of her stunning figure. Her hair was done in cable braids that made a rust-gold crown for her head. With the others, she seemed more relaxed and animated than Naylor had seen her in a long time. But whenever her glance crossed his, he saw tension pull the little muscles tightly about her lips, saw the troubled shadows darken her eyes.

Heap had never gotten over his embarrassment in Charlotte's presence and stood around, shifting from one foot to the other, his Adam's apple bobbing up and down and making him look more like an agitated turkey than ever. It was Louis who finally put him at his ease, opening two cobwebbed bottles of Madeira he had found in a Poydras Street wine shop and pouring fully half of one into Heap's glass. The apartment swam with the delicious odors of shrimp and chicken and gumbo and the baba cakes dipped in rum Angelique was making for dessert.

Naylor wandered to a window, looking down on the Café des Refuges across the street. It was the haunt of the Creoles who had fled from the Negro uprising on Santo Domingo. A group of them stood about the door, hats cocked defiantly, sword canes swinging.

"What is it, Owen?" Louis said. "You seem so restless."

"Blackwell just reached town. We saw him."

Louis exclaimed in surprise. Charlotte's eyes widened, then narrowed thoughtfully. "Surely he wouldn't try anything here," she said.

"Swain's used him before," Naylor answered.

"But there's a constable aboard. The whole police force minutes away."

Heap chuckled humorlessly. "Last time them keelers rioted, the police force couldn't stop 'em."

Charlotte had been watching Naylor all the time. "What's on your mind?" she asked.

He turned to her. "Get out of port before they can do anything."

"You can't!" she said. "You'd be jumping bond. We'd lose the whole case by default."

"What's the use of winning the case, if we ain't got the *Kentucky*?"

She locked her hands together, began to pace. "They won't harm the *Kentucky*. We'll go to Sheriff Finley, request more guards."

"She's right, Owen," Louis said. "We can't take a chance on losing the whole thing, so near to the end. Not only have we beaten the monopoly, we have a full cargo waiting in Natchez."

"What?"

Louis smiled in a pleased way at his surprise. "It is so. Cambre negotiated it for us. Fifty tons of Nassaur coffee, seven hundred bales of cotton Martin Mooney bought on speculation. Cambre said it should give us about nine thousand gross for the one trip."

Captain Abner was gaping at him. "We could make it to Louisville in less'n a month."

Louis nodded, smiling more broadly.

Captain Abner's eyes began to shine with excitement, as he toted it up. "Eight or nine trips a season . . . that'd mean seventy or eighty thousand dollars gross in a year."

Charlotte nodded vigorously. "And it's only the beginning. Remember we've cut our charges a third to get the business. When steam's established, we can go back to the regular rates." She turned to Naylor, seeing the effect it had on him, cheeks glowing. "You realize what we have in our grasp now, Owen."

He walked restlessly to a chair and sat down, staring blankly at the floor. They had talked over probable profits before. Charlotte had quoted to him all the figures Swain had given her, but the actuality of such sums was hard to grasp. It was still whirling through his mind when Angelique led the baby into the room by one chubby hand.

"She want to say good night," the maid told them.

Denise waddled across the room to her father, black

curls bobbing. Louis beamed with paternal affection, kneeling so she could throw her arms about his neck and kiss him. He cooed and gurgled with her, nibbling her pink little ears and whispering endearments in French. Then he told her to say good night to Uncle Owen.

She pouted, concentrating on each step, as she crossed to Naylor. It made her look bowlegged and pompous. Then she began to laugh wildly with success as she reached him, throwing her arms wide and grabbing his knees, trying to climb up. He took her up on his lap. She was all soft and satiny, and her little hands kept pawing at his face. A sudden rush of poignant affection ran through him.

"You look like you're holding a lighted bomb, Owen," Louis said with an indulgent chuckle. "Relax. She doesn't take to many people like that."

Naylor grinned, embarrassed. "I guess I ain't had much practice with kids."

Then, over the top of the curly black head, his gaze met Charlotte's. The candlelight sparkled against her gray-blue eyes, but beneath their surface was a haunted depth that seemed to have no bottom. Her hands were folded in her lap, and he saw how tightly they clasped one another. It took the grin abruptly from his face. Why did they always have to be reminded of that? Why did something as pure and innocent as this child have to be tainted with such a dark question?

He set Denise down. Charlotte came to the baby, glancing at Naylor, then looking away. "Come on, honey. Bedtime."

She and Angelique left the room, Denise waddling between them, each holding a pink hand. Naylor watched them go, a savage anger sweeping through him. How had it all gotten so mixed up? With a child as beautiful as that it should be so simple. It should be *his* kid, *his* wife. He was filled with a painful need for all that implied. Then uncertainty blotted out his anger, and his need. What if she wasn't his child? What rights did he have then? It was the old conflict that always came when he saw Denise, the old sense of hopelessly twisted relationships.

He rose again, too restless to remain still, and walked to the window. The others were discussing freight rates and the possibility of extending the *Kentucky*'s guards to increase her carrying capacity. On the street below, a *belles chandelles* was chanting the price of her wax myrtle candles. In the shadowed doorway of the Café des Refuges a man stood, listening to the chatter of the Creoles on the *banquette*. He shifted slightly, and the smoky light of a street lantern illuminated the grimy skirts of his green frock coat. It made Naylor stiffen.

"Heap," he said.

The keeler looked up, then rose from his chair and came to the window. He followed Naylor's gaze, squinting at the shadowy figure.

"Nicolas Fry," he said.

Charlotte had returned. "What is it now?"

Naylor turned to her. "One of Blackwell's men. Keeping watch on us."

She walked swiftly to the window, staring down. "How can you be sure?"

"No keeler ever goes to them Creole restaurants," Heap said.

"He's there for a purpose," Naylor said. "This proves it. Swain's already seen Blackwell. They're up to something."

Charlotte started to protest, but there was a knock on the door. Louis answered it, admitting Thibodaux. The young lawyer looked haggard, his usually flashing eyes dark and somber.

"Sorry I'm late," he said. "I've been closeted with Bonnet. He's the member of the House who was going to present our petition."

"How did it go?" Charlotte asked.

"I'm afraid our victory dinner is premature. There are ambiguities in the wording of the monopoly grant. They have been construed by Livingston's friends in the Legislature to prove that the *New Orleans* lived up to the specifications. She did reach the limits of the Territory, and no distance beyond that was stipulated. Though she didn't average four knots an hour, she achieved it in certain stretches."

Charlotte's face darkened. "Isn't Bonnet even going to present our petition?"

Thibodaux shook his head helplessly. "The faction favoring Fulton and Livingston is too strong. The *New Orleans* has not been a success as far as steamboats go, but it would take a more complete failure to get the monopoly grant repealed."

They were all silent, with the sense of defeat the news brought. Then a monumental impatience rose up to choke Naylor like cotton in his throat. He'd stood the waiting and the haggling and the legal sparring as long as he could.

"I'm for clearing port, right now."

Charlotte looked sharply at him. "You can't. If we don't beat them here, we'll always be running and hiding."

"How are you going to beat 'em? You won't be able to pay a lawyer next month. Let me loose on that upper river and I'll give you enough money to take this to the Supreme Court!"

"We've still got the court ruling to hope for. It may free the boat. We've got to wait."

"While Blackwell wrecks the *Kentucky*?"

"We'll see that he doesn't wreck it."

"How?"

"Legally. I say we stay and do this legally."

"And I say we get out!"

Her whole body stiffened. Lips tight, voice trembling, she said: "Owen . . . if you try to take that boat out, I'll call the sheriff on you myself."

The savage glitter of his eyes made them look green. He seemed to tower above them in his wrath. "Call him, then. I'm clearing port tonight!"

Chapter Twenty-Six

When Naylor left the entranceway of the Reynaud apartment, he saw Nicolas Fry move quickly behind the group of Santo Domingan refugees talking in front of the café. Without giving any indication that they had seen the man, Naylor and Heap and Captain Abner walked quickly down Chartres. As they turned the corner of Chartres into the Place d'Armes, Naylor glanced back.

"He's following us."

"You'll jist get us thrown in jail," Captain Abner argued. "You know Charlotte'll keep her word. She'll be on her way to the Cabildo in a few minutes. You'll have the whole police force down here before we can shove off. . . ."

"I've got a way to take care of that," Naylor said. "You know how afraid of fire this town is. Heap told me it almost burned down about twenty years ago."

Heap's mouth gaped open. "Owen, you ain't. . . ."

"Not quite the whole town," Naylor said. "Just that old flatboat opposite Saint Anne Street. They're meanin' to knock it apart and use the gunwales for sidewalks. Ain't near enough the other boats to put them in danger."

Heap began to see his point. He grinned broadly. "I got my flint and steel."

"Get lost in the crowd, then," Naylor told him. "You can see the Cabildo from the levee. When the police start across the square, go down and start your fire in the flat. Then make for the *Kentucky* like a greased pig."

They glanced behind. Nicolas Fry was not visible in the

mass of dark figures crossing the square. Heap turned toward St. Anne and disappeared in the crowd.

Captain Abner had to jog trot to keep up with Naylor's long strides. The excitement was beginning to reach him now, too. "What about Blackwell?" he said breathlessly.

"We got the jump on him before," Naylor said. "I'm hoping to do it again. It's my guess he ain't ready yet. If something was going on around the *Kentucky*, Ike would have seen it and come to warn us. It'll likely be a run and jump fight with what men Blackwell has now."

The Faubourg Ste. Marie was the American section that had been built up adjacent to the French Quarter since the cession. Along its waterfront ran Tchoupitoulas Street, lined with the taverns and deadfalls and brothels frequented by the brawling flatters and the keel boatmen. The Red Cock stood three blocks from Canal Street, the border of the French Quarter, a mean, cypress-shingled building with walls made from the gunwales of wrecked flats. Before they reached it, they saw Nicolas Fry following them once more.

The taproom of the Red Cock was typical—a gloomy chamber illumined by the fitful light of sputtering wax myrtle candles and smelling of whisky and molasses and dank sawdust. There was a line of men at the bar, and their talk made a constant mutter in the room. As Naylor headed for the stairs, none of the men paid him any heed. But he saw that one of them had an iron hook for a hand.

"Wheeler's here," he muttered.

Reaching their quarters, they found Thompson asleep and Ike sitting at the window in a dark room. Below, Nicolas Fry was already visible, hurrying down Tchoupitoulas and going directly into the Red Cock. Naylor woke Thompson and told the two men what had happened. They were both as tired as he of waiting. This was something they could understand and cope with, and they were eager for it. Naylor then unfolded his plan.

He was hoping to surprise Blackwell, which would give them one thing in their favor. If Blackwell could call on a handpicked gang, it was a certainty that most of them would have guns. But if he had to depend on arousing the boatmen, the majority of them would not be armed that way. The shack bullies and cut-throats along Tchoupitoulas usually carried pistols at their belts, but this was not typical of a regular keeler. If he had a gun, it was more often a rifle, too awkward to carry around when he went into town.

On the crowded waterfront it would be hard to spot the men Blackwell had set to watch the *Kentucky*. As soon as the fire started, however, Naylor was confident they would reveal themselves. For the boatmen were a childish lot, and the excitement of a fire on the levee would have every man within a mile running toward the scene. If any were left around the Red Cock, it would be close to a certainty that they were Blackwell's men.

They gathered their meager belongings and rolled them into tight bundles. Naylor picked up a chair and smashed it apart on the bunk. He took one of the stout legs, handed another to Thompson. They had four loaded pistols, and he gave one to each man. Captain Abner had been watching at the dark window.

"Fire's started," he said.

They all gathered behind him. Far down the waterfront a rosy glow had begun to silhouette the moored boats and the forest of masts. The men on Tchoupitoulas had already seen it, and their shouts started beating back and forth between the buildings. Figures issued from the doors of deadfalls in a shadowy rush. Shouting, yelling, beckoning, they swarmed down the street, all rushing toward the fire.

In a few moments the exodus had emptied the taverns, the street, and levee in front of them.

"Man in front of the Tin Cup," Ike muttered. "I seen him standin' there yesterday."

Naylor saw the figure in the black shadows of the tavern adjacent to the Red Cock. Then he saw a dim movement among the cotton bales piled along the top of the levee, and finally made out another man up there. Farther down Tchoupitoulas toward the fire a third figure was visible. He had run part way toward the blaze, then stopped. He was walking back toward the Red Cock now, and halted against the wall of the tavern two doors down to light a pipe. These three were the only men in sight.

"Maybe they all ain't Blackwell's," Naylor said. "But we can't take that chance."

He told them to stay at the door a moment and moved down the dark hall to the head of the stairs. Fry and Wheeler were at the bar in the candlelit taproom below. The innkeeper stood at the door, watching the glow of the fire. Naylor moved back to the room, speaking in a swift manner. "Fry and Wheeler are still downstairs. Ike, you and Abner go first. Stop right outside and wait. If either of them get past us, it'll be up to you."

The men went out into the hall. Naylor and Thompson stopped at the top of the stairs. Captain Abner and Ike went on down. The innkeeper turned to look. Crossing toward him, Captain Abner asked: "What is it?"

"Fire on the levee," the keeper said. "Whole damn' town is down there."

Hidden from below, Naylor saw Fry look at the bundled belongings under the arms of Captain Abner and Ike, then glance meaningfully at Wheeler. As soon as Ike and the captain were outside, both Wheeler and Fry left the bar in a rush. Fry was first, and, to reach the front, he had to go past the stairway. Naylor touched Thompson's arm and went down the stairs in a soft-footed run.

Three feet from the stairs, Fry heard the sound. He stopped and gaped upward. Naylor was halfway down the stairs, barely visible in the black shadows. He let the chair leg slide into his hand and vaulted over the banister, dropping right onto Fry. As he fell into the man, feet first, he struck for the top of Fry's head with the club. It made a sharp crack, and Fry crumpled beneath him without a sound.

Naylor sat astraddle the limp body. On hands and knees he looked up to see Wheeler, five feet away. The man had just managed to stop his rush and was yanking a pistol out of his belt with his good hand. Before he could fire, Indian Thompson's knife came out of the blackness above and buried itself between his shoulder blades.

Wheeler's face went blank, and he pitched forward heavily. The gun dropped from his hand as he fell, clattering sharply against the floor. Naylor rose, still gripping his club and ran for the door.

The innkeeper back-pedaled, gaping foolishly. "What the hell?" he shouted.

Naylor doubted if the man was one of Blackwell's gang and ran by him without answering. Ike and the captain were waiting outside, plastered against the wall. The eaves threw black shadows over them, hiding their figures from the man in the Tin Cup. Naylor stood against the wall and started speaking swiftly as Thompson joined them. "Ike, you get that man down toward Canal. Thompson, the one on the levee is yours. Abner, stay here and give us a warning if anything goes wrong. We'll meet on the levee in five minutes."

They all nodded and started moving. Naylor ducked

back inside. Fry and Wheeler were still sprawled on the floor. The innkeeper was behind the bar, pouring himself a drink. Death and brawling were an everyday occurrence along Tchoupitoulas, and, now that the man had gotten over his first surprise, he seemed indifferent to Wheeler's body. "I'll give you five minutes," he told Naylor. "Then I'm goin' to send somebody for the police."

Naylor found the back door and slipped into an alley. He ran through this, climbed a sagging fence, found himself in the stable yard of the Tin Cup. He crossed to the south wall of the building and slid down the moldy logs till he was at a front corner. He could see the Red Cock from here. Even though he knew Captain Abner was in front of the tavern, he could not see his figure in the lightless shadows beneath its eaves. Three feet beyond this corner was the doorway of the Tin Cup. He knew that the instant he stepped into the open, he would be seen by the man in that doorway. There was only one way to do it.

Chair leg gripped tightly, he wheeled onto Tchoupitoulas and went at a dead run for the door. The man only had time to stiffen in surprise, make a bleating sound, and then Naylor was on him. He struck the man across the side of the head so hard that the club broke apart in his hands. The man fell heavily against the door, sagged there for a moment, then began to slide down.

Dropping the broken club, Naylor started for the levee. He knew that Abner would see his running figure and follow. The levee was a parapet of earth, higher than the level of the town, standing like a wall between New Orleans and the river. He ran up its slope to the top, dodging in among the cotton bales. From here he could see the fire. Men were silhouetted against the glow like ants swarming over the levee. Someone was still ringing the alarm bell from the cathedral and a brass-mounted engine was being run across the square from the Dépôt des Pompes, hauled by a whole line of shouting firefighters. Naylor heard someone coming up the levee at a hard run and caught a glimpse of Heap's loose-jointed silhouette.

"Heap," he called softly.

The man slowed down, peered among the cotton bales, then he saw Naylor and joined him, panting and grinning. "That'll hold the police, all right. Looked like every constable in the Cabildo was trying to pull the engine."

"See Blackwell?" Naylor asked.

"On Saint Anne, trying t' git some keelers back here," Heap answered. "I guess he figgers what this could mean."

Thompson trotted in out of the darkness, hefting his club and grinning. "Big Nigrah. He'll have a sore head to-morrow."

Abner was looking toward Tchoupitoulas. "Where's Ike?"

"We can't wait," Naylor told him. He knew that one of the clubbed men was bound to regain consciousness and warn Blackwell. "Heap, go back down the levee a block. When Blackwell comes, let us know."

Naylor turned through the stacked cargo, piled higher than his head. He wended his way into a lane between bales of cotton and came out at the other end near the *Kentucky*'s gangplank. The constable aboard saw him approaching and walked to the bow of the boat.

Naylor stepped onto the gangplank. "Captain Naylor," he said, "coming aboard to get my papers."

The constable stepped up onto the narrow gangplank. "Sorry, Captain, nobody aboard. My orders."

The gangplank creaked and swayed beneath Naylor as he continued on down. The constable spread his legs and dropped a hand to the butt of a pistol in his belt. "Captain, I won't let you aboard."

Naylor knew he couldn't let the man cry out and give them away. He was but three feet from him now. He lunged at the man. The constable tried to jump back and draw his gun, but Naylor struck him before he could get off the gangplank, and it carried them both over the side. The constable hit shallow water spread-eagled. Naylor struck on top of him. Sputtering and spewing, the officer tried to lunge up beneath Naylor. As his head came out of the water, Naylor pulled his own pistol from his belt, caught the man's hair, and yanked his head to one side so he could hit him at the base of the neck. The constable stiffened, going limp. Naylor got to his feet in the muck, and dragged the unconscious man onto the slope of the levee so he wouldn't drown.

Already Captain Abner and Thompson were clattering across the gangplank onto the boat. Dripping mud and slime, Naylor climbed the levee. As he got back onto the plank, Ike came running down from above. He was panting gustily, and there was a bloody gash across his cheek. "Little trouble with that one," he said.

"Throw off all bowlines and stand ready to shove off," Naylor told him.

Leaving Ike to his watch, he ran on back to the waist. They'd had some wood in their cribs when they made the landing, and nobody had bothered to remove that. Thompson already had a fire going in the after box and was stoking hurriedly. Captain Abner had shed his coat and was sweating over the pump. Naylor ran to the forward firebox, threw open the door, and began to chop kindling. Then he got flint and steel and started his fire. The noise around the burning flatboat was like a distant surf in his ears. He was sweating heavily now, as he stoked the box, and soot began to gather in a shimmering black film on his face and arms.

With the fire blazing, he ran to the forecastle and fished out the half dozen keel poles they kept there for emergency. Captain Abner was still pumping water into the boiler.

"Keep it down!" Naylor called. "We want that steam."

"I got to give 'er a few inches or she'll blow us out of the water," the captain answered.

Naylor carried two poles forward. Ike was standing in the bow. He had hauled aboard the hawser, and only the thin line held them to the levee. Naylor dropped the poles in the scuppers on either side.

"If you see trouble, kick off the gangplank and yell," Naylor said. "We may have to pole 'er out yet."

He went back to his firebox, choking it with more wood. Captain Abner was off the pump and had started tinkering with his valves, ear cocked to the *clank* and *groan* of the heating boiler. "Talkin' to us now," he chortled. "Won't be long."

Naylor walked back to the bow, staring down the levee once more. The muscles of his back were stiff with tension. He wiped sweating palms on his pants, leaving long black streaks of soot.

Ike held onto the line, face strained as he glanced astern. "How much longer?"

"Abner's doin' his best."

Twice more Naylor went back to stock his box again. The boiler was beginning to glow now, its plates popping and snapping and spreading their seams. He lost count of the time. It might have been a few minutes; it might have been half an hour. It seemed like an eternity.

Then Heap appeared on the levee, calling to them: "Fry's back on his feet! Got past me on Tchoupitoulas!

Blackwell's already comin' back with him!"

"Come aboard!" Naylor shouted. "We're casting off!"

Heap clattered across the gangplank. There was no time to haul it aboard. Heap and Naylor shoved it off the bow, and the heavy plank splashed into the shallows. Naylor shouted for Thompson, and Ike cut his bowline. Thompson ran forward, and all four men picked twenty-foot keel poles out of the scuppers. Two to a side, they jammed iron-shod tips into the bottom, braced their shoulders against padded knobs, and bent forward.

"Down on 'em," Naylor grunted.

It was a tremendous task for only the four of them to move that boat. They were bent almost double against their poles, straining, gasping, clawing their way along the deck by inches. The blood pounded like a drum through Naylor's forehead with the strain; his eyes stood out in their sockets till he thought the pressure would pop them free like corks. But little by little, groaning like a man in pain, the boat slid backward. On either side of the *Kentucky* other boats were moored, a blunt-browed Indiaman on her port, an ocean-going brig on her larboard. The brig's gunwales towered ten feet above the steamboat's thwarts, and Naylor could see two men standing at the rail, apparently the brig's watch. They had been there since Naylor first boarded the *Kentucky*, taking note of everything. Perhaps they knew what was going on; perhaps it puzzled them. Either way, they had learned the wisdom of neutrality in this town.

"Push your guts out!" one of them called. "You'll get to English Turn in about four years."

The other guffawed. "Wouldn't you do better with a skiff, mate?"

The *Kentucky*'s bow was five feet from shore when the first shouting wave of keelers topped the levee, ran through the baled cotton and other cargo, and swarmed down the slope to the water. Three in the first ranks discharged pistols, but Naylor and his men were poor targets in the darkness, and the balls swept harmlessly past to bury themselves in the forecastle. Naylor heard Blackwell's stentorian bawl ring from the growing mass of figures on the steep levee. "Git into that brig and the Indiaman!"

The watch aboard the brig ran forward, yanking belaying pins from their sockets on the rail. They met the first boatman over the bow and started cracking heads, but more kept coming, by-passing the watch to run for the brig's waist. The binnacle light flared against the yellow mane of the man in the lead—Danny Blackwell. He had a pistol in one hand and reached up to catch the mizzen yards with the other. As Blackwell came up onto the rail directly above, Naylor snatched his pistol from his belt.

Blackwell saw the motion and had to fire while he was still pulling himself up by the yards. It threw his aim off, and the ball *whacked* into the gunwale by Naylor's feet. At the same instant Naylor's pistol bucked in his hand. He saw Blackwell jerk, lose his grip on the yards, and fall across the rail. For a moment he hung there, clutching his thigh. Blood pumped through his fingers, and Naylor could hear his guttural cursing.

"You bastard, you bastard . . . !"

As Blackwell rolled inboard off the rail, another pair of keelers jumped onto the yards. Naylor swept his twenty-foot pole upward in a vicious arc, knocking one of them off the yards and into the water between the boats. The other dropped off the brig onto the *Kentucky*. Landing on all fours, he started to rise and slip a knife from between his teeth. Before he could heave it at Naylor, Heap's pistol blasted from the port. The man stiffened, crying out in pain, and pitched head first into the water.

The steamboat was still sliding backward, and the men on the brig had to run back to the poop deck to keep up. There was another burst of fire. A slug hit the boiler and ricocheted, screaming wildly. Ike was hit, staggering heavily against the forecastle and slumping to the deck. Naylor saw a dim figure climbing onto the brig's taffrail and swung his pole up again. The man had to drop back on the poop deck to avoid being swept overboard.

Thompson and Heap were busy swinging their lethal poles at the keelers trying to drop off the Indiaman on the port side. One of the keelers dropped onto the *Kentucky* from the extreme stern of the Indiaman. Before Heap could turn, the man lunged at him with a knife.

Naylor ducked through the machinery in the waist, driving his pole like a spear at the man. It caught him in the small of the back just as he reached Heap. There was a sharp crack of bone. The keeler's arms flew up, and he was spread-eagled on the rail. Then he pitched off the boat.

All but their bowsprit was out from between the brig and the Indiaman now. Naylor sunk his pole deep and began crawling forward with Heap. A last man made a jump from the Indiaman. Thompson let him reach the deck, then swept him overboard with a full arm swing of his pole. Then they were out in the river.

Naylor saw a keel, sliding out from the *batture* upriver, loaded with keelers. "How's that steam, Captain?"

"Building up," Captain Abner answered. "Just a few minutes, Owen."

"Make it quick. They're starting to come by the boatload."

They kept driving, crawling like huge spiders, grunting and straining and fighting for every step, the sweat pouring off their faces and soaking their clothes. The first keel was bearing down on them now, and a second was pushing off the levee. Slowly, then more swiftly, the gap between the first keel and the steamboat was lessening. Naylor was reaching the top of his pole now. The water would soon be too deep for it. The first keel was coming swiftly, half the size of the *Kentucky*, propelled by a dozen men. She was fully underway now and was scooting down on the steamboat like a greyhound. The second keel was not far behind. Naylor knew there was deep water just ahead, but they could never reach it before they were overtaken. "Captain," he yelled, "we've got to have that steam!"

"You've got it, m'boy, you've got it . . . !"

There was the sudden shriek of the safety valve, the belching cloud of black smoke above the stack, the *clank* of gears and shafts. The whole boat shuddered. The wheel slapped the water. That first keel was only a hundred yards away. Gasping with exhaustion, Naylor drove with the last of his strength against his pole. He could hear Fry on the keel, bellowing at his men. "Down on 'em, you 'coons. Drive these poles through the bottom. Light a fire in your butts."

The space between them narrowed rapidly. Naylor saw Heap pull his pole free and run to the bow to fend off the boatmen on the keel. Naylor staggered after the man. He was so exhausted he fell to his knees once, sobbing for air before he reached the bow.

There couldn't have been over twenty feet separating the two boats now. The boatmen were hefting their poles in the bow of the keel, shouting and cursing at Naylor. Fry ran to the front of the cargo box, bawling his head off for that last spurt from the polers. Then the safety valve stopped shrieking, and Naylor knew the captain had tied it down.

For a moment there was no increase in the speed. Heap and Naylor straightened, tossing their poles high. Then the *Kentucky* shuddered as the wheel picked up a new tempo. With ten feet between the two boats, the *Kentucky* began pulling away.

"Down on 'em, you hosses!" the patroon bellowed. "One more pull, you bastards!"

Gasping with exhaustion, the boatmen heaved against their poles. For a moment they seemed to close the gap. Nine feet. Eight feet. Seven feet. With the boatmen swinging their poles in savage expectancy. With the crew working right off the top of their poles in the deep water. Then the space stopped narrowing. The keelboat seemed to cease moving.

In water too deep to work, the keelers pulled their poles up, most of them sinking to their knees in exhaustion on the cleated runway. Fry let out a mighty curse and turned to look at the receding *Kentucky*. Naylor's legs felt like water, and he dropped to his own knees, utterly drained, unable to think or move. Wheel shuddering, smokestack belching, the steamboat backed on into the river.

Captain Abner stepped from his engine guards, a torn piece of his coat wound about one burned hand. "Can I untie the safety valve now?" he asked. "She'll blow her head off with any more pressure."

Slowly, nauseated with exhaustion, Naylor got to his feet. "It's all right, Captain," he said. "We're free." He turned to Heap, an exultant grin slowly filling his face. "Let's take her up the river."

Chapter Twenty-Seven

Charlotte was hardly fit to live with that next week. For days she seethed with her rage at Naylor for taking the matter into his own hands. The court ruled that the Reynaud-Naylor Steamboat Company was in contempt of court, that they had lost the seizure case by default due to Naylor's actions, and that all officers of the company were liable to a fine of two thousand dollars and a year's imprisonment. Thibodaux countered by quoting the marine law that held an owner not responsible for a master's wrongful acts done outside the scope of his office. Since the boat was seized, Thibodaux claimed that Naylor legally had no right aboard and was thus not acting in his capacity as master. It was a technicality, but Charlotte's warning to the police that night swayed the court in her favor, and she was not jailed.

At the end of the week they heard that the *Kentucky* had reached Natchez and had taken on a cargo. Beyond that there was no word. They knew the steamboat must be in the earthquake area now. Keels were putting into New Orleans every day with reports of new temblors shaking the land. None of them was equaling the December 16th cataclysm, which was becoming known as the New Madrid earthquake. Since its center had occurred in such a vast and uninhabited territory, the full extent of its destruction was still unknown. Many authorities, however, were already claiming it to be the worst quake that had ever shaken the continent. Into this region the *Kentucky* had disappeared.

They heard about Blackwell that first week, too. He had been shot in the thigh by Naylor and was lying in the back room of the Tin Cup, fighting for his life.

With the days wearing on, and no word coming, Charlotte struggled to build the beginnings of a new life in New Orleans. Among the elite of the Creoles in town, she met the same attitude she had found in Natchez. It was something Charlotte had expected. Even Louis seemed resigned to it. If he'd had money, he might have gained *entrée* into the strictly male circle of Creoles, but they were counting their pennies. Louis finally drifted into the group that gathered at the Cafés des Refuges. This was a different class of Creoles than the *chacalatas* whose families had founded New Orleans. Although still proud and haughty, contemptuous of Americans and fiercely loyal to the Bourbons, the experiences of the Santo Domingans in the revolution on their island and their present necessity to earn their living in any way they could gave them a more Bohemian outlook, relaxing the caste system that ruled the lives of the New Orleans Creoles. Thus, for a time, Louis found acceptance in their circle, falling back into his old habits, haunting the cafés and billiard parlors around the Place d'Armes in the company of the young Santo Domingans.

February waned into March, and household expenses and Thibodaux's fees were eating deeply into the few hundred dollars Charlotte had left. She was on the edge of despair when, on March 27th, an agent of Cambre's put in from Natchez. He said the *Kentucky* was there; she had steamed up to Louisville in a record-breaking twenty-two days, depositing her cargo and returning immediately in less than two weeks. It was a history-making trip, even more significant than their epochal downriver voyage, for this—the ability to go upriver, to stem the current of the mighty Mississippi—was the final test. It was conclusive proof of steam's practicability. Yet the bottom was taken from their triumph by Naylor's hand-printed letter.

Natchez
Mar 20, 1812

Dear Charlot and Loois.

Reached Natchez Feb 9 after braking free in N. Orleans. Litle Ike killd in fite with Blackwel & we all morn him. Cambre rong about N's cargo at Natchez. N wood only give us 20 tons cofee & few teerces Tanners oil as sort of test. Getting his cotton downriver still didn't proov we cood do it up.

Same in Looeyvil. Evrybudy afrayd 2 try this newfangled contrapshun. Only 2 passengers & 40 tons salt for down trip. Think Swayn & Lgstn. hav put preshur on at Natchez. Nobody will yet trust steem. Enclsd. is bill of layding for up & down trips, list of Xpnses & insurance bill.

Your 60% of net sent with Cambre's agnt. Pay him 5% comishun.

Owen

After paying Cambre, Charlotte's share amounted to less than three hundred dollars. It was a bitter disappointment to her. Cambre was apologetic for Nassaur's change of heart, but he agreed with Naylor. Much of the failure was undoubtedly due to pressure brought to bear by the monopoly. Both Swain and Livingston had powerful friends in Natchez, and those that couldn't be persuaded through friendship could be bought off. The combination of this and the natural fear and mistrust of such a new idea were defeating them on every hand. It brought Charlotte close to that desperation she had known when they had faced ruin in Natchez.

Louis didn't help. It came to a head one morning shortly after Naylor's letter, while Louis was dressing. The single new suit he'd been able to buy on their arrival was growing worn and shabby from constant use. Finishing with his cravat, he put his hands into his pockets, and she knew he was hunting for money. He took them out again, empty. His handsome young face flushed irritably.

"Haven't you handled the purse strings long enough?" he asked. "My friends know I come to you for every cent I spend. I can see the smirk on their faces every time I buy a drink. I'm tired of being treated like a kept man, like a child. . . ."

"Then why don't you stop acting like one," she said. She saw the surprise on his face and went on thinly: "I know you've been brought up in a different world than I have, Louis. It's probably never entered your head to get a job, but if we don't get some money soon, we'll be out on the streets. If you go on playing the gentleman much longer, your daughter will be starving to death."

She saw his face go pale, his shoulders pull together. She had used it deliberately, knowing it was one of the few things left with which she could reach him. They had lost so much these last years. She sometimes thought his love for Denise was greater than his love for her. He looked down at the baby, playing on the floor. Her black curls peeked from a pink bonnet; her cheeks were round as apples, and her little hands were doll-like in their chubbiness.

Charlotte saw a muscle twitch in Louis's cheek. He looked at her with miserable eyes. "What can I do?"

It was so typical of him. Would he always be so helpless?

Charlotte turned away to hide her anger, trying to keep it from her voice. "You might try Cambre. He has a lot of connections."

So he tried Cambre, and the man finally found him a clerk's position, paying eight dollars a week, in one of the Creole commission houses along the Toulouse. He had to deal with the Kentucky boatmen, and on the second day he took offense at something a patroon said, slapped his face, and demanded satisfaction. The man knocked him down and took his business elsewhere. Louis was fired. Cambre got him another job, and again Louis's instability and pride and hot temper caused him to lose it within a week. By wheedling and cajoling and using Denise against him, Charlotte finally got him to look for a job himself. He went to make the rounds of the business houses on Toulouse.

It was the middle of April, and the warm weather was already coming to New Orleans. Charlotte had taken a chair out onto the iron balcony overlooking Chartres. Dusk shrouded the street below; the lanterns had already been lit. In the treacherous pools of light they cast, she saw Louis's familiar figure coming down the *banquette* from the square. His clothes were rumpled, and his face had a loose, wild look to it that told her how drunk he was. Instead of coming to the apartment, he turned into the Cafés des Refuges. She knew what it meant. It deepened the sense of desperation in her. There had always been a way out before. Now she seemed to face a blind alley.

A few days later a packet came from Natchez with word that Naylor had been forced to leave the week before with only a few tons of cargo. Charlotte knew their money would run out before he returned. She spent a sleepless night trying to see her way clear. She thought of selling their share in the boat. It stirred angry rebellion in her. She couldn't submit so completely to defeat; it was the boat they were still fighting for, as much as anything else. She had too much faith in it to give up yet. And who would buy now? If the public wouldn't ship, they certainly wouldn't put money into it. She could finally reach but one valid conclusion. It was grasping at straws, a last possibility. She had to find the shippers herself.

The next day she went to Cambre. Despite his failure in closing the Nassaur contract for them, she knew he was acquainted with all the important shippers in New Orleans. He dubiously gave her a list, and she started her calls. It was bitterly discouraging. Meeting them, Americans and Creoles, she got an idea of what Naylor had been up against in Natchez. Some openly ridiculed steam; others evaded and quibbled; still others simply said no. She got so she could tell which of them were acting under their own convictions, which were being influenced by the Livingston-Fulton faction in town. Either way, when she reached the end of the list, she had to admit complete failure.

Then, just as an off chance, Cambre mentioned that Harold Warwick was in town. With the war spirit reaching a fevered pitch along the river and sentiment growing against the Tories, Warwick was having a hard time finding bottoms for his cargoes. It put the germ of the plan in Charlotte's mind. She realized what a gamble it would be, but it was a gamble based on her judgment of Warwick as she had known him in Natchez. If she didn't take it, they could only last a few more weeks.

Cambre told her Warwick was staying at an apartment on St. Anne, one block from the Place d'Armes, and it was his habit to rise and breakfast on the square about ten. Thus Charlotte managed to be shopping in the Place d'Armes that next morning when the man came to Dupre's coffee shop. It must have seemed an entirely accidental meeting to him. His narrow face showed a momentary pleasure, then stiffened into a pale wariness. He gravely tipped his broad-brimmed planter's hat. She gave him a dazzling smile.

"You'll have to visit us, while you're in town, Mister Warwick," she said. She saw his surprise. Her smile widened. "You are thinking of that unfortunate party in Natchez. Admit it. You had a morbid curiosity. Like Hannah Maddox, you came to gawk at the wanton Louis had found in Natchez-Under."

There was no bitterness in her voice, only irony, and it took him off guard. He nodded. "You strike me true, *madame*. I have regretted it since."

"You shouldn't," she said. "I think that in your place I should have done the same thing." He looked up, surprised again. Then she laughed, an infectious little chuckle, and he couldn't help joining in. "Now," she said, "tell me the truth. Don't you Tories find it rather lonely in this place, with all the sentiment against the British?"

"Why do people always try to pigeonhole a man's politics?" he asked. "My uncle fought with Washington at Valley Forge."

"And your brother is a captain with Wellington," she said. "It isn't your politics I'm interested in. But if you'd like some stimulating company, why don't you visit our apartment this Saturday evening. We're having some of our Santo Domingan friends in after the theater. You'll find that most of them are royalists and hate Napoléon. And since England is fighting Napoléon, they look upon her as an ally." She saw the wariness leave his face, and she gave him a rueful smile. "And I promise you, Mister Warwick, this time there will be no uninvited guests from Natchez-Under."

Louis was incredulous when she told him. Such an affair would take most of their remaining money. She was past arguing with him much, or even explaining. The money was in her possession, and she would use it as she saw fit. For his part, would he please choose carefully a dozen of his friends from the Cafés des Refuges?

Angelique haunted the market for days, getting a recipe from Choctaw Indians for gumbo, picking over the venison and the wild hog and the canvasback brought in from Lake Pontchartrain by the Cajun hunters. Charlotte helped her in the kitchen, concocting the traditional flavors for the ladies—weaving orange peel into dainty baskets, dipping it in boiling syrup, setting it aside to harden, afterward filling the baskets with bonbons and nougats and pralines. The day before the party the kitchen was steeped in the juicy odors of wild hog and papabotes and chickens turning on their spits in the brick fireplace. In the smaller pots on the trivets, the *roux* and the gravies and the gumbo simmered. Louis made three trips to the wine shops on Poydras for the cobwebbed bottles of Madeira and Amontillado and Jamaica rum. The silver epergnes in the parlor were filled to overflowing with flowers Charlotte bought in the Place d'Armes. Angelique was flushed with excitement, declaring that Charlotte would shame the cotillions Gaspar Reynaud had given in the old days.

On the evening of April 15th, they came. Titi Montiasse, the famed fencing master from Exchange Alley; Pierre Labatte, who had once owned a thousand slaves and who now had but one coat to his back; the Marquise de Varenne, who had been the richest woman on Santo Domingo and was now a *modiste* on Chartres Street; a score more, all who had once been rich, famous, titled. They were a gay and brilliant crowd and were admirably suited to

331

Warwick's taste. It was the marquise who had made Charlotte's gown, a gossamer satin robe of French gray. A square carnelian brooch rode the exposed swell of her breasts, and the flesh of her arms, above the long kid gloves *à la mousquetaire,* shone snow white in the soft light of a hundred candles.

Charlotte had hired four violinists from the St. Philip Theater Orchestra, and after dinner the parlor was cleared for dancing. Louis was on the balcony, drinking and smoking with Montiasse, and Warwick gallantly asked Charlotte for the first dance. As he held her in his arms, swinging her around to the measured paces of a *contredanse,* she saw the flush slowly rise in his face.

"Madame," he murmured, "you might tell your husband how dangerous it is to let anyone but himself dance with such a ravishing creature."

Her smile held provocation and a promise. "The town must be getting under your skin, Mister Warwick. You were never so gallant in Natchez."

"I feel even more remorseful for my unforgivable actions that evening," he said. They swung around, and he glanced at the handsome silver epergnes, filled with flowers, the glittering cut glass on the sideboards, the expensive wines on the table. "Swain must be misinforming me," he said. "He told me you hadn't made a cent out of the *Kentucky.*"

She smiled enigmatically. "He has reason to misinform you."

"But I was in Natchez when your boat left this last time. Naylor hardly had ten tons of cargo."

"There are a hundred more towns on the upper river," she said. "If the shippers at Natchez are afraid to trust steam, it is not we who suffer. But somebody in Natchez loses six thousand dollars every time the *Kentucky* goes upriver."

"Loses?"

"You pay a hundred dollars a ton to ship by keel, don't you? We charge sixty. The *Kentucky* carried a hundred and fifty tons. That's a difference of exactly six thousand dollars."

She saw that she had struck home. Over their *café diabolique* he admitted that Swain's advice had kept him from seeing it in those terms. The exorbitant insurance rates and the failure of the *New Orleans* had made him afraid of steam. He had a cargo of Jamaica coffee rotting in a Natchez warehouse right now for want of a boat. It was one of the reasons for his trip to New Orleans. Charlotte could see that he was on the hook, but she knew she could not press him. Indifference was her bait.

Two days later Warwick was along with a small group of Santo Domingans who attended the St. Philip Theater with the Reynauds. He invited Charlotte and Louis to drive with him the next afternoon to Lake St. Charles, but Louis quarreled with Charlotte about money the next day and left the house. Boldly Charlotte went alone with Warwick. His interest was obvious now. He was no doubt weighing the possibilities of shipping on the *Kentucky*, but the prime attraction was Charlotte. He had undoubtedly heard from the Creoles how strained the relationship was between Charlotte and Louis and had drawn his own conclusions. She was surprised how deliberately she could use this. Although she felt little attraction for the man, she kept leading him on. She had learned the art of conversational fencing from Swain. Whenever Warwick turned the discussion to her, she turned it back to the boat. The first impression of the *Kentucky*'s success that she had planted in his mind at the sumptuous dinner party was taking its effect.

Then, in June, Warwick got news about the last keel he had sent north. Strangely enough, it concerned Blackwell. The wound Naylor had given the man had finally healed, but his leg would never be the same. Blackwell had hobbled around New Orleans, seeking a keel, but no owners would hire a cripple. He had finally managed to get to Natchez, approaching Warwick, who even then was hard put to find bottoms for his cargoes. Blackwell had handled many boats for him, and Warwick agreed to give him a chance. But the leg was still causing Blackwell pain, and he'd been drinking heavily to ease it. Now the news reached Warwick that Blackwell had been drunk all the way upriver and had finally run the keel on the rocks at Big Chain, losing every pound of cargo.

"It's the last straw," Warwick said. "You've convinced me that steam is the only way, Charlotte. If you can profit so handsomely from it, so can I. I'm willing to give you a contract to ship a hundred tons of coffee I've got in my Natchez warehouses."

For a moment Charlotte felt distinctly giddy. If Warwick only knew how close it had been. Her handsome profits on steam amounted to exactly twenty dollars left between them and starvation. But then she recovered herself and persuaded Warwick to advance them ten percent of the freight charges, and send the contract with Cambre to Natchez. When Naylor put in there in July, he had a cargo for his boat. That trip netted them almost five thousand dollars.

Charlotte began entertaining on a more lavish scale. The Reynaud apartment soon became the center for the social outcasts of the city—the Natchez Tories, the Santo Domingan refugees, the American businessmen who could not break through the wall of Creole hostility, even some of the picaresque smugglers from Barataria, among them the colorful Jean Lafitte who attended several *soirées* at the apartment. During the worst of summer half the town seemed to flee the heat, taking packets to the cooler bluffs of Natchez or the fashionable resorts on the lake, but Charlotte remained in town, patiently cultivating the shippers and commission men and whoever she thought could help her.

It was during this time that they heard President Madison had presented his war message to Congress. The reasons cited were violations of the flag on the high seas, confiscation of ships, illegal impressments of United States seamen, blockade of our shores, the obnoxious Orders in Council, and inciting the Indians against our borders. It caused a great flurry in New Orleans. Many of the Creoles, with their Bourbon sympathies, were against any war. Warwick thought it was stupid. England, he claimed, didn't want war. They were already staggering under a public debt of a billion pounds incurred by fighting Napoléon. If Madison had a minister in England, he would know that the British merchants were against it, were clamoring for a re-opening of trade. Give the ministry a little time and they would re-open the Orders in Council.

Charlotte's reaction was a confused one. Her political allegiances were vague. She had previously lived in New Orleans variously under three different flags; the town had belonged to the United States only nine years now. She knew she didn't want war, but she had little understanding of what it would mean to them.

A few days later, still early in July, Warwick invited her out to meet an American shipper who had a cargo of sugar and rum. They were to see the man at seven in the evening, at a little café just off the Place d'Armes. Warwick and

Charlotte took a table from which they could see the swirl of color and noise that always filled the square at this hour. Past the flaring torches of the coffee stands flowed an endless crowd of blanketed Choctaws and garlanded Creoles, trappers in buckskin and red-shirted flat boatmen, pigtailed mariners, and laughing mulatto girls. They had just gotten their coffee when Charlotte saw the familiar figure of Kenneth Swain in the crowd. He wound his way through the babble with the easy grace, the unconscious balance of the inveterate swordsman. An octoroon at one of the fruit stands said something to him. He tipped his hat, smiling ironically.

"Swain," Warwick said ruefully. "I think he knows every woman in New Orleans."

Passing the door, Swain caught sight of them. He paused, smiling wryly at the stiff hostility in Charlotte's face. Then he entered the café, bowing gallantly before her.

"As Poor Richard said . . . 'Love your enemies, for they tell you your faults'."

"Your fault is in your misjudgment of a woman, my friend," Warwick told him.

"And you have turned on me and taken unto the enemy," Swain chided him.

Warwick held his hands out helplessly. "I've got to get my cargoes north. If your boat won't do it, some other must."

Swain winced. "Don't rub it in." He had been watching Charlotte all the time. "Are we still bitter?" he asked.

"That would be small, wouldn't it?" she said.

"And you are anything but that," he told her. "I'm surprised you'd be out tonight, with Blackwell so close."

She frowned. "The last I heard he was in Louisville."

"It's a sad story," Swain said. "The insurance companies

wouldn't underwrite any boat he commanded up there. He couldn't get a keel. Couldn't even take a pole on a downriver boat, with that leg. As I understand it, he finally joined Commodore Nash and his shipweckers at Cave-in-Rock. Their crimes grew so heinous that the militia broke them up, and Blackwell had to flee the state. He's down here again. I saw him on Tchoupitoulas, drunk as sin, throwing Planter's Bank notes right and left. It's my guess there's a boatmen's riot building down there."

Concern darkened Warwick's eyes. "Then it *is* dangerous for you to be so close," he told Charlotte. "Blackwell blames Naylor for all this, you know. He's vowed to kill him. And he identifies you very closely with Naylor. . . ."

He broke off, as the new sound blended with the babble of the square. It came first like the subdued roar of a distant surf, seeming to center at the levee. One by one Charlotte saw the diners turn to look, frowning, questioning. Then, somewhere far off, a woman screamed. It cut through all the other sounds—even the unidentifiable roar—bright as a knife blade flashing in the sun. The tinkle of glassware and babble of questioning voices in the café ceased abruptly. The scream wavered pitifully and fell back into rougher sound and died in it.

Charlotte stood suddenly. For she recognized that roar. She had heard it before too often at Point Coupée, at Baton Rouge, at Natchez-Under. A sick apprehension ran through her. "It's the boatmen," she said.

She saw the blood drain from Warwick's face. He rose, catching her arm. "We'd better get out. . . ."

There was a general rush toward the front door, as others realized what it was, and Charlotte and Warwick were caught up in it. Charlotte knew the immense destructiveness of these boatmen when they went on a rampage.

She had seen them completely destroy Tunica Village. It was one of the scourges of the river. With their brutal, volatile natures, they were like a keg of dynamite with an exposed fuse. Anything could set them off—a woman who refused their advances, a fight among themselves on the levee, a drunken suggestion in a tavern—and it would sweep like wildfire through the waterfront, gathering them by the hundreds.

As she reached the door with Warwick, she caught sight of them—a wild mob, sweeping across the square from the river, red-shirted, black-booted, cursing, laughing, crazy drunk, driving everything before them. A gang of them ran against one of the coffee stands. It collapsed before their rush, torches falling to the ground, the mulatto owner squealing like a stuck pig. At the same time, across the square, a tavernkeeper tried to slam shut the door of his dingy building. A trio of men rushed against it, ramming it open. They grabbed the tavernkeeper and turned him out into the mob, where he was thrown back and forth among them as they tore off his clothes. He stumbled free, pants dragging from naked shanks, and ran wildly toward Chartres.

Then, in the lead on the side of the square nearest the café, Charlotte saw Blackwell, the beaver cap with the red feather in it hanging far back on his head, the long blond hair, burnt so many taffy shades by the sun, the primitive face, wild and flushed with drink. He moved in a hobbling run at the head of the mob, dragging his left leg with each step. Bits of his drunken bawling broke through the roar of the other boatmen.

"Here to celeybrate the war, damn you . . . ! This is me and no mistake . . . ! Ring-tailed roarer, Salt River squealer . . . fearsome critter that walks like a 'gator, swims like an eel, and makes love like a mad bull . . . git my hands on a woman or 'll spile rotten as hog side . . . !"

The jam of diners blocked the door. Warwick released Charlotte's elbow, trying to fight his way through. The boatmen were within a hundred yards of the café now, shouting, wrecking, brawling. Panic swept the crowd within the café while their struggles to break through a door separated Charlotte from Warwick. She lost sight of him, stumbling backward, almost falling over an upset chair. Then someone caught her elbow. She turned to see Swain's face, pale and calm as ice.

"Shall we assay the rear?"

"What about Warwick?" She looked helplessly through the struggling crowd, unable to see him.

"He can take care of himself," Swain said. She glanced at Blackwell, only a short distance from the door now. Swain saw the look. He had to shout to be heard above the tumult. "You have but an instant, Charlotte. It would be disastrous to let Blackwell catch you here."

She sent a last frantic look into the crowd for Warwick, then answered the pressure of Swain's hand. The rear door opened onto an alleyway that led to Chartres Street. There was no sign of the boatmen here, but the street was choked with people, fleeing the riot. Swain hailed a passing hack, and the driver pulled up, holding his prancing, frothing horses while Swain helped Charlotte in. As the door swung shut, the coach lunged ahead, jarring Charlotte back against the seat. They rocked and clattered through the streets, turning off Chartes into Toulouse. Charlotte settled back, as the coach slowed down, with the sounds of the riot fading behind.

"They'll probably have to call out the militia to quell that one," Swain said.

She saw that he was studying her quizzically. One of the street lanterns splashed light through a window as they passed. For a moment the edges of his hair made a brazen glitter beneath his hat brim. Then the light was gone, leaving his face statue-pale in the shadows. The remembered handsomeness was there, the bold cynicism.

"Humble pie, Swain," she said. "I must thank you."

He moved closer. "Don't you wish . . . sometimes . . . that it could be as it was?"

She was surprised that she could feel no hostility toward him now. He had touched something in her. She felt a genuine wish for the carefree gaiety his old badinage had brought. "You were a valued friend, Kenneth."

"And could be again." He bent toward her, the faint and pleasant odor of him, an intensely male blend of fine leather and expensive whisky and Cuban tobacco. "Perhaps this isn't the time to speak, Charlotte. But I must take advantage of the opportunity. Livingston has authorized me to make you an offer. For your half of the *Kentucky*, we will pay you twenty thousand dollars in cash, and give you a ten percent share in the corporation."

She settled back, breathless with surprise. She had learned enough about marine law to see how this sale would give the monopoly a virtual control of the *Kentucky*. The law looked upon the employment of a ship as a matter of public concern; in a question of employment or non-employment, the courts would always decide in favor of the former. Thus, Naylor could not block the Fulton combine by refusing to carry their cargo. He would be in their power, and the success of the *Kentucky* would make up for the failure of the *New Orleans*, would give Fulton and Livingston a boat to secure the monopoly and complete their domination of the river. Yet it signified something else to her. She remembered Swain's duplicities and was wary. "Is the monopoly admitting defeat, Kenneth?"

"Hardly. I'm sure you have a perfect gauge of what this means, so I can be frank with you. We admit that the *Kentucky* being free on the upper river, doing what the *New Orleans* couldn't do, has been a blow. But it is in no way a defeat, Charlotte. Plying only between New Orleans and Natchez, our boat looks to net fifty percent on the original investment in this first year alone. We have plans for building another boat immediately. The monopoly is still in effect. Sooner or later we will defeat you. We're simply offering you the easy way out . . . for both of us."

For a moment—remembering all of Naylor's antagonisms, remembering how he had fought her every foot of the way, how he had ignored her wishes at every turn—she felt an insidious temptation.

Swain continued. "You seem to have triumphed temporarily, with Warwick and his cronies. But you know how precarious the whole thing is. What if the war starts? Anybody trafficking with Tories then would be next to a traitor. The British would blockade this coast so tight not even Jean Lafitte could smuggle you in a cargo. Your whole business would collapse."

She knew he was right. She remembered her miserable desperation when there had been no cargoes for the *Kentucky*, when they had faced complete defeat. With the *Kentucky* operated by the monopoly, all that would be obviated. Anybody owning ten percent of the corporation would be fixed for life. In a single stroke, she would have what she had fought for so long. Perhaps Swain sensed her weakening. A change came to his face. It was one of the few times she had seen it so devoid of its irony, its mocking cynicism. It gave him a strangely young and vulnerable look.

"Charlotte," he said, "I've waited years for this moment. I would have spoken long ago, but I understood you too well. A man couldn't come to you with empty hands. Now I can offer you what you want. Sell your half. Between us we'll have twenty percent of the monopoly. We can go anywhere in the world . . . New York, Paris, London. You don't know what living is, Charlotte. This is a squalid hamlet in comparison. You've wanted escape from Silver Street. I give it to you now. . . ."

She looked at him in complete surprise. He covered her hand with his. A tingle ran through her body. His eyes were shining.

"What you had with Louis is over now. You may have thought you loved him once. But I've seen what's happened to you in these last years. Your marriage is beyond salvaging, and you know it. He isn't enough for you, Charlotte, never was. You need someone who can satisfy your depths, your fires, your every need. . . ."

Somehow his voice, trembling with excitement, took her back to Louis and those first wild promises he had made in the illusory romance of their courtship. She pulled back, looking into his narrow face, her own excitement fading. The mockery, the cynicism, the sense of past tragedy, the fabulous rumors of his origins—all had served to surround Swain with an aura of mystery and romance. He had always intrigued her; their relationship had filled her with a sense of standing on the brink of something exciting, dangerous, forbidden. But now the illusion was shattered. He stood revealed to her, a man no different than a hundred others she had known, with all their fears, their desires, their ambitions, petty or grandiose. With the intrigue gone, there was something cheap and tawdry about sitting in the shrouded coach, pressed against the musty plush by his body, looking into his taut, excited face. It brought into focus the betrayal he offered. Naylor had fought, too, and Captain Abner, and all the others. She would be sacrificing their dreams, in attaining her own.

"Swain," she said, "we've reached the apartment."

His eyes were blank a moment. He slowly drew his body away, looking at her. His lips compressed till the grooves lay like knife wounds at their tips. Then the defensive armor of cynicism returned to his face. "Would you have liked me better, had I remained the lost Dauphin?"

She moistened her lips. Her voice was barely audible. "Yes, Swain," she said.

He bowed his head till his face was hidden from her. *"Madame,"* he said. He remained that way a moment, then turned to climb out of the coach.

She allowed him to help her down. They could still hear the sounds of the riot, but it did not come in the steady, surf-like roar now, and Charlotte knew it was being broken up. A troop of mounted militia passed them at a gallop, heading toward the Place d'Armes. Swain saw her to the vestibule. He removed his hat.

"At least consider my first offer," he said.

She glanced at him. A sense of guilt hung between them. His revelation had left them both vaguely embarrassed. She nodded. "I will."

He looked into her eyes a moment, then he turned and went back to the coach. She walked slowly upstairs, still a little shaken by the devastating glimpse of a man who had always been such a mystery to her.

Louis was in the sitting room, at the open window. She knew he had seen Swain bring her home. There was a single lamp burning. His clothes were rumpled, and his face was puffy and sullen. When he turned at her entrance, he swayed a little, and had to touch a silver epergne by the window for support. "You should warn me when you mean to return with your gentlemen friends," he sneered. "I would contrive not to be in evidence."

Reaction to the riot had left her nervous, in no mood to argue with him. "You know what's going on," she said. "You know exactly why I've had to do this. Why are you home so early, anyway? Are your Santo Domingo friends getting tired of a kept man, too?"

His face drained of blood. He stared at her with eyes like holes burned in a blanket. His arm twitched, and for a moment she thought he would hit her. Then he turned and stalked for the door. He bumped into a marquetry table and knocked it over, almost falling. He lurched against the mantel, mumbling a curse, and then stumbled across the room and out. She stood a moment without moving, sick with anger and humiliation. Then she shut the door, dropped her carrick on a chair, walked dismally to a window. A year ago, six months ago, he would have broken down, would have apologized, would have been a little boy again, in such desperate need of her help and strength. Was Swain right? Was Louis beyond salvaging now?

She had clung to the hope that somehow, when the *Kentucky* began paying off, when they had begun to live like normal people again, Louis could regain what he had lost. But somehow the money wasn't the complete answer, for either of them. She glanced around the room. It was the same Chartres Street apartment, but they had furnished it more sumptuously, as befitted their growing station. Charlotte's efforts at cultivating Santo Domingans had done more than get cargo for the *Kentucky*. It had created for her a circle of vivid, cultured, stimulating friends such as she had never known before. No matter what was happening to the foundations of her marriage, on the surface at least it was treated with respect. All this—the respectability, the identity at last with a group of decent people, the dignity of marriage—represented the sum of what she had sought for so long. In every respect she had at last wrought for herself a way of life she had dreamed of down in Natchez-Under.

Chapter Twenty-Eight

In the second week of July, 1812, New Orleans learned that war had been declared by Congress. The excitement in the town was intense. But, aside from the uprising of the Creeks along the Tombigbee and an immediate blockade of the whole Gulf Coast by the British, there was no military movement against New Orleans itself. As the ferment died down, a feeling grew that the main operations would be confined to the Canadian border.

This was agreeable to Kenneth Swain, who took a cynical view of the war. His main concern was with Charlotte. Her rejection of him had been a blow, but he was convinced that he had merely timed it wrong, had been mistaken in making acceptance of him so contingent upon her relinquishing the *Kentucky*. She was not yet ready to give up the boat. It was Silver Street, standing between them once more, making her reject the rapport which he was certain still remained between them. Only when she was on her knees would she come to him. He had waited this long; he could wait a little longer.

In the middle of July came a story that took the war news off the front page for a day. Some Choctaws, fishing in a bayou south of Natchez, had found the corpse of Colonel Benjamin Seeley, one of the first territorial delegates to Mississippi. He had left New Orleans two weeks before with his annual cotton money, five thousand dollars in Planter's Bank notes. It branded Danny Blackwell. For it was known that Blackwell had come down the Trace about the same time Seeley had left New Orleans. A few days after Seeley's disappearance, Blackwell had fomented the riot, leaving hundreds of Planter's Bank notes in the wake of his drunken frolic on Tchoupitoulas Street. Governor Claiborne put a price on Blackwell's head, but Blackwell had disappeared from the waterfront.

After the furor died down, the rest of Swain's year was taken up with Thibodaux's suit against the monopoly. He and Livingston worked mightily for postponement of the case till the second Fulton boat, the *Vesuvius*, should be finished in Pittsburgh.

The year 1813 came with the war news good and bad. General Hampton met ignominious defeat in Montreal, and Wilkinson's planned invasion of Canada fell through. Owen Naylor stayed with the *Kentucky*, carrying supplies to St. Louis in connection with the efforts being made to plant a string of forts along the upper Mississippi. With the British blockade cutting shipping to nothing in New Orleans, these government contracts were the only thing that kept Charlotte and Louis alive.

Then the *Vesuvius* was launched, arriving in New Orleans on May 16th. To Swain's disgust, she was hardly different than the *New Orleans*—a deep-draft boat with an upright Boulton-Watt-type engine in her hold. Amid much fanfare, she loaded on freight and passengers and left on her upriver voyage in July. They got word she had passed Natchez, and Livingston expressed high hopes that at last they had a boat to beat Owen Naylor. Shortly afterward, those hopes were shattered by a double blow. On July 14th, the *New Orleans* ran on a snag two miles below Baton Rouge and was sunk. A few weeks later they got the news that the *Vesuvius* had run aground on a bar four hundred miles north of Natchez and could not be gotten off.

It was not much of a surprise to Swain. It only convinced him more than ever that the true key to the problem lay not only in defeating Naylor but in obtaining the *Kentucky*. To this end, he had been watching Louis Reynaud carefully. Although everything was in Charlotte's name, Swain still felt that Louis was the weakest link in her armor. Livingston had mentioned loopholes in the Code Napoléon that might be used against the Reynaud-Naylor Steamboat Company, if Louis's name appeared on any of the documents or contracts, or there could be such a thing as a letter from Louis, luring Naylor back to New Orleans.

Swain knew the Creole psychology to be a precariously balanced thing at best. Louis's disintegration had started with his marriage. His weakness had forced Charlotte to dominate, and that domination had sucked the manhood from him in a dozen insidious ways. Being cut off so completely from the life he had known only hurried the process.

In the summer of 1814, Swain heard that the young man was being seen less and less at Charlotte's glittering *soirées*, had ceased to haunt the Cafés des Refuges. All the Santo Domingans knew that Louis was little more than a kept man, and the condescension and patronization implicit in such a situation had apparently corroded his pride till he could no longer face it. Early in October, Dominique reported to Swain that Louis was now frequenting a deadfall on Tchoupitoulas Street called the Tin Cup. Swain decided it was time to make his move.

On the evening of October 5th, he and Dominique took a hack to the waterfront north of the Vieux Carré. The Tin Cup was a miserable barrel house that angled out toward the levee. Leaving Dominique by the coach, Swain entered the dingy taproom, swimming with its foul stench. The bar was merely a pair of flatboat gunwales placed across two barrels. At one end a pair of keelers were mauling a pock-marked jade. Farther back in a corner, Louis Reynaud and a woman sat at one of the round tables. Reynaud had his elbows on the table, leaning slackly against them. His eyes were blank, glazed, bloodshot. Beneath the clay-blue stain of his beard, the flesh of his puffy jowls had an unhealthy color. It took Swain a moment to recognize the woman as Sanite Dede. It came as a distinct surprise to him. In her middle thirties, this free woman of color who had been the Reynaud housekeeper seemed ageless. Her face was still smooth and unlined as stained ivory; the shape of her body beneath the simple calico was as firm and slim as a girl's. Swain could understand why Louis had come here. Sanite Dede was the only thing left of his old life—a symbol of the security and protection and happiness he had known. It was his return to the womb.

Swain walked to the table. The woman had cat eyes, shining in the gloom. Their unwinking stare had always disturbed him. She did not speak, but Louis became aware of Swain and raised his head. He had trouble focusing his eyes. Then he stiffened in his chair, rage making his face ugly.

Swain smiled, pulled out a chair. "Haven't you learned who your friends are yet?"

Louis shoved his chair back, coming to his feet. But he swayed forward and had to put his hands flat against the table to keep from falling. His slack lips worked a moment before any sound came. "Swain. . . . You don't get out. . . . You have my cartel. . . ."

"I've come to offer you my help, Louis. . . ."

With a shrill cry, Louis lurched from the table, arms flailing wildly. Swain stepped back to avoid the clawing hand, and Louis fell to his knees. Sanite Dede rose swiftly.

Then she stopped, watching Louis. He remained on his knees a while, swaying back and forth. Finally he turned around, got to his feet, stumbled to the table. He had to put his hands on it again to keep from falling. His breath made a sobbing sound in the room. He remained that way a moment, swaying, then he slumped into the chair again. He seemed to have forgotten Swain. He stared blankly at the bottle. He reached for it, missed, his whole body sliding forward against the table, his head sinking into his arms. He did not lift it again.

Swain looked at him, knowing a moment of regret. Louis had been a good friend in the early days. Gambling and wenching and wassail such as Natchez would never know again. "Perhaps we can get him upstairs," he told Sanite Dede.

She did not answer. She rose, swaying sinuously as she came to him. Her hand was like a claw on his arm, pulling him insistently away from the table. When they were out of earshot, she spoke in a hissing voice: "Louis got nothing left. Only Sanite Dede."

He nodded. "And, perhaps, the child."

He thought Sanite Dede would understand; she knew how Louis loved Denise. It had become almost an obsession with him, these last years. Louis must have realized how steadily and inevitably he was losing Charlotte's love and respect; the knowledge was part of what had contributed to his degeneration. The baby was the only one left who gave him love, fully and unquestioningly, making no demands on a manhood he had lost, oblivious of all the other insidious pressures and conflicts at work. But as Swain mentioned the child, he saw an expression suddenly leak through Sanite Dede's ivory mask—jealousy and resentment so intense it startled him. The woman's voice was vitriolic. "He no got

Denise," she said. "Owen Naylor got Denise."

Swain stared blankly, uncomprehending. "What?"

Her eyes glowed vindictively. "You tell Louis. He kill me, if I tell him."

"Tell Louis what?"

"That day before the wedding. Where she was."

"Where she was?"

"*Madame* Reynaud. With Owen Naylor."

All the way back to the Vieux Carré, Swain's head spun with the possibilities. Had it been merely a fiction of Sanite Dede's hate and jealousy, an attempt to cut the last bond between Charlotte and Louis? Or could it be the truth? It was logical that Sanite Dede should know of such a thing. Perhaps Pepper Annie's drunken babblings had given her a hint. Or perhaps she had guessed it from her contact with Charlotte. Whatever the source, if it was true, it gave him a powerful weapon.

He wanted to discuss it with Livingston and so had directed the driver to go to the company office in the Vieux Carré. The lights were lit, and Swain went in. Toby Garret sat behind the desk. John Montgomery was ensconced in one of the leather wing chairs.

"Gentlemen," Swain said, "is Ed about?"

Toby seemed unusually reserved. "Livingston's with Judge Pine, trying to get a further postponement."

"A pity. I had something for him."

"We have something for you, too," Montgomery said. He rose, lips tight and gray. "We were just about to seek you out, Swain." He walked to the desk, putting his hand down on an opened letter in front of Toby. "One of the Wilkinson letters, written to Aaron Burr in October of Eighteen Oh Four."

A cottony dryness touched Swain's mouth. "Indeed?" he said. "How did it fall into your hands?"

"One of my clients," Toby said. "A former officer under Wilkinson."

"The letter mentions you, Swain." Montgomery's face grew pale with its wrath. "What it reveals would give the government a new case against Burr. You'd be prosecuted with him. If there are other letters like this in existence, there's no telling when it will break. We'd lose half our stockholders if one of our officers was mixed up in such a scandal. There's still bitter feeling against Burr in certain quarters down here. We'd lose our strongest support in the legislature. Claiborne would no longer be with us. It could wreck us."

Swain pursed his lips, studied his sword cane. Then, condescendingly, asked: "What do you propose?"

"That you break all connections with the company," Toby said.

"We'll buy your shares and make public announcement of the severance," Montgomery said.

"What if I won't sell?"

Montgomery's voice trembled. "We'll take it to court. Our petition will make it clear why we want to sever connections with you. That way it will be a certainty that your connections with Burr will come to light. This way, you have at least a fifty-fifty chance."

Anger ran through Swain like the burn of acid. This Puritanical popinjay, this backwoods mechanic—telling him what to do—his slender fingers closed tightly about the head of his cane. "What if the company was strong enough to stand such a scandal?"

"It never could. Public opinion is against us. The courts are beginning to question the validity of Fulton's monopoly in New York. Naylor is making our boats look silly. . . ."

"That's the whole point. Naylor is the crux of your problem. And if I have something now that will stop him for sure. . . ."

"I won't have any more of your violence," Montgomery said. "Setting Blackwell on Naylor that last time almost cost us Claiborne's support."

"This won't be violence. . . ."

"It certainly won't. Livingston will be here at nine this evening. So will you, with your contracts, your stock certificates, whatever other papers you have. The announcement of your termination will be in the papers tomorrow. Your game's up, Swain. I think you know it."

Montgomery was wallowing in a vengeance he had sought for years. Swain couldn't let him be fulfilled.

"My dear Montgomery, I don't give one pinch of owl dung for what you think."

In the hired hack, with Dominique riding as footman, heading back down St. Anne toward the square, Swain gave way to his reactions. For a while his frustrated anger at Montgomery and a gnawing sense of defeat made a sickly sweet taste in his mouth. The Wilkinson letter had come as a shock that he couldn't deny. When Wilkinson had been court-martialed and then acquitted in 1811, Swain had been confident that all his own connections with Burr had been buried.

Yet he could not let this be a defeat. Down here, Ed Livingston had final word as to whether Swain should remain in the corporation. Under the present circumstances, the man probably agreed with Montgomery and Toby that Swain was too dangerous to remain. Yet Livingston was more of a realist than the other two. If Swain had in his possession the weapon to ruin Naylor, he was confident that Livingston would welcome him back with open arms. With the *Kentucky* in their service, the monopoly would be strong enough to withstand any scandal.

As they turned into Chartres, Swain stopped the coach to buy a St. Honoré from a coffee stand at the corner. Then he went on to the Reynaud apartment, leaving Dominique with the coach.

Angelique answered his knock. "*Madame* no here."

"Tell her who is calling, my Pontchartrain papabote, or you shall find *gris-gris* hanging at your front door to-morrow."

Angelique looked scandalized. "Someday, *miche*, you sorry you laugh at voodoo."

She backed away, not closing the door completely, and he heard her petulant voice speaking to Charlotte. Without waiting further, he pushed into the entrance hall. Beyond was the parlor and Denise, playing with her dolls on the floor. And Charlotte. Her hair was piled in a rusty tiara on her handsome head, glowing and scintillating with a life all its own. She wore a gown of jaconet muslin and a long pelerine that was crossed over the front and held in at the waist by a sash. It emphasized the curve of her hips, the proud shape of her breasts. These last years had brought her a poise and a pride, had made a stunning woman out of a remarkable girl. He savored it for a moment, without speaking. He genuinely regretted what he was about to do. Yet he knew what a corner he was in and could see no other way out. He held up the St. Honoré.

"A peace offering."

She almost smiled. "For me . . . or Denise?"

"I have something else for you," he said. He bent over, holding the pastry out to the child. She rose from her dolls with a pleased cry, stretching up greedy little hands.

"*Merci, m'sieu,*" she said. "*Quelle merveilleuse pâtisserie, elle ressemble tout à fait le bateau à vapeur.*"

Swain tilted his brows. "So fluent already."

"Louis's influence," Charlotte said. "He spends hours talking with her in French."

"I never saw such a fond father."

She sat down, folding her hands carefully in her lap. There was neither hostility nor warmth in her face. She looked at Angelique, and the maid discreetly retired to another part of the apartment. "What will it be, Swain?" Charlotte asked.

He moved to a chair, lifting the tails of his bottle-green coat, carefully seating himself. "The cash offer has been upped, Charlotte. Twenty-five thousand for your share of the *Kentucky.*"

A shadow seemed to cross her face. He took it for hesitancy. Then she shook her head. "We're doing quite well with the government contracts."

"Then may I give you an alternative?" Smiling, he looked down at Denise, who was gurgling happily as she licked the puff paste and chocolate-cream filling off her chubby fingers. She was a beautiful child—curly black hair, apple-ripe cheeks. Swain bent forward, taking her chin gently between thumb and forefinger, turning her face toward the window. He could see no change in the jet black of her eyes, but he said: "Have you ever noticed, when the light catches them just right, how green her eyes look?"

Charlotte did not answer. He could hear the distant *clop-clop* of hoofs and the rattle of wheels on the street outside. He looked up at her. All the blood had left Charlotte's cheeks. They were pale as wax. She was staring at him with wide eyes, unable to conceal any of her shock. He straightened, feeling a distinct triumph. She moistened her lips. Her voice came in the barest of whispers, containing intensely restrained rage.

"Swain," she said. "Swain. . . ."

He dipped his head. "I thought it would be like that. A secret that could ruin your whole life."

Charlotte rose sharply, as if unable to bear the pressure sitting down any longer. She was controlling herself with a visible effort. Her nostrils were pinched, and her lips pressed together so tightly a white ridge of flesh surrounded them. "Get out," she said. "How can you even suggest such a thing? Get out . . . !"

"It's no use trying to put up any pretense, Charlotte," he said. "We both know what it would do to you if it got out. It would wreck your marriage. The little girl would be branded for life. Louis might well kill Naylor when he saw him next. . . ."

A tremor ran through her. "You won't breathe a word of it, Swain. Do you hear? Not a word."

"Then you'll sell out?"

"How can you ask that?"

"You have no alternative," he said. He saw her eyes change focus abruptly, going past him. Without understanding what it meant, at first, he went on: "Sell out today, Charlotte, or tomorrow all of New Orleans will know that Denise is the child of Owen Naylor."

Her eyes widened. There was a glassy light to them, and she was still staring beyond him. It made him turn.

Louis stood in the door to the entrance hall. He was still drunk, swaying, blinking his eyes at Swain, as if in an effort to understand what he had heard. He spoke thickly. "What did you say . . . Swain?"

Swain held up his hand. "Louis . . . I. . . ."

It finally penetrated Louis's drink-logged mind. Swain saw the young man's face contort with a blinding rage. The sound that left him was shrill and broken, like the cry of some animal in agony.

"*Cochon!*" Louis screamed. He lunged at Swain, whipping the sword out of his cane. "*Animal vous,* Swain! Bâtard!*"

It was the attack of a madman. All Swain could do was jump backward, throwing his chair over in Louis's path. Louis tripped on it and fell to his knees. It gave Swain time to whip free his own sword. But Louis was already jumping to his feet again, with that crazed sound. It gave Swain no time to get down on his legs; all he could do was retreat, executing a series of desperate parries.

Louis abandoned all strategy, attacking insanely, using no feints, lunging and thrusting time after time. It would have been suicidal for Louis if Swain had been able to gain his guard for an instant, but he was still off balance, retreating across the room. He backed into a chair, upsetting it. Louis's blade missed his head by an inch, hacking a chip from the marble mantelpiece. Swain's own blade caught in a hanging, ripping it to the floor. He heard Denise bawling and saw Charlotte running across the room toward her. Not wanting to get caught against the wall, he backed through the open door onto the landing. Out there, Swain finally got down on his legs. It allowed him to parry a thrust and engage. In his rage, Louis had no patience to spar. He wildly gave Swain an invitation. Swain accepted, feinting for the flank. Louis barely executed his parry, rushing his riposte. Swain lunged backward, dropping his blade to parry.

His whole response was based on the fact that Louis was too enraged to feint. The youth's entire attack up to this point had been a series of wild thrusts, but even as Swain

357

dropped his blade, he saw Louis's blade flashing into a new position. Too late, Swain realized the riposte had been a feint. Louis's blade was silver when it went in—crimson when it came out.

Swain felt himself buckle in the middle. Pain ran through his belly like a core of fire. Then he was stumbling backward, and the stairs were beneath his feet, somehow, like shuffled cards, and no matter how fast he moved his feet, the cards kept shuffling, so he fell, and tumbled down the stairs, down the circular stairs, like a big fish, flopping over and over, with the agony tearing him apart in the middle every time he turned. Then he lay at the bottom, on the black-and-white marble squares, and looked up. Louis's face was floating down from above, as in a dream, a wildly contorted face, with a sword blade flashing in front of it. Somehow Swain realized the man was not finished yet.

Swain's sword lay beside him on the marble, and he got it in his hand and caught hold of the newel post, clawing his way up until he stood on his feet. Then he stepped away from the post to meet Louis's wild rush as he came down the last three steps. Only half a lifetime of grueling practice in the *sale d'armes* of Exchange Alley kept Swain from sustaining another thrust, as he blocked Louis's attack. Lunge, thrust, parry. Riposte, parry, counter-riposte. They were like movements in a dream, while Swain backed carefully across the black-and-white marble squares, with his life leaking swiftly through the pale fingers pressed against his stomach. It was strange that he felt no pain now. He couldn't even feel his legs. But he must be down on them, for Louis had not broken through his guard. The clash of blades and the tattoo of Louis's feet and the pumping huff of their breathing all sounded far away. Then he was in the street, with Dominique's black face gaping at him from beside the coach, and the Santo Domingans chattering like a covey of excited birds in front of the Café des Refuges across the street. Swain was growing dizzy, and Louis's wild figure seemed to lose definition before him.

There was not much time now. He knew what he had to do. Like an echo from the past, his own voice seemed to float through his mind. *It is not our opponents, but our own bad habits that will one day kill us.* Swain parried and retreated and engaged. He lifted his elbow, giving Louis the invitation in tierce. Louis accepted it with a savage cry, going automatically into his triple feint. His blade made the blinding flash toward Swain's head, his chest, his belly. Swain parried each feint. Then, even before his third feint was finished, Louis was executing that telltale shift of weight from right to left foot.

Swain's third parry and riposte were one movement. Too late, Louis tried to recover. The lunge he had advertised with his shift carried him onto Swain's blade clear up to the hilt. Swain released his rapier and stepped aside to keep from being carried to the ground with Louis, as the Creole pitched heavily onto his face. Swain stood still a moment, staring emptily at the body sprawled in the street with two feet of bloody blade protruding from his back. Then Swain turned and walked carefully to the *banquette.*

He was dimly aware of Charlotte, running from the door, dropping on her knees beside Louis. Swain had to sit down on the edge of the *banquette.* Everything was spinning. His shirt front was soaked with blood, and there was a buzzing of bees in his head. Then he realized he wasn't sitting. He was lying, in the street, on his back, with Dominique bending over him. The Negro's cheeks were wet with tears.

"*Miche,*" he said hopelessly, "*miche . . . ?*"

359

Swain tried to smile. "A pity, Dominique. So much magnificent villainy left undone."

It was November in Kentucky, and winter was coming. The timber was leafless and rimed with frost and standing like a skeletal host on the banks of a tobacco-brown river. The rain beat into the fallen heaps of gum leaves, filling the naked forest with a smell like a tanning yard. The birds were gone, having flown south in black triangles against the sky, and the bears and the raccoons and the spotted rattlers had holed up. The bitter chill was like a pressure, holding a man to his fireside most of the day.

This was what Naylor met, when he returned to Louisville after spending two months transporting a thousand pigs of Galena lead between St. Louis and Pittsburgh. He found orders waiting from General Harrison. He was to stay in Louisville till a load of saltpeter came overland from Mammoth Cave, then transport it upriver to the gunpowder factories at Pittsburgh. It was a welcome respite from his unending river runs.

Evadne was there for him, as she had been upon his every return during these last years. She seemed a natural part of the pattern of his life. Theirs was a comfortable, tacit relationship that needed little explanation or justification. He knew that by all rights she should have satisfied him completely, should have been his wife by now. Yet there was that restlessness in him that would not let him abide port for long, would not let him settle down, would not let him accept the full measure of comfort and contentment she could give him. He knew what it was. Although Evadne had never mentioned it again, she knew, too. Charlotte was still in his system. Remembering the bitter antagonisms that had come to them even in those moments of passion, he wondered if it wasn't closer to hate. That was the dark current running beneath their placid existence as they once more took up the threads of their lives in November of 1814. Despite it, there were moments of fulfillment with Evadne, when ecstasy and rapport drowned the memory of Charlotte, and there were long hours of contentment in the taproom with his friends and his crew.

The talk there concerned itself mostly with the host of rumors that had filled the air these last weeks. The British and Canadian newspapers made no secret of the fact that a huge expedition had sailed from Plymouth for the Caribbean. There were more than fifty warships and transports, carrying the picked veterans of Wellington's peninsular campaigns. News was always weeks late, but it was known that Andrew Jackson had conquered the Creek Indians in the south and was now moving against Pensacola. If the British expedition landed anywhere on the Gulf, he would be there to meet them. But what could Jackson's handful of backwoodsmen do against the formidable veterans who had defeated Napoléon?

It was a gloomy picture, but it wasn't the only news moving through the river towns that winter. Another steamboat had been built in Brownsville earlier in the year. She was the *Enterprise*, seventy-five tons, and she had made two trips to Louisville during the summer. Early in December she showed up again, commanded by Captain Henry Shreve who announced that he was headed to New Orleans with a load of ordnance and military supplies for General Jackson. Naylor went aboard to inspect the boat and was immediately impressed by Shreve. He warned the man of the Fulton monopoly. Shreve felt that the precedent Naylor had set would allow him to buck Fulton. The monopoly had already received a blow in the death of Chancellor

Livingston, and public sympathy was moving more and more against it. The more independent operators who challenged the monopoly, the weaker its hold would grow. Naylor wished the man luck and stood on the levee, watching the saucy little boat churn its way out to the Falls. It filled him with a new restlessness, as he walked back to the tavern.

Three days later, still waiting for the saltpeter from Mammoth Cave, he and Heap and Captain Abner were seated at their usual corner table, when a woodsman in a deerskin hunting shirt and moccasins with flaps halfway to the knees entered the door. He looked around the room, saw Naylor, and shambled toward the table. He was immensely tall, lean as a whip, with a face cured by wind and sun till it had the look of old rawhide.

"I understand you be the man with the steamboat contraption that air goin' t' run us down the river t' N'yawleens."

Naylor looked up into shrewd blue eyes. "I've got a cargo of saltpeter for Pittsburgh."

"Keels can take it up," the man said. "And Gen'ral Harrison won't court-martial you when he hears what you done. I'm Captain Dave Mint, and I got two companies o' Kentucky militia to take down the river. Ain't a one cain't take the rag off the bush at two hunnert yards. With the British fixin' to jump us down there, I figger these men'll be worth thar weight in gold to Old Hickory."

Naylor shook his head. "My boat would be seized. I ran against the Fulton monopoly in New Orleans. I'm still wanted down there."

Captain Mint spat contemptuously. "I heard about these damn' gov'ment contractors, sittin' around on their asses and cleanin' up the gold while us iggerant farmers was out gittin' kilt, but I never thought I'd see one in Kentucky. . . ."

Heap was on his feet, anger cracking the marble-smooth surface of his face into a thousand fine wrinkles. "You come to the right place if you want a fight, Mint."

Naylor put a hand on Heap's arm, stopping him. "Never mind, Heap. Mint's right. Jackson probably needs these men worse in New Orleans than Harrison needs his saltpeter at Pittsburgh. A keel would never get the men south in time."

Captain Abner's eyes began to gleam excitedly. "We could put them ashore a few miles above New Orleans. Swain'd never know we were there."

Naylor looked at Heap, and a grin broke out over the keeler's face. "My pole's tossed, Owen."

"Mint," Naylor said, "you've got yourself a steamboat."

It was already evening, and they promised to get up steam at dawn. When Naylor finally went upstairs, he found Evadne sitting in a rocker by the bed, darning a pair of his socks. It so typified the quiet depths of their relationship that he knew a poignant reluctance to tell her he was leaving again. He paced restlessly to the window, looking down on the waterfront. Her black, heavy-lidded eyes followed him like a faithful dog's. There was something of the eternal earth mother in her utter, animal quiescence. By contrast it made him think of Charlotte. How different the two women were, one fighting so bitterly and unceasingly for every step she took, the other resigned to whatever life made of her. Yet he wondered if Evadne, by fighting as bitterly as Charlotte for what she wanted, could have bound him any closer. Perhaps it would have driven him away. Maybe Evadne sensed that. Maybe she had a deeper understanding of him than Charlotte.

Finally he turned and told her what had happened. He saw her underlip grow slack and full. It was the look others took for sulkiness, but he knew the deep streak of fatalism it held, making her accept the changes of her life with as little resistance as the earth accepted the cycle of seasons. He expected the same acceptance tonight and walked to her, but, as she rose to meet him, he saw something new in her eyes. She stood gazing up at him, the change spreading from her eyes into her face, something almost wild.

Suddenly his name left her in a sobbing way. "Owen!" The petulant shape left her mouth, her eyes drew almost shut, and she came into his arms with all her weight, sobbing his name again. "Owen . . . Owen. . . ."

It was a release she had never shown him before. She was clinging to him in desperation, her body working against him like a frightened animal.

"Don't take on like that," he said helplessly. "It's just another little trip. I've gone so many times before."

"Not downriver." Her fingers were digging into him, and there was a sound of utter misery in her voice. "Always to Saint Looey or Pittsburgh or up the Miami, but not downriver, not down there."

He knew what it was now. Charlotte was down there. It made him realize how strongly this fear must have abided within Evadne, working at her and gnawing at her and waiting for this moment to release it, this day when he should go downriver again. He twined his hand in the abundance of her dark hair, pulling her cheek against him, trying to soothe her. She wouldn't be soothed. She kept on pulling at him, working her body against him, sobbing his name.

It was a thing of hysteria, contagious in its abandonment. It touched a corresponding emotion in him, a sympathetic sense of poignant loss. Then the emotion changed identity. The cushiony pressure of her body working against him turned it to passion. He was stripping off her dress, while she still sobbed and clung to him. The lamplight made a pink-white glow against her heavy-fleshed hips. His fingers dug into the soft back. She was no longer sobbing; she was pleading with him, incoherently, gasping his name, moaning. The hysteria, the savage release of everything that had been trapped in her for so long made for an abandonment he had never seen in her before.

When it was over, when she lay beside him, spent, breathing shallowly, her face slack with exhaustion, her black eyes closed, he felt a shudder run through her body.

"I'll pull a blanket up," he whispered.

"Never mind," she said. "It won't do any good." Her voice was barely audible, rusty with hopelessness. "Winter's comin', Owen. Why does it always seem to be winter . . . when you go away?"

Chapter Twenty-Nine

They left the next morning at dawn, loaded to the guards with ragged, tobacco-chewing militiamen. It was a load that made the boat sluggish going through the Falls, and every man on deck was soaked to the skin by the time they reached Shippingport. As they put ashore to drop the pilot, a horsebacker came down the waterfront from the direction of Louisville. It was the stable boy from the Red Feather. He said the mail rider had put in from Lexington just after the *Kentucky* had shoved off. There was a letter from New Orleans for Naylor. It was from Thibodaux.

New Orleans, La.
Oct. 7, 1814

Mon Ami,
   I have, indeed, a sad duty to perform. *Madame* Reynaud will communicate with you later but at the present time is much too disturbed by her grief. In any event, on Oct. 5 Kenneth Swain and Louis, undoubtedly quarreling over the monopoly, had an affair of arms, both dying as a result of their wounds. . . .

There was more, but Naylor stopped reading. He stared emptily before him, letting the dull shock run thin and die. He could not force sorrow. Under other circumstances, he and Louis might have been friends. There had been something about Louis that made you want to like him, despite his weakness, his instability, but too much had stood between them. All Naylor could think of now was the pathetic figure Louis had made during these last years—in comparison with the gay, charming youth he had been when Naylor had first known him. Then the real significance of this blotted out all other reaction. Charlotte was free. It filled him with a deep restlessness, a need to be on his way that ran through his body like a fever. Then it made him turn to look back through the white mist, toward Louisville, remembering how Evadne had acted. To her, the fact of his going downriver was symbolic of a return to Charlotte. In the passion and abandonment of Evadne's release, it was almost as if she had sensed how complete her loss was to be.

Why hadn't he sensed it, too? If this was to be the last time between them, why hadn't he known it, why hadn't he been able to feel the pain as she had felt it? He knew a futile anger at himself, at the mysterious patterns of life that had thrown them together and had allowed him to hurt her like that. Yet she would have had it no other way. He knew that. Whatever the circumstances, she had wanted him, and he had been as helpless. He hadn't really understood what was in him. He had wanted to do the right thing by her, had hoped for the day when he could go to her, cleansed of the maddening ferment over Charlotte. It filled him with a sense of helplessness and of life's enigmatic cruelty. He shivered in the chilled air and drew his blanket coat closer about him as he climbed back to the wheelhouse.

The journey down was an endless succession of chilly fall days with the cañon-like shores of the river gradually lowering to an endless prairie land. Then it was the mouth of the Ohio, and New Madrid, a half-sunken, dying town, still clinging to the river that had not yet swallowed it. On December 20th, they had to stop at Natchez for fuel. Naylor had a few minutes with Pepper Annie. She was almost blind now, and her mind was wandering.

"Damn' bitch, runnin' off, leavin' 'er poor old aunt. She could make a hunnert dollars a day, a body like that. A thousand. But what? No-o-o. Got t' be pure. Waitin' around f'r that puke, Louis Reynaud. He'll never marry with 'er. Charlotte! Git off your lazy tail 'n' come down here 'n' serve these keelers. . . . ."

Naylor tried to leave some cash with the barman, but the man said Charlotte had been sending money regularly. Then he told Naylor that Angelique and Denise had arrived yesterday and were staying with the Prevals. Thousands of civilians were fleeing New Orleans, and there had been only enough room on the already crowded boat for two more. Charlotte had sent her maid ahead, with Denise, meaning to follow as soon as she could find a place on another keel. There was still more fuel going aboard the *Kentucky*, and Naylor took another precious half hour to go to the Prevals. They greeted him graciously and took him to the parlor where Denise was playing with her dolls. She looked up at him shyly. He sat in the chair beside her.

"Don't you remember me, honey?"

Her cheeks flushed suddenly, as memory rushed in on her. "*Oncle* Owen!" She stood up, the shyness leaving her, coming to him with outstretched arms. He took her on his lap, feeling that awkwardness again. "*M'avez-vous apporté un bateau à vapeur, Oncle Owen? J'en veux un qui soufflé de la fumée comme le* Kentucky. *Maman a dit que vous voyagez par toute la rivière. . . .*"

"Make it in English, honey," he said. "You know I'm just a dumb river man."

Preval chuckled. "She asked if you brought her a steamboat."

"It's down at the levee, honey. Maybe Uncle Preval will take you in the coach so's you can see it from the bluffs."

"Will you ring all the bells for me?"

"And whistle the safety valve," he said.

"Papa was making a toy boat for me. He never got to finish it. Will you go get him on the steamboat? He had a fight with a man and they ran downstairs in the street and I could hear them yelling. *Maman* says he won't ever come back, but I want him to finish the toy boat for me, *Oncle* Owen. . . ."

Naylor glanced at Preval. The man shook his head and turned away, pacing across the room. Denise's childish mind had already jumped from Louis to her dolls. As she prattled on, Naylor looked at her face. It was the old question, the old search. Yet he could see no change. She had Creole hair, blue-black, filled with dancing lights. Her eyes were flecked with that hint of elfin mischief he had first seen in Charlotte. Then an impatient anger swept him. What did it matter? Louis's child or his, what did it really matter? From here on out Denise would be his. Whether or not she was his flesh and blood, he would be her father in every sense of the word. She would be his daughter, as Charlotte would be his woman. It all went together, and the past didn't matter. He felt a need, fierce, possessive, and lifted Denise in his arms and held her tightly against him. It was like a revelation. The sense of kinship and identity that flooded him was an answer to all the questions, all the doubts that had plagued them through the years, and he knew they would never come again.

"The child must be good for you, *m'sieu*," Preval said. "Angelique has told me you are not one to grin often. . . ."

The memory of it stayed with Naylor the rest of the way downriver, filling him with an even greater eagerness to see Charlotte. They reached Baton Rouge the next day. The town was under a pall of gloom. There had been a naval engagement at Lake Borgne. The British had triumphed and were now ashore with an overwhelming force. It convinced Naylor that the main battle was not far off, and Mint's men might be too late if he put them ashore anywhere short of New Orleans. He held a council with Heap and Captain Abner and the crew, and the vote was unanimous: the hell with the monopoly, they were going to New Orleans.

They ran all night with half a dozen men on the bow, holding pine-knot torches, and with Heap taking soundings. The dawn of the 22nd was chilly and wind-whipped, with a fog covering the river like gray smoke. The pale sunlight made a silver shimmer on the forest of masts that broke through the pearly mist. When the Kentuckians realized it was New Orleans, their shouting and hoorawing made a bedlam of the boat.

Remembering the seething waterfront from his last trip, Naylor was surprised at the desolation of the levee. Half the quay space along the Faubourg Ste. Marie was unoccupied and what keels were moored there seemed loaded wholly with ordnance and military stores. But most of them were lumbering flats that would never go back upriver, or Indiamen and coasting schooners with the green scum of their waterlines revealing how long the blockade had held them here. The cannonade of exhausting steam had already proclaimed the *Kentucky*'s arrival from far upriver, and there was a crowd awaiting their landing. They warped the steamboat in between a rotting brig and a keel loaded with pyramids of round shot and kegs of powder. The Kentuckians poured off the boat onto the levee, with Mint bawling hoarsely in a futile effort to form them into some semblance of ranks. As soon as they were ashore, a crowd of civilians replaced them, swarming aboard the boat and pleading with Naylor to take them upriver. Then Naylor saw Thibodaux, fighting to get through. The young lawyer had to shout to be heard over the babble.

"The *Vesuvius* is aground again, and Shreve's gone back upriver for Jackson," Thibodaux said. "I knew it had to be you when they told me another steamboat was landing."

Naylor told Captain Abner to keep steam up and shove off if they were threatened. Then he dragged Thibodaux into an after cabin and closed the door on the noise. The lawyer removed his hat, wiping his sallow face with a handkerchief. "You don't have to worry about being seized," he said. "Didn't you get my letter of November Twenty-Ninth?"

"We barely got the letter you wrote in October."

Thibodaux clapped him on the back. "Then I have the honor of telling you in person. On the 18th of November, the district court ruled that the Territory had exceeded its authority in granting the monopoly."

"Is that the final decision?"

"Ed Livingston had the case removed by a writ of error to the Supreme Court. But with Chancellor Livingston dead and the monopoly in such public disfavor, I have no doubt the verdict will be upheld. You've beaten them, my friend. Even Charlotte has to admit it. If you hadn't broken free so you could supply us with the money to keep fighting, it would never have happened. But now the river is free."

Naylor was silent. Somehow he couldn't react the way he should. A man ought to shout or sing or get drunk or bust up a barroom. It was that big. It was the best thing that had happened since the launching of the boat. Maybe it was too big to grasp all at once, or maybe he needed to share it with someone.

"Am I safe ashore?" he asked.

"There is still that contempt citation against you and your crew for breaking court. You're subject to arrest ashore. I don't even think I could get you free on bond. Our only hope lies with General Jackson. It has to do with the military situation here."

Thibodaux went on to explain. There was a fear that the British would try to move their warships upriver. They had a formidable force—the huge *Tonnant,* mounting eighty guns, one of Nelson's prizes at the battle of the Nile; the *Royal Oak,* the *Norge,* and three other seventy-fours; the fifty-four-gun *Gorgon* and the *Annide* of thirty-eight, and a score more men o' war. If they ever reached New Orleans and attacked from the waterfront, the city would surely fall. The only thing between them and the city were the forts commanding the Mississippi some sixty miles below the city, and they were dangerously low on supplies and ammunition. The British had moved a heavy force of artillery and infantry above the forts, cutting them off from the city. The only way they could not be reached was by the river. Keels had tried it and had failed. Jackson was looking for another boat capable of getting past the British batteries.

"We have precedent," Thibodaux said. "Jackson has promised complete pardon for all past crimes to Lafitte and his Baratarian pirates, in return for their help in the defense of New Orleans. I'm sure he would be willing to set aside your contempt charges in return for the service of the *Kentucky.*"

Naylor called the crew in and told them.

Captain Abner wiped his nose with a greasy thumb, giving them a toothless grin. "Better'n rottin' in jail."

"We've come through the New Madrid earthquake and beat off every keeler on the Mississippi," Heap said. "Them British batteries won't amount to a 'gator's tit."

"My pole's tossed," Thompson said.

"Then it's a deal," Naylor said.

"I'll go to Jackson immediately," Thibodaux said. "In the meantime, you'd better not show your face till we have your official clearance."

But Naylor could not stay aboard. A few minutes after Thibodaux left, he told Captain Abner to keep steam up, and went ashore. The signs of war were everywhere. A crowd of Negroes, apparently free men of color, were gathered beneath the levee, trying to elect a captain for their company. At the corner of the Place d'Armes a ragged knot of buckskinned men from Coffee's brigade stood dipping snuff and spitting tobacco and making obscene jokes about the redcoats. A group of young Creoles issued from the Cabildo, singing the "*Marseillaise*" and "*Chant du Départ*," muskets canted proudly over their shoulders. Behind them appeared one of the constables who had been with Sheriff Finley when Naylor had been arrested before. Naylor ducked into Chartres before the man saw him. As he hurried through the crowded street toward the apartment, a feeling of breathlessness, of constriction came to his chest. It was almost three years now. Would it be any different? Had Louis's death really changed it? Would the animosity, the struggle, the strange paradox of attraction and repulsion still exist between them?

He tried to shake off the doubts, tried to recapture the certainty he'd first felt upon hearing that Louis had died. She was free now. Nothing stood between them. He crossed the black-and-white marble of the entrance hall, ascending the spiral staircase. He stopped before the door, with its ornate carving of Phoebus and his chariots. There was sweat on his palms. He knocked.

It seemed an interminable time before he heard movement from within. Then the door was open. Charlotte stood before him. Her eyes went blank with surprise. For a moment, with her red lips parted, she didn't make a sound. Then the word left her, barely whispered. "Owen."

The sight of her brought the blood thick and hot to his throat. He was at a complete loss for words. He knew a simple urge to take her in his arms, to sweep every constraint from between them with one move, to know the passion and pain and sweetness that should be rightfully theirs now. But he was looking at her dress—high-necked, long-sleeved, black for mourning, and it suddenly blocked the urges in him, reminding him with sudden impact how recently Louis had died.

"Charlotte," he said. "I heard . . . Thibodaux. . . ." He trailed off, making a helpless movement with his hand.

She had recovered from surprise. She moistened her lips. "I know," she said. "Charles wrote you about Louis." She paused, seeming to search for something in his face. Her cheeks looked drawn, pale. She made a meaningless little gesture. "Come in," she said. "The parlor."

He followed her. At the mantel, she turned to him. Her lips were compressed, giving her face a deep strain. He had the feeling of that intense constraint between them. He knew it was more than the symbol of the dress now. The barrier of all the past years rose up, shadowy, intangible, yet impregnable as a stone wall. Charlotte's chin rose. Always more articulate than he, more ready to put their conflict into words, she said: "This is going to be a hard meeting, Owen. We might as well accept it."

He took a step toward her. "Why does it have to be? You

certainly can't hold it against me about the boat. . . ."

"You mean jumping port? Of course not. That was so long ago. There are so many other things. . . ." She broke off. She clasped her hands, turning to walk to the window. With her back to him, she said: "I think I'd better tell you about Louis first. Swain had found out about you and me. He came and threatened to tell whose child Denise really was. Louis walked in on it. You know how much the baby meant to him. I think it was the only thing Swain could have done to enrage Louis enough to attack him."

It shocked Naylor. "How did Swain find out?"

"I can only guess. Sanite Dede killed herself on Tchoupitoulas the next day. I learned Louis had been seeing her."

"You mean she told Swain?"

"I can think of no one else in a position to know. Annie must have said something about you and me, when she was living with us in Natchez. Sanite Dede began adding two and two, keeping it as a last weapon to get Louis away from me. I never realized why she hated me."

The irony of it struck him with bitter force, that Sanite Dede could have been so sure Denise was his child, that Swain could have used it as the truth—when neither he nor Charlotte had ever really known themselves. He wanted to tell her what had happened to him in Natchez, wanted to make her see it as he did, the three of them belonging together, despite the past, the way they had belonged from the beginning. He searched her face for some break, some sign that she would help him smash the barriers for the last time. But the ridges of strain still compressed her lips and wariness made a brittle shine in her eyes. The silence was a stiff and uncomfortable thing, and again words were a veil behind which their emotions stirred and tried to break through.

"Charles told you we've beaten them?" she asked.

"Yes."

She tried to smile. It looked stiff and false. "Aren't we silly? Something we've fought for all this time, and we take it like this."

"Maybe it's too big to grasp right away."

"Maybe." She moistened her lips again. "What about the contempt charges?"

"Thibodaux's seeing Jackson. He thinks Jackson might give me a pardon in return for my services with the *Kentucky*."

She nodded. "Shreve is already working for Jackson."

"This is downriver, Fort Saint Philip."

"What?"

He took a step toward her, unable to spar any longer. "Charlotte, this is crazy. We're. . . ."

"What did you say about Fort Saint Philip?" The bite of her voice stopped him. The gray was gone from her eyes, leaving them almost black. "You aren't going down there?" she said. "The British have reached the river between New Orleans and the forts. A pair of keels were blown out of the water, trying to get through."

"The *Kentucky*'s five times as fast as a keel."

"There are hundreds of British sympathizers in town, Owen. They'd know the minute you left. You wouldn't have a chance."

"And if Saint Philip don't get those supplies, New Orleans might not have a chance. . . ."

"You won't do the town any good by letting them blow up the boat. You had no right to make such a deal."

"The crew agreed, Charlotte."

"What about me? What about Denise?"

All his breathless expectancy, his hope, his anticipation

was swept away. Her eyes danced with anger, and the surface of her face was hard and brittle as an enamel mask. His voice was abruptly bitter. "Would you rather be rich in a British colony or poor in the United States?"

A hot flush ran into her face. "It hasn't got anything to do with my patriotism. I've fought too long to lose everything on such a hopeless gesture."

A gust of raw anger ran through him. "You can't set the police on me this time."

She laced her fingers together, speaking in a bitterly restrained voice. "The Fulton interests have a standing offer for my share in the company."

"Is that a threat?"

"What else can I do?"

There was a ridge of white about his lips. He knew now what the constraint had been between them. It had little to do with the proximity of Louis's death, or her mourning. It was about their antagonism, bitter as ever, lying in wait, and the source of that antagonism. "Charlotte," he said. His voice trembled. "When I heard Louis had been killed, I thought you were free at last. I thought I could come down here with nothing between us, start all over again, the way it should have been from the beginning. I was a fool."

She started to speak. He wouldn't let her.

"Louis wasn't really what stood between us," he said. "You're still afraid of Silver Street. It's spoiled everything you ever touched. You wanted me as bad as I wanted you. But you took Louis because you were afraid."

"Owen. . . ."

"Look what it did to Louis. Maybe he wasn't much to begin with. But he could laugh, he had a million friends. . . ."

"What else could I do?" Her voice broke. "He would

377

have had us in the gutter."

"What's wrong with the gutter? Maybe he would have found himself there."

"How do you know, how do you know?"

"I don't. All I know is what you did to him. Taking over all the decisions, using his own weaknesses against him when you wanted something, using your body when everything else failed, sucking the guts out of him. . . ."

"Owen!"

"You made a drunk and a kept man out of him. Now you want to make a coward and a traitor out of me."

"Stop it, stop it!"

Her voice was shrill, close to hysteria. She turned from him, her shoulders bowed and pulled tightly together. He could see how deeply he had struck home, but it gave him no sense of victory. The room was deadly quiet. Neither of them moved. Finally she turned back to him. Tears made silvery tracks down her cheeks, but there was no sound of crying. He had never seen her so defeated. She spoke in a husky, strained voice.

"What you say is untrue. There is more to love than momentary passion. But, even if you're right, even if suppose I'd quit fighting Silver Street, as you say? Suppose I'd come to you on your own terms? Have you ever thought of anyone but yourself, of what *you* want?"

No hope would rise in him. He looked emptily at her a long time. Finally in a dull voice he said: "Let's do our supposing about right now. Say I take the boat downriver. Say she gets blown up. Say I get out alive. What then? For you and Denise? Another boat? You know what a gamble it was. You know how I lived. We wouldn't have a cent. Saint Louis or Natchez or New Orleans, it's all the same. It's all Silver Street. Years of it. Even if we make the grade. Could you face that, Charlotte? Could you let Denise face that?"

She did not answer. A little muscle worked in her throat. Her lips closed, and the blood left her cheeks until they were wax-pale and her eyes grew wide and luminous and tortured. He wondered if she had looked like that in Natchez, on the day so long ago when she had made her choice between him and Louis.

"I thought so," he said. He looked at her a moment longer, with his eyes blank and dead. Then he turned and went out.

Just outside the French Quarter, a few blocks up Girod from the river, narrow muddy streets where sidewalks made from old flatboat gunwales sank beneath the ooze. Gable-roofed buildings shouldered together, tipsy as old men leering at a passing tart. There were saloons where a man could get murdered as quickly as he could get drunk, deadfalls where he could lose a year's wages at the turn of the cards, brothels where a picayune would buy him a meal and a woman and a room for the night. There was an average of six killings a week. It was a half mile square of the nearest thing to hell on earth. The swamp was the ultimate destination of every boatman on the river, their drinking and frolics along Tchoupitoulas and the waterfront only preliminaries to the wild debaucheries they indulged in within the confines of the swamp. Gangs of them filled Girod Street, stumbling in and out of the dives, gawking at the women who stood in doorways or called from upstairs windows.

Danny Blackwell could see it all. He could see it from where he stood in the shadows of an alley. Twenty feet away, one of the Carondelet's lanterns creaked on its hook, spilling a pool of smoky light into the street. Its backwash flashed now and again against the silvery surface of Blackwell's eyes and made them gleam like those of a hunted beast in the maw of its cave. He had been closer to a beast than a man these last years. His hair was a wild and tangled mane that fell clear to his shoulders, no longer variegated with the pale sun streaks, for he hadn't been out in the sun for months. On his primitive jaw was four inches of bristly blond beard, honey-brown at the edges from spilled food and liquor.

Standing there, he shifted his weight the wrong way, and a dull throb of pain ran up his left leg. It was always with him. It had been with him that rainy night the Kentucky militia had come down on them at Cave-in-Rock. The militia had hanged Commodore Nash and the other boat wreckers. Blackwell had been one of the few to escape. A thousand miles of walking down the Trace with that leg had followed. He was half insane with it when he met Colonel Seeley. Not knowing who the man was, just seeing the fat saddlebags and guessing at the money inside, he had clubbed the man to death, sinking the body in a bayou. He had gotten drunk in New Orleans and played the fool, scattering the telltale banknotes all over town. After that it was the swamp, and the flimsy protection of its boast that for twenty years no officer of the law had dared set foot within its boundaries. He was living like a rat in its hole, frying in the summer and freezing in the winter, a shack bully in one of the taverns till he got so drunk one night he killed the owner.

He was sleeping in a stable now, so hungry there wasn't any bottom to his belly. His leg ached so much he'd do anything to get a drink, and, every time it hurt, he remembered who had done it. Remembering Naylor had been the core of his life, these last years, his pain, and his hatred, and the knowledge that someday he would see Naylor again.

He hardly saw the man move out of the traffic. Not till he was a foot away did Blackwell recognize him. Harold Warwick, in all his Tory elegance—a long dress coat with lapels to the hips and a sugarloaf hat with a drooping brim that all but hid his shrewd blue eyes. He stopped before Blackwell, smiling secretively.

"Loan me a dollar," Blackwell said thickly.

"That won't buy you much of a woman. Wouldn't you rather have a thousand?"

Blackwell began to breathe heavily. "Don't joke, Warwick. I want a drink, and I want it quick."

"Did you know that Naylor has just put into port?"

Blackwell gazed at him a moment, without reacting. Then he felt the pound of blood through his temples, seeming to join the throb of pain in his leg. He made a husky sound, and his whole massive weight tilted forward. Warwick stopped him with a hand on his chest.

"Why not make it worth your while, Danny?"

Blackwell's eyes were almost closed. His voice sounded thick and strained. "I been waiting almost three years, Warwick."

"If you do it when and where I say, Danny, you can make a thousand dollars."

The man's insistent voice finally penetrated Blackwell's seething mind. He settled back a little. His eyes were squinted and bloodshot, staring at Warwick.

The man smiled. "Naylor is going to take supplies down to Fort Saint Philip for Jackson," he said. "We would rather he didn't."

"You and the British," Blackwell said softly.

Warwick merely smiled. "Being only suspected of British sympathies, I haven't had to go into hiding like so many known Tories. There are others of my same ilk, in positions to acquire such knowledge as this concerning Naylor."

Blackwell was letting it go through his mind. A thousand dollars. A chance to escape. And Naylor. It began to uncoil an excitement in him such as a woman could never bring. His eyes grew to silvery slits; a wolfish smile peeled his lips off his teeth, ugly and malicious and totally devoid of humor. Warwick saw it and nodded with satisfaction.

"The boat will be too well-guarded to get aboard at the levee. How about farther downriver?"

"I know a place down there." Blackwell was almost talking to himself. "Willow Channel. They'll have to pass so close to shore I could wade out to 'em."

"That will fit our plan to a nicety."

Blackwell was thinking of Naylor now. His eyes turned bleak and savage. He was looking beyond Warwick, and his voice was guttural with anticipation. "Just what is your plan?"

Chapter Thirty

At eight o'clock, Owen Naylor was aboard the *Kentucky*, standing in the wheelhouse, staring emptily at the city. At any other time the levee would have been crowded—young Creole dandies and their sweethearts out for an evening stroll, *belles chandelles* selling their wax myrtle candles, boatmen crossing into the square. But tonight New Orleans was shrouded in the threat of attack. Few lights showed, the top of the levee was almost deserted, and the crowds usually filling the Place d'Armes were gone. Not even the telltale creak of the high-wheeled carts could be heard, or the familiar clatter of hoofs on cobbles. It meant little to Naylor. He was still thinking of Charlotte. It had been a bitter blow to find that nothing had changed, that the old barriers still held them apart. He had seen what he called her fear of Silver Street before, and he should have known. It was all that simple for Owen Naylor. It never occurred to him that they were so far apart in so many ways that a moment's passion years ago could not possibly mean anything to Charlotte now and that it should mean nothing to him.

He moved out the door, pacing the dark boiler deck. There were no riding lights on the brigs and keels moored on either side of the *Kentucky*, but he could hear them straining at their moorings, and the muttering talk of men aboard came to him out of the darkness. Despite his anger and defeat, he thought again of what was driving Charlotte. It was more than her own fear now: it was fear for Denise. If the *Kentucky* were destroyed, it would leave them both

383

destitute. Was he justified in risking the boat, under any circumstances? He shook his head savagely. There was so much more involved. Why couldn't Charlotte see that? A whole city. Maybe a country. New Orleans was the key to all the trade on the river. If the British occupied the town, it would give them virtual domination of the Mississippi.

He was still pacing the deck, torn by conflict, when Captain Abner appeared at the head of the forecastle stairs. "We better get started changin' the escape pipes, Owen. Ain't much time left if we're goin' downriver tonight."

Naylor said: "Little while longer, Captain. Something stuck in my craw."

They both looked toward the levee as someone called softly. Naylor saw shadowy shapes, moving in the night, and the gangplank trembled under many feet. He and Captain Abner went down to the main deck. Near the bow they met Charles Thibodaux with a dozen buckskinned soldiers coming aboard behind him.

"Jackson promised the pardon, Owen," Thibodaux said. "He's sent Lieutenant Harris and some men to help you load."

Lieutenant Harris was long and lean, wearing a conglomerate uniform of captured British Wellingtons, a ragged pair of rawhide leggings, and a faded blue coat with the horizontal tape and blind buttonholes of the regular Army. Naylor knew he had to make his decision now. Memory of the torture in Charlotte's eyes went through him in a poignant rush. "I didn't have the right to make this deal," he said. "There's another owner involved. We can't take the boat down."

Surprise fluttered over the lieutenant's cynical, snuff-brown face. Then he spoke in a disgusted Tennessee drawl: "Mistah Naylor, when Old Hickory gives an order, hit's done carried out. He's done commandeered this ship. Hit's goin' downriver, whether you're on it or not."

Naylor looked at the dozen Tennesseans crowded behind Harris. These were men who had just come out of the bloody Creek War, grim and ragged and tough, long rifles held casually in their arms, skinning knives stuck through their belts. A feeling of helplessness stole through him. He looked at Captain Abner.

The old man displayed toothless gums in his rueful smile. "Looks like it's outta your hands, Owen."

"The boat won't be ours if we get back," Naylor said. "Charlotte threatened to sell out to Fulton if we went downriver."

A hurt look meant to reassure filled Thibodaux's face. "No she won't, Owen. I've talked to Charlotte since you did. She's changed her mind."

"No matter what you say," Naylor snapped, "I think she would." They stared at each other for a moment pensively. This might presage a turn of events Naylor had never expected. Then, in a miserable voice, he said: "All right, Lieutenant. Get to work."

In ten minutes the boat looked like a beehive. At Naylor's request, Harris sent for a couple of Army blacksmiths to help Captain Abner build an expansion tank to muffle the thunderclaps of escaping steam. They knew that in 1803 Oliver Evans had tried to launch a steamboat from New Orleans, shipping the machinery from the East. Failing, the engine had been put into a sawmill and the hull left to rot. They got a requisition from Jackson's headquarters for the Evans boiler and then spent frantic hours locating the mill. They cut a hole in the deck beneath the main cabin and lowered the boiler into the hold where it would act as the expansion tank. Then they ran a pipe through the boiler and out under the stern wheel. It was a jerry-built job with ragged joints and dubious seams, but Captain Abner thought it would hold up for one trip. They rigged guards to block the sparks in the stack and ran up scantlings and enclosed the engine room in a cabin to cover the clash of gears as much as possible.

While this was going on, Harris brought aboard an old Creole named Taussat who had been bringing brigs and Indiamen up the hundred treacherous miles of river from the Gulf for the last forty years. Taussat saw the uncertain expression in Naylor's eyes and cackled like a hen.

"I have almos' eighty years, *m'sieu*. I have sleep with every woman in the swamp, drink more wine than there is water in the river, seen everything life has to hold. If someone can save our beloved city, who has less to lose than I?"

Naylor grinned and clapped him on the shoulder. "Come up in the wheelhouse, then, and show us how it goes."

While Naylor and Heap were in the wheelhouse, studying the charts and learning the lower river from the old man, the troops were knocking together cribs in which to stow the cannon balls. High-wheeled carts began to appear on the levee, loaded with powder and shot, their axles dripping tallow that had been applied in an effort to reduce the usual creaking. A line of militia formed to pass the shot down—eight- and twelve- and twenty-four pound balls—and then came the powder, the kegs being rolled down the levee and across the gangplank and into the after cabins. Finally came the all-important fuses for the nineteen-inch mortars, so vitally necessary for the defense of Fort St. Philip. Together, all of these munitions might prevent passage of any British battleships up the Mississippi in order to attack the American fortifications from the river.

Slowly the *Kentucky*'s freeboard disappeared, till only inches of gunwale remained above the water. As they worked, the fog common in January began to drift in off the river. Soon the mist was so thick a man could stand in the bow without being able to see the levee a few feet away. When the sweating, cursing Tennessee militia was finished loading, they helped Naylor and his crew secure bales of cotton to the guards with iron hooks, completely covering the exposed sides of the vessel. It would provide meager protection from the shore batteries, but it was the best they could do. While Indian Thompson was firing up, Harris picked out the six men Jackson had given him to protect the boat, and the others trooped ashore. The fog was so dense now that Naylor could not see the river from the wheelhouse. He placed Heap on the bow to take soundings, with Taussat to help direct him. He put four militiamen in a line from the bow to the forecastle, and the two others on the forecastle stairs. That way, they could pass Heap's soundings and Taussat's directions up to Naylor at barely more than a whisper. Lieutenant Harris joined Naylor in the wheelhouse. The mist pressed against the windows like a milky wall, and now they could not even see their own bow. Naylor looked ashore, thinking of Charlotte again. It made his face gaunt and bleak. Then, deliberately, he pulled on the bell chord for dead slow astern.

Naylor and Harris both waited tensely for that first exhaustion of steam. The success of the whole voyage would stand or fall on whether Captain Abner had effectively silenced the engine. There was the muffled *clank* of gears from the enclosed engine room, barely audible to Naylor. Then the escape pipes let off their first steam. Used to the cannon-like report, Naylor was hardly prepared for the soft coughing noise from underneath the stern. As it was repeated, he realized this was all the sound the escaping steam was likely to make.

"If they hear that ashore, they'll think hit's a' 'gator grunting in some bayou," the lieutenant said.

Slowly the *Kentucky* eased away from the levee, swinging gently to Naylor's wheel. The boat shuddered as Captain Abner labored to reverse his engines. They slid almost soundlessly past the lone line of boats anchored at the waterfront. Then the city was behind, and they were on the open river. It was a tense journey through the milky mist, with Heap's soundings passed up the line of militiamen in husky whispers every few minutes.

Some of the time the fog was so thick that Taussat resorted to the keelboat trick of banging a board against the hull. The time between the sound and its echo told him their distance from shore. But as they drew near the British lines, he had to give that up and rely on his uncanny knowledge of the river. They passed alongside the *USS Louisiana* cautiously, its spectral looming presence like a malignant hulk, guarding entrance to a dark netherworld filled with monstrous, unknown dangers. The *Kentucky*'s wake, lapping against it, was a whispering, mocking echo. Naylor had lost all sense of time since they'd been under way. His knuckles ached from gripping the wheel, and his eyes burned from staring into the fog. Finally Heap came up from the main deck.

"Might as well spell you, hoss," he said. "That Taussat don't need my soundings. He can smell his way down these reaches."

As Naylor gave the wheel over to Heap, they heard the stutter of distant rifle fire ashore. Then a Congreve rocket arched into the sky, lighting the fog for a few moments even so far away.

"Think it's started?" Naylor asked Harris.

"Not the big fight," the lieutenant replied. "Probably Hinds an' his Mississippi Dragoons cuttin' a hunk outta the British line."

Naylor was watching the rocket light fade into darkness ashore. "How many men has Jackson got now?" he asked.

"About four thousand."

"Thibodaux told me the British were nearly ten thousand."

Harris glanced at him, then spat disgustedly. "I know what you're thinkin', an' you're wrong. I done been with Jackson two years now. I'd give you ten to one in his favor. I was at Fort Bowyer when them redcoats attacked, an' I know how they operate. So does Jackson. He's done planned his breastworks so they'll have to come across low ground to reach us. An' they'll come square an' massed. Like a bunch o' tin soldiers without sense enough to duck and scatter when they start getting knocked over. They'll be mowed down, mistah. If they fight like they done at Bowyer, you'll see killin' like you never thought could happen."

Harris looked off at the hidden shore on their larboard. The firing had ceased, and the silence was oppressive. "Kentuckians behind them breastworks, mistah," he said. "Tennesseans. Four thousand of 'em. And not one cain't but hit the head of a nail at two hunnert feet. Our batteries are just as good. Baratarians on them there cannons. Lafitte's men. You couldn't find better gunners, anywhere. They'll match Pakenham's guns, ball fer ball, an' still shoot his pants off." He spat again. "We'll win this fight, mistah. They'll be tellin' about it fer a long time to come."

389

The man's confidence was infectious. "When you talk like that, I hope we get back in time to be a part of it," Naylor said.

Harris frowned at him. "That don't sound like the jasper what didn't wanna come downriver."

"I told you," Naylor said, "there's another owner."

Harris nodded. "A beautiful one, at that."

"You've seen her?"

"When she came aboard."

"What?"

"This evenin'. About the time the fog come up. I warn't goin' to let her on, but that Thibodaux told me who she was."

"That's funny," Naylor said. "I didn't see her."

Harris appeared surprised. "You must've. You're the one she said she wanted to see."

Naylor stared emptily at the man, a dark premonition running through him. "Did you see her leave?" he asked.

"Hell, no. I was up to my neck loading that shot."

Without answering, Naylor wheeled and went down the forecastle stairs. Half formed as it was, the idea had run like a shock through his whole body; he couldn't quite believe it, but he had to find out for himself. Reaching the main deck, he opened the makeshift hatch they had put in the engine room cabin. Captain Abner and Indian Thompson were soaked in sweat, blackened with ashes.

"You been outside?" Naylor asked.

"Only to stoke the forward firebox," Thompson replied.

"See anybody?"

"Just that sentry Harris put on the main deck." Thompson scowled. "Somethin' the matter?"

"I don't know." Naylor shook his head. "Just keep your eyes open."

He went aft, looking into the main cabin. The dark interior was jarred with each muffled explosion of steam that shot into the expansion tank. The seams were beginning to leak, but it wasn't dangerous yet. He stepped out on deck again. He heard soft footsteps farther aft, and the breath blocked up in his throat. They were approaching him. The muscles of his shoulders stiffened with tension. It was crazy, he told himself. It couldn't be. Yet, why else would she come aboard?

The figure of a man moved out of the swirling fog. Catching sight of Naylor, he jerked his rifle up. Naylor's pent-up breath flowed out in a husky tide. "All right, soldier. It's Naylor."

The man approached dubiously, rifle pointed at Naylor's mid-section. Two feet away the muzzle sagged. "Sorry, mister. Guess I'm a little jumpy."

"Seen anything funny?"

"Heard somethin' . . . about a mile or so back . . . when we passed through Willow Channel. I was up in the waist. There was a thumpin' near the stern."

"Why didn't you report it?"

"I couldn't find nothin'. Figgered we'd run against driftwood."

It wasn't what Naylor wanted, and his mind wouldn't stay with it. "You checked all the cabins?"

"Not since we loaded up. What's wrong?"

"Nothing," Naylor said impatiently. "You better get on your rounds. Tell us next time . . . thumping or anything."

"Yes, sir."

The man moved up toward the waist, turning to cross the deck abaft the forecastle. Naylor started toward the stern. A faint creaking dead ahead stopped him in his tracks. Vaguely, through the dense mist, he saw the door of the after cabin open. The figure was like a wraith, seeming to float out, slowly resolving itself.

Charlotte stopped two feet from him. She had on a wool carrick. Her face above it, in this misty darkness, was but a ghostly illusion to Naylor. She spoke in a subdued voice. "We heard you talking. What is our position?"

He took a step nearer, his voice tight with strain: "Charlotte? What are you doing here? . . . and who's *we?*"

"Charles Thibodaux. We came on board together. We talked, and I know now you were right. I was wrong. This is something we have to do . . . for our country."

Her voice broke, and she made a sobbing sound. He took her in his arms and could feel the proud swell of her breasts burning through the heavy carrick. Without understanding it yet, he kissed the pale face. For him it was the passion and the pain and the sweetness again. He tried to kiss her on the lips, but she resisted, pushing him away.

"Owen . . . what are you doing?" she protested sharply.

"Charlotte," he said, trying to take her in his arms once more, "why did you do it this way?"

"Do what?" she asked, pulling farther back.

"Come aboard?" He dropped his arms.

"Because we thought it would be the only way you'd believe me . . . that I had changed my mind . . . that I know you're right."

"And Thibodaux?"

"He's a very close friend . . . already before Louis died . . . and even more now."

"I should have stayed." His voice was tortured. "I should have given you a chance to talk."

"You were right, Owen. About the fear of Silver Street. I was afraid. Charles convinced me how wrong I was . . . how unfair to you . . . to our country. He even offered to buy out my interest in the *Kentucky*, if it would make me feel better about it. He's already done so much for us, Owen, with pressing the lawsuit . . . getting you the promise of a pardon for performing war service. I just didn't see it clearly until Charles and I talked about it. Heap had talked to him when you docked . . . about Evadne Archer . . . how she's now with your child. And this time, Owen, it really will be *yours*. Not the way we let our foolish questioning run wild about Denise . . . who always has been my child with Louis. I knew I had to make my choice. If you were willing to risk your life, even knowing Evadne was with your child . . . well, now I've made my decision. I'm here where I belong . . . on the *Kentucky*."

He looked into her face and saw, despite the dimness, the truth that was there. The way he had wanted it to be upon his return this time—with nothing standing between them, as pure and burning and bright as that first time south of Natchez—he realized now that had only been the comet's tail of a ridiculous, passionate, obsessive dream that was irrevocably over. He understood, as he hadn't before, the acute anguish Evadne had felt upon their parting, and now he knew *why*—although it seemed dreadfully unfair that Heap should have known, when Evadne had not told him. Perhaps she hadn't told him because she had been certain that he was leaving her for Charlotte.

"Owen . . . we're good as partners . . . as friends. I want more than anything to keep it that way . . . always. We were both very foolish . . . once . . . so long ago. And we've both suffered for it . . . over and over again. I never told Louis . . . and that was my mistake . . . because in a way it was what cost him his life . . . learning about it the way he did from Kenneth Swain . . . something that wasn't true but which Swain made sound so dirty and low. You're wrong

about Louis, too. He was not a bad man . . . just in some
ways a weak one . . . in ways he couldn't help. He liked you,
Owen, and thought highly of you. You did not have his education or his social position, but he thought in many ways
you were far more of a man than he could ever hope to be.
He didn't die protecting me, Owen. He died defending the
reputation of our daughter. I am sure Denise will know and
understand that when she is older. In his way her father was
also very much a man."

It was tearing him apart inside, but Naylor's mind
jumped now to the present danger. "Thibodaux is here with
you?"

"Yes. I left him in the cabin. I wanted to speak with you
alone. I felt I owed you that, Owen."

"We've got to get you off."

"Why, how close are we to the British?"

This stopped him cold, as nothing else had. He knew
what she meant by that question, and, therefore, why she
had waited to reveal her presence on the *Kentucky*. The
British batteries were perilously close. Were they to put
Thibodaux and Charlotte ashore now, they might well land
right in the lap of a British bivouac.

"This what you want?" he asked incredulously.

"It was part of Charles's arrangement with General
Jackson that he accompany you on the *Kentucky* for this
voyage. I couldn't let him do that alone . . . not when you
thought I was standing in your way, and I wanted you to be
sure that I wasn't . . . that I approved what you were doing
. . . that it was something *both* the owners were doing . . .
wanted to do." She moved closer to him as she was
speaking. He could make out her strained, pleading expression now. "I'm not afraid of losing the *Kentucky* any more.
I'm afraid of losing what's on board . . . of losing the war

. . . of losing our freedom."

Naylor was incredulous no longer. This was so typical of her. The risk of the British batteries probably wasn't significant to her. Violence had been such an integral part of her life in Natchez-Under. Still, he was unwilling to let her go through with it. "We'll put about. We'll take you . . . and Thibodaux, if he's willing . . . back far enough to be safe. . . ."

"You can't," she said. "Charles has given his word, and I'm where I want to be. You'd only lose time . . . too much time. It would be daylight before you got back far enough."

"But I. . . ."

Sound from the bow cut him off. It was Lieutenant Harris's voice. He was hidden by the mist and the night but was apparently addressing Captain Abner through the opened engine room hatch. "Taussat says we're passing through them willow islands now. The Scud's dead ahead. We won't use the bell from now on. Just throttle down to dead slow ahead."

Captain Abner assented, and there was the thump of the hatch closing. On the heels of that sound, a strangled cry came from the stern. Naylor wheeled that way, bypassing Charlotte as he ran headlong down the deck. Rounding the after corner of the cabin, he almost tripped over a sprawled body. It was the sentry, blood leaking from a gash in his head. The next instant, Charles Thibodaux, having come out of the after cabin to see what was the cause of all the commotion, had joined Charlotte in coming up behind Naylor. Harris was only a short distance behind them.

Naylor was shaking the sentry. "What happened? Can you hear me?"

The man groaned. His face squinted, tight with pain. He

was barely coherent. "Man hidin' in the paddle box . . . jumped me. . . ."

Naylor was on his feet, speaking abruptly to Harris. "Go up the starb'rd. Get your men going over the boat. Don't miss a square inch."

Harris looked at Charlotte and Thibodaux. "What about them?"

"Get back in the cabin . . . both of you . . . and put out any lights," Naylor ordered. "Don't come out again till I say. . . ."

"It can't be a British boardin' party," Harris affirmed. "There'd be more men. . . ." He could make out the savage anger blazing in Naylor and wheeled, running forward.

Bending to get the fallen sentry's loaded rifle, Naylor felt he could not spare another instant. He knew that whoever had struck the sentry couldn't have come up the side on which he and Charlotte had been standing. Charlotte and Thibodaux were heading back to the after cabin on the starboard side as Naylor ran around to the larboard and jerked open the first door. This was the storeroom behind the after cabin. Whatever he did now would have to be fast. They were getting too close to the British batteries to risk any lights. He plunged about in the storeroom, stumbling over kegs of powder and cribs of shot, swinging the musket in vicious arcs. It banged against the walls, clanged off lead balls in the blinding darkness, but nowhere did it come up against a man. As satisfied as he could be that the room was empty, he darted out again. Charlotte and Thibodaux would keep the after cabin secure. He could hear Harris's soft, excited calling from forward, and the dull thump of feet on the forecastle stairs as the militiamen ran down to the main deck. A sudden flare of light from forward caught his eye.

Running past the muffled clank of gears within the engine room, he saw the light blaze under the open forecastle. One of the militiamen shouted, on the starboard side, and there was more thumping of feet and surprised calling.

"Shut up!" Harris called angrily. "You want them redcoats to hear us?"

All the while Naylor was running up the deck. He was ten feet from the forecastle, just athwart Number One firebox, when he saw the figure illuminated by the growing flames. The ruddy light silhouetted the man, turning the shaggy edges of his blond hair to a tangled yellow halo. He had a torch in one hand and was applying it to the bales of cotton they had stacked around the powder. In that instant, Naylor understood what had happened. That thumping the sentry had heard in Willow Channel had been Blackwell, boarding them. The man meant to light his fires and drop off and swim to one of the islands. When the British batteries opened up, the boat would be downriver from the islands, and Blackwell would be safe.

The knowledge sent a rush of raw anger through Naylor. Still running forward, he swung the rifle up and fired at Blackwell. The hammer dropped, and the spark flashed up from the flint, but there was no explosion. Naylor realized that he had dropped powder and ball out, swinging the gun around the cabin. Blackwell was looking at Naylor now. The patch lay like a black stain on Blackwell's left cheek. His good eye glittered with murderous hatred.

Lieutenant Harris rushed into the forecastle, a pair of his troopers behind. Blackwell threw the torch at Harris and wheeled to run for the larboard gunwale, dragging his leg with each plunging step. Naylor swung the rifle high to club the man. Blackwell saw him in the last instant and ducked under the blow, butting Naylor as he ran into him. The man's skull seemed to tear a hole in Naylor's body. He was thrown violently against the wall, dropping the rifle in his agony. While he was still pinned there, Naylor was deafened by a thunderclap of sound. An instant later a roaring crash shook the *Kentucky* from stem to stern. The boat shuddered and yawed so violently that both Naylor and Blackwell were pitched from their feet. Rolling over, grappled to Blackwell, Naylor heard another roar from the distance. This time he saw the flash from shore. Then another rending crash made the steamboat shudder, and he realized what it was. The shore batteries had caught sight of the fire aboard and were using it as a target.

Blackwell sought to tear free, but Naylor caught him, slamming a blow at his face. The pitching and yawing of the boat rolled them toward the stern. Kicking, struggling, fighting for a hold that would give him the advantage, Naylor had flashing glimpses of the action on the foredeck.

The fire was still blazing in the forecastle. Its light revealed Harris and the pair of troopers frantically rolling the flaming cotton bales overboard. A round from the shore batteries swept through the three men, chopping them down like grain and smashing into the engine room. Steam shot up from the engine with a hissing roar, and someone within the shattered cabin began a muffled screaming. The two militiamen lay bloody and broken in the wreckage on deck, and Harris was crouched on his knees, a dazed look on his face, clutching a smashed arm to his belly. Thibodaux wasn't in the after cabin any more, if he had ever gone there at all. He was up front, dumping the last of the burning cotton bales overboard, the flames singeing his clothes and body.

Naylor and Blackwell were finally wedged against the after cabin and could roll no more. Naylor scissored his legs on the man and flopped up on top. With the roar of the guns and crashing of shot creating a continuous bedlam all about them, Naylor struck at the man's face. He felt his knuckles split lips against teeth and then break the teeth themselves. He struck again and again, blows that would have beaten an ordinary man into a dazed helplessness, but Blackwell was still struggling viciously when a round of shot crashed into the after cabin. Smashed scantlings and a piece of heavy roof beam fell across Naylor's back and head, stunning him.

Blackwell drove up out of the smoking débris. Naylor sought to grapple him, and Blackwell sledged a knee into his groin. Naylor's face went ashen with agony, and his will flowed out of him like water. Blackwell staggered to his feet, kicking Naylor viciously in the ribs. It flopped Naylor over on his back, and Blackwell jumped on top of him, stamping his chest, slamming a boot into his face. Pain was a bright and roaring thing in Naylor's head. Blackwell lunged up, the gouging nail glittering like a scimitar. "Now, Naylor!" he bawled.

The lunge had lifted Blackwell off Naylor for just an instant. It freed Naylor's left leg, and it was all he had left. He kicked it viciously into Blackwell's crotch. Blackwell lost all control. His nail gouged deeply into Naylor's eye, but he was rearing back in a helpless spasm at the same time, roaring sickly with pain. Agony shot through Naylor's eye, blinding it. He caught at Blackwell, heaving the man off him entirely. Naylor could not see out of his right eye and the left was blurred, but he could hear the shuffle of Blackwell's boots as the man sought to rise and the wheezing sound of Blackwell's labored breathing. Sick with the pain shooting along his optic nerve, Naylor drove himself at Blackwell. His pawing hands caught one of those boots as it smashed into his face again. He clawed his fingers around it and threw the last of his consciousness into the effort. His jerk, feeble as it was, spilled the man. Blackwell tried to kick free as he fell, but Naylor hung on. Wheezing and mewing with pain, Naylor crawled up the man's body. Blackwell fought him, but Naylor kept his weight on the man, countering each twist of the body, weakly blocking the blows. He heard the thump of the pitman over his head and felt water splash into his face by the ten-foot paddle buckets. It made him realize that their struggle had carried them clear to the stern. Blackwell was hanging over the taffrail.

Naylor knew he didn't have the strength to finish the fight any other way. He twined his left hand in Blackwell's long yellow hair. With his other hand he got a grip on the man's clothes. As Blackwell sensed Naylor's intent, he erupted in a new spasm of fury. He sledged blows at Naylor, clawed and fought to tear loose. Unable to spare the strength to block the blows, Naylor took them all. Jarred by them, sickened by them, sobbing with the effort and the awful force of his concentration, he dragged Blackwell inch by inch across the thwart.

A fountain of water spewed from each bucket in the giant paddle wheel, drowning Blackwell. Coughing and retching, he went into a last insane paroxysm to get free. Naylor's body rocked to the punishment of hammering fists, clawing nails, madly kicking boots. His head was roaring with the detonation of the shore batteries, the crash of shot into the *Kentucky*, the crackle and scream of smashed and falling upperworks. Then the first paddle bucket hit Blackwell's head. Blackwell's body went rigid beneath Naylor. Naylor gave another heave, and Blackwell's body went deeper into the wheel. The second bucket hit him, snapping his whole head violently downward, twisting it into the grotesque angle of a broken neck. A shudder ran through the arched body, and then Blackwell went completely slack beneath Naylor. The third bucket dragged him down into the churning water.

Naylor crouched on hands and knees, too drained to move. The thunder of British guns sounded astern now, but another salvo raked the ship. The boat rocked in a spasm, and there was a scream and clang of metal on metal. The pitman set up a wild vibration that shook the whole craft, and the thumping of the wheel went crazy. Then, with a groan of wood and a whine of straining guides, it all came to an abrupt stop.

The silence was frightening in its intensity, after the endless bedlam. Naylor got to his feet, supporting himself against the shattered wall of the after cabin. The fire was out in the forecastle. Fog and night shrouded the boat once more. It was a wounded craft, losing steerageway as it drifted downriver with the current, listing to the larboard and drawing more and more water.

Naylor stumbled through the smoking wreckage toward the bow, sick with reaction to the battle now. There was a great fear in him, making his voice shake. "Charlotte!" he called. "Charlotte . . . !"

"Owen." Her answer came from the bow. She materialized out of the milky fog, Charles Thibodaux following her. "I didn't think we'd ever get the fire out."

"Had to throw some of the powder overboard to keep it from the flames," Thibodaux affirmed. "Sorry."

Another distant salvo crashed from the shore. The British were firing blindly now, with no flames to light the boat. Their volleys were searching the river methodically and any minute might strike home again.

Lieutenant Harris was picking his way forward from the forecastle, bloody arm inside his coat. "We aren't out of it yet," he said.

"Put what men you've got left on the pumps," Naylor told Harris. "You, too, Thibodaux." Then, looking at Charlotte, he said: "Can you make it?"

She nodded stiffly. "I'm all right. Somebody has to tend to the wounded. Go about your work, Owen."

He squeezed her arm reassuringly, grinning at her. Then he ducked inside the gaping hole in the wrecked engine room. He could barely see Indian Thompson, sprawled over a fuel crib. Captain Abner was rubbing tallow on his naked upper body. "Damned shot blew away the safety valve," Abner said. "Steam boiled Indian like a lobster."

Thompson grimaced in pain. "Don't pay no heed to me. Git her under way again."

Captain Abner glanced at the mangled mess of crosshead guides and connecting rods. "It might be done. See if you kin find that spare pitman in the cabin, Owen . . . and some packing for this damned boiler. They almost blew it off the timbers."

A quick inspection of the damage gave them slim hope. The cotton bales had warded off a lot of the fire. Naylor found a dozen six-pound balls buried in the bales near the bow. The angle of British fire had caused the bulk of the shot to sweep across the deck rather than drop through and puncture the bottom. With every able man on the pumps, they fought to keep the *Kentucky* afloat while Captain Abner repaired the engine. For half an hour they drifted down the fog-bound river with the booming of the British guns falling farther and farther astern. Captain Abner finally got the engine started again. Crashing and banging like a factory gone mad, they steamed on down through the fog.

Dawn light was beginning to pervade the mist when the ghostly ramparts of Fort St. Philip loomed ahead. The *Kentucky* came around sluggishly, listing profoundly to larboard, and ran headlong for the beach. Fifty yards from shore there was a wild screaming from the engine. Captain Abner threw himself flat, shouting wildly for the others to do the same. Thibodaux, now on deck with Charlotte, pulled her down with him. The cylinder head let go with a detonation like a sixteen pounder. Flying metal whistled over Naylor's head and smashed through the wrecked cabins. At the same time there was a grinding crash as the bow ran full speed toward the beach. The *Kentucky* slid onto the low sandbar and squatted like a stubborn hen on her eggs. Then there was only the melancholy sigh of steam escaping the boiler joints.

The troops of the fort had heard them coming from upriver. They appeared out of the fog, led by Captain Charles Wollstonecraft, tall and hungry-looking. "You have saved our lives, Captain," he said. "We didn't have enough dry powder and fuses to stop a British skiff from passing the fort."

Soon lines of troops were passing the kegs of powder, boxes of fuses, and rounds of dully gleaming shot ashore. Thompson, Harris, and the wounded militiamen were transported to the fort on litters.

"You son-of-a-bitch!" Naylor said to Heap. "Why didn't you tell me about Evadne?"

"Wasn't sure how you'd take it," he replied simply.

They were moving to higher ground where Charlotte and Thibodaux were already standing. Naylor's face was stiff and raw, and his body ached all over from the beating it had taken. Captain Abner joined the group. They stood silently, looking at the sinking boat. Finally Neville Heap said:

"Ain't there no way o' savin' her?"

Captain Abner shook his head sadly. "She's a tired old gal, Heap. Ain't a piece worth salvaging."

"We'll build another one," Charlotte said.

Except for Thibodaux, everyone looked at her with surprise. But the calm conviction in her eyes was a contagious thing, and Naylor started to grin, despite the hurt it brought to his bruised face. "Twice as big," he said.

"With what for money?" Captain Abner asked.

"I suppose with what I would have paid Charlotte for her interest in the *Kentucky*," Thibodaux said, smiling. "More, maybe. I'm sure I can raise it. The *Kentucky* has played a vital rôle in saving New Orleans from rape and pillage by those damned redcoats."

"In that case," Heap said, fishing out a twist of garlic, "we'll build one twice as beautiful."

Naylor could not help smiling, reflecting his amazement at what a shrewd businesswoman Charlotte had proven herself to be. He had been wrong about her so many times. He had been wrong about her again. He could only hope Thibodaux would be man enough for her.

"We'll build one twice as fast," Captain Abner said, and chuckled.

A feeling of comradeship and strength passed through them, and suddenly they were all laughing together. Naylor could see that they were as confident of building a new boat as Harris was—as they all were, really—that Jackson would win this war. When Naylor looked out at the broad, looping Mississippi, just beginning now to materialize out of the mist, he felt like he owned the world. Sure, it was a constant struggle, and there were great losses along the way, but you just had to keep on, that was all, had to persist, and, if you did and you proved strong enough, you would win out in the end. While there was no way Naylor could know it, at that very moment, with the image of Denise foremost in her mind, Charlotte Reynaud was thinking the very same thing.

About the Author

Les Savage, Jr. was born in Alhambra, California and grew up in Los Angeles. His first published story was "Bullets and Bullwhips" accepted by the prestigious magazine, Street & Smith's *Western Story*. Almost ninety more magazine stories followed, all set on the American frontier, many of them published in Fiction House magazines such as *Frontier Stories* and *Lariat Story Magazine* where Savage became a superstar with his name on many covers. His first novel, *Treasure of the Brasada*, appeared from Simon & Schuster in 1947. Due to his preference for historical accuracy, Savage often ran into problems with book editors in the 1950s who were concerned about marriages between his protagonists and women of different races—a commonplace on the real frontier but not in much Western fiction in that decade. Savage died young, at thirty-five, from complications arising out of hereditary diabetes and elevated cholesterol. However, as a result of the censorship imposed on many of his works, only now are they being fully restored by returning to the author's original manuscripts. Among Savage's finest Western stories are *Fire Dance at Spider Rock* (Five Star Westerns, 1995), *Medicine Wheel* (Five Star Westerns, 1996), *Coffin Gap* (Five Star Westerns, 1997), *Phantoms in the Night* (Five Star Westerns, 1998), *The Bloody Quarter* (Five Star Westerns, 1999), *In the Land of Little Sticks* (Five Star Westerns, 2000), and *The Cavan Breed* (Five Star Westerns, 2001). Much as Stephen Crane before him, while he wrote, the shadow of his imminent death grew longer and longer across his young life, and he knew that, if he was going to do it at all, he would have to do it quickly. He did it well, and, now that his novels and stories are being restored to what he had intended them to be, his achievement irradiated by his powerful and profoundly sensitive imagination will be with us always, as he had wanted it to be, as he had so rushed against time and mortality that it might be. *The Devil's Corral* will be his next **Five Star Western**.